"*The Divine Proverb of Streusel* is a sw
layers of heartbreak and healing, forgiver
dom . . . and recipes! You'll want to slow u~...

Julie Klassen, bestselling author of *The Sisters of Sea View*

"Sara Brunsvold's *The Divine Proverb of Streusel* is a lovely novel filled with faith, love, and honesty. With its sweet details, memorable characters, and much-loved recipes, readers are sure to savor each page."

Shelley Shepard Gray, *New York Times* and *USA Today*
bestselling author of *Her Heart's Desire*

"Sara Brunsvold's latest novel is an absolute feast for the reader's heart. Not only does it provide recipes to try in the kitchen, but it also lays out the ingredients for rediscovering your heritage and reconciling the most broken relationships. With relatable characters facing the all-too-common recklessness found in families throughout generations, this story feels less like a novel and more like sitting at a beloved grandmother's table with a slice of strawberry rhubarb pie. *The Divine Proverb of Streusel* is a superb delight."

Janine Rosche, bestselling author of *With Every Memory*

"In *The Divine Proverb of Streusel*, Sara Brunsvold pens a tale richly flavored with the wisdom of generations past that will leave you hungry for simple times and simple truths. Brunsvold gently folds in life lessons discovered in both the strengths and weaknesses in the recipe of one's lineage, leaving your heart full of goodness and grace as you turn the final page."

Amanda Cox, Christy Award–winning author
of *The Secret Keepers of Old Depot Grocery*
and *He Should Have Told the Bees*

Praise for *The Extraordinary Deaths of Mrs. Kip*

The
DIVINE
PROVERB
of
STREUSEL

Books by Sara Brunsvold

The Extraordinary Deaths of Mrs. Kip
The Divine Proverb of Streusel

The

DIVINE
PROVERB

of

STREUSEL

A NOVEL

SARA BRUNSVOLD

Revell

a division of Baker Publishing Group
Grand Rapids, Michigan

© 2024 by Sara B. Brunsvold

Published by Revell
a division of Baker Publishing Group
Grand Rapids, Michigan
www.revellbooks.com

Printed in the United States of America

Library of Congress Cataloging-in-Publication Data
Names: Brunsvold, Sara, 1979– author.
Title: The divine Proverb of Streusel : a novel / Sara Brunsvold.
Description: Grand Rapids, Michigan : Revell, a division of Baker Publishing Group, [2024]
Identifiers: LCCN 2023019301 | ISBN 9780800742997 (paper) | ISBN 9780800745608 (casebound) | ISBN 9781493444748 (ebook)
Subjects: LCGFT: Christian fiction. | Novels.
Classification: LCC PS3602.R865 D58 2024 | DDC 813/.6—dc23/eng/20230522
LC record available at https://lccn.loc.gov/2023019301

Most Scripture used in this book, whether quoted or paraphrased by the characters, is from the King James Version of the Bible.

Some Scripture is from THE HOLY BIBLE, NEW INTERNATIONAL VERSION®, NIV® Copyright © 1973, 1978, 1984, 2011 by Biblica, Inc.® Used by permission. All rights reserved worldwide.

Published in association with Books & Such Literary Management, BooksAndSuch .com.

Baker Publishing Group publications use paper produced from sustainable forestry practices and post-consumer waste whenever possible.

24 25 26 27 28 29 30   7 6 5 4 3 2 1

For Dad.

What was sown years ago continues to multiply.

NIKKI WERNER'S
Family Tree

Henrietta Schoenborn
GREAT-GREAT-GRANDMOTHER

Georg Schoenborn
GREAT-GREAT-GRANDFATHER

Lena (Schoenborn) Baumann
GREAT-GRANDMOTHER

Otto Baumann
GREAT-GRANDFATHER

Emma (Baumann) Straub
GREAT-AUNT

Ann (Baumann) Werner
GRANDMOTHER

Henry Werner
GRANDFATHER

Wesley Werner
PATERNAL UNCLE

Christopher Werner
FATHER

Lydia (Ellis) Werner
MOTHER

Hannah (Werner) Shaw
SISTER

Nikki Werner

One

The message left little reason to believe Nikki Werner still held significance in her dad's life. After four months of the little girl inside her heart crying for her dad to come back, four months of wondering if he could hear those cries, she had received her answer. It was loud, clear, and immortalized on social media.

She reread the text from Hannah. The words had not changed.

Thought you should know.

The picture underneath had not changed either. A screenshot of a post. Their dad in a light gray suit, boutonniere pinned to the lapel, standing next to a white-clad woman neither of his grown daughters had ever met.

She replied to her sister.

It's like he doesn't care.

Did he? About any of them? At all?

Outside her classroom window, a gray-bellied cloud swelled in all directions, inflating like a balloon against the steel-blue morning sky. An unwelcome blemish invading a tranquil sea. It billowed and rolled, blown by the same invisible wind that churned the treetops. The world advanced at a dizzying pace, no thought to the weary or brokenhearted.

Four long months had passed since her dad had packed a bag and walked away from her mom—from all three of them. They were hollowed of everything they thought they knew of him, of family, of love. How much more would they have to unlearn?

Billow and roll.

The classroom door whined on its hinges. Tracy Brown stepped through and thrust two paper coffee cups above her head. "Raise your praise, Miss Werner, it's the last day of school! Woo!" She'd donned those canvas sandals middle-aged women like her loved so much and a "Salvy for Perez-ident" T-shirt. Both spoke to her summer dreams of no dress code and plenty of Kansas City Royals baseball games.

Nikki roused a smile in response, but there was no point hiding anything from Tracy. A high school calculus teacher for seventeen years, Tracy spotted consternation in the younger set the way a hawk spied a mouse.

Predictably, Tracy's expression mellowed. She lowered her arms. "That's not the face a teacher should be making five hours from final bell. What happened? Is it Jacob's mom again about his grade?"

Nikki shook her head then held up her phone.

Tracy padded over. Her mouth dropped as she read. "He got *married?*"

"Apparently."

"When?"

"According to this post of his new wife, this past Saturday."

"Oh, sister. I'm so sorry." Tracy sank into the chair next to Nikki's desk—the same spot she claimed every Thursday morning before students arrived—for a "Gab and Grace session," as she called it. The life-giving thirty minutes of prayer and mentoring that had sustained Nikki through her first year at Northwood High.

Nikki gave a shrug. "His choice, right?" A throb pressed against the backs of her eyes.

"Doesn't make it right, or easy."

No, it didn't. Nikki chewed her bottom lip and laid her phone facedown.

"Want your latte?" Tracy asked.

"No, I'm not in the mood." Quickly she added, "Hand it over."

With a sideways grin, Tracy slipped the cup into her hand.

The first sip went down smooth, a warm, centering presence reminiscent of those hopeful days of first semester, back when her only prayer request was how to whet her sophomores' appetites for the nation-shaping literature of Faulkner and Ellison and Twain. Back when she was oblivious to her dad's affair.

"Want to talk about it?" Tracy asked.

Nikki thrummed her fingers on the cup sleeve. She shook her head.

"Want to scream about it?"

A small smile tweaked her lips. "Kinda."

"I would too. Think your mom knows about that?" Tracy gestured toward Nikki's phone.

"Not sure."

"Hopefully she doesn't find out through social media."

"She's been off it for a while. We both have. Ever since—" The rest of that sentence tasted too sour.

"Since the truth came out," her friend finished.

Nikki nodded. That day had been the heaviest of her life.

"You can't do anything about his choices," Tracy said. "Only your own. And I suspect this summer is going to be filled with bright and glorious choices for you. Especially with a certain beau." She winked, a clear diversion to other topics. To Isaac.

The throbbing behind Nikki's eyes speared into her chest. It happened every time he came up. Like the pain her mom felt had suddenly transferred to her. "We don't know that Isaac is going to propose."

Tracy peered at her over the rim of her glasses. "Don't we?"

Nikki pulled her cup closer. "It's not a guarantee, anyway."

"Do you want him to?"

"Yes," she replied a little too quickly.

Tracy tilted her head to the side in that tell-me-more posture she had perfected.

"I do love him. And I have thought of us being married. But . . ."

"But it's a lot on top of a lot?"

"Yeah."

"Have you told Isaac this?"

Nikki shifted in her seat. "No."

Tracy reached over and cupped Nikki's hand. "Probably a conversation to have sooner rather than later. Men are the worst when it comes to mind reading."

"You'd think they'd evolve past that."

"You'd think." Tracy chuckled and glanced at her watch. "Nearly time for the circus to descend. Let's get you fully caffeinated and reasonably cheerful." She raised her cup for a toast. "To summer."

Nikki grinned, tapped her own cup against Tracy's, swallowed another fortifying drink. But the depths of her soul remained as clouded as the sky.

Billow and roll.

◆ ◆ ◆ ◆

Weeks had passed since his brother had answered any of his calls, but that didn't stop Wes Werner from dialing Chris's number again. "A brother is born for a time of adversity," Proverbs 17 taught, and if what Aunt Emma said she saw on social media was true, his kid brother sank deeper every day. The spiral was evident even from Wes's vantage point clear on the opposite side of Missouri.

Had Lydia seen the photo? Had the girls?

The divorce was barely a month old.

He placed the phone to his ear and stepped out onto his front porch. The midmorning sun coaxed melodies from the winged singers in the century-old oak tree at the edge of the yard, a source of endless adventure when he and Chris were boys. The gentle slopes of the Werner farm rolled into the distance.

The other end of the line rang. And rang. Ignored.

Voicemail picked up. Again.

Wes filled his lungs and held the air in place as he waited for the beep. He prayed the words would come with at least moderate coherence and grace.

Beep.

"Hey, Chris. Wes. Think about you every day. And your family. Spoke with Aunt Emma. She told me you and, uh, Sheryl? Is that right? That you all moved to Oklahoma and you're about an hour from her." He paused. "She also said you may have . . . bigger news. Hoping we can talk. Give me a call."

As soon as he hit the red End button, more words rushed to his lips, a half minute too late.

I want you to be happy—and whole.

I love you.

My heart is heavy.

Words that would be unheard by anyone other than God. At least until—unless—Chris called him back.

◆ ◆ ◆ ◆

The final bell rang. Nine hundred high schoolers roughhoused and laughed their way to summer freedom. Soon after, Nikki slid into her Malibu. Tracy wanted her to go out for a "celebratory and completely unhealthy amount of spinach dip," but Nikki declined. The ache in her head begged for a quiet place.

She intended to drive to her apartment, crawl under the covers, and sleep off the day—the semester. Instead, she ended up parked behind her mom's car in the driveway of the two-story colonial in the heart of Kansas City, Missouri's northland. The house that had been home for all of Nikki's twenty-six years. The Werner family hub, and the core from which every branch of her existence stretched.

The FOR SALE sign in the front lawn had donned a new addition: a red rectangle with bold white letters. CONTRACT PENDING.

Her entire Werner life had ebbed away, piece by rotted piece. Nothing left whole. Nothing left untouched.

13

She stepped into the afternoon sunshine.

The shades of the living room's picture window were open, as if the house grasped at any light it could find to chase away the darkness that had settled over it. One of her earliest memories had happened at that window. She'd been four years old, nose practically touching the pane, waiting for her dad's car to turn into the drive.

She gritted her teeth against the pang and pushed forward, up the front steps. She reached for the handle of the storm door and stopped. The inside door stood open, allowing an unobstructed view into the house. Her mom knelt in the middle of the furniture-less living room. A large cardboard box sat in front of her, a stack of framed pictures on one side and a pile of dish towels on the other. She stared at the picture in her hands. Just stared. Like she tried to believe their family had ever been happy.

Such moments had caught Nikki several times over the last four months too. Moments when she saw a picture or relived a memory and the daunting question rose once more: Would anything from that point forward ever be joyful enough to capture and frame for posterity?

Slowly her mom lifted a dish towel and shrouded the picture. The ripple of grief knew no end.

Nikki drew in a breath, then knocked on the storm door.

The noise startled her mom, whose surprised expression slowly melted to one of confusion. She rose and came to the door. "Nik? What are you doing here?"

What was she doing there? What was it that had made her drive twenty-five minutes out of her way? Was she, too, grasping at any light she could find? Any semblance of the life that had been theirs only months ago?

Her chin began to tremble.

Instantly her mom wrapped her arm around her and pulled her inside. "Come on, baby. Let's have some coffee."

❧ *Two* ❧

"Guess who called me." Aunt Emma had a way of starting a phone call with little prelude, as if her seventy-seven years was reason enough to move things along.

Wes laid his pen down on his desk, welcoming the excuse to not focus on projected feed bills for a moment, and leaned back in his office chair. "I can only guess Chris."

"Spot-on. He called me not more than five minutes ago, mad as a wet hen. I take it you contacted him?"

"Tried to. Left another voicemail."

"Well, you finally poked the bear, it seems. He said we all need to mind our own business, especially me since I'm not his mother."

Wes winced. An awful thing for Chris to tell his aunt—his godmother at that—who had unfailingly doted on them both their whole lives despite the distance.

"He also said he and Sheryl will no longer be coming for dinner on Sunday."

"I really stirred things up, didn't I?"

"You did what a big brother is supposed to do. We just have to keep asking for that divine whack to the side of the noggin. That's what you had to do with some of those Army boys during your sergeant days, yes? I bet you asked for a good many divine whacks for that bunch."

15

Several names of privates rose from his memory banks. "In so many words, yes."

"That's because you're a good and decent man, Fritz."

Warmth tingled his face, as it always did when she endeared him with encouragement and the pet name she had given him as a baby because he "looked his heritage from hour one." She never failed to leave him with a measure of maternal tenderness, a precious thing for a son without a mother on this side of heaven.

"Wish there was more I could do," he said.

"Me too. It was so much simpler to get through to you boys when you were little. Grown men are impossibly hard to convince the sky is blue. Present company excluded, of course."

"Of course."

"Hope you get ready, though. Chris may be mad enough to call you back this time."

"Standing guard."

"Good." She let out a singsong sigh. "Tell me something pleasant before I get all kinds of gray here. How's the new house? I'm still waiting on those pictures you promised to text me."

"I know. I'm behind on that. Been busy moving in."

"You said your new house is near the machine shed?"

"Sort of in between the machine shed and the old farmhouse. From my living room window, I can see the old place and the pasture across the road, which lets me keep an eye on my herd."

"Rowdy bunch, no doubt. Figure out your plans for the farmhouse? Last time we talked, you were thinking a respite getaway for veterans."

"Maybe. Or a furnished rental. Affordable housing—and everything else—is hard to come by around here anymore. Especially this year. Have a board meeting at the electric co-op tomorrow, and I suspect we'll learn that even more members have fallen behind on payments."

"Bless them. Times have never been easy on rural folks. I'm sure you'll figure out what's best, for the co-op and the farmhouse."

"Regardless, the farmhouse needs a face-lift," Wes said. "Some

16

paint at least. Maybe new flooring in the bathroom and kitchen. Nothing drastic. Want to keep the character."

"I couldn't bear it if you didn't," she replied. "I'll always have a soft spot for that little house too. That's usually the case with your childhood home, though. It served us both well as youngsters, didn't it?"

"One of many reasons I came back after the service."

"It's why your mom came back too, and brought your father with her. There is something powerful about that slice of earth. I like to think in her final days, my sister's mind still convinced her she was in that kitchen. She kept it so warm and full of coffee cake for any company that came to her door. Wouldn't it be something if she greeted us at the gates with her smile and a warm cinnamony slice? It's not scriptural, but it's a comforting thought."

The mere mention of his mother's baking made him long for the scents and sounds of her at work. Had it really been almost fifteen years since he'd had any food produced by her seemingly tireless hands?

Another singsong sigh. "Well, I best be getting. It's almost four."

"Bocce ball practice?"

"Yep. The Lutheran Ladies of the Lawn have a tournament we intend to dominate this weekend. The boys are quaking in their orthopedics—I can feel it. Our team T-shirts arrive tomorrow."

He laughed. "Text me a picture."

"You first."

"Right. Me first. Have fun at practice with the LLLs."

"Love you a bushel, Wes."

"And a peck."

◆　◆　◆　◆

Before Nikki had a chance to take one sip of her coffee, all the pent-up emotion tumbled out of her in a mess of exhausted tears.

Her mom wore the same knitted-brow expression that had welcomed a thousand confidences over the years. It seemed unfair to load down a woman who already had so much to carry. The hollows

17

of her cheeks were more pronounced. The curve of her back more noticeable. More white streaked through her light-brown locks, which she wore in an unraveling ponytail.

Still, her mom took it. She reached across the table and wove her fingers into Nikki's. "I know it's been hard these last several months—at school and at home. Summer break is coming at the best time, isn't it?"

Nikki wiped her cheeks and nodded.

"And Isaac gets back from his work trip tomorrow?"

"Right."

She squeezed Nikki's hand. "That's something to look forward to. I wish I could make things easier for you in the meantime."

"I should be making things easier for you, Mom. You have far more on your plate. Selling the house, moving to Salina with Hannah, new city, new job to find . . . Dad." One syllable, a giant, barbed tangle of hurt.

Her mom looked down at the table. The angle put emphasis on the dark circles under her eyes, evidence of the layer upon layer of loss, none of it her choosing. Regardless, she stroked Nikki's hand with her thumb, the self-sacrificial act of comfort from mother to child.

"Have you heard from your dad?" she asked.

Nikki's shoulders stiffened. "No. And I'm not sure I want to after seeing the latest post."

"What post?"

Nikki froze. Her mom had not seen it. Of course she hadn't. She hadn't been anywhere near social media. For as gutted as Nikki was, her mom might break in two.

She took a breath and prayed for mercy to engulf her mom before the news did. "Dad got married on Saturday."

Her mom's lips parted. The helpless look in her eyes was sheer torture. "Did he—" Her voice cracked. She swallowed and tried again. "Is it . . . her?"

The name was like a curse word. Never would Nikki say it. She nodded.

Her mom drew her hand away, tucked it into her lap.

If Nikki could, she would rewind to the day she was born and take back every word she had ever said that was less than respectful toward her mom. Take upon herself every insult her mom had ever endured, if only it meant her mom could feel relief. Why couldn't she?

Slowly, stiffly, her mom reached for her mug, her voice quiet and strained. "Better drink up before it gets too cold."

The ache behind Nikki's eyes pounded once more. As her mom took a long, slow drink, Nikki lifted her mug to her lips. The now-tepid coffee was Lydia Werner's signature preparation, a dark roast blend slightly sweetened by a douse of whole milk. Her dad never wanted any other kind of milk in the house. Whole was what he grew up with on the farm, and that was what he wanted to grow old with too.

They had done a lot of things as a family because of his preferences. They always watched whatever sport was in season on Sundays because that was his pastime. And they visited the Werner family farm in Eddner, Missouri, only on Christmas Day, driving three hours there in the morning and three hours back that night. Their lives had long been framed closely with his. In all the ways that cut the deepest, they still were.

Her mom set her mug on the table, cradled it in both hands, and stared at the light-brown liquid.

Nikki relegated her mug to the end of her place mat and cleared her throat. "Mom? You okay?"

"Fine, baby."

It wasn't fine. It was maddening. The boxes around them served as witnesses to her mom's growing shame.

"I can stay, help you."

Her mom shook her head. "I'm done for the day. Have to meet the Realtor soon."

"When is the closing?"

"Two weeks." Her mom's eyes traced around the kitchen and the living room beyond to spots now blank of photos and furniture but baked with history. "Two more weeks to pack up twenty-nine years."

Nikki dipped her head. The pain between them was so large it sucked up their air, commanded far more space than the memories themselves. "How are you getting through this, Mom?"

She tilted her head to the side, eyes moistening. "Your Grandma Werner had a saying she loved. She'd say, 'Do the next thing.' She picked it up from a radio show she listened to." Her mom stroked the handle of her mug and looked at Nikki. "That's what I'm doing. The next thing. It's the only thing I can do."

Nikki shook her head. "You shouldn't be reduced to this."

Tears dripped over her mom's lower lids. She looked away. So weary, so defeated.

Nikki clenched the edge of the place mat. "I bet if Grandma was still alive, she would have a few things to say about all this." It was conjecture. Grandma Ann had died when Nikki was only twelve, too soon for Nikki to have formed any memories of her besides Christmas Day in her farmhouse, which always smelled of baked ham and possessed a brand of peace that every other place dreamed of. "Do you ever wish Grandma Ann was still alive right now? That she was here to speak up?"

Her mom shook her head. "Grandma's thoughts wouldn't have made a difference, Nik."

She didn't argue, but surely they would have.

If only someone would set her dad straight. Soon.

◆　◆　◆　◆

"Chris, please." Wes tried to speak into the spews of anger from the other end of the line. "I'm only trying to help you."

Silence.

"Chris?" Wes pulled his cell phone from his ear. The dreaded words cut across the screen: call ended.

He sighed and put his phone facedown on the armrest of his recliner. He pushed up and traced over to the window looking east, toward the old farmhouse a football field's length away. It hadn't been that long since he and Chris lived under that roof, learning the value of family, obedience, and above all, faith. It hadn't been that long ago that Chris seemed so in love with his wife and daughters.

Things had fallen so far, and Wes was helpless to stem the tide, no matter how bad he wanted to.

He rubbed a hand down his face, the callused skin of his fingers bristling against his beard. It was all in God's hands. Still, the same three words pinged in his soul: *Be the help.* The phrase his mother had given him to take into his enlistment. It had stayed with him for his thirty years in, and for the last seven back in Eddner.

Be the help.

"How, God?" he whispered.

No answer came, as if God trusted him to discern the way. He had faith sharpened by war, by witnessing the brightest good bloom among the sharpest thorns of depravation. But God should have known by then how dense Wes really was.

❖ ❖ ❖ ❖

The throb of her head demanded a still, quiet place at long last. A place to escape the unceasing churn. Nikki drove south toward downtown and her tiny studio apartment in the River Market District.

Happy hour was in full swing. She slowed to a crawl several times, navigating through the bustle of people between shops and restaurants—Vietnamese, Chinese, Thai, Brazilian, Italian, Ethiopian, Mexican, Indian, Middle Eastern, Eastern European, and the requisite barbecue. A cross section of the world in one square mile, a contemporary nod to the district's past as a steamboat port for dream-bound settlers.

After several minutes of circling her block, she found a spot not far from her building. The street noise, usually a comfort, seemed louder, aggressive. The clack of a train on the riverfront, the rumble of the electric streetcar, the whir of cars squeezing through the narrow streets, the grind of a bicycle chain. They shoved into her already overcrowded mind.

She jogged the last leg to the door leading up to her apartment. Her four hundred square feet were nestled in the northwest corner of the third floor, above China-Town Grocery. The only window opened to the fire escape on the north face. The wide, muddy Missouri River roiled in the middle distance.

She dropped her purse and work bag next to her kitchenette and sank face-first onto her bed. Her feet, still in her flats, hung off the side.

Maybe in the confines of her little home she finally could float away to solitude, find the kind of peace held amid the tall grass of a sunny pasture where only butterflies and fleet-footed deer roamed. Far from all that raged within and around.

She let herself press deeper into the pillow and closed her eyes.

Three

The chime of an incoming video call roused Nikki from a shallow sleep. Dusk soaked the city outside her window. Hours had passed.

She fumbled for the lamp on the nightstand, then rushed for her phone still tucked in her purse by the kitchenette. At the tail end of the fourth ring, she finally had the device in hand.

Isaac.

Quickly she finger-combed her hair, then accepted the call.

As soon as his face appeared on the screen, his cheeks lifted toward his praline-colored eyes. "Hey, beautiful." His voice was like soothing honey.

She smiled into it. If only she could sink into it too. "I miss you."

"I miss you too."

Despite the lift of her heart, a vague stir started in her gut.

Isaac lay back on his hotel bed and tucked an arm behind his head. His shirtsleeves were rolled to the middle of his forearms, tie long gone, but his jet-black hair was still neatly held in place by gel. Garmin didn't require him to dress so formal; the desire stemmed from hero worship of his pastor grandfather.

"How was the last day of school?" he asked.

"No one acted up."

"Not even that one kid, the one with the mom who emails 'suggestions'?"

"Not even him."

He laughed. "Sounds like a great day. And now summer. Freedom!"

The word grazed against her. Freedom did not describe what she felt. She lowered onto her bed and rested against the pillow. "How were your meetings?"

"Really great. In fact, I have news." His grin grew. "I was offered the senior project manager role."

Nikki sat up straight. "You're kidding! Isaac, that's amazing. I'm so proud of you!"

His eyes twinkled, the pure joy of life falling into place. He spoke of what was next, of the brighter future, the bigger opportunities. Of all the things they hoped for. All the what-ifs of the day before started to take realistic shape for the days to come.

"And with the new salary," he said, "I could definitely afford a mortgage."

The stir in her gut quickened.

They had scouted neighborhoods. Mapped routes to work. Measured the distance to stores, hospitals, and the homes of his extended Sarn family. The path to their future revealed itself stone by stone.

Her parents surely had planned and imagined their years together. They had searched for houses until the colonial came into view, had kicked around ideas for the future. Never did they imagine betrayal. Or abandonment.

Her mom had fallen in love, then into divorce at a time in her life when she should have expected only security. She never saw it coming.

Nikki wrapped her free arm across her stomach and held on tightly.

"Nik?"

She lifted her chin. "Mmm?"

"You okay? I seem to have lost you for a sec."

24

"Sorry. Yes. Just tired."

Isaac lowered his brow. "Something on your mind?" Before she could answer, he shook his head at his own question. "Of course you have a lot on your mind. How is . . . everything?" The missed beat clearly indicated which "everything" he meant.

She shrugged. "It's hard. That's all."

"That's all?" he asked gently.

"Yeah."

For a moment he watched her, eyes searching her face.

"I'm just tired," she assured him.

At last he nodded. "You should rest then. I have an idea. I get in about four tomorrow. I'll pick you up and take you out. Anywhere you want to go. Maybe that Lao bistro?"

She grinned at the memories. Her first taste of his heritage food. Their first kiss.

He grinned back. "That's the one. We'll order nam khao and extra spring rolls. And maybe we can pick up where we left off in our conversation last Friday."

She fought to keep the grin in place. The conversation had been about ring design. The stir whipped into an ache.

"What do you say?" he asked.

"That— Yeah. That sounds great."

◆ ◆ ◆ ◆

Coffee could not compare to drinking in Scripture at sunrise. It was as true in the desert as it was on a two-hundred-acre plot in northeast Missouri.

Wes sat on his porch swing, Bible open to Ephesians in his lap. Rich orange and pink hues collided on the eastern horizon. The birds' songs of praise rose from the branches of the oak at the end of the front yard. Indelible words from the apostle Paul cycled through the space around him: "I urge you to live a life worthy of the calling you have received. Be completely humble and gentle; be patient, bearing with one another in love."

He closed his eyes, silently reciting the words as the birds chirped along their up-down scales. He pulled in every drop of wisdom that opened up to him. Humble. Gentle. Patient. Bearing in love. He asked to have it all toward Chris.

At last he exhaled. Every morning, he said thank-you to the Creator of all. Every morning, he meant it a little more.

He rose from the swing and went inside to make himself a fast breakfast of instant oatmeal topped with butter and bacon crumbles. His doctor had instructed him to stay away from salt and fat. Having both astride tasteless heart-healthy grains was as far as he cared to wander.

Around eight o'clock, he texted the long-overdue photo of his house to Aunt Emma, then loaded up his gray Silverado and followed the long gravel driveway past the old farmhouse and toward the unpaved county road slicing through the Werner land. His small herd of Angus milled about the gate of the pasture across the road. Their rust-red heads turned his way when he pulled up.

"Already waiting for me, aren't you, girls?" he said as he climbed down from his cab. He toted the five-gallon buckets of corn feed from the bed of his truck to the troughs inside the gate and spread the contents evenly for the girls. It took several trips to unload all four buckets, but none of the cows dared try for the open gate during feeding time.

When the buckets were empty and the cows occupied, he retrieved a fresh salt-lick block from the truck bed and slipped it into the holder on the fence post near the gate. One of the cows, a lighter shade than the others, ambled over to investigate.

"Morning, Connie."

She flicked her ears against invisible nuisances. Her yellow ear tag cut through the air, flashing the "17" written on the front in his own hand. She took Wes in with her dark eyes. His father once told him that certain cows, like dogs, have an undeniable ability to understand humans. Connie was one of the few in Wes's lifetime that fit that description.

"Brought the good stuff for you today. Tell that rascal of yours to come on over."

As if on cue, the bull calf bounded out of the crowd and came toward his mother. He stopped when he saw how close she was to Wes. In the two weeks since his birth, he had grown in thickness considerably, owing entirely to the rich spring grass.

Wes backed out of the gate and latched the chain. "All yours, big guy."

The calf kept a wary eye on him. For her part, Connie strode to the salt lick, unafraid. Her long, tannish tongue stretched toward the block as her tail glanced to the right and left. Step by step, her calf padded up to her side. Like his mother, he twitched his ears. Unlike his mother, he had no tag to flash, his future on the Werner farm yet to be determined. By the end of summer, before he turned four months, Wes would decide whether to sell him or raise him as a steer.

Wes squatted and reached through a gap in the gate, palm up. "Come on," he called to the calf.

The young one considered, even took a step, then quickly dodged behind his mother.

Wes chuckled. "Fair enough. Maybe next time." Before returning to his truck, he stroked Connie between the eyes and wished her a good day.

The co-op board meeting started at nine o'clock in Redmont, the nearest "big" town. He had just enough time to get there.

A mile from home, he crested a hill and came upon the hamlet of Eddner, a piece of the Werner family for longer than the farmstead itself. First came the cemetery, many of its headstones chiseled with the names of saints with whom he shared blood. In the distance, the steeple of Hosana Lutheran Church held a silver cross aloft. Underneath it were the remaining buildings of a once-bustling settlement. A freestanding parish hall, the parsonage, the defunct one-room schoolhouse that he and Chris—and their parents—attended for elementary school, the teacher's cottage, and several sheds. Most of the buildings donned a matching, pristine-white clapboard.

Cottonwoods and elms partially shaded the schoolyard. Shirts on the clothesline behind the parsonage served as the only sign of human presence on a Friday morning. Sunday mornings and Thursday night 4-H meetings at the schoolhouse brought more activity.

The grass of the cemetery needed a mow ahead of the Memorial Day weekend. Later that day, he would need to bring up his small tractor and brush hog to get everything shipshape. Final resting places deserved to be as respectable as possible, especially for that holiday. War had taught him that.

For such a tiny, almost forgotten spot on earth, Eddner held so many treasured pieces of Wes's life. Nearly as treasured as those found in his parents' old farmhouse. Chris didn't understand his desire to preserve their childhood home. But much like with Eddner, too much lived under the surface to be completely disregarded.

Wes would find a way to keep the house relevant into the future. One way or another.

◆ ◆ ◆ ◆

The co-op manager, Roy, clicked to the next slide of his presentation. "Here is a snapshot of the monthly totals so far this year," he said. "The black bar on each month shows the total number of accounts, which you can see remained steady over this time period. But I know we are all more concerned at this point with the red bar—the past-due accounts."

The red bars had inched upward month over month. Though April seemed to level off, if not fall a fraction, the total was still too high.

"With summer right around the corner and customers ramping up use of cooling devices for both themselves and their livestock, we could see this number continue to climb," he added.

Board members weren't allowed to know the identity of the at-risk customers, though it was not a leap to assume those red bars represented people whose homes they had been to—neighbors, former classmates, fellow farmers, maybe congregation mates.

People whose livelihoods rose and fell with agricultural commodity prices and who lived at the mercy of the weather.

"Economics always hit hardest on the people who can least stand against it," lamented the chairman, a slightly hunched seventy-something named Otis Harman, voice husky from age and wear. "Is there a way to soften the blow for our folks? What haven't we tried, Roy?"

Roy gripped the back of the chair in front of him. "Our options are few, ladies and gentlemen. Remember, we are for-profit. We have bills to pay too. We need to protect our bottom line."

"We need to protect our community first," Otis shot back.

Wes spoke up, a softer edge to his tone. "The co-op exists for all of us. It's why it was founded. People banded together to bring an essential need to our area when no one else would."

"And during the Great Depression, no less."

All heads turned to the far end of the table. Joyce Kindstrom, bakery manager for Redmont's only grocery store, held her gaze to Roy's. "We owe it to those who sacrificed to build this co-op to continue keeping the community first."

"Amen!" Otis replied. Others echoed.

Amid the murmur, Joyce flitted her eyes toward Wes. Her lips tilted upward.

Quickly he turned back to the chart and adjusted his reading glasses. Despite all his best efforts, he had not figured out how to dissuade her grins of interest. That part of his life was long over. It had started wilting the moment he left Ada behind.

After another hour of discussion and respectful debate, Otis adjourned the meeting. Wes gathered his papers into his portfolio, already switching his mental energy back to his farm, where only cattle and a long list of to-dos would keep him company.

Several directors stopped on their way out of the boardroom to pat him on the shoulder and congratulate him on the new house.

"Thank you. Stay well," he returned to each of them.

The interaction happened several times in a row, enough to

distract him from the fact that Joyce waited by the boardroom door, a foil-wrapped tin in her hand.

Wes girded himself and slowly proceeded to the door. Otis and Roy were deep in conversation. Everyone else had left. A minimal audience was still too much of an audience.

Joyce smiled wide as he approached, her perfectly set teeth gleaming between soft pink lips. Straw-colored hair edged her jawline. As a girl sitting a row apart from him in the Eddner schoolhouse, she'd seemed more interested in Chris. Every girl had seemed more interested in Chris.

He nodded to her politely and mumbled, "Morning, Joyce."

She held out the tin. "A housewarming gift for you."

"Thoughtful of you. Thanks." He took the tin, careful to avoid her hands lest he give the wrong impression.

"Rhubarb pie," she said. "We had a fresh shipment come in at the store, and I thought I might as well put it to good use for an old friend. Of course, I did save some back for my 4-H girls to practice canning, but I know how much you like rhubarb."

"I do. Yes."

"Hope it's better than those Hostess things you normally eat." She laughed. Lines formed parentheses around her mouth. Deep-set crow's feet whiskered on her temples. Despite what beauty magazines claimed about such signs of age, Joyce seemed to possess more refined grace than any woman in town. A grace that riled a certain place in Wes's chest, against his better judgment.

He cleared his throat, drawing himself back to the moment. "Very thoughtful," he said and started to take a step forward.

Joyce held out her hand for him to pause. She glanced toward Otis and Roy, then leaned closer. "I heard about Chris." She held up her left hand and wiggled her empty ring finger.

"How did you . . . ?"

"I'm connected with Chris on social media. I saw the pictures his wife posted from the party they had. Reception, I guess you'd call it."

Another reason to avoid social media. The backhanded stunts people pulled were dehumanizing. If Joyce was seeing the family business blasted on social media, Lydia and the girls surely had too.

Joyce glanced down, hesitant. "His wife—Sheryl—posted some things about your family."

The Holy Spirit tugged the reins of his tongue. Heeding the words of a fool never led to good. But it was his family Sheryl talked about. He couldn't stop himself. "What did she say?" he asked.

Joyce worked her bottom lip for a second. "That you all were narrow-minded and, in so many words, heartless."

Judgment from a woman who had never met him or, to his knowledge, any Werner except Chris.

He nodded. "Yes, I suppose she would say that."

"For what it's worth, no one who knows your family would ever think of you all that way." She glanced again at the other men before adding, "Especially about you."

Heat crawled across his cheeks. Her pie in his hands, her compliment clanging in his ears . . . It didn't take an overly intelligent man to do the math.

He held up the gift and nodded. "Thanks again. I better get going."

"Before you go." Joyce reached for his arm but pulled back before her fingers could land. "If you need help with your parents' old house—you know, cleaning it up and getting it ready for whatever's next—I hope you'll let me know. That little house has such special memories for me too. Your mother was always so sweet to me. I'm happy to help in whatever way you need."

He shifted his weight from one foot to the other. "Well, actually . . ."

"Oh, maybe you have plans already? I should have asked that first."

Only one word came to his lips. "Yes." Internally, he cringed. Lies tasted like vinegar.

Joyce nodded. "Of course. I understand. The offer stands, though. See you at church." She smiled brightly. Too brightly. Like a spotlight directly on his indiscretion.

"See you," he said, then turned and walked out of the room.

Outside, as he crossed the parking lot to his truck, he fought the urge to hang his head. What he needed more than ever were some plans for that house.

Four

T he kinks in Nikki's neck testified to unreleased tension burrowed deep in her muscles. The bedsheets pulled loose from the corners bore witness to the restlessness that had invaded even her sleep. She forced herself to rise long enough to call Principal Washington and ask for a personal day. It was the only one she had used all year, and the fact it fell on an end-of-term teacher workday took the edge off the guilt. She wasn't missing any classroom time. Then she silenced her phone and hid under the covers.

Finally, a little before ten, she trudged to the bathroom. She cringed at her reflection in the mirror above the sink. Mussed chestnut hair, drooping eyelids, dark half moons at the tops of her ivory cheeks. A mess. She met her own eyes. The same brown shade as her dad's peered back at her.

She cut her gaze away and flipped on the tap. The bite of cold water on her face chased away the gathering thoughts.

That was what she had to keep doing: chasing away the thoughts of her dad, of her mom, of the impending conversation with Isaac that night—of everything. If she kept her hands moving, the thoughts would be silenced.

She changed into cotton sweatpants and her old Kansas State T-shirt and set her hands to the only task she could find: cleaning.

From top to bottom, side to side, front to back, she attacked her tiny abode with vigor. Scrubbed the shelves of the fridge. Swept away the cobwebs from the corners. Stripped the bed. Wiped the smudges from the windowpanes. Took a toothbrush to the white caulk between the shower tiles.

Sweat formed on her brow as her apartment took on a clean and cozy feel reminiscent of Grandma Ann's farmhouse. Only snatches of her grandma remained in her memory. The way she threw open her arms when Nikki walked through her front door, the pitch of her laugh, the crisp cleanness of her home. She always seemed to have a towel within reach, ready to sweep up crumbs or tidy up a spill.

Nikki moved her scrub pad in circles, the way Grandma Ann used to run a wet washcloth over the table after Christmas dinner. The smile on her grandma's face was a product of the joy she'd found in providing her family a comfortable space to slip back into whenever the occasion arose. Which didn't come often.

What a difference it would have made if Nikki had known her grandma more, known what she was like on a normal day. Did she ever long to know Nikki more? Did she ever say as much to her son? Did he listen?

Nikki scrubbed harder, until the thoughts skittered away.

◆　◆　◆　◆

By one o'clock, the apartment gleamed. Nikki made herself a spinach grilled cheese and sat on the ledge below her lone window. Full sun danced on the current ripples of the river. She closed her eyes and attempted to soak in the moment of stillness. The roar of an airplane cut through. The rumble grew louder as the vessel approached the downtown airport less than a mile away. Then a train whistled.

She sighed and opened her eyes. So much for a peaceful lunch break. She took a bite, then another. The sandwich was salty-greasy in all the best ways. The result of the technique she had worked to perfect.

She licked the oil off her fingers, glad her grandma was not around to see such a lack of couth, then padded over to the nightstand to grab a tissue. The box moved with the pull of her hand, butting against her phone lying facedown, where it had been from the moment after she ended the call with Principal Washington. Though part of her wanted to leave it that way, another part needed assurance her mom didn't need anything.

She picked up the phone and turned it upright. A text from Tracy.

Heard you took the day off. Hope you are
getting good rest. Text me if you need anything.

She smiled and put her plate on the bed to type back.

You're the best.

Another unread message waited, sent early that morning. From Isaac.

At the airport. Only a few more hours until I'm
home. Can't stop thinking about you—about us.

A sharp pain sliced through her. He loved her so much. He wanted things women dreamed of their man wanting. So why did it hurt? Why did that churn start again?

If only someone would tell her what it all meant. Someone who had been there before on the edge of forever. Someone like her older sister.

She noted the time. Twenty after one. Maybe she could catch Hannah at a good time. She dialed her sister's number and waited through the rings.

"Hey there," Hannah answered.

"Bad time?"

"I have a meeting in a few minutes, but I can talk. How are you? Tough day yesterday."

"Shocking day." She told Hannah about the visit with their

mom, the hollow of her cheeks, the crumpling of her spirit when the news of their dad sank in.

"Oh, Mom." Hannah sighed. "I can't even imagine what she's going through."

Nikki moved back to the window and sat on the ledge. The sunbeams warmed her face. "Do you think she regrets getting married?"

"Regrets? That's pretty strong."

"Wouldn't you feel that way if you were her?"

"Nik, what's going on? Is this about you and Isaac?"

"No, I just . . ." She might as well confess. "I suppose it is."

"You and Isaac are not Mom and Dad."

"I know, but . . ."

"But what?"

Outside her window, the current billowed, rolled with a strength that sank boats. "How did you know Tyler was the one?"

Hannah paused as if drumming up the best, most careful advice she could on the spot. "Love is often confused with infatuation. I found him attractive, for sure, and I felt all the butterflies and all that. But the real way I knew was because I trusted him. With everything, I mean. Trusted him with my heart, my money, my fears, my sadness. I trusted him to see the worst of me, the ugliest pieces, and still choose me."

Despite the clarity the answer brought, the pain stabbed again. Nikki lowered her head against it.

"You okay, Nik?"

"I'm fine. Thinking, is all."

"Listen, I have to get to my meeting, but can I ask you to do one thing?"

"What's that?"

"Whatever it is you're thinking about, tell Isaac."

Nikki chortled. "My mentor teacher said the same thing."

"Wise woman. Call me later if you want."

"Thanks for talking."

"Always."

They said their goodbyes and hung up.

Nikki was left once more with the hours between her and Isaac. Hours that dwindled quickly.

The walls slowly closed in.

◆ ◆ ◆ ◆

Tracy would tell her to pray. But the more the minutes marched toward four o'clock, the stiffer her hands became, refusing to fold. They were too busy trying to hold up the mass that pressed in on her, heavier, colder, harder. Squeezing the air from her lungs, making her mind scream.

If her hands wouldn't move, then her feet could. She grabbed her purse and keys and headed down to the street. She could walk. To wherever, for however long. Walk and keep walking. Let the bustle of the neighborhood fold her in, hide her in the shadows.

She started down her block, toward the heart of the district where her favorite coffee shop waited. Small pleasures made days better.

But the cacophony of the River Market seemed louder than the day before. Closer, invasive. It was everywhere she turned, on the right, on the left, above, below, behind.

Her feet chose a new direction. Toward her car.

She started driving. Through the downtown streets, then onto an interstate that wound into the suburbs. She kept driving, followed the interstate until it spilled onto another, which eventually spilled onto another. From one edge of the city to another, she traced along the never-ending white line, hour after hour. The white noise of tires thrumming on pavement. She stopped for gas and a taquito from the roller, then returned to the wheel.

The sun tiptoed toward the horizon. Still she drove. Past the same exits, the same junctions. Past four o'clock. She stopped again, texted Isaac.

I can't do tonight.

Then kept driving.

Her phone rang. She ignored it.

Six o'clock. Seven. Eight.

Pinks and reds swathed the western horizon. She turned onto I-35 North, the white line cutting upward at a diagonal through the city. Within minutes, farmland stretched in every direction. Exits grew farther and farther apart.

Miles passed. The sun pulled the covers over its head.

Her phone rang again.

She let it go to voicemail.

The junction with US Highway 36 approached, the Iowa border less than seventy miles beyond.

She took the exit and paused at the stoplight guarding the intersection. To the left, the entrance ramp to the southbound lanes with traffic flowing back to the city. To the right, a long white line leading eastward to the opposite side of Missouri, to the larger, wider, muddier Mississippi River.

To Grandma Ann's farm.

She tightened her grip on the steering wheel.

A semitruck approached from behind. Its headlights grew bigger and bigger.

Left, home. Right . . . where?

The semi stopped behind her, diesel engine rumbling through her windows.

She pulled in her breath. And turned right.

◆ ◆ ◆ ◆

Wes would have been asleep already had it not been for the pie. One slice for lunch, two for supper, and the lure of a fourth proved too strong to resist. He left his bedtime reading behind and lumbered to the kitchen.

No one needed to know how much he enjoyed Joyce's rhubarb pie. Especially not Joyce.

Plate balanced in one hand, he settled into his recliner and clicked on the television. The screen kicked on to the first half of

Shane. The time on the satellite box ticked to 10:37 as the Technicolor wonders of the Alan Ladd Western splashed across the room and mixed with the buttery glow of the floor lamp next to his chair.

He had barely taken a bite when headlights began to crawl up the driveway. He paused mid-chew. No one would be out this far this late if they weren't lost or in need of help.

The headlights hesitated at the turn for the old farmhouse. Then, as if the driver could tell the house was empty, the headlights proceeded toward his partially illuminated living room window.

He rose, muted the television.

The headlights slid to a stop behind his truck. Moments later, he opened the front door to find a young woman under his porch light, with an unkempt bun and sweatpants, arms clasped across her torso, and eyes a strikingly familiar color.

"Uncle Wes?" she asked.

He blinked. It couldn't be. "N-Nikki?"

She nodded.

Often he had prayed for her; rarely had they spoken. Now she stood before him, waiting with water-rimmed eyes. No one followed her to the door. No other car inched up the driveway. So many questions to ask. All he could get out was, "Why . . . why are . . . ?"

She shook her head. "I don't know." Her expression pleaded, the same cry of a wounded buddy in a hospital bed, silently begging for Wes to explain the purpose behind the pain.

He needed to do something, to be an uncle. "You, uh . . . you want . . ." For lack of words, he motioned toward the living room and stepped aside.

She dipped her head and brushed past him, out from the broad night, away from whatever had chased her to his doorstep.

Palpable heartache trailed in her wake.

❀ *Five* ❀

U ncle Wes was taller than her dad, was squarer in the shoulders, and had dark hair that had fizzled to gray mixed
with specks of white. The salt-and-pepper carried forward to his close-cropped beard, and in between was skin leathered
by the sun. He moved past her to the recliner, where a plate of pie
waited on the seat. Scenes of an old Western played silently on
the television.

"I, uh . . ." He put a thick hand on the hip of his flannel pajama
pants, rippling the blue T-shirt above it. "Quite a surprise, you
coming."

She pulled her arms tighter against her ribs. "I'm sorry I'm
disturbing you."

"No, no. Not disturbing. You're always welcome." He grabbed
the remote from the arm of the chair and powered off the TV. "I'm
just surprised."

That made two of them. She had not walked on Werner land in
fourteen years and had little reason left to do so. Still, something
about that plot of earth had drawn her.

"I wanted somewhere to think," she said. It was the thinnest
of explanations she could give. It was the only explanation she
could give.

After a moment, he nodded, as if he understood perfectly. She took in a deep breath and let it out slowly.

They stood in silence for several beats. At last Uncle Wes asked, "Want some pie?"

He asked for no further explanation, no further qualification. He unhesitatingly made room in his life and home for her, something her dad withheld.

To that, she nodded. "Yeah."

◆ ◆ ◆ ◆

Nikki needed a place to think, she had said. Needed it so much she had driven across an entire state in the dark to find it. She may not have understood why she landed in Eddner, but Wes did. Family roots pulled on every human heart, no matter how broken. Yet more proof he could not let his parents' old place go barren.

He set his plate of pie on the breakfast bar between the kitchen and dining room and headed to the opposite corner to get a slice for Nikki.

"New house?" she asked.

"Moved in last week."

"Still has that fresh-drywall smell." She trailed around the dining table, evaluating the digs. "Pretty bare bones in here. Not a lot of pictures on your walls. Except for these guys." She stopped before two framed grayscale portraits overlooking the table, one of a man and the other of his wife.

"Know who they are?" he asked.

"Grandma's parents. Otto and Lena Baumann."

He lifted his brow. "Impressive."

"Grandma used to have them hanging in her living room, so I would see them every Christmas. They always looked so stern, like we were having way too much fun without them."

He grinned. "Sounds about right."

"You ever meet them?"

He gathered the full plate and a fork and brought them over to the bar. "Otto died when I was still young. Lena before I was born, before my mom and dad moved to the farm, actually."

She frowned. "Really?" More questions obviously lingered, but she left them where they were and came over to the bar. "Thank you for the pie. What flavor is this?"

"Rhubarb."

She poked the tines of her fork against the softened pinkish-red chunks. "Don't think I've ever had rhubarb. Is it a favorite of yours?"

He turned slightly and nodded toward the tin, now more than half empty.

"Apparently so." She chuckled. Her fork slid easily through the flaky crust and filling, then clinked against her plate. At the first bite, her eyes widened. "Wow, that is tart. Good, but tart."

"Makes you know you're alive," he said, taking in a forkful.

"Did Grandma make rhubarb pies for you as a kid?"

"Cakes mostly. Apple for pies, usually. Used to have two trees on the west side of the farmhouse."

"Oh yes, I remember those."

A ringtone bounced through the room. Nikki looked at her purse sitting on a nearby barstool. Throwaway calls rarely came in the middle of the night.

"Need to get that?" he asked.

She twisted her lips to the side. "I'll call them back."

The rings ran their course. Silence resumed. Nikki fiddled with her fork, staring at her pie.

"Does anyone know where you are?" Wes asked.

The fork in her hand caught the overhead light with every movement. "No," she admitted at last.

She was a grown woman, entitled to move about as she pleased. But clearly whatever she ran from had followed her. With everything going on with her parents, it was probably best to not let it fester.

He cleared his throat. "Maybe call back now."

Her eyes flitted up to him, then lowered again.

"Nikki," he said, "I'd be more comfortable if you called now."

The fork twirled once, twice. Finally she set it down and reached into her purse.

He turned to the side, offering her a shield of privacy.

"That was my mom." Her voice tipped up at the end, a clear note of surprise.

He hung back as she rose from the stool and headed for the living room. The phone was to her ear before she rounded the corner.

◆ ◆ ◆ ◆

"Nikki! You had me worried! Isaac said he couldn't get ahold of you."

She bowed her head, stepped closer to the front door, farther from her uncle. "I'm sorry, Mom. I didn't think Isaac would call you." She gritted her teeth. He shouldn't have involved her mom— her already fragile mom. But it was understandable why he did.

"Where are you? Are you okay?"

One of those questions was easier to answer than the other. "I'm fine. I'm . . . in Eddner."

"*Eddner?* What on earth?"

"I don't know, Mom. Honestly, I don't. I only know that I needed a place to think."

"So you went to Eddner? I don't understand."

If she couldn't explain it to herself, there was no hope of explaining it to her mom.

"Are you at the farm?" her mom asked.

"Yes. With Uncle Wes."

"Let me talk to him."

"Mom, I—"

"Give him the phone." Not since Nikki was a child had she received such a sharp command. Slowly she turned and trailed back to the kitchen.

Uncle Wes looked up, a question written across his brow.

She held out her phone. "My mom wants to talk to you."

His Adam's apple bobbed. In measured movements, he took the phone in his callused hand. "Hello?"

Her mom's voice was a mere muffle, a formless sound seeping through the narrow space between the phone and Uncle Wes's ear.

Nikki hovered near her plate, lifted up her fork, then set it down again.

"Yes, Lydia, long time . . . Yes . . . Not a problem at all."

Clearly they were talking about her and the imposition she thrust upon him.

For a while, her mom carried the conversation, saying many words that only Uncle Wes could hear. He sprinkled in a "Yes" or "I understand."

Nikki picked up her fork again, poked at a piece of rhubarb.

"Really, it's no problem," he said. "She's welcome . . . Yes . . . Yes . . . Will do . . . Nice talking to you too, Lydia. Did you want Nikki— Okay. Yes. Goodbye." He ended the call and met her gaze. "She wants you to call her tomorrow. She's going to bed."

She took the phone from his outstretched hand and waited for more. But he betrayed no confidences, no secrets of what they had discussed.

The partially eaten slices waited on their plates. The night deepened around the house. The clock on the stove ticked deeper into the eleven o'clock hour. Time for all of them to think about bed.

Uncle Wes scratched his chin. "My, uh, my spare bed is still in the farmhouse, if you're okay with sleeping there." He had told her mom she was welcome, that it wasn't a problem. But it still cost him.

"More than okay," she said.

He nodded. "I'll walk you down when you're ready."

Mercy upon mercy. The way family should be. She was safe with him in that place. The promise of it settled around her, invited her to exhale. She was in the presence of family who understood what family meant.

She laid down her fork for the last time. "Ready."

◆ ◆ ◆ ◆

A three-quarter moon cast enough light to make the white gravel of the driveway glow against the drape of darkness between yard lights. Overhead, the bold stars hung like fireflies just out of reach. A bullfrog's deep-throated croak resounded from the pond across the road.

The plastic grocery sack swung against Wes's thigh, the spare toiletries he had managed to scrounge up poking at his pajama pant leg with every tap.

Nikki shouldered her purse and the gym bag from her trunk, a single change of clothes inside—the only thing she had brought with her besides a head full of worries and fears, the magnitude of which Lydia had shared a glimpse. It wasn't only the divorce that had made Nikki run, her mother had said. God only knew how ensnared Nikki must have felt with everything pressing in on her. God only knew how much he related, especially when it came to the hopes and desires of a certain young man waiting for her back in Kansas City.

"Sure you don't want me to move my car?" she asked.

"It's fine for tonight."

Neither of them broached the question that was slung over them: *What happens in the morning?*

In the distance, a muffled whistle blew from a freight train finding its way through the countryside.

"I hope you know how much I appreciate all you're doing, Uncle Wes."

"Glad to help."

They turned left at the elbow of the old driveway. The gravel had long worn away, exposing the dirt underneath, the kind that stuck to the ribs of vehicles with the stubbornness of broadleaf weeds. The drive ended abruptly at the spot where the old chicken coop once stood. A narrow sidewalk older than Wes himself joined up with the drive there.

He led the way up the walk toward the L-shaped white clapboard house on the outer edge of the yard light's orb. The boards of his mother's beloved porch creaked under their feet in greeting.

Using his hip to prop open the screen door, he dug the keys from his pocket. "Usually keep it locked, just to be safe."

The latch clicked. The door whined on its hinges as he pushed it open.

"Come on in." He flipped on the light and set the grocery bag on the small table next to the door. Nikki stepped inside.

Most of the furniture his mother owned remained, in mostly the same spots they had always been—all relics from the 1990s era, with loud rose-adorned upholstery in reds and blues. A couch and armchair, coffee table and area rug. The only addition he'd made was the squat media console underneath the now-empty television bracket.

"Bought a lot of new furniture for my house," he explained. "Left all this thinking I might rent out the place. Needs a good face-lift, though."

Nikki set her bag and purse on the floor and pointed to a stack of boxes in the corner by the picture window. "Still packing up some things?"

"Yes. Boxes in the front bedroom too. But those over there are from the attic. My mom's stuff, I believe. Need to go through it yet. Hope it won't be in your way much."

"Not at all." She stepped forward to the kitchen off the back of the living room, the hardwoods awaking under her feet. "I can almost smell Christmas."

He followed her to the entrance of the galley kitchen. "Left some cookware I didn't need. No food, though."

She surveyed the room—the dark-brown cabinets, old-school Formica countertops, appliances that had lasted more harvests than the combine. At the opposite end of the room, tucked in the open space under the windows overlooking the backyard, was the oak table. The centerpiece of every family meal, with an intricately carved pedestal and skirt and a slit down the middle where a leaf could be inserted. She studied it as if resurrecting scenes long finished.

After a moment, she turned to him. "Suppose I should get settled in."

◆　◆　◆　◆

Before he left, Uncle Wes had dug sheets and a towel from one of the boxes slung against the wall of the larger bedroom. The towel now hung in the bathroom, and the sheets lay folded with precise military creases on the foot of the bare twin mattress in the smaller bedroom. The bed was the only piece of furniture in the room besides the chest of drawers. The walls boasted the same old beige paper with muted gray pinstripes. The paper had faded with time, except for those spots where something once hung. If she closed her eyes, she could drum up which FFA plaque or baseball all-star poster fit into which square or rectangle.

Her dad had slept in that room. Spent his entire childhood there, admiring those posters, counting those stripes, staring up at that ceiling as he dreamed of things beyond those four walls.

That innocent boy was no longer.

She clenched her jaw and swatted the light switch down. She would sleep on the couch.

In the only bathroom, tucked between the two bedrooms, she did her best to strip off her makeup from the day using the bar of soap from the supply of toiletries Uncle Wes had given her. She brushed her teeth with the extra toothbrush and tube of tooth-paste. The holdovers of tart rhubarb yielded to the minty tooth-paste. When she finished, she returned to the living room, to the quiet she had driven two hundred miles hoping to find.

She lingered behind the couch, fingers tracing over the threads of the crocheted afghan lying across the back. For the first time, she stood dead center in the decision she had made. The wee hours amplified her aloneness. Cricket songs seeped through the windowpanes. Each note pealed with a reminder of how far she was from home, from her mom, from her neighborhood, from everything that was hers.

From Isaac.

Surely her mom had told him by now where she was. Her phone waited in her purse by the front door. She had no answers for him, though. Not yet. And certainly not the ones he longed to hear—and deserved to have his girlfriend say. He wouldn't wait forever. Every love had its limits. The past four months had taught her that.

She swallowed against the rising cries, against the billow and roll. Somehow she would find a way to explain to Isaac why she couldn't have dinner.

Somehow, God willing, that moment would come soon.

Six

Orange splintered across the inky eastern horizon, seeping steadily upward and outward. Wes closed his Bible and exhaled. The facade of the old farmhouse captured a faint tint of the sky. Between those walls, Nikki slept. The niece he barely knew but whose decision to run echoed his own.

"Lord," he whispered, "if I'm truly to be in the middle of this, please go there first. Because I'm going to need all the guidance I can get. Amen."

The swing chains clinked as he rose. He had sought the wisest counsel of all. It was time for the second-wisest. As he headed inside to make his morning oatmeal, he called Aunt Emma's cell. By the time he reached the kitchen, she'd answered.

"Didn't wake you, did I?"

"Please. Who do you think gets up the roosters?"

He chuckled and retrieved the instant rolled oats from the pantry. "Glad you're up. Had an interesting development last night."

"Oh?"

"Nikki showed up."

"Nikki? Chris's Nikki?"

"Knocked on my door in the middle of the night. Alone. Red eyes. Lost look. Said she wanted a place to think."

"Sakes alive! What brought that on?"

As he prepped his oatmeal for the microwave, he recounted the major points of his interaction with Nikki, and with Lydia.

"Bless her heart," Aunt Emma replied. "It has to be difficult."

"She stayed in the farmhouse last night. Seemed to remember the place fondly."

"I'm sure she does. Your mother always loved having her for those brief Christmas visits."

He set his bowl in the microwave and punched in a cook time of one minute. "She and I don't really know each other, though. Haven't seen her since she was a girl. I have no idea what to say to her."

"Just keep doing what you're doing, Fritz. She clearly feels at peace with you, and she clearly needs somewhere peaceful to be right now. Besides, I can think of no one better who understands what it is to be young and have the screws put to you."

He shifted his weight from one foot to the other. "Not sure I'm the model she needs in that department." Especially when it came to the situation with Isaac.

"Hogwash. There's a big fat zero percent chance that her showing up at your door was a coincidence. What's that Bible verse about God comforting us in our pain so that we can comfort others? You have been specially selected for an important role in this season of her life precisely because you understand."

He swallowed. The timer counted down steadily, closer to breakfast, closer to the time he would be face-to-face with Nikki again.

"Take this chance to get to know her," Aunt Emma said. "Make up for lost time."

The microwave dinged, like a loud punctuation on the end of her directive.

"You have far too much confidence in me," he said.

"And for that I will never apologize."

◆　◆　◆　◆

Maybe it was being on the farm. Maybe it was the way the couch cushions sagged and peaked in all the wrong places. Whatever it was, Nikki woke before the sun had fully crested the horizon. She opened the side slots of the picture window and soaked in the early morning. Light spread its silent wings over the gentle hills and fenced pasture in the distance across the road. All of it serene as a postcard, as comforting as her deep memories had claimed it was.

Still, below the surface festered a reality that it couldn't last. Choices needed to be made. Messages returned. Explanations given.

She drew in a breath, blew it out slowly, asked for strength. A request she should have made the day before.

She pushed away from the window and went to her purse still sitting by the door. She picked up her phone and woke it from sleep mode. A low-battery warning appeared. Less than two percent power. Her charger, along with every other essential, was still back in Kansas City.

She cleared out the warning and used what little juice remained to open the text thread with Isaac. His last message had come through after midnight.

What's going on?

She grimaced. What could she say? Nothing seemed good enough or truthful enough. He deserved a reply of some kind, though. Something to let him know her heart still sought his.

I'm sorry. I will call soon.

Shame pooled in her chest as she powered down her phone and slipped it deep into her purse, out of sight. Had it not been for the footfalls on the porch, she would have stayed hunched over.

A knock fell on the door. She smoothed her hair, then stepped over to open it.

Uncle Wes was already fully dressed in a button-down plaid shirt, jeans, and faded cowboy boots. In his hands was a ceramic cereal bowl. "Brought you breakfast."

"That's so nice of you." She stepped aside to let him enter.

His gaze caught on the couch, the pillow and the afghan splayed across the cushions. Though he didn't say anything, his eyes held questions.

She shut the door and kept them on the topic at hand. "What's for breakfast?"

"Oatmeal. Hope you like it."

"I do." She took the bowl. The outside was still wonderfully warm, but the crumbles of meat scattered on top made her pause. She lifted her gaze to his. "Is that sausage?"

He shrugged one shoulder. "I ran out of bacon."

She blinked. The man ate his fruit between crusts and his oats saturated with meat. It didn't get more bachelor, more farmer, than that. She nodded politely. "Thank you."

He rocked onto his toes, clearly weighing what to say next. "I, uh, I was needing to go to town to get some things. Wondered if you want to go, pick up anything you might need."

The implication was clear in his invitation. She tapped the side of the bowl. "I suppose we should talk about how long I'll be staying."

He hooked his thumbs through his front belt loops. "You're welcome to stay the weekend. Or however long. No rush."

Indeed, the rush was not on his end. Nothing about him or his farm dealt in rush, and it was a salve she didn't want to lose.

"How about the weekend?" she said. It was Memorial Day weekend, long enough but short.

He nodded. "Good with me."

She grinned. First decision made, the first stone in whatever path she had wandered onto. "In that case, I will definitely go to town with you. I have lots of things I'll need."

"Good, then." He took a step toward the door. "Need to feed my cows and take care of a few things. Half hour okay?"

"Sure. Wait, you have cows?"

He pointed out the picture window. "In that pasture across the road. About twenty head."

"I figured you had crops."

"I cash-rent the fields to a local boy."

"You mean like a lease?"

"Basically. He pays me to use my land and equipment. Helps him get started with farming and gives me income off the fields I'm too old to farm anyway."

"I wouldn't call you old, Uncle Wes."

"You haven't seen me in the cold."

She laughed.

For the first time, her uncle showed his smile. It dimpled one cheek and squinted his eyes, the way Grandma Ann's used to.

"Half hour?" he confirmed.

"I'll see you then."

◆　◆　◆　◆

Sausage did not belong on oatmeal. Bless Uncle Wes, but no. Sausage did not make her favorites list to begin with, let alone atop mushy grains. Nikki used her spoon to push the meat crumbles to one side, then to strip back the sheen of fat the meat had left behind. The underlayers were bland but at least reasonably normal.

She stepped over to the picture window as she ate. The pasture came into better view the more she leaned to the side. Five reddish cows grazed at the edge of the pond. The others must have been off somewhere else.

Uncle Wes drove by in an ATV, five-gallon buckets strapped in the back cargo area. Hopefully his cows ate something healthier than he did.

She scooped more of the untainted oats and chewed. A few minutes later, only a puddle of milk and the clumps of sausage remained. She turned for the kitchen, a plan to discard them already hatching, but the stack of boxes in the corner of the living room caught her eye. The flaps of the top box stood open, presumably where Uncle Wes had left off. Curiosity pulled her closer.

Inside were the remnants of life one would expect to find. Old report cards, letters, photo albums, small jewelry boxes, several books. Two rolled pieces of cloth were wedged among them.

She set the bowl on the coffee table and lifted out a photo album. The pages held black-and-white square photographs, the kind antique cameras produced. Dozens of moments in Werner family history reflected back at her, each one telling a story she had never heard, never knew existed, never had anyone willing to tell her.

Most of the faces she did not recognize, except for one. Great-Grandma Lena. She was more slender than her framed portrait indicated. Though she kept a stoic expression in every photo, her lips seemed to tip up in some, eyes taking in the world around her with interest and care. The collection of photos offered a peek into her life.

Lena with a little girl outside a barn, chickens pecking at the ground around their feet.

Lena holding up a baby quilt for the camera.

The farmhouse looking crisp and new.

A mutt standing guard next to a vegetable garden, the farmhouse and the two apple trees Uncle Wes had mentioned visible in the background.

Lena in her kitchen, a rose-speckled apron covering her dress, mixing bowl in one hand and baby in a matching dress on the opposite hip. The baby girl had the same dark hair and eyes.

Nikki slid the photo from its sleeve and read the penciled inscription on the back: Lena and Ann, 1937. She turned the photo back over, meeting the stares of her great-grandmother and grandmother. The kitchen in which they stood was the same one that was mere feet away from her. The home Grandma Ann had experienced as a tender sprig had become her home in adulthood as well. A type of inheritance most people in the world never enjoyed—Nikki among them.

She tucked the photo back in its place, then shut the album and laid it on the floor. One of the rolled cloths in the box had the same floral print as the apron Great-Grandma Lena wore in the picture with her daughter. Nikki pulled it out and let it fall open.

It *was* the apron.

"Wow." She laid it on the couch and returned to the box for

the other rolled cloth. Another apron, solid blue with gingham pockets and lace trim. She draped it over the first one.

The books called to her next. Books always called to her. All of them were small, almost pocket size, except for one, a thick blue book with *The Lutheran Hymnal* written in gold on the spine. One by one, she pulled the smaller books from the box. The first had a rich burgundy hardcover, the front emblazoned with ornate gold lettering that clearly wasn't English.

Seid Sturk in der Herr.

"That has to be German."

The yellowed pages contained more of the ornate font, all German, except for two short lines at the bottom of the title page: "Concordia Publishing House, St. Louis, Missouri, 1889."

She leaned closer to the page, waiting for her eyes to stop playing tricks on her. But the date indeed claimed the book in her hands—in excellent condition—was 130 years old.

To think it had been in an attic for who knew how many of those years.

She slipped it back into place and pulled out the next one, also in great condition. The cover was an earth brown with the same gold font for the title: *Danz und Theaterbefuch*. According to the title page, Concordia also published it, in 1888.

The third book, though, certainly looked its age. The headcap over the spine was so frayed along the edges it had nearly separated from the book. The wordless black cover was worn to a near gray.

She cradled the fragile headcap in her left palm and gingerly opened the book. In the top right corner of the inside page was a tidy, penciled inscription: "Henrietta Schoenborn." Nikki frowned at the unfamiliar name.

Throughout the book, the text was grouped together in stanzas and labeled with cardinal numbers, like a hymnal without music notations. All in German. Published by Concordia, 1904.

Lastly, she lifted out the Lutheran hymnal, the only book written in English. Published by Concordia, 1941. In the top right corner of the inside page, another inscription, in ink: "Lena Schoenborn."

"Great-Grandma was a Schoenborn?" She could only guess at the pronunciation. German may have been her ancestors' native tongue, but it was a garble in her own mouth.

The questions for Uncle Wes grew.

She replaced the hymnal and quickly searched through the other items. The report cards were all for Grandma Ann, who was dinged a few times by her teacher for her penmanship and "proclivity for daydreams." Tucked next to the cards was a simple, soft-cover composition notebook with a glued spine. The kind a little girl in a one-room country schoolhouse might use.

Nikki eased it from its spot and opened to the first page. Tight inked handwriting filled the spaces between the blue lines.

April 7, 1951

Of all the things our immigrant mothers carried with them to the rollicking hills of middle America, three things withstood the pressures of time and assimilation: faith in One True God, hope for better things, and love of butter.

The first was their stay, the second their nourishment, and the third their salve, unspeakably useful.

Remember this and consider the contents of this book—a humble but well-positioned common book of Old World ways for the modern home. The wise listen to those who have already learned and lived. "Forsake not the law of thy mother: for they shall be an ornament of grace unto thy head, and chains about thy neck" (Prov. 1:8–9).

The meager words in this book, such intangible things that they are, are the only earthly wealth our mothers could leave all their own. But the riches within them are far greater than the hollow gains *of this world, which are such a dim substitute. I pray you follow in our mothers' lead.*

May God be your Rock the rest of your days, and butter be your joy.

The letter was unsigned.

Nikki's lips parted. This was no child's notebook, no child's thoughts.

She started to turn the page, to see more, when a faint rumble outside the window drew her attention. Uncle Wes zipped by, headed back to the house. She still needed to brush her teeth and dress.

She laid the notebook on the couch next to the aprons. The most intriguing book of all would need to wait.

❧ *Seven* ❧

A few minutes before nine o'clock, Wes fired up the Silverado with Nikki sitting shotgun. Eight miles stretched between the farm and Redmont. Eight slow miles of county roads to follow Aunt Emma's advice. Ask Nikki questions, she'd told him. Memorize her answers. Love her accordingly. Aunt Emma had made it sound so easy.

They rolled down the driveway, then Wes made the left onto the county road. Connie watched them pass from her spot by the feed troughs. Her boy took off from her side and bumbled along the fencerow after them.

Nikki chuckled. "Looks like someone wants to go with us."

"Ornery little guy," Wes said. "Keeps his mom busy."

"Which one's his mom?"

"Lighter-colored one back there. Connie."

"You name your cows?"

"And number them. For state registration."

They passed the corner of the pasture, where the perpendicular fencerows met. The calf came to a halt in the crook.

Nikki turned in her seat and watched him pine for adventure. "Does he have a name?"

"Haven't registered him yet. May sell him later this summer."

"He still deserves a name, don't you think?"

"Hadn't thought about it."

The road slipped between woods on either side. Wes shifted to fourth gear, settling in at the cautious speed. A dust cloud kicked up behind them.

"Do you like living away from people?" Nikki asked.

"Depends on which people."

"Fair point. But in general. You live closer to cows than to neighbors. Is that the way you like it?"

It was the way he had it. No one else to join him on the farm, to keep it breathing as long as possible. "Like it fine, I suppose. You like the city?"

Nikki looked out at the untamed thickets rambling by her window. "Any other day I'd probably say yes. Now I'm not so sure. A lot has changed in a short time."

Unlike the men with whom he had experienced the counted and uncounted casualties of war, she bore wounds for which she had not enlisted. The evidence of her refusal to sleep in her dad's room was a testimony to how deep those wounds ran—and their accompanying bitterness.

He gave his attention to the road ahead, to the next curve, and kept his grip locked on the steering wheel. If only Chris had eyes to see.

A short while later, they topped the hill by the cemetery, Eddner stretched out beyond it.

Nikki took in the place. "Did you know the last time I was here was for Grandma's funeral?" She paused before adding, "Dad never wanted to come again."

Though she didn't turn his way or seem to expect an answer, Wes nodded. He did know. He knew far more than she could imagine.

He knew the echo of the church bells over the open fields. The joy of the pipe organ at a wedding processional. The elation of little boys playing baseball in the schoolyard. The twitter of birds in the trees shading the parish hall. The cushion of the fescue carpeting his parents' graves.

He knew the Chris of Eddner days had been slowly buried by layer upon layer of unhealed hurt.

None of this could he tell her. Because none of it was she ready to hear.

He slowed for the T intersection at the northern edge of the hamlet. Nikki's gaze was fixed on the steeple.

"Do you still go to that church?" she asked.

"I do." He eased into the left turn.

She looked straight ahead, to the gravel road lacing between the fields of verdant young corn. She said no more about Eddner, asked no further questions. But all of his experience told him that silence was a veil around the hardest questions of all.

◆ ◆ ◆ ◆

According to the city limit sign that passed by Nikki's window, Redmont boasted a whopping three thousand residents. Large enough for two factories, defunct railroad tracks, and a Mexican restaurant.

Uncle Wes followed Main Street through town. American flags hung from every light pole, their shadows swaying on the sidewalk. The heart of town squared off around the two-story county court-house and its sprawling lawn.

Several blocks north of downtown, four stone grain elevators with peeling white paint pushed up to the sky, the tallest structures in Redmont. Within shouting distance of the elevators, Uncle Wes turned into a shopping center anchored by County Mart grocery store on one end and Dollar General on the other. The buildings' aluminum roofs shot the sun back at itself, forcing shoppers to squint against the dueling powers.

Uncle Wes pulled into a spot roughly halfway between the two stores. "Not many clothes stores around here," he said. "We could go to Hannibal if you need. About fifteen minutes from here."

"This is fine. I'm not here to impress anyone." She slid down from the passenger seat into the cool morning air. The burn of summer was still a ways off, despite the racks of blue plastic wading pools at the entrance of Dollar General.

The store had more of a clothing selection than she'd expected. She secured two calf-length maxi dresses that complemented her sneakers surprisingly well, a three-pack of low-cut socks, underwear, and two sports bras for less than thirty dollars. Uncle Wes managed to find an off-brand phone charger that, God willing, would not catch her phone on fire.

He insisted on paying for everything. She insisted he'd done enough, but he gave the cashier crisp bills anyway.

After dropping off the purchases at the truck, they crossed over to County Mart. The front windows featured a hodgepodge of advertisements announcing sales on charcoal, fried chicken gizzards, and live bait available in the meat department.

The scent of fresh bread enveloped them as soon as they walked in. Uncle Wes pulled a cart from the corral and led her into the store. Though he quickly walked past the bakery section, she lingered. Square tables draped with red gingham displayed various breads alongside pastries and desserts. One table prominently displayed clear plastic containers of rhubarb pie. A large yellow sign declared MADE WITH LOCAL PRODUCE.

She stopped and admired the wares. "Is this where you got your pie?"

He turned the cart back to her, glancing toward the bakery counter, where a teenage attendant filled an order of donuts for a customer. "No, I, uh, a friend brought it to me."

"Want another one? My treat."

"That's okay." His eyes darted to the counter again. "Like strawberries? They're on sale this week." He turned the cart toward the adjacent produce section.

He had taken only two steps when an apron-clad woman came around the corner, headed for the bakery. Her face brightened, lips parted to reveal her beautiful smile. "Wes. Fancy seeing you here this morning."

The handwritten name tag affixed to the top hem of her apron had a tidy print similar to the one on the table sign. Joyce.

"Morning," Uncle Wes replied.

"I see you have a shopping buddy."

He cleared his throat. "My niece."

Joyce's brow pinched. She looked between them. "As in Chris's daughter?"

Nikki's own smile fell. She quickly mustered all the social decorum warranted for the situation and extended her hand. "I'm Nikki. Pleasure to meet you."

"Joyce Kindstrom." She grasped Nikki's hand. "I grew up with your uncle. Well, and your dad."

Nikki nodded and broke their grip.

"Your grandma was my after-school babysitter for a while. Spent a lot of time with her cooking while her knucklehead boys were off helping their dad." Joyce glided her twinkling eyes to Uncle Wes. "Sure was a sweet time."

He looked down at the cart.

"Are you visiting for the weekend then, Nikki?"

"I am."

"Very nice. Helping with the farmhouse?"

Uncle Wes had mentioned he was giving the farmhouse a face-lift, preparing it for the future. She would need something to occupy her anyway. So she nodded. "Yes."

Her uncle shot her a look.

"That's wonderful," Joyce said. "I'm sure he appreciates it. Might I suggest some pastries to keep up your strength? Got plenty to choose from here."

"Actually, I was thinking about one of these rhubarb pies. Since Uncle Wes is almost out."

Joyce's eyebrows shot up. She turned to Wes. "Gracious, Wesley! I just gave you that pie yesterday!" Her shoulders bobbed with laughter.

His cheeks tinged red.

Nikki narrowed her eyes at him. Suddenly, the pieces clicked into place. His eagerness to move beyond the bakery. His inability to look at Joyce for long. The woman's eyes sparkling like stars. Nikki grinned, the backstory taking clear shape.

Joyce glanced at the bakery counter. "I should get back. Poor Mikayla has been alone for too long. Nice to meet you, Nikki. I hope to see you at church tomorrow."

The plot thickened. Nikki's grin notched upward. "See you tomorrow."

Joyce went her way, and Uncle Wes pushed the cart forward. Nikki followed after him, biting the inside of her lip to keep from giggling.

Well into the produce section, as they approached the strawberries, Nikki sidled up to him. "She made you that pie, didn't she?"

"It's not what you think."

"Isn't it?"

He stopped, looked at her. A sternness flashed in his gaze but melted as fast as it had come. He continued to walk. "Let's get those strawberries."

Whatever her innocent jest had roused within him, he evidently wanted it to remain hidden. If she was going to repay him for all he was doing for her, she needed to give him the same assurance of security he provided her. Family did not hurt family.

Perhaps they both needed that more than they could express.

◆　◆　◆　◆

Wes had spent half the morning with Nikki, and still he had yet to uncover much of anything about her except she liked frozen burritos. Nikki, though, had learned more about him than he cared to have out in the open, namely about Joyce.

He tapped his thumb against the steering wheel as Main traced them through downtown once more. Saturday morning traffic had ticked up as lunchtime approached. Main twisted to the left and finally intersected with the county route near the city limit, a spot marked by the factory on his side and the John Deere implement on hers. Tractors, combines, headers, planters, and balers lined the grassy lot, all in that signature green.

Nikki studied the implement. Suddenly she sat up straight and pointed out her window. "Uncle Wes, how do you say that name?" Her finger targeted the surname cutting across the building's aluminum facade.

"*Shin-burn* is how I've always said it."

"Schoenborn," she repeated. "Are we related to a Henrietta Schoenborn?"

That was a name he rarely heard anymore. He made the turn onto the highway. "She was my mom's maternal grandmother. Why? Where'd you see her name?"

"In one of the books in Grandma's things. I may have snooped a little."

"Nothing secret in those boxes," he said. "Look all you want. Henrietta's name was in a book?"

"One of those super old books written in German."

He blinked. "Old German books?"

"You didn't see them? It looked like you had started going through the box."

He shook his head. "Grandma had lots of things I haven't gotten to yet, though."

"You should see these. They're over a hundred years old. Did Grandma speak German?"

"Your great-grandmother, Lena, was the last generation to speak it around here. Spoke it as a child, anyway. Not sure how much she remembered when she was older." Another casualty of war—World War I, specifically. An uncounted casualty suffered on the home front. How different pre–World War I Eddner—and Redmont—must have been.

The county road opened up to the highway. Thick trees interspersed with fields protected by barbed-wire fences. For as much as the landscape had changed since Lena's time, the society had changed far more.

"Will you take a look at the books when we get back?" Nikki asked. "Maybe together we can figure out what they are."

Hopefulness tinted her expression. A hope to learn more about the things she'd missed out on. Things that potentially could answer questions she didn't yet know she had.

He nodded. "Be glad to."

◆ ◆ ◆ ◆

As Uncle Wes stepped over to the corner of the living room to retrieve the books from the box, Nikki put away the food. Frozen burritos, fruit, milk, and packets of her own oatmeal. Enough sustenance to last her through Monday.

"Did you find them?" she called toward the living room.

"Yes," came the reply.

She riffled through the yellow Dollar General sacks until she found the charger. The plastic packaging required scissors from the drawer and careful attention not to slice her fingers. Eventually, she freed the cord and brick and hooked up her phone to an outlet over the counter. Before long she would have the ability to call Isaac. Before long she would need to come up with something to say.

She walked away from her phone as the stir threatened to start.

In the living room, Uncle Wes sat on the couch with two of the books in his lap. He had the burgundy one open in his hands, studying the title page.

"Any clues?" She joined him on the couch. The aprons and notebook still lay on the opposite end.

He pointed at the last words of the title. "Could be wrong, but I believe *der Herr* is 'the Lord.'"

"So it's a faith book?"

"Must be. Concordia is the publisher for the Lutheran Church–Missouri Synod. Hosana, my church, is a member. The book must've been aimed at synod congregations."

"All of these would have been, then. Concordia published them all."

He exchanged the burgundy book for the brown *Danz und Theaterbefuch* and examined its cover. "Seems it's something about theater."

"Doesn't sound very faith-y."

He shook his head and opened to the front matter. After a moment, he tapped the page. "Description here references C. F. W. Walther. He was a pastor and president of the synod. My mom used to talk about being in the Walther League, kind of like a youth group."

"Maybe the book bemoans the worldly wiles of the theater."

"Knowing Walther, probably. He was pretty conservative." He laid the book aside and gingerly opened the crumbling black one.

"That one's in the worst shape even though it's the youngest," she said.

He paused on each page to scan its contents. "Looks like a hymnbook."

"That's what I thought."

"Would make sense if it was. People used to bring their own hymnbooks to church. It wouldn't have spent much time on a shelf."

"All of these books must have had special meaning to someone," she said.

"Agreed. Books weren't something a farmer usually spent money on back then. They were a rarity."

The statement pierced her. Someone upstream in her family had treasured books even more than she did. "We have to find out what these are. The books someone chooses to keep tell you a lot about their character."

"We could find an English-German dictionary at the library, maybe."

"That's it! A translator! We can use Google Translate."

He frowned. "Google translates languages?"

"Google does everything."

He huffed, clearly having his own opinion on the matter. He looked at the hymnbook in his hands and nodded. "Let's go up to my house. We can use my laptop."

Eight

es brought his laptop to the breakfast bar and let Nikki have at it. He stood over her shoulder as she worked. For each book, she typed the title, subtitle, and description from the front page into the "German" box on the screen. Google did the rest, breaking the code of the Fraktur font that old German texts loved so much and displaying the translation in the "English" box. Modern technology filling in gaps that the passage of time and generations had left behind.

According to Google, the burgundy book was titled *Be Strong in the Lord*.

"'Joyous words of remembrances for Christian young people,'" Nikki read from the screen. She looked up at him. "Someone loved devotionals."

"Seems so."

The brown book's title translated to *Dance and Theatergoing*.

"You were right, Uncle Wes. This book is connected to Walther. Apparently it contains two lectures he gave over four occasions on the topics of dance and visiting the theater."

In other words, the book was not just a family heirloom, it was a valuable record of church history. Wes shook his head in awe. He had lived in that farmhouse for years without ever knowing that treasures were boxed away above his head.

Last came the black book. Nikki typed in the information,

Google working the translation as she progressed. At the end, she sat back and read, "'Church hymnbook for the Evangelical Lutheran congregations of the Augsburg Confession. Found therein are church hymns and teachings of Dr. Martin Luther.'"

Doctrine and worship together. No wonder the book was so worn. It would have been used at church and home. Wes gently lifted it from the countertop. The Fraktur font carried forward into every page, foreign in every way. But what his mind could not grasp, his soul leaned toward. The jumble of markings were proclamations of praise to the same God he worshiped, the same promises he believed, the same hope he pressed toward. And there on one page he landed on, the name written identically in both languages: Jesus.

"Amazing," he whispered.

"That's the book with Henrietta Schoenborn's name in the front," Nikki said. "Do you think the other two belonged to her too?"

"Probably." He laid the hymnbook with the others. "Makes sense. She must have passed them to Lena, who must have passed them to my mom."

Nikki smoothed her fingers over the brown book's cover. "Kind of crazy how fast things change, isn't it? In one generation, an entire language is lost. Makes you wonder what else goes with it."

They both jumped at the ring of his phone.

"Sorry about that." He reached into his back pocket and pulled out his phone. The screen lit up with the caller's identity. He sucked in his breath. "It's your dad."

Nikki whirled around. Her mouth, smiling moments before, clamped shut.

◆　◆　◆　◆

Uncle Wes paced the length of the dining room, listening with far more patience than Nikki would have. The muffled words on the other end were loud and sharp, and they hardly stopped. Uncle Wes had to talk over them to get any reply in.

"Yes, actually, she is here," he said. Long pause. "No, I didn't ask Lydia to call you. She obviously thought you should know."

Nikki clenched her teeth. *Thought you should know.* She had encountered those words recently too. She closed the laptop, the happiness of the previous thirty minutes gone in an instant.

"Chris, I'm not choosing sides. I'm just—" He went quiet again, clearly cut off.

She put her fist to her mouth.

"Yes, I did," Uncle Wes replied. "Because she's my niece." His tone was firm, protective. The uncle who had defended his country set a clear perimeter around her, fenced her in on all sides. The very thing her dad was supposed to do. Dads weren't supposed to be the enemy needing to be kept out.

She balled her fist tighter. Tears sullied her vision.

"It doesn't matter how long," he said. "Not to me, it doesn't."

Her throat constricted.

The next pause was long, charged. And then her uncle replied, "No, Chris. It's up to her."

How dare her dad. How dare he shove his way into where he didn't belong when he wasn't dad enough to stay where he was supposed to be.

She pushed back her stool, stacked the books, and marched down to the farmhouse.

Uncle Wes shouldn't have to fight her battles. Surely her phone would have enough charge. Enough for a truth-laced text long overdue.

◆ ◆ ◆ ◆

SATURDAY, MAY 25, AT 11:34 A.M.

Nikki

If you're going to give Uncle Wes a hard time about my being here, stop to consider why I would want to be here at all. If anyone chose sides, it was you, when you chose to leave. You chose the side away from us, the side with a new wife. If that's where you want to be, fine. Just stay on your side. Goodbye, Dad.

Nikki thrust open the screen door of the farmhouse and pounded across the porch toward the yard. Wood smacked against wood. Her pulse thrummed in her ears. Her hands shook. The last two words coursed through her like the ocean thrusting its waves against the shore.

Goodbye, Dad.

Words he had not given her the space to say before. She had to carve it out for herself. Because God forbid he actually talk to her instead of around her.

The sidewalk led to the driveway, which led to the outbuildings beyond Uncle Wes's house. Her shoes fell hard against the gravel. She passed the three-walled machine shed with Uncle Wes's equipment. Passed the aluminum grain bins and the large white barn, to the edge of a cornfield. Short green stalks sunned their floppy leaves in straight rows almost perfectly perpendicular to the fence.

Nikki followed the fencerow, her feet beating down the grass.

What roiled inside her begged to be set free, like magma churning below the surface. She walked and walked, until only the barn's roof was visible. There, in the solitude, it finally roared out. Her scream echoed across the expanse. Again and again. Each scream wanting to be loud enough to reach Oklahoma but not strong enough to get there. They faded into the distance, absorbed into the nothing. Coming to nothing.

She fell silent, heartbeat slowly calming. Breath steadying.

She would never be like her dad. Never. She would keep her promises, live in integrity.

Which meant she had a phone call of her own to make, to someone she needed to talk to instead of around. Isaac had waited too long.

She lifted her face to the sky. Not a single cloud. Open blue. Free. The irony was bitter.

She inhaled long and deep, holding in the air for a beat. Then she turned back to the farmhouse.

With every step, her stomach knotted more. By the time she pulled open the screen door, it felt like a rock.

She picked up her phone, closed her eyes, promised herself she could do it. Her thumb quivered as she tapped Isaac's name.

One ring.

Two.

Three.

Finally, his voice, thick and taut. "Hello?"

"Hi."

Silence.

She lowered onto the couch, her legs too wobbly to stand. "I'm so sorry, Isaac. I should have called you to tell you where I was."

"Glad you're safe. I was worried."

"I know. I'm sorry. I'm planning to be back Monday night. Maybe we could do something Tuesday?"

"Have to go back to Portland next week."

"Oh."

"I was going to tell you that last night. One of many things I wanted to talk to you about."

The knot tightened. She hunched against the pain. "I guess we did have a lot to talk about."

"You do understand that's really what hurts the most, don't you? That you're not telling me things? It's not the fact you didn't call. It's the fact you didn't tell me about what was going on. Your dad getting remarried is kind of a big deal. I know how much that must be killing you. Yet your mom was the one who told me, not you. Why?"

"I . . . I was still processing it."

"I can help you with that, Nik. I want to help you with that. I love you, and I thought you loved me."

"I do love you."

"Then why the hiding? Why the lack of honesty?"

The pain of the knot seeped upward, grabbed hold of her heart.

"I asked you twice if something was wrong the other day," he continued. "I could tell there was. You chose not to be honest. Then when I come home, you run away. Two hundred miles away. How am I supposed to interpret that?"

Her face burned. "I'm sorry."

Silence.

"Tell me where we are now, Nik, because I'm confused."

"I still love you, Isaac."

"That's great, but it doesn't answer my question."

For so long, her greatest security had been in his embrace. Somewhere along the way, a fear had weaseled in, whispering the question, "But what if it's a snare?"

She blinked back tears. They came where words failed.

"Fine, I'll answer for both of us." His tone was biting. "Honestly, I am so angry right now. So angry. I think I need space of my own. You be wherever it is you want to be, and I'll tell my boss I am available after all to stay in Portland the next twelve weeks until this project is done. That was the other thing I was going to talk to you about. There. Decision made. We'll both have space to figure out where we go from here. Sound good?"

"Isaac—"

"Fantastic. Goodbye, Nikki."

Call ended.

She stared in disbelief at her phone.

The reverberations of his words pounded against the inside of her skull. They did not fade. They did not absorb into the nothing.

She folded herself into a fetal position on the couch and sobbed.

◆ ◆ ◆ ◆

For the third time, Wes went out to his porch and paused. The farmhouse sat still and quiet in the midday sun. Should he go check on her?

Clearly she had overheard the conversation, or at least enough of it to piece things together. That was why she'd stormed out. The danger of pain was it isolated the sufferer, enfolded the person into its world. The cruelest kind of POW camp.

But should he go to her?

"I'm not trying to drive a wedge between anyone," he had insisted to his brother. He was only trying to be the help.

Chris had a few choice replies to that, all of them laced with resentment. Resentment stemmed from insecurity, a cry for help in itself.

Wes stepped off the porch, the farthest he had yet gone.

Sometimes the best way to help was to get dirty by the mess. Other times, though, it was best to let the one hurt decide when to ask for help.

He sighed. Then went back inside.

◆ ◆ ◆ ◆

The sun filled the spot on the wall where Uncle Wes used to have his TV. The brackets were still there, but the wall itself was blank, stripped of what used to be. The console underneath, empty. Everything taken away, every piece. Like her family home, stripped and empty.

Like her mom.

Like her heart.

All the pieces of her life broke off bit by bit. Slipped through her fingers even as she had her palms to heaven in a plea for mercy. How had it all fallen apart so quickly? How had it gotten so completely out of her control? How would she ever get through it?

Her mom's reply to that very question floated back. It comprised the words from Grandma Ann herself. *"Do the next thing."*

"It's the only thing I can do," her mom had said.

Brave words from a brave woman. The kind Nikki needed to be.

She pulled herself into a seated position, wiped her eyes, sniffed. Do the next thing. It would be her response too. What else could she do?

She started to stand. The items on the foot of the couch, near where her head had been, caught her eye. Great-Grandma Lena's aprons and the notebook. She sat back down and brought the notebook to her lap.

Cupping the spine in her left palm, she flipped to the last page with writing. In impeccable handwriting along the top line, the author had written "Anise Christmas Cookies (Springerles)."

Between the title and the ingredients list was a note stretching to the midpoint of the page. The first line declared, "Sometimes the hardest thing in the world to do is to keep trying to do something for which natural talents are lacking."

Nikki furrowed her brow, turned back a few pages. Another recipe, titled "Crispy Egg Noodles (Spätzle)." Preceding the ingredients was another note, capped off by a proverb that said, "Whoso putteth his trust in the Lord shall be safe."

She turned back page by page. More recipes titled in both English and German and prefaced by a note. Written in the same hand, the same ink, as if captured in one sitting rather than accumulated over the course of time.

Scalloped potatoes (Kartoffelgratin). Red cabbage with apple (Apfel-Rotkohl). Potato pancakes (Kartoffelpuffer). Applesauce (Apfelmus). Beef rolls (Rouladen). Fried pork patties (Schnitzel).

Finally, she landed at the first recipe. Within the beautifully lettered words was the introduction and recipe for something called egg hash (Hoppel Poppel).

Nine

Egg Hash (Hoppel Poppel)

It is tempting to think the role of home cook is little more than servanthood, a fate of labor relegated to the unimportant of society. But the work set before us is the work ordained for us by a God who sees no inequality of worth. We can either decry our humanly lot and shout, "Unfair!" or we can trust and obey and ask, "What good can I bring to this space? What joy can I weave?" For our work carries reward from heaven, which far exceeds any recompense on earth.

Generations ago, a home cook somewhere deep in Germany asked those questions, and what resulted was this classic dish now known in households across the country, a symbol of comfort and hearth. "This . . . that she hath done shall be spoken of for a memorial of her" (Mark 14:9). Only keen artists create masterpieces from unflashy ingredients like these. Many a mother carried the proof of this truth to her table when times were lean and her family depended on her ability to make enough from little. Such artistry flows in your veins too. Let such example be your guide. "Every wise woman buildeth her house" (Prov. 14:1), and "the house of the righteous shall stand" (Prov. 12:7).

I pound potatoes, peeled, chunked, and boiled
I pound cooked meat (diced ham, bacon, sausage)
I bell pepper, diced
butter
half an onion, diced
7 eggs, beaten
salt and pepper
parsley for garnish

Fry potatoes in butter, flipping to lightly brown both sides. Add more butter, then the onion and bell pepper. Cook until onion is translucent. Add meat. Continue to fry and mix until potatoes are browned and meat is warmed. Pour in beaten eggs. Cook until eggs are set. Season, garnish, and serve.

Few times had words on a page instantly captured her. The eloquent prose dismantled all presumptions of a Missouri farm wife, which was who surely wrote it. Rich, intelligent, and suffused with insights only maturity could yield.

Prose, perhaps, taught from reading.

Nikki laid the notebook open on the couch and searched the photo album she had perused earlier. Finally, she came to the picture of Great-Grandma Lena in her kitchen wearing the rose-speckled apron, baby girl on her hip and a smile on her lips. A singular moment in 1937. Had she penned the words, folding her love of cooking with her proximity to the "Old World ways"?

Had thoughts of the notebook swum in her head even as she held her baby girl? Thoughts of how she wanted to help shape her daughter's life, to connect her to the family and heritage they shared? Thoughts that Nikki's father seemingly didn't have.

The visages of her mothers stared back at Nikki from the snapshot, their dark eyes to her own, as if whispering to her to save the last remaining thread of the family tie.

She whispered back, "Do the next thing."

She propped up the notebook and the picture on the kitchen counter, then strode back to Uncle Wes's house. With any luck, he had plenty of potatoes.

◆ ◆ ◆ ◆

Nikki pulled the top loop of Great-Grandma Lena's apron over her neck and tied the strings at the base of her spine. The handsewn apron fit as if it was meant for her shape, an affirmation that her great-grandma's world, like her uncle's, had space for her.

The notebook rested in the cookbook rack. The picture of Lena holding Ann perched against the backsplash, their eyes fixed on her.

"You're going to help me with this, right?" The most complicated thing she'd ever made was spaghetti—from jars and boxes.

The two mothers' gazes stayed strong and sure, eyes radiating even in aged print.

Nikki took up the large russet potato. "Let's begin."

The other ingredients waited in a line along the counter, all swiped from Uncle Wes's supplies, including the last of his bulk sausage. If it wasn't on oatmeal, she could hopefully stomach it. The egg hash sounded like the epitome of a farmer's go-to meal. The kind of breakfast skillet that Midwesterners adored, but without the cheese.

Almost immediately, the recipe's author proved to have left holes. The recipe called for peeled, chunked, and boiled potatoes but failed to clarify how large the chunks should be or how long to boil them. The chunks had started to crumble to the touch by the time Nikki removed them from the heat and drained the water.

Similarly, the recipe called for butter in which to fry the potatoes but did not clarify how much. She lobbed off about a third of the stick of butter and held it up for Lena. "Think this is enough?"

Her great-grandmother gleamed back.

She dropped the fat portion into the hot pan in slices. They wilted and glistened over the surface. A sizzle rose like a glorious song when she added the potatoes, the theme of a masterpiece unfolding. Excitement grew in her belly. The artistry said to be in her veins awoke from its dormancy.

Every step in the process wove a new layer of flavor, texture, aroma, and confidence. Even with hazy instructions, she made something out of little, like the women before her. She invoked the same come-home scents they once created at their stoves. Every pat of butter added to the pan was a piece of creativity given freely, a nurturing of the family tie.

She cracked the eggs into a small bowl and beat them until frothy, the circular movement of her arm coaxing loose the knots in her neck muscles.

The potatoes browned a little too dark and the diced veggies turned a little too soft, but it didn't matter. She tossed in more butter, loosening all the bits from the bottom of the pan, then added the cooked sausage. After giving the meat a chance to warm up, she poured in the eggs. The blanket of liquid muffled the crackle. The recipe did not say how to cook the eggs, only to cook them until set. All her former egg cooking involved scrambling, so using a spatula, she cut figure eights through the pan until the eggs formed a soft, pale-yellow bind.

She snapped off the burner, dashed the top of the hash with salt, pepper, and parsley. At last she stepped back.

Her first-ever German meal. Her first-ever real connection to the women who had labored in that small galley kitchen before her.

"We did it," she told them.

◆　◆　◆　◆

At exactly one o'clock as instructed, Wes knocked on the farm-house door. The last of the rhubarb pie rested in his left hand. The faint scent of fried potatoes seeped through the open living room windows.

Floorboards creaked. Hinges whined. Nikki pulled open the door and smiled. "Hey, Uncle Wes. Come on in."

He stepped over the threshold. Every window was open, call-ing in the cool afternoon breeze to play with the aromas from the stovetop. The twangy crooning of Reba McEntire wafted from a radio on the console in the living room. Apparently Nikki had been doing more digging in the boxes to have found it.

Nikki waved him forward, into the kitchen. "Lunch is ready."

The counters showed evidence of a hardworking cook—used dishes, a butter wrapper, the cores of an onion and bell pepper, and a skillet filled with an egg-potato mixture. On the table, two neatly set places.

"You've gone to a lot of trouble," he said, slipping the pie into an open spot on the counter.

"It was no trouble at all. Ever had hoppel poppel?"

"Can't say I have."

She reached onto the counter and retrieved an antique-looking notebook. "Found these recipes among Grandma's things too." She handed him the find, opened to a recipe. The yellowed pages spelled out a dish that perfectly described what waited on their plates.

"All kinds of surprises in that box," he said.

"Do you recognize the handwriting?"

He shook his head.

"I was thinking it might be Great-Grandma Lena's."

"Could be." He flipped through some of the pages before hand-ing the notebook back to her. "Intriguing."

"Exactly." She placed it in the cookbook holder. "Ready to eat?"

They took up their places at the table, Nikki sitting taller and straighter than she had been. The square of her shoulders a boon to his own.

"May I pray for us?" he asked.

"Please."

They bowed their heads, and he gathered the words to his lips. "Father God, thank you for this food. Thank you for this time we have together. May both bless us in ways we cannot yet see." He paused before adding, "Thank you also for the family you have blessed us with, both those who are in this room and those who are not. Amen."

Nikki's "amen" was soft, her glance knowing.

But it was the right thing to pray. It was always the right thing to pray. God willing, he would find a way to share why.

The first bite of hash was a collision of buttery, crisp potato, slightly charred along the edges, and sausage crumbles encased in puffs of eggs.

"Delicious," he said.

"Thank you for letting me steal your potatoes. And eggs and sausage and—well, everything."

"I'm glad it was there when you needed it."

They ate to the country rhythms wafting from the radio.

After a few moments, he broached the subject he had debated over. "About that call earlier."

"Don't worry about it."

"I'm sorry you heard."

She shrugged. "He doesn't have to understand why I want to be here. And I've told him as much."

He lowered his fork to his plate. "You talked to him?"

"Texted."

It wasn't hard to guess what the message said. He could ask, but knowing wouldn't change anything. What was said was said. He scooped up a piece of eggy sausage.

"Uncle Wes, may I ask you something?"

He nodded.

"Do you really need help refreshing the farmhouse?"

Before answering, he washed down his food with milk. "Maybe. Why?"

She tapped the tines of her fork on a potato cube. "I was thinking, I have the summer off."

Her meaning became clear. And her running made him squirm. "I thought you had . . . other things back in KC?"

She dipped her head, the pause pregnant. "He has summer plans, apparently."

Her words, her posture, revealed another conversation had also taken place since that morning. Yet another echo of his own past.

Hurt had multiple dimensions.

Nikki staying for the summer could make things worse. Could drive Chris further away too. But he had promised her she could stay as long as she needed.

Either he was a man of his word or he wasn't. Either he truly was selected to serve a role in this season of Nikki's life, as Aunt Emma contended, or he wasn't.

Which did he believe?

He gathered another bite. At last he met her gaze. "Be glad for the company, Nikki."

◆　◆　◆　◆

The rest of the meal passed without much meaningful talk, aside from his ideas on how they might fix up the farmhouse. If he was supposed to say something with meat, the words refused to muster.

He thanked Nikki for lunch and headed back to his house. As he descended the farmhouse porch steps, he pulled out his phone and checked his messages. A text from Aunt Emma awaited him.

Behold! The tournament VICTORS! Throwing
ourselves a parade.

She ended her message with five smiley-face emojis wearing sunglasses. Below it was a picture of five senior ladies in matching hot-pink shirts holding a trophy.

He chuckled into the afternoon air. Leave it to her to do something to lighten any day. He tapped the phone icon next to her name, then waited through the rings as he continued down the sidewalk. When the other end of the line connected, noise exploded through the speaker. Crowds talking, music blaring, and Aunt Emma's voice attempting to rise above.

"Don't hang up!" she called. "Sit tight!"

Wes held the phone away from his ear until finally the background fell quiet and Aunt Emma's voice came through clear.

"There," she said. "I stepped out to the parking lot."

"Catch you at a bad time?"

"Not at all. The girls and I went out for burgers and beers. Don't tell our pastor. Of course, he'll probably find out anyway. We posted a few of those selfie photos on the social media. Too bad you're not on it. Old women with beers and insufficient knowledge of technology make for interesting results."

He laughed and turned onto the driveway. "Glad you're celebrating. Big win must feel pretty good."

"One step closer to world domination. How goes it on your end? Any victories to celebrate on the bonding front?"

"Don't know if we'd call it a victory, but Nikki decided to stay for the summer."

"That's definitely a major advancement. What led to that decision?"

He recounted the call from Chris, including the way Nikki overheard and holed up in the farmhouse. "On top of that, I believe she had some kind of further falling-out with her young man back home."

"You mean they broke up?"

"Don't know, honestly. Didn't press."

She tsked. "A broken heart upon a broken heart. The poor child. Sounds like a summer on the farm might be the best thing for her."

Maybe Aunt Emma was right, and his worry was unfounded. It was just the summer, after all. Not a complete life change, like the decision he had made all those years ago. That remained a key difference between their stories.

He reached the edge of his yard and started across the grass. "She said she'll help me get the farmhouse spruced up."

"Hope you take her up on that."

"Definitely will. She's also intrigued by an old notebook full of recipes she found in Mom's things. German recipes, all handwritten. Does that sound familiar?"

"Handwritten German recipes," she repeated slowly, as if to comprehend the phrase from all angles. "I can't on earth think what those might be."

"The notebook was mixed in with a few books printed in German, each of them more than a hundred years old. One of them has Henrietta Schoenborn's name written on the inside cover."

"Well, I'll be. Mother Schoenborn?"

"I wondered if all the books belonged to her," Wes said as he stepped inside his house.

"Maybe. Mother Schoenborn loved books. As a child, I used to admire them when we went to her house for Sunday afternoon visits. I was never allowed to touch any of them, mind you. I stared longingly at them from across the room, imagining the worlds they contained that would allow me to escape from the drudgery of adult conversation."

He settled into his recliner and kicked off his boots. "You never saw your grandmother reading them?"

"No, but that doesn't mean she didn't. I also rarely heard her speak German, but that doesn't mean she didn't. If I think hard enough—and that's a dangerous thing at my age—I can almost remember the way she greeted us in German when we arrived at her door. That's the only time I heard her speak the language. No one else would have understood her anyway by that point. I'm sure you know the Great War changed everything in Eddner. Speaking German, dressing German, being German could spell trouble in those days."

"Mom told me a few of those stories," he said.

"How many of these books are there?"

"Three, not counting the notebook. They all have something to do with the Lutheran Church."

"Those have to be Mother Schoenborn's, then. I wonder how Ann ended up with them and I never knew. The notebook, though—I'm not sure where that would have come from, or the recipes. We didn't eat much German food."

"Us either."

"Though come to think of it," she said, "I do remember my mother making some kind of cake with a streusel topping. Kind of like coffee cake but not as much cinnamon. Do you remember it? Ann made it a couple of times when you boys were young."

"Doesn't sound familiar."

"Maybe you were too little to remember. I'm too old to forget and you're too young to recall. Ain't life a hoot? The cake is a lot of work, if I remember correctly. Ann gave it up after a while. Goodness, I haven't thought of that cake in years! Now I'm salivating."

"You should get back to your burger, then. Your friends are probably wondering what happened to you."

"Nah, they found a dartboard. They're occupied."

He chuckled. "Competitors through and through. But still, I should let you go back to your well-earned celebration. Thanks for taking my call even in the middle of it. And I love the team shirts."

"Of course you do. I designed them." Her laughter rang through the phone. "All right, I can take a hint. I'll get off here and go make sure the LLLs still have all their eyeballs. Tell our niece I said hello."

"Will do. Aunt Emma?"

"Yes?"

He weighed his words, let his gaze travel to the front window and the old farmhouse beyond. "How well would you say someone needs to know someone else before they speak into their life?"

"You mean like, say, an uncle and his niece?"

He didn't respond. He didn't need to.

"Listen, my darling boy, a broken heart knows when it has found a place of truth. So speak. And never grow weary of doing good. Hear me?"

"Yes, Aunt Emma."

"Hugs around both your necks."

Ten

"The whole summer?" Her mom's voice tipped up. "Are you sure that's what you want to do?"

Nikki lowered herself onto the porch step, holding the phone to her ear. The sun had dipped behind the roof of the barn, beginning to draw away the vividness of the clear day. "Through July 28, more specifically. That will give me a couple of weeks before school starts."

"That's a long time, Nik."

"Nine weeks. A little over nine. I can pay all my bills online."

"That's not what I'm worried about."

Of course it wasn't. Nikki dug her toes into the tread of the step. "Isaac knows, Mom. Kind of. It was his idea, in a way."

"What are you talking about? What happened?"

Recounting the exchange with him for her mom cut nearly as deep as the original conversation.

"What does that mean for you two?" her mom asked. "Are you still together?"

Nikki tucked her free arm against her stomach, pressing on the ache there. "I think we're on a pause."

"Oh, baby."

She blinked away the tears pushing into her vision. Across the road, the cows ambled carefree among the reeds.

86

"When does he leave?" her mom asked.

"Sometime next week, maybe Tuesday, after the holiday."

"Call him before he goes."

"I've already talked to him."

"Talk some more."

"And say what? I've said everything."

"Say what you're thinking. That's what he wants."

Honesty. The only thing he asked for, expected. "What if that's what drives him away, Mom? What if I tell him the truth, that I don't know what I want? That I don't even know myself anymore? He would still think I'm hiding."

"Do you not trust him to believe you?"

The question hooked into her. "I . . . I don't know."

Her mom was quiet for a moment. "Sounds like you have a lot of thinking to do. Maybe this summer is exactly the gift you need."

She brought her knees to her chest, wrapped her free arm around them. "I'm a mess, Mom."

"We all are, baby."

They talked logistics, what Nikki needed from her apartment that could be mailed.

"I'll go over there tomorrow," her mom promised.

"Thank you."

"Besides fixing up the house, do you have anything else planned? Hannibal is nice. I'm sure you remember it was Mark Twain's boyhood home, the setting for *Tom Sawyer*. That should entertain you."

"I might explore at some point. I also found some old recipes I think came from Great-Grandma Lena. I made one for lunch today that was pretty good. I might make more."

"Wish I could be there."

Nikki tightened her hug around her knees. "I do too."

They said their love-yous and goodbyes.

Long afterward, Nikki sat on the steps watching the cows mill about the pasture as the day drew to evening. Her first of many full days in a place she'd never expected to be.

◆ ◆ ◆ ◆

The silent Sunday dawn light poured onto his porch. Wes trailed his finger under the Ephesians verse once more because God, in his providence, was speaking plainly.

Get rid of all bitterness, rage and anger, brawling and slander, along with every form of malice. Be kind and compassionate to one another, forgiving each other, just as in Christ God forgave you.

The words wrapped themselves around him, tucked him into their center.

His niece was angry enough to stay. His brother was angry enough to leave forever. Bitterness smoldered around him on all sides. Only by the grace of heaven would it be snuffed out.

He prayed for Chris to hear, and if he couldn't hear, then to see. If he couldn't see, then to feel.

He prayed for Nikki, that the caliber of bricks Chris had used in the wall between himself and their father would not be used by Nikki to build her own wall. One father is all anyone gets.

He prayed for his own heart to be protected from the malice, the infectious weapon the enemy had perfected and used in stealth. He prayed, as always, for wisdom.

"Lord, in your timing," he finished.

Then he rose from the porch swing and carried his Bible back inside. His Sunday suit waited on its hanger, and the living room light of the old farmhouse had switched on.

◆ ◆ ◆ ◆

Uncle Wes picked Nikki up for church dressed in a brown suit matched with a white shirt and blue tie—the colors of earth and sky—with a woodsy cologne to boot. He opened the truck door and held out his hand for her as she stepped up into the cab. His

Bible, worn at the edges, lay on the console, stuffed with little papers and marked with sticky tabs.

She strapped on her seat belt and folded her hands in her lap. Bible—she needed to tell her mom to send her Bible too.

Uncle Wes came around the truck and heaved himself into the driver's seat.

"Anything I should know?" Nikki asked. "About church, I mean."

He turned the key in the ignition. "Like what?"

"Like any unwritten rules about when to stand and sit or which pew to sit in. That kind of thing. I've never been to a Lutheran service before, not counting the funeral."

He looked at her, palm on the knob of the gearshift. "Ever?"

"Not that I recall."

"You'd remember," he mumbled, then shifted into gear. "The order of service will be in the bulletin. Only church members can take communion. Other than that, you'll be good."

"And the people? Are they nice?"

"Yeah." The truck rolled forward. He gave it gas.

"Is that a 'yeah' as in 'you're going to fit right in'?"

"You're a Werner. You already do."

"But they don't know me."

He chuckled. "What do you think your grandma's favorite topic was?"

Warmth covered her, erasing every question of whether Grandma Ann had wished for more time with her.

The cows nibbled on their feed, hardly looking up as the truck passed by the pasture. The road twisted through the woods and up the hill on the back side of Eddner.

As they passed the cemetery, Uncle Wes nodded in the general direction of the headstones. "Need to go to Hannibal today to pick up Memorial Day wreaths for my parents. Want to come?"

"Sure."

They turned right at the T intersection and followed the road in front of the teacherage and schoolhouse, into the heart of Eddner.

Jagged rows of vehicles glinted in the gravel parking lot between the parsonage and church. Every adult present had donned their Sunday finest that clearly did not come from Dollar General. A band of children in polished loafers and Mary Janes played tag, zipping across the concrete landing at the bottom of the church steps. Everyone was bathed, shaved, groomed, and perfected for the holiest morning of the week.

If the pictures in Grandma Ann's photo album were any indication, every generation of Hosana Lutheran worshipers came bearing their best. Best clothes, best appearance, best reverence. As it was with Henrietta, so it was with Lena, then Ann, then Wes. Nikki needed to ask her mom to send her dresses too.

When Uncle Wes had parked, he gathered his Bible and asked her if she was ready.

She smiled. "Born ready."

◆ ◆ ◆ ◆

More than a few heads turned to watch Nikki walk alongside Wes to the church steps. A small circle of white-haired ladies, church purses hanging from their forearms, swung open to a line so they could all see the passing duo. Each of them nodded to the younger Werner.

Otis Harman strolled up to them, his ancient navy blazer sagging off his hunched frame. He never dressed up for co-op board meetings, only for church. "Morning there, Wes. Who you got with you today?"

"My niece Nikki."

One of Otis's eyebrows lifted. "Niece? Chris's girl?"

Behind Wes, the church-purse ladies murmured.

The smile on Nikki's face pinched. The same reaction she'd had when Joyce referenced her lineage.

Wes quickly diverted to a safer topic. "She's staying with me this summer. Helping me with the house."

"Very nice. You remember where my hardware store is, I reckon. You let me know what you need."

"I certainly will."

They talked of his hope to turn the farmhouse into a rental. Throughout it all, Nikki looked around, at the church, at the grounds, at the people who smiled from a distance.

"It's a good thing you're doing, son," Otis said. "Doing your mother proud, I'd say."

"I appreciate it."

A white sedan pulled into the parking lot and inched across the gravel. A cross dangled from the rearview mirror. Joyce.

Wes moved toward the steps. "Better show Nikki to her seat."

Otis reached out a gnarled hand and patted Wes's arm. "Good talking to ya."

"You too."

The older man walked away. The sedan came to a stop in a spot facing the front door.

"He seems nice," Nikki whispered.

"Very." Wes turned them to the steps before Joyce could exit her car.

◆　◆　◆　◆

Nikki quickly lost count how many times the pastor turned between the altar and the congregation. Every time he turned, his white cloak brushed the tops of his shoes. His emerald-green stole horseshoed his almost nonexistent neck.

"Beloved in the Lord!" he said, projecting as high as the rafters and as far as the swinging doors to the narthex. "Let us draw near with a true heart and confess our sins unto God our Father, beseeching him in the name of our Lord Jesus Christ to grant us forgiveness. Our help is in the name of the Lord."

The pipe organist ground out the first notes of the response, cueing the seventy-some worshipers.

"Who made heaven and earth," they chanted in unison, emotionless despite the rise and fall of the melody, as reverent in their sanctuary as they were in their fields.

The mothers before her had said those words, initially in German, eventually in English. The same responses to the same tunes lifted from the same spartan wood pews.

A portrait of Jesus hung above the altar. He was barefoot, walking on clouds, robed in white with a soft red sash, arms uplifted as if inviting all to behold him and lift their praise. Tiny flames swayed from the austere candelabras on either side of his feet.

"I said, I will confess my transgressions unto the Lord," the pastor called.

Uncle Wes slid into the melody of the sung response, not needing to look at the order of service in his bulletin for direction. "And you forgive the iniquity of my sin," he sang amid the others with a steady baritone voice.

Despite where his heart may have been, his eyes betrayed where his mind circled. Frequently his eyes drifted to the woman two rows in front of them. Joyce wore a royal-purple wrap dress paired tastefully with a light gray scarf. Her hair was perfectly manicured. Overall, significantly more regal than the humble County Mart bakery matron of the previous day. Beautiful, in fact.

Nikki grinned.

To her right, the frosted glass of the arched windows diffused the streams descending from the sun and shut out the earthy aroma rising from the fields surrounding the church property. A sanctuary caught between glory and ground, populated by a congregation who seemed to hold the two in balance with practiced discipline. The inside of the church boasted clean arches and polished wood. The church building had a firmness to it that reminded worshipers of their smallness against the hard world and offered a reprieve from the deepest agony of it.

Both Henrietta and Lena had had hymnbooks of their own. They had taken them to Hosana and back home, a piece of home to church and a piece of church to home. To them, those were not two separate places but a continuation of each other. Neither place could stand without the other.

Somewhere in the family line, that cord had been snapped apart.

Not long after that, a marriage dissolved. An extended family divided. Snap. Snap.

What would the mothers of the past say if they knew Nikki, as their daughter, sat in their church reciting their beloved words and didn't know which graves in the cemetery belonged to them?

❧ *Eleven* ❧

The congregation spilled onto the landing at the bottom of the steps and split into their usual after-church chat groups. The kids raced to be the first to scramble up the stone marquee between the evergreen bushes, the way Wes and his friends used to. Some things never changed.

No sooner had Wes led Nikki down the steps than Trennen Voepel approached, all gangly and big grin.

"Morning, Wes!" His young cash renter jutted out his hand. His grip was firm and strong.

"Trennen. Didn't see you before."

"Got here late. Had to sit in the back." He turned to Nikki, smile widening. "Heard you had company."

Wes straightened. The look in Trennen's eyes was a universal language.

The young man switched his handshake to Nikki. "I'm Trennen."

"Nikki. Wes's niece."

"Pleasure." He held on to her hand—and gaze—a mite too long.

Wes cleared his throat. The young man withdrew his hand.

"Trennen's the one who rents my fields," Wes told her. "You'll see him on the farm from time to time."

"Accurate," Trennen said, focusing on him. "In fact, you might

94

see me Tuesday morning. My parents and I are headed to St. Louis later that day, so I was going to swing by before we leave to check on the back twenty. Won't disturb you, will I?"

"Not at all."

"Cool." Trennen's eyes wandered to Nikki, then ricocheted back to Wes.

Dave, a Hosana deacon, strode up to them. "Fellas, got a minute? We're going to have a quick deacons meeting."

"Sure." Wes turned to Nikki. "You'll be okay?"

"Of course. I'll just hang out."

He and Trennen followed Dave to the group of men gathered in the shade on the far side of the landing. On the way, he kept his attention on his shoes to avoid the woman in purple standing a few yards away.

◆ ◆ ◆ ◆

The Trennen kid gave her one last look before he followed Uncle Wes. His blue eyes stood out from under his brown hair. He couldn't have been more than a year or two out of college. A scrawny farmer on the start-up, with the bronzed complexion to account for his hours outdoors.

A trio of older women toddled up to Nikki.

"So you're Chris's daughter," said the middle one, apparently the leader.

A fine choice for introductions. She forced a smile. "I'm Nikki."

"You're staying in Ann's old house."

Small talk clearly was not her priority. "I am. I'm helping my uncle fix it up this summer."

"Is that right?"

The other women looked on as if feeding their questions telepathically to their leader.

"You probably didn't know Ann all that well, did you?"

"Not really. I have good memories of Christmases together."

"She talked about you."

"A lot," the shorter of the two companions added. The taller one nodded.

"She said you loved getting Big Red gum on your birthday," the leader said.

Nikki grinned. "I did." Even the card would smell like cinnamon.

"She got all of us ladies to send gum to our grandkids for their birthdays," the leader said.

"I did Juicy Fruit," the shorter companion reported.

The taller one pointed to her chest. "Wrigley's."

Grandma Ann, the original influencer. Nikki chuckled.

"We got all the updates on you and your sister at Tuesday morning quilting," the leader explained. "All us ladies loved to talk about our families. Best day of the year for Ann was when the school pictures arrived in the mail." She traced her finger in the air the length of Nikki. "You look a lot like her."

"Same coloring," the shorter one said.

"I've said that about you since you were a little one in pigtails," the leader claimed. "Where is your sister these days?"

"Salina. She's married now, for two years."

"How lovely." She pulled the straps of her purse farther up her forearm. "Crying shame about your parents. Your grandmother would have been heartbroken."

Nikki's smile faded.

From across the landing, Uncle Wes's gaze caught hers. His brow furrowed.

"Marriage used to mean so much more than it does these days," the leader continued. "People seem to throw it away like it's a used paper towel."

Nikki folded her arms over her stomach, fought to keep the polite smile on her face.

"I taught your dad in Sunday school." The leader's tone brightened as if she had not just dragged Nikki through a land mine. "Him and Wesley both, actually. The Werner boys couldn't have been more different from the get-go. Wesley was so compliant, picked up everything very quickly. But that Christopher, he was a rascal. Always looking for ways to sneak out to the playground. Once he did it right in the middle of the sermon." The trio laughed at the shared memory.

"Henry got so cross at him," the shorter woman said.

"About tanned his hide right off," the taller one recalled. "Right there on those steps."

More chuckles.

Nikki rolled her bottom lip under her teeth.

Suddenly an arm wrapped around her shoulders. "Nikki, I thought that was you!" Joyce squeezed her to her side.

"You know her, Joyce?" the leader asked.

"I do, Mrs. Rothfuss. We met yesterday. Isn't she a doll?"

"Every bit as pretty as Ann said," the older woman replied.

"I hope you ladies don't mind, but Wes sent me over to get Nikki for him. Mind if I steal her?"

"Of course." Mrs. Rothfuss gave Nikki a nod. "Very nice to have met you, Nikki. Hope to see you again soon."

The companions nodded farewell.

As Nikki stepped away from them guided by Joyce's arm, she realized how shallow her inhales had become.

Joyce led her toward the group of men. Uncle Wes's frown deepened.

"What did he need me for?" Nikki asked.

"He didn't send for you, actually. That's a small lie on my part that I'll ask for forgiveness for later." She stopped and turned to Nikki. "I figured you wanted a change of topic."

Nikki could have hugged her right then and there. "Thank you."

Joyce patted her shoulders before peeling her arm away. "We all need a wingman, as they say." Her giggle was as lyrical as her smile.

◆ ◆ ◆ ◆

It wasn't Wes's imagination. Nikki had been disturbed by something Mrs. Rothfuss and the other ladies said. He had planned to step away from the deacons, even started in Nikki's direction. Then Joyce swooped in, deftly moving Nikki closer to him. She kept his niece there with her, protected, while his meeting continued, as if she could read his mind.

Joyce's gaze traveled to his and locked. The first time they had been face-to-face all morning. The purple brought out the gold of her hair.

He inhaled sharply and pulled his attention back to the discussion at hand. He had to concentrate on the things needing concentration.

When the meeting ended, he approached the women slowly, attempting to keep his focus mostly on Nikki. "Sorry about that," he told her.

"It's perfectly fine. Joyce makes great company." She grinned.

"If I'm great company, it's because you make it easy." Joyce lightly patted her arm.

Despite his own will, his eyes drifted to Joyce's. Their hazel depths shone back at him. A wave of heat rushed down to his toes.

"Thanks again," Nikki told her.

"Of course. Glad we got to talk some."

Joyce deserved a thanks from him too, for being there when he could not. He managed only a "Have a great day." Hopefully she could read between the lines.

Joyce didn't seem to mind. She smiled as they started for the truck. "Enjoy the rest of the pie," she called after them.

Nikki laughed and looked up at him. "You do realize you will never live that down."

"Probably not." They reached the truck.

"And Joyce really is good company," she added.

Before he could form a reply, she cut to the left, toward the passenger door.

◆　◆　◆　◆

Stomach full of leftover hoppel poppel and an hour to kill before they left for Hannibal, Wes sat in his recliner and called Aunt

Emma to catch her up on the latest. He told her about the hash and Nikki's plans to make more of the dishes.

"She's taken with this notebook," he said.

"So am I, and I haven't seen it!"

"She also lit up when I told her how much her great-great-grandmother loved books. Nikki's a literature teacher. Don't know if you knew that."

"Seems like I did. Either way, it makes perfect sense that she is. Ann would talk about finding the right books to give her for Christmas. If memory serves, as a little girl Nikki had a particular fondness for Judy Blume . . . or maybe Beverly Cleary. One of those. Then when the Harry Potter books came out, your mom was first in line at the bookstore in Hannibal to purchase copies. She probably elbowed more than one pubescent boy out of the way. Just kidding, of course. She didn't elbow anyone. She had a heavy purse."

Wes laughed. "Sounds more like something you would do."

"It does, and I did." Her hummy chuckle was as bright as the early afternoon. "I was a terrible influence on my sister. I was never much of a reader, though. Nor Ann. Funny what skips generations. Don't you wish you could have known Nikki better as a child? If it hadn't been for Ann's updates, I don't think I'd know her at all."

Wes agreed. Whatever news his mother received about the girls she had shared far, wide, and immediately. Her frequent letters to him during his deployments were his primary connection to the extended family. Chris rarely reached out in those days.

"Did Nikki go to church with you this morning?" Aunt Emma asked.

"She did. Several people commented how much they enjoyed seeing her. They knew her through Mom too."

"Those are good people for her to talk to. They surely have lots of stories about Ann and Eddner to tickle her fancy."

"Nikki does seem increasingly curious about our family history. Except for things related to Chris."

"That'll change the more stories she hears, don't you think?"

"Only if she wants to hear them." If the incident with the church-purse ladies was any indication, the odds seemed small.

"I bet you a thick dollar she will eventually," Aunt Emma countered. "Readers usually have a keener interest in the experiences of others, especially of those who came before. I think that's why she's so taken with the notebook. It's helping her discover the stock she comes from and what it means to bear her name. Clear as day she desires to learn that."

"Suppose you're right."

"I am right. It's one of my greatest qualities. Learning our family history is going to be a good thing for her. Family history has a way of putting our own lives into perspective. None of us walk a path entirely of our own making. Which means you, sir, have a task ahead of you."

"What's that?" he asked.

"Let the people of Eddner into this with you. Encourage them to tell Nikki stories and answer her questions where you can't. The more people the better."

"I will," he promised. But quietly he prayed that "more people" would not have to include much of a certain pie maker.

◆　◆　◆　◆

"You're where?" Tracy's tone mimicked Nikki's mom's in nearly every way. "How did that happen?"

"It's a long story," Nikki said as she continued her search through the notebook for supper ideas. They were leaving for Hannibal in less than twenty minutes.

"Tell me the gist, at least. Last I knew you were taking just a day off. Now you're telling me you're not coming back until the end of July."

"I didn't plan it this way. It sort of happened spur of the moment. I needed somewhere quiet for a while, away from everything."

"Everything? As in *every*thing?"

Nikki chewed her lip. The silence answered for her.

"Mmm." Tracy's one short sound verified the message had been received. The full message and all its implications, particularly about Isaac.

Nikki turned a page and smoothed her fingertips down the paper. Though right in front of her, the written words did not register, her mind too busy attempting to predict Tracy's opinion. What her mom thought of her decision was one thing, but what Tracy thought was another. For the first time, someone objectively outside the drama had an invitation to weigh in. Someone she respected, and who was close enough to tell her that she was doing exactly what the woman on the church landing had lamented—potentially throwing away something of value. She held her breath.

Whatever Tracy truly thought of the decision, her only response was, "Is there anything I can do?"

Nikki exhaled. Knowing when to speak and when to let Nikki make her own choices was one of Tracy's most admirable traits.

"That's actually why I called you," Nikki told her.

They discussed what in Nikki's room needed to be cleaned or locked up for the summer. Tracy wrote it all down and read back the list to confirm.

"That should do it," Nikki said. "I'll call Washington on Tuesday to let him know. Thank you. I really appreciate it."

"Happy to help." Tracy paused. "You know, sister, I've watched you do a lot of growing this past year. It strikes me that God has more in store for you. I hope this summer will clarify even more than you think it will."

The comment resounded through her. So much had already changed. Much more was bound to change. For better or worse.

"I hope so too, Tracy."

◆ ◆ ◆ ◆

Painting supplies were fairly quick and easy to pick out. It was the wreath selection that took up the largest percentage of their shopping time. Uncle Wes took great pains to evaluate every option on the shelf, deliberating the colors and flowers—but not the price tags. After several minutes, he chose a rose-adorned wreath three feet in diameter for Grandma Ann. Grandpa Henry's wreath, a manly red-white-and-blue arrangement of carnations, mums, and irises, was a comparatively paltry one foot in diameter.

"Trust me, he won't mind," Uncle Wes assured Nikki as he set the far less ornate wreath in the cart. "He would've rather had the money."

Nikki grinned.

The last leg of their trip required them to cross the full length of the supercenter to the grocery section for the ingredients she needed for supper. The front wheel of their cart dizzied itself crazy as they walked.

Nikki pulled up her list on her phone. "I need eggs, bread crumbs, paprika, parsley, ground beef, and ground pork." She turned to Uncle Wes. "I don't know if I've ever had ground pork before. Have you?"

"Pork burgers," he said. "At the fair."

"Are they good?"

"Juice drips down your hands."

"Yeah, I'd say that's good."

They arrived in the grocery section and rounded the endcap of the baking and spices aisle. Their cart nearly smacked into another one wheeled by a demure white-haired lady.

Uncle Wes came to a squeaky halt. "So sorry."

At first the senior lady startled. Then she looked up at him with beaming recognition. "Wesley!" The shorter companion from the church landing, still in her Sunday dress. Her purse rode in the child's seat. "I nearly plowed you over!" She giggled.

"Should've been more alert myself, Mrs. Dutzow."

The woman—at last named—noticed Nikki standing beside him. "And your niece is with you. How nice. Hello again."

"Hello."

"You all headed to the cemetery?" She gestured with an arthritic finger at the wreaths.

"After this," he confirmed.

"Us too. My niece and I." She motioned behind her.

At the other end of the aisle, selecting a bag of flour from the shelf, was Joyce.

Uncle Wes took a subtle step back. Nikki bit her lip to rein in her amusement. Small towns were a trove of plot twists.

"Wesley, you sure did pick out a pretty wreath for your mother," Mrs. Dutzow continued, clearly chattier when not under the headship of her leader.

He listened but looked between her and Joyce, who approached with flour in her hands and a glow in her expression.

"She adored the roses you would send her on her birthday," Mrs. Dutzow said. "Such a sweet son. Always taking care of her despite being so far away."

"I, uh, I did my best."

Joyce was to them in a few more strides, gaze flitting between the new arrivals. "Looks like everyone's in Hannibal this afternoon."

Nikki waited for Uncle Wes to respond. When he didn't, she spoke up. "We needed to get wreaths for Grandma and Grandpa and groceries for supper tonight."

"They're beautiful." Joyce's eyes twinkled. "And what's on the menu for tonight?"

"German hamburgers, from a recipe I found among Grandma Ann's things. She had a notebook full of them, all German dishes."

"How interesting," Joyce replied. "I don't remember her making many German dishes. Do you, Wes?"

He briefly met her stare and shook his head. "Not really."

"We didn't eat much German food coming up either," Mrs. Dutzow cut in. "We ate whatever we could. You a good cook, Nikki?"

She shrugged. "Not the worst. But these recipes, I'm discovering, aren't always the clearest when it comes to instructions."

"Probably because they were passed down orally," Mrs. Dutzow said. "My mother didn't write down any of her recipes. It was all from memory."

Joyce nodded. "Daughters learned mostly by shadowing their mothers, didn't they, Aunt Pauline?"

"It's how I learned. Learned to cook and sew and tend the babies by working alongside my mother. That's not how it's done nowadays, though."

"Times have changed." Joyce's eyes darted to Uncle Wes, who shifted his weight.

"Just go with your instincts," Mrs. Dutzow advised. "That's what the old cooks had to do."

"And you can give me a call if you get stuck," Joyce offered. "I'm happy to help if I can."

"I appreciate that. Thank you."

Joyce set the flour in her aunt's cart. "We should let you finish your shopping. Nice to see you both again."

"Same to you," Nikki said.

Uncle Wes silently moved farther to the side to let them pass.

When they were gone, Nikki leaned close to him. "Funny how we keep running into Joyce, huh?"

He cut his eyes to her, then pushed the cart forward. "Small town."

Twelve

A narrow gravel drive horseshoed through the Hosana Lutheran cemetery, routing so close to some headstones that one wrong move meant Wes's truck tires might snag against one. He pulled to a stop near the top of the horseshoe, under the shade of the only tree. Nikki helped him retrieve the wreaths from the back seat.

The cemetery was a half acre, cut into the cornfield that edged up to the schoolyard. The quaint spot soaked in the symphony of Sunday afternoon stillness and birdsong. The headstones ran in perfect lines perpendicular to the county road. Stones of remembrance for saints who had gone before, first to the Missouri prairie and then on to glory. Their lives only a blip and yet memorialized by those who followed.

Wes led his niece into the grass freshly cut under his blades two days before. They wound through the headstones marked with names she had encountered already in her time in Eddner. Rothfuss. Dutzow. Schoenborn. Several stones were complemented by bouquets or wreaths for people whose descendants still lived in the area. The Baumanns were on the west side of the horseshoe. And the Werners, three generations of them, took up most of the third row inside the bend. Wes stopped in front of a slab of carved granite covering adjoining gravesites.

Henry James Werner, Ann Ruth (Baumann) Werner

A pair of cherubs held a long cloth banner between them.

Joined in lives and hearts, May 14, 1960

Wes knelt and began unpacking his father's wreath from its cardboard frame.

Nikki squatted next to him. "Grandpa was young when he died."

"Sixty-six. Heart attack." The cardboard flaps snapped out of their joints. He pulled away the backing enough to expose the plastic ties securing the wreath, then took out his utility knife and sliced.

"What was he like?" Nikki asked. "I was only eight when he died. I don't really remember him."

Wes took his time removing the ties. Of all the topics Chris would have kept close to the vest, their father would have been the most hidden. The day it all came to a head—when Chris had reached his breaking point—left an indelible mark on them all. Chris only fifteen. The shouting match. Their father red-faced, vein bulging down the center of his forehead. Chris's white knuckles. A swing that fortunately missed. The screen door slammed so hard the hinges broke. His mother staring out the kitchen window for hours. She had kept her vigil at their family table every evening until Chris returned five days later. He never went to church with the family again, just to break their father's pride a little more each Sunday.

Wes freed the smaller wreath from its last tie. The cardboard padded onto the grass. "Grandpa knew what he liked and what he didn't."

Above his father's side of the headstone stood a wire post with a hook at the top. He stood and settled the wreath onto it.

"What did he like?" she asked.

He finished adjusting the wreath and met her gaze. "Farming. Church. Rain. Pretty much in that order."

"What about his family?"

He knelt next to the larger wreath. "Some days."

"Was he hard to get along with or something?"

The ties on his mother's wreath were larger, requiring more ardent cutting. "Most of those old farmers were tough. Had to be. Tough meant survival."

"Not much time for sentiment?" she concluded.

The first tie snapped apart. "Unless you count anger."

Nikki lowered onto the grass, sitting cross-legged. The pinch of her brow indicated her attempt to process the glimpse of her grandfather.

People might depart the world, but the emotions they wrought did not.

"He was a good man, Nikki. Hardworking, taught me a lot. But he held on to things he shouldn't have. In the end, it cost him a lot."

He finished freeing the wreath and hung it on the hook over his mother's grave. It undulated gently over the words carved in stone.

Loving wife and mother

"Grandma wasn't like that, was she?"

Wes slipped his hands into his pockets. "No."

"Do you still miss her?"

"Very much."

"Do you miss him?"

The grip of grief pinched his windpipe. He swallowed hard to chase it away. "Very much."

"Even though he was such a crank?"

Some things could only be understood when seen from the other side of a choice. He had chosen very differently than his brother had. Wes had chosen to find a way to love. Self-protection was never a savior from pain. Only forgiveness could be.

"Yes," he said. Then he faced her fully. "Nikki, I want you to tell your dad you're staying for the summer. He needs to hear it from you."

Her mouth drew into a hard line. She looked away.

They stayed in silence.

A gray junco came to rest on a headstone several yards to their right. Juncos had been one of his mother's most consistent visitors to the bird feeder outside her kitchen window in the winter months, bringing her delight on dreary days. The bird turned its head toward Nikki, took her in with its dark eyes. It hopped once atop the stone, then sailed on outstretched wings.

At last Nikki sighed. "I'll think about it."

◆ ◆ ◆ ◆

German Hamburgers (Frikadellen)

Home should be where peace comes to roost. But peace is never an uninvited guest. As the keeper of the home, you must invite it daily. Bring it in, give it the place of honor, sit with it until you are filled with its tenderness. Turn away the indignation that will invariably come to your door too, pounding in its loud and obnoxious way. Resist its advances. Leave it cold on the porch. If it crosses your threshold, it will only steal and destroy. Even feeling the corner of its shadow upon your skin will rev your mind like a steam engine, and always in the wrong direction. Through prayer and petition and productive use of your two hands, ask for peace and you shall receive it. God's peace is the glorious antidote that stills the heart, and "a sound heart is the life of the flesh" as well as the home (Prov. 14:30).

3 slices stale bread

1 cup water, lukewarm

6 tablespoons butter

1 medium onion, diced

1 pound lean ground beef

1 pound ground pork

2 eggs

½ tablespoon paprika

½ tablespoon each salt and pepper

1 tablespoon parsley

About 1 cup plain bread crumbs

Melt 2 tablespoons of butter in skillet and fry onions until translucent and lightly brown. Let bread soak in water for a few minutes. Gently squeeze extra water from bread and crumble into a large bowl. Add meats, eggs, seasonings, and onions. Mix well with your hands. Form 8 equal-size patties. Press top and bottom of each patty into bread crumbs and set aside.

Melt 2 tablespoons of butter in skillet. Brown 4 patties on each side for about 2 minutes. Then reduce heat, cover, and cook for 8–10 minutes, flipping patties occasionally. Repeat for next 4 patties. Serve with whole-grain or stone-ground mustard.

◆　◆　◆　◆

The onions shimmied in the buttery pan, slowly giving up their whitish hue. The bread soaked nearby, returning to a pliable dough-like substance and yielding a slight yeasty smell. The sounds and scents that many souls had attached to home and the peace within.

As the keeper of the home, you must invite it daily.

The words stood out the first time as well as the third. Such a responsibility to bear. If what Uncle Wes indicated about Grandpa Henry was true, inviting peace was a practice Grandma Ann had known well. All those Christmases of food and gifts and grateful prayers were built on top of discord buried from Nikki's view.

The kitchen must have been a refuge for Grandma Ann. The place where she could escape to create something hearty amid the gray, where she fought off the advances of her husband's anger by putting her hands to the task of mixing in steady, soothing motions. Every revolution of the spoon a petition for the storm to pass, for the billow and roll to break and the sun to reclaim the hills around the farm. The glorious antidote of God's peace would come and still her heart.

Nikki switched off the burner and let the onions cool, then pressed murky water from the bread slices. The glob of reconstituted dough did not crumble so much as pull apart in small clumps. She dropped them into a large glass bowl. The eggs, seasonings, and meats went in next. Last, the onions, sliding easily from their pan.

She glided her hands down the edges of the bowl, under the mound of ingredients, and squeezed. The meat gave as easily as putty in her grasp. She worked her way through the bowl, mixing handful by handful. Steady, predictable motions, the kind that slowed minds and stilled hearts, focusing them on what mattered.

She divided the mixture into roughly even patties, coated them in bread crumbs, then set them on a sheet of foil. As the butter melted in the pan, she washed her hands and grabbed her phone.

Uncle Wes had asked her to tell her dad that she was staying in Eddner. If that was what it took to ensure that the peace of her home was protected, then that was what she would do.

She opened the text chain with her dad—to which he never responded—and added a new message.

Staying here for the summer. It's peaceful.

Send.

❦ *Thirteen* ❦

The bread-crumb coating crackled under Wes's fork as he sliced into the meat patty. Juices trickled out, carrying a few specks of the herbs. Except for the crunchy exterior and visible seasoning, the creation Nikki had put on his plate was nearly identical to the thick, quarter-pound burgers at the Huck Finn Dinette, the ones that made his doctor look disapprovingly at him over the rims of his glasses.

He lifted the first bite into his mouth as Nikki watched with knitted brow. The crisp-tender composition was reminiscent of fried chicken, a perfect marriage of texture and savory flavor.

"What do you think?" she asked.

According to her research, which she'd shared with him as they prepared to eat, the correct way to say the dish's name was *frick-a-deln*. However it was pronounced in German, only one English word seemed appropriate.

"Tasty," he replied. "Really tasty."

A grin spread across her face. It smacked of Chris. He used to grin that way as a boy, usually when he had done something to please their mother. That grin had all but disappeared by the time Wes left for basic.

Nikki took up her fork and began cutting her own first bite. "Which do you like better, this or the hoppel poppel?"

"I like meat."

She laughed. "Spoken like a guy."

That was almost certainly a compliment. He would accept it as such, anyway.

Nikki took her first taste. A pause. Her eyes widened. "That *is* good! Where has this been all my life?" She quickly cut off another chunk.

Undoubtedly, his brother would have shared their opinion of their supper.

In between bites, she asked, "Were you ever stationed in Germany?"

He shook his head. "Been to the Munich airport, but never Germany proper."

"I hear it's beautiful."

"The airport was nice."

She chuckled as she picked a fresh apple slice off her plate and snapped it between her teeth. "I think I might make a recipe a week while I'm here. There's lots to choose from." She nodded toward the notebook sitting in the cookbook holder. "What else do you like besides meat?"

"Sugar."

"Could've guessed that. You'll be happy to know there's plenty of cookie recipes."

Aunt Emma's mention of her grandmother's special dessert came back. "Any cakes?" he asked.

"A few. Why? You like cakes better?"

"I like it all."

"Fair enough."

They steadily worked through their frikadellen. Splotches of grease dotted his plate. In between mouthfuls of meat, he ate his apple slices. No sense making his doctor too upset.

"Uncle Wes," Nikki said, "can I ask you a personal question?"

"Sure."

She met his gaze. "Why did you choose the military?"

The question made him freeze.

That was the trouble with letting someone close enough to share space and meals. Hiding eventually became too hard to do. It was inevitable that Nikki would learn how their stories paralleled, but it seemed to come so soon, so offhandedly.

He took a moment to finish chewing, carving out the time to formulate a response. At last he swallowed and answered, "Didn't want to stay on the farm."

"Because of Grandpa Henry?"

"Mostly."

"What else was it?"

He lifted his napkin and wiped his mouth. "There were a lot of expectations. From my dad primarily, but also other people. I didn't want to be what those expectations pegged me to be."

"Which was what?"

"Here, all my life. As a farmer. A country boy who saw little of the world. A 'good son.'" He hesitated. "A husband."

At first she frowned. Then her lips parted. "Oh."

He reached for his cup of milk and brought it closer.

"What was her name?" she asked.

The name had not rolled from his tongue in years. Maybe more than a decade. Suddenly there it was again.

"Ada." He turned the glass with his fingertips. "Ada Juergen. We dated throughout high school."

Nikki rested her arms on top of each other in the narrow space between her plate and the table's edge. "Did she break your heart?"

He rubbed his forefinger on the glass and shook his head.

"*You* were the heartbreaker?"

More than thirty years had passed, and yet he could not shake the image of Ada's face when he'd dropped her off after senior prom. The streaks of mascara. The ruined corsage on her wrist. The echoes of her furious words. She had refused to hear that he wasn't ready. That forever was longer than she thought. That he needed a chance to figure out who *he* wanted to be. She cried that he was "ruining everything." The revenge rumors began to fly that very night, solidifying his belief he needed to move on and keep moving. Away from anything that tied him down.

"Did you love her?" Nikki asked.

"Thought I did. But sometimes love alone isn't strong enough to fix everything that's broken, or straighten out all that's crooked." Tap, tap on the glass. "Sometimes I wish I would have handled it differently. With Ada, and with my dad."

She studied him, a wrinkle forming in the middle of her brow. If the revelation struck too close to home, she didn't let on how much. "How long after you broke it off did you enlist?"

"About two days."

Her eyebrows shot up.

His mother's had too. His father's eyes had narrowed. His brother had left the room.

"Seems unlike you to be so rash," Nikki said.

He shrugged. "I was a kid who wanted out. Of everything."

"You must have enjoyed the Army, though," she said. "You stayed in."

"It grew me in more ways than I can count." It had taken him multiple decades and tours to realize his dad had been right about the farm and what it could offer.

"Did Grandpa and Grandma like that you chose the military?"

"Not at first. Grandpa especially, as you can imagine. They had bigger worries, though."

"Like the farm?"

"The farm . . . Your dad."

Nikki closed her mouth. A coolness descended over the table. "Guess he's been hurting people for a long time."

Wes let go of his glass and leaned toward her. "He's been hurting for a long time. There's a difference."

Her eyes cut to him. A retort clearly clamored to rush across her lips, rattle its sword.

He held his breath, gripped the shield of faith tighter.

After a moment, she lowered her gaze to her nearly empty plate. "I think I want some pie." Her chair's legs dragged against the floor as she rose.

The wall was blunt, a thick protection around her most vulnerable spot.

Somehow he needed to find the one loose stone.

◆ ◆ ◆ ◆

After supper, without being asked, Uncle Wes took up position at the sink and began washing dishes, something her dad, despite all his faults, would do for her mom. The gesture fired the sting in her chest. She had shut Uncle Wes down on her least favorite topic. They hadn't spoken much since. Surely he understood. It was too soon, too painful.

She eased over to the linen drawer next to the sink and selected a clean "warshrag," as Grandma Ann used to call it. "Mind if I wet this?" she asked.

He took one hand from the sudsy water and swiveled the faucet closer to her. He peeked her way.

Quickly she dipped the rag in the running water and wrung out the excess.

"Got a lot left over." He pointed at the sheet pan on the counter with six uneaten patties. "Plans for them?"

"Lunch the rest of the week, I guess."

"Could give some to Trennen when he's by on Tuesday."

"Sure." She walked over to the table. Like Grandma Ann used to, she started in the middle of the table and swept the rag toward a corner, bringing crumbs together in one spot.

Behind her, the faucet turned off. The metal frying pan clinked against the stainless-steel sink. Water sloshed.

She carefully pushed the collection of crumbs over the edge into her waiting palm. As she turned for the trash can at the end of the counter, Uncle Wes looked up from his work and caught her gaze.

"Maybe you could do more of that," he said.

"Of what?"

"Share the German food you make with people around Eddner."

The crumbs loose enough to fall tumbled into the trash can.

She brushed off the rest with the edge of the rag. "You mean like deliver it to their houses?"

"I mean have them over. To eat."

She folded the rag and let the offer roll around her mind. It seemed to come from beyond him. He did, after all, willingly live miles from people. "You'd really be okay with having people over?"

He swiped the pan with a scrub pad. "They probably have great stories to tell."

She laid the rag on the counter and smoothed it flat. "What if it was Joyce?"

"Joyce?"

"She offered to help me figure out the recipes."

He looked down at the pan, slowly trailing it again with the pad. "If, uh, if that's what you need." After a beat, he lifted his gaze to hers. His eyes held every indication he meant what he said, regardless of whatever discomfort he was about to feel.

She smiled.

He smiled back, though tightly. Yet another example of him putting himself aside.

Which made the story of Ada and enlisting all the more intriguing.

◆ ◆ ◆ ◆

"Good, beautiful morning to you, Fritz!" Aunt Emma's cheerful tone almost made up for the dreary bacon oatmeal globbed in Wes's bowl.

"Good morning, and happy Memorial Day," he answered as he trudged his spoon through the mixture.

"Memorial Day. Yes. Somehow that slipped my mind—forgive me. This is probably more of a reverent day than a happy one for you. Attending any events today?"

"Not this year. I took wreaths to Mom and Dad yesterday, though."

"Did Nikki go with you?"

"She did, and we ended up talking about Dad."

"Look at you diving right into the family history. What all did you tell her?"

He rested his spoon on the side of his bowl. "That he was a hardworking man but that hardness carried over to other areas of his life."

"Nice, diplomatic way to put it."

"I hope it helps. She has so many assumptions about Chris and why he avoids Eddner. She's not willing to move past those yet."

"Give it time. People prefer to hang on to their own view of things far longer than they should, particularly about their own family. Your brother's like that too. Henry's never been his favorite subject either. Ironic how history repeats itself in the same family even one generation later."

He toyed with his spoon handle. "Was thinking about that last night. Seems there's another side to it."

"How so?"

"Dad was never willing to share with Chris about his experiences. He left us both to wonder and assume. Now Chris is doing the same thing with Nikki."

A beat went by. "That's a very astute observation, Wes."

"Maybe you're rubbing off on me."

"It's about time." She chuckled.

The levity brought a grin to his lips.

"Goes to show," she continued, "you never know what God can do with the memories we let others into."

Absently he stirred the oatmeal, the conversation with Nikki over supper releasing with the steam. Ada had not been a topic he had planned on discussing.

Before he had deployed to Desert Storm, he asked an old classmate if he had heard anything about Ada. They were in their late twenties by then. The classmate told him she had moved away many years before. Only once more, in his short-lived presence on social media, did Wes attempt to learn what had become of her. She had married, become a mother. All the things she had ever wanted.

Someone else had fulfilled the promise she'd wanted from him. Someone else had stepped into the hole he had left, and he never had a chance to tell her that was all he'd ever wanted for her—to be happy. Maybe she wouldn't have believed him anyway.

He could lead men into war, but he could never find the courage to reach out to her.

Aunt Emma broke into his memories. "Have you talked to Nikki about fixing up the house?"

"Will talk specifics soon. Told her I'd come up with a list."

"It's nice that she wants to help you."

"She said she enjoys painting, which is good. There'll be plenty of that."

"If she applies the first coat in a W shape, you'll know she's not lying. Did she make any more of those recipes?"

"Last night she did. Made German hamburgers. They were delicious. She agreed to give the leftovers to Trennen, which led to a whole conversation about hosting different people from Eddner for meals. Could be a way for them to tell her what they know."

"Clever idea!" Aunt Emma said. "Oh, to be a fly on the wall at those meals. You tell her she can count me as part of the Eddner community too. I haven't lived there since I was seventeen, and obviously I can't be there for the meals, but I would be happy as a clam to share. She can call me anytime. Think she would?"

"Hard to say."

"Mmm, that's probably true. I doubt she remembers me. I haven't had any contact with her since Ann's funeral. I might need a good ol'-fashioned incentive for her to dial my digits. Let me think on that. In the meantime, please insist to her that I'm full of good things."

"It's all I ever say about you, Aunt Emma."

"Good boy."

Fourteen

Early strands of pale light reached through the living room window and spread themselves around the couch. Nikki pulled the afghan closer to her chin, shielding her bare arms from the chill of fresh morning. In place of rhythmic train clacks and the low hum of interstate traffic, an ocean of quiet, wide and deep. Enough to sink into forever.

The alarm on her phone chirped into the silence.

She pulled her phone off the coffee table and swiped off the sound. The notification disappeared, but another one instantly took its place. From her photos app. ONE YEAR AGO TODAY.

Her breath caught.

It was a picture of her and Isaac, ice creams in hand. The Day of Dessert, they had called it.

Her thumb hovered over their smiles, lingering on the edge between running away and leaning toward. Finally she tapped.

The collection of photos from the day opened, and she scrolled through. Each pic pulled her deeper into the memories, deeper into the ache for what was.

Her and Isaac with cookies half the size of their faces. Isaac with an ornate milkshake served in a trendy mason jar. Her with vanilla bean cheesecake topped with strawberries and caramel drizzle. The entire day—breakfast, lunch, dinner, and snacks—they had driven to various points of the city, to bakeries, restaurants, and ice cream shops, eating nothing but sugary delights, then rating each one on a scale of one to five and posting them on social media. Hundreds of likes.

"We should start a blog," she had suggested.

"*Desserts of Kansas City,*" he had named it.

The burn in her chest crawled up to her eyes. She blinked it away and switched over to her text stream with Isaac. So much to say to him. So much to plead. So much to get themselves back to, even if there were two hundred miles between them. They couldn't end like Uncle Wes and Ada. She couldn't run forever.

Her thumbs paused over the screen, poised to type whatever needed to be said. Nothing came. Her mind was frozen by the yearning.

She scrolled through the stream of their previous conversations, through the "Good morning, babe" messages and the "Can't wait to see you" promises. Through the weekly updates of funny things her students had said, and his occasional challenge to "guess what this corporate acronym means."

On March 3 she had texted,

Love you forever.

He had texted back,

I'll love you longer.

She pinched her face against the hard welling within her chest.

"*Sometimes love alone isn't strong enough to fix everything that's broken.*"

Uncle Wes was right.

Love pulled her back to Isaac, but whatever had pushed her to Eddner still dug its shoulder into her stomach, refusing to relent.

She switched her phone to sleep mode and kicked off the afghan. Before the tears broke over her lashes, she folded the blanket and turned on the radio. The country music drowned out all the reminders of Kansas City.

Do the next thing. It was all she could do.

◆ ◆ ◆ ◆

On Tuesday morning, Wes handed Nikki the sheet of notebook paper on which he had listed and numbered the tasks for the farmhouse. "Want to know what you think," he said.

She sat with one leg tucked under her on his mother's couch, free hand digging into a box of Life cereal. His mother would have asked if she wanted a bowl, a subtle way of telling her guest that she was getting crumbs over everything, namely her own sleeping place. Obviously Nikki still opted for the couch at night with only the old afghan for comfort, despite a bed being available.

He stayed silent on both points and let her crunch her way through the list that attempted to organize her weeks—her months—in Eddner. Nine items in all, several marked by a star to represent the ones on which he would take the lead.

Task 1: Inventory boxes from attic.

Task 2: Take unneeded items to charity.

Task 3: Paint and re-hardware bathroom cabinets.

Task 4: Replace bathroom flooring and baseboards.*

Task 5: Replace faucets in bathroom sink and tub.*

Task 6: Sand, paint, and re-hardware kitchen cabinets.

Task 7: Replace kitchen flooring and baseboards.*

Task 8: Paint walls in bedrooms, bathroom, kitchen, and living room.

Task 9: Clean house inside and out.

Only Nikki could say if she was comfortable with the amount and type of work ahead.

As she read, he moved the first box from the attic onto the floor, then opened the second. Inside were old clothes decades out of fashion, three pairs of women's leather heels stiffened from lack of care, a collection of *Our Daily Bread* devotional booklets from the late 1950s, and several issues of *The Lutheran Witness*, the oldest from 1934. Underneath all that, a King James Bible. The edges of the pages had turned golden brown but were straight and smooth, unbothered by use. The black cover was uncreased. He opened it to the first page.

"This Holy Bible is presented to," the printed text read. On the lines provided, a handwritten script revealed the sacred Scripture had been a gift to his mother from "your loving sister" for Christmas 1958. Two years before his mother married his father.

For some reason, his mother had kept it out of rotation, protected and preserved, the way Henrietta had kept the German books. They served as markers of family history, denoting a path between generations that, until then, had long been covered in weeds, forgotten.

"This looks like a full summer." Nikki's voice tore him away from the page.

He laid the Bible on top of the clothes and turned to her. "Hope it's not too much."

"Not at all. Happy to do it, and I'll get started today." She slipped the paper onto the coffee table and rose from the couch. "What're your plans for the day?"

"Need to check the fencerows."

"Trying to keep the cows in?"

"And wildlife out."

She hugged the cereal box to her side. "I could help with that too, if you want."

"It's nothing special."

Her expression fell slightly, a clear signal he wasn't picking up on what she was really asking for. "Maybe not," she said, "but I would see more of the farm that way."

Of course she would. He nodded. "You have your pants?"

She glanced down at her dress. "Do I need them?"

"Unless you like the feel of thistle."

"I'll change."

◆　◆　◆　◆

Nikki held open the gate as Uncle Wes eased the truck into the pasture. Once through, he signaled for her to close and chain it. The squeal of hinges called across the open pasture, empty of the red-hide herd.

"Where are the cows?" she asked as she climbed into the cab.

"Probably down farther. We'll see them eventually." He shifted into first and made a sharp turn to the left to follow the fencerow. Despite the slow speed, the thick brush and hoofprint-pocked ground jostled them in their seats.

Uncle Wes surveyed the posts and the panel of woven wire hooked between them, his left elbow slung over the sill of his open window. His toolbox and roll of extra wire jangled in the truck bed.

"How large is this pasture?" Nikki asked.

"About fifty acres. Ends at the river bottoms."

The midmorning sun glinted off the hood of the truck. She squinted against the glare. "What made you come back to farming? You were so eager to get away from it."

He was quiet for a moment. "Like I said, the Army grew me in many ways."

"It made you miss farming?"

"The land more so. Made me see it the way Grandpa did, what it meant to him."

"Which was what?"

Their gazes met, his sincere. "Wholeness."

The answer touched down in her soul. A refrain it knew intuitively.

He returned to his examination, driving them along the line in bumpy quiet.

They had driven for a solid five minutes, looping back south along the row, before the first cow appeared. She ambled out of the trees at the precipice of a gentle downward slope. In the basin of the valley below, the rest of the herd strung themselves across the waving grass.

"There're the girls," Uncle Wes said, a note of pride in his voice.

He traced along the fencerow at a snail's pace, eventually easing down into the bottoms. He occasionally glanced at his herd. "Seems everyone's here."

"That's good," she said.

"Very."

The bottoms banked at a ravine guarded by a row of thirsty trees on either side. He came to a stop. "Gotta look on foot." He turned off the engine and stepped out of the truck. Nikki followed.

They trudged through the grass, tiny white moths taking flight as their hiding places were disturbed. The fence angled down into the ravine and stopped suddenly in the middle. It picked up again in full force on the other side. Strung between the two end poles were four strands of barbed wire. In the ravine bed, a serpentine of opaque water wound around parcels of sooty rock. The branches overhead watched their reflection in the placid surface of the pools.

Uncle Wes planted his hands on either hip. "River's low."

"That's a river?"

"Sometimes a river," he said. "When it rains enough. It's South River. Runs out of the Mississippi about fifteen miles northeast of here."

"So it flows that way?" She swept her hand toward the fencerow.

He nodded. "Ends a few miles away. This is its last breath, you could say."

"Or the place it found its rest."

He looked at her, clearly as surprised as she was at the lyricism. "Suppose I can relate."

"Me too."

A rustle of grass behind them made them turn in unison. The bull calf had broken from the pack and trotted over to the truck.

"Probably expects food," Uncle Wes said.

"Think he'd like frikadellen? We have plenty."

He chuckled. The breeze danced the grass against the calf's knobby knees.

"I still say he needs a name," she said.

Uncle Wes started for the truck, her cue to shadow. "What would you name him?"

"He's a bull, so maybe a strong German moniker like Ludwig or Heinrich. Something stalwart."

"Stalwart, huh?"

Their steps synched, grass crunching under their soles.

The calf lowered his head and moved one back leg behind him, as if preparing to turn on his heel. The anxious stance could not hide his muscular frame. He was rugged and hard-wearing, like the Eddner settlers who had found their resting place on the land that now fed him.

"How about Bonhoeffer?" Uncle Wes said. "The Lutheran pastor who resisted the Nazis. That's stalwart."

"Bonhoeffer," she repeated loud enough for the calf to hear.

The animal lifted his head, ears tilting up. He clearly liked it too.

"That is indeed stalwart," she said. "I like it. Bonhoeffer."

They neared the truck. It was the closest she had ever been to a bull calf. Or any calf. He appeared to be about hip height from hoof to spine. Still a baby.

She slowed her steps, reached out her hand.

Bonhoeffer stared at her for a moment. Then he flipped himself around and cantered back to wherever his mother grazed.

Off to tell his mom about his new friend.

◆　◆　◆　◆

Only a few places along the fencerow required any kind of adjustment. Nikki stood by Wes's side, overseeing the toolbox and knowing which implement to pass him when he asked for it by name. Chris undoubtedly had taught her that, unwittingly preparing his daughter for the summer of labor ahead.

About an hour after they had embarked, he pulled into the driveway. A familiar white F-150 sat outside the machine shed. Trennen emerged as Wes parked.

"Morning!" the young man called when they stepped out.

"Morning, Trennen." Wes met him halfway as Nikki gathered

her things and headed into the house. He pushed his cap back on his head. "Just starting out?"

"Yeah, about to fire up the Polaris." He gestured to the blue ATV.

"Corn's been looking good from what I've seen."

"It's the beans I'm more concerned about," Trennen said. "Hoping to double-crop with winter wheat, but only if the soil's not shot." He looked over Wes's shoulder at where Nikki once stood. "How's your niece doing?"

"Since Sunday? Fine."

"She liking it here?"

"Believe so."

Trennen nodded, looked down at the Polaris keys looped around his fingers, then tentatively back at the driveway. "How old is she anyway?"

Wes shook his head. "No."

"What? I didn't—"

"You didn't have to, son. The answer's no."

Trennen pursed his lips, spun the keys around his finger.

"Thought you had a girl in Hannibal anyway," Wes said.

"It's . . . complicated."

Wes jutted his head toward his house. "That's more complicated."

The boy sighed. "Fine. Thanks for killing all my hopes and dreams."

"Somebody had to."

Trennen smirked and started to walk away.

"If you need some lunch, we have extra German hamburgers."

Looking over his shoulder, Trennen asked, "What are German hamburgers?"

"Basically a breaded hamburger. Nikki made them from a recipe she found. Pretty good."

"I'll pick one up when I head out. Thanks." He proceeded to the shed, waving as he went. Off to his fields and his burgeoning future.

Trennen knew what he wanted in life—in his career, in his

home, in his relationships—and didn't shy away from taking good risks. The complete opposite of Wes at that age. Or any age.

Stunning how a kid could be so inexperienced and yet have a better head on his shoulders than a middle-aged man.

❊ *Fifteen* ❊

Nikki left a plastic container of frikadellen in Wes's re-frigerator, then returned to the farmhouse to work on the boxes. "I'll have them done today," she promised.

No doubt she would.

Wes, meanwhile, hunkered down in his office with his laptop and the month's invoices and receipts. Bookkeeping was never his thing until it absolutely had to be.

Half an hour into his number crunching, his phone came alive with an incoming call. He reached for it, then froze.

Chris.

Two rings. Three.

He prayed for grace, then answered. "Morning."

"I hear Nikki's staying with you all summer." His tone was hard.

"You talked to her?"

"She texted me."

Wes grimaced. Another text. Texting was the cheap way out.

"Don't suppose you or Lydia had anything to do with her decision?" Chris asked.

"We left it up to her. I think Lydia and I were both surprised, to be honest."

"But you didn't exactly discourage her."

"She can make her own choices, Chris."

"Yes, she made it perfectly clear."

A taste of his own medicine. It was as bitter to him as it was to everyone else.

Wes rubbed his chin and leaned back in his chair. "She's helping with the farmhouse," he explained. "She's also taking the opportunity to learn more about our family. What she's heard so far has been an eye-opener, especially about Mom and Dad."

The hint was not so subtle. Still, Chris didn't touch it.

"So she's not going back to KC at all this summer?"

"That's a great question for Nikki." As in, he should call his daughter, have a real conversation. One of them really needed to make the first move.

"She doesn't want to talk to me, Wes. She made that crystal clear too."

Bitter, bitter medicine. As gently as he could, Wes replied, "She doesn't understand your choices either."

A long, heated pause.

Chris's tone was tight. "You know what? You're right. She doesn't understand. But does she even want to? She has shut me out. All three of them have. And I—" He stopped, clearly fighting back a press of anger. So much hidden behind it, so much driving it. Chris had always been more like their father than he would admit.

Chris sighed heavily into the phone. "Look, Wes, the real reason I'm calling is to ask for help."

Wes lifted his chin. "What kind of help?"

"I would . . ." The words seemed difficult to get out. "I would like to see Nikki. Talk to her face-to-face."

Wes eased into an upright position, his chair creaking with the change. That was a big step for Chris. A good step.

"Will you help— Will you bring her to see me for Father's Day?"

Hope pinched. "Chris—"

"She won't come by herself, okay? I know I've messed up too much for her to ever do that. But if you come, then . . . then maybe she will."

Wes didn't have to be a father to feel the fresh fissure in his brother's heart. Wes, who had missed most of Nikki's life, had more influence over her than her own father. No amount of his empathy for Chris, however, would change her heart.

"You can't force things like this, Chris."

"I'm not trying to force it."

"Then why are you calling me instead of her?"

Several beats went by. At last Chris replied. "Do you honestly think she would take my call?"

He had a point. The likelihood seemed small, at least at the moment.

"Please, Wes. Help me?"

Wes rubbed his hand down his face and let it drop to his lap. "I'll plant a seed."

That was the best he could promise.

◆　◆　◆　◆

As soon as Wes handed Trennen the container of German hamburgers, the boy tore the lid off and scarfed down a patty with the aggressive efficiency of a soldier in the mess hall. Wes stood nearby and sipped his coffee. It had taken nearly five years to break himself of the speed-eating habit after retirement.

When the last bite had disappeared down his gullet, Trennen licked his fingertips and sighed contentedly. "Tell Nikki those're amazing."

Wes shook his head. To be young and heartburn free. "I'll walk you out."

He escorted Trennen to his truck, then followed behind it as the boy drove down the driveway. Trennen's compliments weren't the only thing he needed to relay to Nikki.

The farmhouse windows were open, inviting in the gentle temps.

Nikki answered the door with a dish towel in her hands. "Just washing up from lunch. Did you eat already?"

He nodded.

"Come on in."

A Neal McCoy song played on the radio. A row of empty cardboard boxes sat open-mouthed on the couch. Their contents had been sorted into piles on the floor.

"You finished going through the boxes?" he asked as they headed for the kitchen.

"About twenty minutes ago," she said over her shoulder. "Then I stopped for food. You sure you don't need anything?"

"I'm sure." Wes paused at the doorway and leaned against the frame, the spot he had taken up countless times when his mother cleaned up after meals or as her cookies baked in the oven.

Nikki returned to the sink and rinsed the soapy water from her plate. She set it on another dish towel to dry, the way his mother used to do, her favorite program playing on the old Zenith AM/FM radio by the flour canister. His mother's hands would move with a honed precision, methodical and poetic. Dip, wash, rinse, set. An even cadence that assured him the earth still spun the correct direction, despite what anything else led him to believe, and everything would be all right. Everyone was all right. Especially her. Sometimes a son needed that assurance.

Wes folded his arms. If only his mother could be there to assure him everything would be all right after he said what he came to say.

He cleared his throat. "I had a call."

Nikki brought a fork up from the water and took the dishcloth to it. "Who from?"

"Your dad."

Her hands paused. "What did he want?"

"Said he got your text."

She resumed wiping. The tines were well past clean.

"He'd like to see you. For Father's Day."

She flipped on the faucet and ran the water over the fork.

"It, uh, it might be good for you two to talk."

She turned off the faucet. "Why would I talk to him when he shows such little interest in talking to me?"

"He is interested. He wants to see you."

Nikki cut her eyes to him. "So interested he went through you to ask me?"

Wes dipped his head.

"Exactly." She set the fork on the towel and pulled the stopper from the sink. The drain swallowed the water in loud gargles.

He took a small step toward her. "Nikki—"

"I can't, Uncle Wes." She grabbed the free towel and dried her hands. "I can't and I won't. If he calls again, you can tell him that." She dropped the towel in a ball on the counter and stalked past him to the living room.

He sighed, slid his hands into his pockets.

Avoiding pain often caused more pain. Something it had taken more than half his life to understand.

◆ ◆ ◆ ◆

Disappointment had colored Uncle Wes's expression, but her answer would have to be what it needed to be. Her dad couldn't expect to be accommodated at his convenience. It wasn't right. It wasn't fair. It wasn't how things worked.

Nikki picked up an empty box and knelt with it next to the giveaway pile. Behind her, cowboy boots thumped on the wood floors. The top of her head tingled under Uncle Wes's gaze. She braced for round two.

Instead, he asked, "Need help?"

He had let it go, let it be what it needed to be. Every day, he gave her a new reason to respect him.

Slowly she turned and picked up a plastic freezer bag of photos from the coffee table. She handed it to him. "You could take a look at these and tell me what you want to do with them."

He took the bag from her outstretched hand. Their fingers did not meet, but their gazes did, briefly. A quick exchange flashing between them.

We're okay?

Yeah. And she meant it.

He settled into the armchair and opened the bag.

"There are some interesting ones in there," she said as she started to pack up the giveaway items. "Saw some of Grandma's sister."

"Do you remember Aunt Emma?" he asked.

"Dad would take calls from her occasionally. I only met her the once, at Grandma Ann's funeral. I assume she's still alive?"

"Lives in Oklahoma."

She turned to him. "Oklahoma? Near Dad?"

He nodded. "About an hour."

"Was that intentional? Him moving there?"

"Believe it's where Sheryl's from, isn't it?"

She shrugged, grabbed a pair of navy pumps, and thrust them into the box. "I wouldn't know." Her dad had married a woman whose last name was a mystery, along with virtually all other biographical information. With stiff movements, Nikki rolled several old shirts and stuffed them into the box.

"I think it's a good thing your dad is near Aunt Emma."

Roll, stuff. "Why's that?"

"He's always loved her. She's a good influence."

She tossed several angel statuettes on top of the rolled shirts and peeked at Uncle Wes. The way he said it naturally raised the suspicion Aunt Emma was an ally.

"She said she'd be glad to help answer questions about the family, by the way," he told her. "You could call her. She texts too."

She rested her hands on the edge of the box. "Aunt Emma texts?"

"She does a lot of things that may surprise you." He pulled a photo from the bag and held it out. "One of my favorites."

Nikki latched on to the white scalloped edges of the square photograph and brought it close. Two little girls stared back at her, so similar in features yet distinctly their own person. The young Ann possessed a stronger nose and smaller eyes and stood at least a foot taller than her little sister. She also had a more reserved smile—lips closed, cheeks barely lifted. In contrast, Emma's stretched so wide that nearly every baby tooth showed and her eyes almost disappeared. A baby doll hung from her pudgy hand. They wore matching peacoats, frilly white socks, and Mary Janes. The farmhouse porch sprawled behind them, two rockers sitting listless under the awning. The penciled caption on the back read "Ann and Emma, 1946."

"Were they close?" she asked.

"Only time I saw your grandma truly at ease was when Aunt Emma came to visit. We rarely took vacations, but having her back in town was the next best thing."

That smile frozen on Emma's face affirmed his claim.

Nikki handed the photo back to him. "Think she knows anything about the notebook or the recipes?"

"You should ask her." He gently laid the photo on the coffee table. His fingertips lingered on the edge, as if he didn't want to move away from whatever memory had painted his mind. Aunt Emma, bringing a reminder of life to the farmhouse when it was needed most. Aunt Emma, able to stand where Grandma Ann could not, be a voice where Grandma's no longer rang.

And that could prove to be as advantageous as Uncle Wes insinuated.

◆ ◆ ◆ ◆

"Were your ears burning yesterday afternoon?" Wes asked Aunt Emma as he set his oatmeal bowl in the sink.

"Why? Spreading rumors about me again?"

"If you count telling Nikki you were on standby, then yes. She was shocked to learn you text."

She laughed loudly. "Imagine if you told her I email too. Might just send her over the edge. Does this mean I should wait by the phone for her imminent call?"

He briefly turned on the tap and sloshed water into the bowl. "Still hard to tell. Some things she dives into and other things she's slow on the uptake."

"Sums up my entire existence, Fritz."

He chuckled and dried his hand on the dish towel.

"Anytime she's ready, she can reach out," Aunt Emma said. "Unless I get bored of waiting. We'll see which comes first."

"If it makes you feel any better, you're not the only one she's hesitant to speak to. Chris called me yesterday, wants to see Nikki for Father's Day. You can imagine her response when I asked her about it."

"Why didn't he ask her himself?"

"That was her point too."

"It's a fair one." She tsked. "Shame, that whole situation. But Chris has made his bed. He'll need to sleep in it a while yet. Hard as it is, we need to let him. The good news is God's not afraid of an attitude. That divine whack will come in due course—to all the skulls that need it."

Wes leaned against the counter and switched the phone to his other ear. "Nikki's resentment runs so deep, though. I'm equally concerned about that."

"Me too."

"I pray I can speak when I need to, Aunt Emma." The middle was the one place he disliked being almost as much as the Saudi desert. When it came to the people he loved, though, the middle was apparently unavoidable.

"Your tongue will untie at the right time," she assured him. "I have no doubt."

"Hope you're right." He lowered his head, tapped the back of his heel against the toes on his other foot.

"Wesley," she said in that pay-attention tone, "have I told you how proud I am of you?"

He lifted his chin.

"You have taken on a role that so few brothers and uncles would take on. Your mother would be so proud of you too. She wouldn't be surprised one bit that you care as much as you do. She saw things in you long before you ever realized they were there."

A tingle spread across his chest. No matter how old, a boy never stopped wanting to make his mother happy.

"I miss her every day," he said.

"I know you do. I do too."

His mother had been gone for so long, yet he still caught himself walking into the farmhouse expecting to see her in her chair, guiding a needle through the hem of his dad's pants or brushing a broom across the floorboards. The day before, he had gone down to the farmhouse to measure the bathroom for new flooring and trim. He swore he caught a glimpse of her through the living room window, folding clothes on the couch. But it was Nikki. It took a solid minute for that fact to register.

He cleared his throat of the gathering tension. "Speaking of Mom, Nikki finished sorting through the boxes of her things from the attic. Do you remember giving Mom a Bible in 1958?"

"I do. It was a Christmas gift."

"Hope you don't take this the wrong way," he said, "but I don't think she used it much."

"No, she didn't. She was more into other things than Scripture back then. She left the Bible at the farmhouse when she moved out. Mother held on to it for her. I think she had a feeling Ann'd come back to it eventually."

"Sounds like there's more behind what you just said."

"Tell Nikki to call me, and I'll spill."

He grinned. "Well played."

❧ Sixteen ❧

O n Wednesday afternoon, Nikki stood over the coffee
table, a freshly arrived box waiting. She held the scissors
in one hand and her phone in the other.

"I can't believe my things got here so fast," she told her sister
through the speakerphone. She opened the scissors, sank the tip of
one blade into the tape along the outer edge of the box, then sliced.

"She told me Sunday she was going to overnight them to you,"
Hannah replied.

Nikki turned the box and sliced through the tape on the other
edge. "You talked to her Sunday?"

"We went to help her finish packing. She plans to move this
weekend."

"But that's a full week before closing."

"She wants out of KC, Nik. We'll take her back for the closing,
but she wants to be out of there sooner."

The top flaps of the box were hidden by a sheet of white paper
on which her mom had written the farmhouse's address. The usually precise penmanship had a noticeable wobble as if written
haphazardly—or in exhaustion. Literally everything had been
taken from her mom, down to the way she wrote her *r*'s.

Nikki guided the scissors blade between the flaps and cut. "How
did she look when you saw her?"

"Like she needs a month off."

Even a year off wouldn't be enough.

Nikki laid the scissors on the floor and pulled open the flaps. Inside, her toiletries, shoes, and a few books (God bless her mom) were tucked carefully among her clothes. Regardless of what it cost, her mom kept thinking of her daughter's needs.

"Dad asked me to come see him for Father's Day," she told Hannah.

"He did?"

"Correction—he didn't ask *me*. He asked Uncle Wes to ask me."

Hannah huffed. "Nice."

"Did he ask you too?"

"No, but I think Mom living with us has something to do with that."

Nikki pulled each clothing item out of the box and laid them over the back of the couch in groups according to type. Jeans, dresses, skirts, shorts, tops, even her swimsuit and towel. Her mom had thought of every possible scenario.

"Are you going to meet him?" Hannah asked.

"No. Would you?"

"It'd be really hard." Hannah was quiet for a moment. "Part of me would kind of want to. I mean, it's Dad, but it's *Dad*, like he used to be. There's a part of my brain that says he'll always be *Dad*, you know? I don't know how to turn it off."

Nikki's gaze drifted to the armchair, the spot where years ago, when she was five or six, she'd sat on her dad's lap waiting to open Christmas presents. He'd worn his favorite cable knit sweater that left imprints on her bare arms. Her head fit perfectly in the spot where his broad shoulder met his neck, where the Hugo Boss cologne was thickest. His wet kiss on her hair. The flight of his laughter. The weight of his arms around her, protective and tender. Proud.

If she tried hard enough, maybe she could reach out and touch the vapor of the dad who once was. The dad that little girl knew. Before everything started to slide away.

Her throat tightened. "Do you ever imagine what you might say to him if you did see him?" she asked her sister. "How it would feel?"

"Sometimes," Hannah said softly.

The musk of cologne, the scratch of sweater, the vibration of his voice in his chest—they all faded into the distance. Gone. Because what was could never be again. The only words Nikki could imagine saying all came with exclamation points.

She turned her back on the chair and continued to unpack. "Let's change the subject. What else is going on?"

They talked about Hannah's job, Tyler's rec league soccer, and highlights from Hannah's favorite show. All the things that convinced them life moved forward. Then Hannah's tone grayed.

"There is one piece of news I've been debating telling you. Mom says I should, but I'm not sure."

Finished with the box, Nikki lowered onto the arm of the couch. "Sounds ominous."

"Not ominous necessarily." Hannah paused. "Isaac called me Monday."

Air stalled in her lungs. "W-what did he want?"

"To talk about you. You and him together, more specifically."

Needles of pain pricked the backs of Nikki's hands. Surely he had already left for Portland. "What did he say?"

"He wanted my opinion on whether you and him still have a future. Whether this stay in Eddner was really about our parents or if it was something else."

In other words, he wanted to know if she was being honest. Because he did not trust her to tell him herself. Her chest ached. "What did you say?"

"I said what I believe, Nik. That you love him very much, you just need time to find your way again."

Tears rimmed her eyes. Her sister had put into words what she couldn't. Hopefully Isaac heard them. He was not a ghost, not a thing of the past. He was her present. Her future. He was the one who looked at her as if she were the only star in the sky. Who led her by the hand into every restaurant. But who wanted more than she could be to him right then.

Her heart screamed. "I don't want to lose him, Han. But I . . . I don't know what to do."

"Tell him that. He needs to hear it. From you."

It echoed the advice her mom had given her. But it wasn't that simple. Love alone would not fix what was broken.

What else was needed, though, remained a frustrating mystery.

❖ ❖ ❖ ❖

Do the next thing.

It was her guidepost the rest of the day. Blocking out all other things, Nikki took the step immediately in front of her. The ache hung low around her, thick and heavy. Still, she stepped.

She claimed her grandparents' old bedroom as her own. No more couch sleeping. She put away her clothes in the closet and shoved all the boxes Uncle Wes had left in that room into the smaller bedroom, where the bed still sat empty. She peeled the twin-size mattress off its frame and slid it on its side across the hall, away from the faded pinstripe wallpaper and into the sunnier front bedroom. She brought the bed frame in pieces and reassembled it so the foot pointed to the window looking into the front yard. She dressed the bed with sheets and the afghan from the couch.

She ate the last of the egg hash for supper with the company of the next recipe and the shopping list for the next day—a list that included more ground beef and potatoes.

At last, with the bedroom windows darkened by the night and her hands stilled by the lack of tasks, she settled into the cocoon of sheets. In the middle of the quiet, Hannah's words resurfaced.

"He needs to hear it. From you."

The simple advice for a complex problem.

A few words would not fix everything. They would not heal and cover. But they were, in themselves, a step. The next thing.

Whatever else was needed to fix the brokenness, at least it was clear love was essential. She could act on that. She could invite peace and ask, *What good could I bring to this space?*

She pulled in a deep breath, let it out slowly, then picked up her phone from the pillow beside her.

Words had never seemed like such inadequate vessels as much as they did in that midnight moment. After several starts and deletions, a line from one of her favorite novels rolled to her thumbs.

> Though I am far away, my heart is with you.
> Forever. Please forgive me.

Send.

She put away her phone and lifted a silent prayer for the words to be received.

◆ ◆ ◆ ◆

Aunt Emma didn't answer Wes's call over Thursday breakfast. When lunchtime rolled around, he tried again. His call rang through to voicemail. That time, he left a message.

"Hey, Aunt Emma. Checking in. We're headed to Redmont this afternoon. Picking up groceries and hardware for the bathroom. Nikki's got better taste than I do, I'm sure you're pleased to know. She's hoping to get the bathroom cabinets spruced up by Sunday, before her first Sunday supper. And no need to ask—I'll send you pictures of our progress. In fact, I'll text you a picture of where we're starting too. Call me back."

After he hung up, he searched for the picture he'd taken of the bathroom earlier that week and sent it to her along with a message.

> Re: my voicemail. What the bathroom looks like now. It's "basic," Nikki said. Can only go up from here.

The last sentence was the hope of many things in his Werner life.

◆ ◆ ◆ ◆

The bell over the door chimed as Wes entered Harman and Sons Hardware. The late-afternoon hum of Main Street slowly faded as the door eased shut behind him.

The teenage girl at the cash register quickly slid her phone into the pocket of her tan apron and smiled. "Hello, Mr. Werner."

"Greta." He pulled a shopping cart from the stack near the entrance. "Otis around?"

"He's in the office. Want me to call him for you?" She reached for the handheld two-way clipped to the waistband of her jeans.

"That's all right. I'll catch up with him eventually."

"Yell if you need anything."

Having grown up coming to Harman's, Wes practically knew the store by heart. It had not changed much in five decades. It still wore the pungent cologne of wood and chemicals—the intoxicating harbinger of things to be built and improved, of sweat and muscle about to be spent. Only the aroma of freshly tilled soil compared.

The bathroom hardware comprised half of an aisle in the back left of the store. Nikki had texted him pictures of knobs and pulls to use as a guide for what she envisioned.

"Brushed nickel would be perfect with a faux-granite vinyl floor tile," she had told him. Such descriptive words for things that were essentially gray. Her texts also noted the sizes of each item needed, as well as the estimated ounces of paint needed to cover the simple vanity and over-the-toilet cabinet.

Out of Harman's limited selection, the closest knob was a mushroom shape with a raised center. He put four knobs in the cart along with two coordinating drawer pulls.

In the paint aisle, he easily located the silver matte spray paint Nikki wanted for the bathroom mirror frame as well as the primer and ultra-white semigloss enamel for the cabinets.

Before heading to the checkout, he added a few paint trays, which he had neglected to get from Hannibal, stirrers, and 120-grit sandpaper. Everything else Nikki would need, he had at the house.

Hopefully. Though giving Otis more of his patronage would not be a bad thing.

As he neared the front, the office door to the left of the register swung open. Out shuffled Otis, who quickly spied Wes and plodded over to greet him.

"They're letting anybody roam these parts anymore. Afternoon to you, Wes."

They shook hands.

Otis nodded at his cart. "Planning on some painting, I see."

"Nikki's working on the bathroom cabinets."

"She here with you?"

"Dropped her off at County Mart to get what she needs."

"Glad you have her help. Think you'll get the house done this summer?"

"Should, God willing."

"I hope you do rent it out, son. We need more of that kind of thing around here, the looking out for one another. Speaking of which . . ." Otis glanced toward Greta, then leaned in close to whisper, "Joyce makes a pretty mean pie, doesn't she?" He winked.

Heat trailed across Wes's cheeks. Of course Otis had seen the interaction after the last co-op meeting. How could he not?

Wes adjusted his grip on the cart handle. "Suppose she does."

The elder patted Wes's shoulder. "You're a blessed man."

Wes forced himself to smile. It would be rude not to. But if it were possible, he would sink through the polished concrete floor.

If accepting a pie from Joyce set tongues to wagging, sharing an entire meal with her at his house was bound to do more.

◆　◆　◆　◆

"Here's what I'm planning to make this Sunday." Nikki zoomed in on the picture she had taken of the beef and potato recipe and slid her phone across the bakery counter.

Joyce leaned in, her apron bunching at her chest. Her lips moved slightly as she read to herself. "Hmm. Never heard of it. Sounds good, though."

Nikki brought her phone back across the counter. "I'm glad you think so, because I was wondering if you would be willing to come over and help me make it—and eat with us."

"Wow. Really?"

"You said you'd be willing. Plus, I was hoping you could tell me more about my grandma. You knew her pretty well, right?"

Joyce grinned. "She was one of my favorite people ever. It's been a long, long time since I was in her house." She stared off to the side, grin lingering. Then she straightened and pulled her hands off the counter. "Is your uncle okay with this? I know he likes to keep to himself."

Nikki nodded. "He's okay with it all. Inviting people to eat with us was his idea."

Joyce's eyebrows nearly shot off her face. "I'll be. Wonders never cease." She giggled, smoothed her hair behind her right ear.

How long had she hoped? How long had she watched Uncle Wes from a distance, wondering if he ever looked her way? What if she knew he did?

"What time would you like me to be there Sunday?" Joyce asked.

"Five would be great."

"Five it is."

In every great romance ever written, love always had a way of returning itself to the giver. Eventually.

Nikki bid Joyce goodbye, then navigated her cart between the bakery display tables. When she reached produce, she checked her text messages. For the third time that day.

Isaac hadn't replied.

◆ ◆ ◆ ◆

Uncle Wes assured Nikki it was "fine" that Joyce would be their guest on Sunday evening. "Perfectly fine," he insisted, then abruptly segued to proper sanding techniques for cabinets.

She harbored her suspicions but listened to his instructions as they knelt on the floor of the small bathroom. The room was not any wider than the bathtub and barely twice as long.

"Be sure to clean the cabinets well first," he said. "Paint won't stick well to grime."

"Get rid of the gunk first. Got it." Nikki positioned herself in front of the vanity with a spray bottle of warm water mixed with dish soap in one hand and a microfiber cloth in the other.

"See the buildup back here?" He pointed to the far side of the vanity shadowed by the toilet. Years' worth of dust had accumulated and stuck to the faded paint. The humidity from showers had created a sticky surface that dried like glue around the particles. "Should come off with a good scrub," he said.

She gave the shadowed area a good douse, then scrubbed with the cloth. The solidified dust snagged at the cloth and cut at her fingertips but eventually began to give way.

"Needs a lot of elbow grease," Uncle Wes said.

"I don't mind. It'll be good for me."

"Wish more recruits had your attitude."

She laughed and squirted additional liquid onto the wood.

He rose, giving her more space to work. He retrieved a flathead screwdriver from his nearby toolbox and started to remove the doors from the cabinet above the toilet.

They worked in unison, a team. Sharing the same goal, the same vision. He had brought home every piece of hardware and the paint she had requested, demonstrating his inherent trust in her.

She paused in her scrubbing and turned to him. "Thank you for letting me be part of this process."

He glanced her direction. "You're free labor for me. Thank *you*."

"All the same, I appreciate it." She returned to the vanity. Her hand moved slowly against the wood in a clockwise circle. "When I was little, Dad would sometimes have me help him around the house fixing things. Eventually, though, he just did it without asking me. He said he could get it done faster alone." Her hand stopped circling. The pointed retort from her dad when she was fifteen still cut years later. A bid for attention—for value—dismissed outright.

A screw clattered to the floor. Her gaze connected to her uncle's. If anyone understood pointed retorts from a father, he surely did.

He recouped the escaped screw, tucked it into his front pocket, then locked in on the head of the next screw. As he twisted, he spoke. "I know your dad wasn't—isn't the easiest man. He's made a lot of hurtful choices. But I hope you remember . . . he's got a judge already."

The screw popped loose and fell into his waiting hand. He looked down at her. His stare burrowed his words deeper into her heart.

She was the first to return to her work. She spritzed, scrubbed.

In no world did it make sense for her to simply turn a blind eye to everything—all the things her dad had never apologized for and likely never would. Such offenses couldn't simply be wiped away like that.

But she kept those words inside and scoured harder, attempting to get rid of all the gunk.

◆　◆　◆　◆

On the way up the driveway to his house that evening, Wes called Aunt Emma for the third time that day, too eager to tell her the latest to wait for her return call from his earlier message.

Once more, his call rang to voicemail. At the beep, he shared the news of his loosened tongue.

"I think she understood what I was getting at," he told her. "She at least looked contemplative for a second."

Perhaps it was feasible that he could get Nikki to agree to a compromise on Father's Day. He still owed his brother an answer.

"Nikki's an amazing worker, by the way. You'd be impressed. She also found someone to help her with the recipes. Call me when you can, assure me you're staying out of trouble."

Seventeen

Hannah moved her phone slowly through each room of their childhood home, capturing the emptiness in vivid detail for Nikki on the other end of the video call.

"Never thought it would come to this," Hannah said.

"Me neither."

Hannah switched the light on in Nikki's old bedroom, the click echoing through the blank space.

A knot curled in Nikki's stomach. The walls, floors—life—stripped. "It looks so foreign."

"I know."

"Where are we going to go for Christmas? Or birthdays? Or any holiday?"

"My house, I guess." Hannah switched off the light and stepped into the hallway.

"It's not the same, though," Nikki said.

"It's not. But maybe we can start new traditions." Though her sister turned her voice to a happier note at the end, her heartbreak was evident.

The camera swayed with Hannah's steps. Eventually, the living room came into frame. Their mom and Tyler set to-go boxes of Chinese food on a picnic blanket spread out where the couch and coffee table once were. The last Friday night in the house. The last night, period. The U-Haul waited in the driveway.

"Here's Mom and Tyler," Hannah said. Both of them looked up at the camera and waved.

"Hey, guys," Nikki called.

"How's the house reno coming?" her mom asked.

"It's hardly a reno," Nikki said. "More like a face-lift. We started with the bathroom. I have the cabinets sanded and primed. Here, take a peek." She switched the camera to point at the cabinet doors propped up on five-gallon buckets in the living room, drop cloths underneath. The can of paint and the brushes waited next to them. "I'll do a coat on these tonight, the second tomorrow, and then the sealant on Sunday."

"You sound like a regular DIY-er," Tyler said.

She pointed the camera back to herself. "I'm learning a lot, that's for sure. Uncle Wes is a great teacher."

Hannah switched to selfie view as well and sat on the floor so all three of them could be seen. "Learn any more about Great-Grandma Lena?"

"Working on it." Nikki told them about inviting different Eddner people over to eat. "A lady in the church, Joyce, is going to help me cook the first meal, hopefully more."

"You have a lot of good things going there," her mom said. "I'm glad."

"I do regret not being with you all, though. For closing, and for . . . everything."

Her mother shook her head. "You are where you need to be, baby. I believe that."

"Me too," Hannah said.

"For what it's worth, me three," Tyler added, drawing a laugh from the group.

"On a related note," her mom said, "have you talked to Isaac?"

Nikki's chest pinched. "I've texted him, but . . ." The rest of the words spoke for themselves.

"Keep trying," her mom said. "He's probably reading even if he's not replying."

Three sets of eyes looked expectantly at her through the camera.

All three people clearly shared the same opinion. But none of them lived in the stark silence of unreturned texts.

"Okay," she replied, not having the courage to promise.

They talked several more minutes, then exchanged goodbyes.

When the call ended, the silence returned. Floating through it, sliding in close like an old friend, was the reminder *Do the next thing.*

When in doubt, when in fear, when in far too deep, it was the only thing she could do.

She cranked up the country music station. Then she picked up a paintbrush.

◆ ◆ ◆ ◆

"Now, Fritz, don't get mad."

Quite a way to start a conversation, let alone well into the night. Wes muted the ten o'clock news and sat up in his recliner. "What's going on, Aunt Emma?"

"I want to explain why I didn't call you back sooner. It's because I had a bit of a spill yesterday and needed to hang out in the hospital—"

"The hospital?" He shot to his feet as if prepared to run to Oklahoma in one go.

"Only for a tiny bit," she said. "And only for the purpose of repeatedly assuring those tiresome medical folks that I am, in fact, fit as a fiddle."

"But what happened?"

"It's the silliest thing. I tripped coming out to my garage and got a little kiss from the fender of my truck. I saw stars, and not the good kind."

"Aunt Emma!"

"Oh, stop your fussing. You sound just like my son did when he came to help me get cleaned up. He insisted I go to the ER. I have bruises down the left side of my face, and I needed a few stitches above my eyebrow. The sweet nurse who sewed me up said that's where boxers often get stitches. So there you go. I'm practically Rocky."

"But you're okay?"

"Can't keep a good woman down. Doc says the bruising will fade in a few weeks. Meanwhile, I'm having a grand ol' time making up stories for the strangers who do double takes. I told the LLLs that I'll make up a story about taking a bocce ball to the eye and living to tell the tale. We have a game tomorrow afternoon, and I think the intimidation factor will work in our favor."

He chuckled. "If it works, though, please don't make scuffles with automobiles a pregame ritual."

"No promises. On to better things. How's it going over there? Sounds like from your messages the house project is moving along, and maybe the niece situation."

He settled back into his chair. "Both are going in a mostly good direction, I think."

"I'm glad you spoke up to Nikki when you did."

"Not sure it actually did make a difference. She still seems very . . . determined."

"Probably an apt word for it. Keep saying what needs to be said, Wes. None of us learn the first time."

No truer words had ever been spoken.

"Who is it that's helping Nikki with the recipes, by the way?" she asked.

"Joyce Kindstrom. You may remember her aunt, Pauline Dutzow."

"Pauline, sure. Seems I remember a Joyce too, though. Is she about your age?"

"She is."

"That must be who I'm thinking of then. Your mom used to talk about a young woman named Joyce."

"She did?"

"Many times. She said there was a young woman from church who used to check in on her while you were in the service."

He blinked. Not once had his mother mentioned anything of the sort to him.

"The way Ann talked," Aunt Emma continued, "it sounded

like they were pretty close. She described her as an angelic beauty, inside and out. Does that sound like the right person?"

He could barely get his mouth to work. "Mom was, uh, a good judge of character. I won't argue with her."

"If it is the same person, I'm glad she's on Nikki's side."

"Yes," he said, softer. "Good thing."

They talked for a few more minutes before Aunt Emma excused herself for her last dose of ibuprofen for the day.

"Have to be fresh for the game tomorrow," she said. "Tell the niece hello for me and that I do answer my calls. Eventually."

"Good night, Aunt Emma."

"Sleep tight, my boy."

◆ ◆ ◆ ◆

It was all Wes could do to not let his gaze drift toward Joyce during Sunday service.

Angelic beauty? He refused to answer that question. But he could not refuse the fact his mother had called her that. She'd never called Ada that.

Somehow Joyce had received the honor. Somehow he had never known. Joyce's connection to his mother had deeper roots than the surface showed.

When had that happened?

"Let us pray," Pastor Vark called across the pews. He led them through the responsive prayer calling for heaven's mercy, then through the hymns lauding its grace. The organ pipes lifted high the tinny notes. Flames flickered on the altar candles. The Savior held up his scarred hands. All evidence of the sacred purpose of why Wes was there, of the eternal life on the other side of the veil.

And yet his mind wandered to the earthly past—the afternoon snacks Joyce had shared at his mother's table, the games together in the schoolyard, the small group discussions in youth fellowship.

And then, again and again, his eyes wandered to the tender profile of the woman two rows in front of him. The woman who would be back at his mother's table in a matter of hours.

151

◆ ◆ ◆ ◆

Beef Sauce for Mashed Potatoes (Haschee)

Welcoming others into our homes is a ministry that cannot be overrated. No matter how small, how lacking in finery, how old or new, our homes are gifts to be shared generously, opened to friends and foes and foreigners without partiality. How incredible to think that the space between our four walls can be where others set down their burdens and rest, if only for a meal. We can cheer and comfort the empty so they leave filled, soul and body. "He that watereth shall be watered also himself" (Prov. 11:25).

Butter
Half an onion, diced
1 teaspoon minced garlic
1 pound ground beef
½ pound mushrooms, sliced
1 bell pepper, diced
3 cups beef broth
1 tablespoon stone-ground or spicy brown mustard
Paprika
Basil
Salt and pepper
1 tablespoon cornstarch
1 tablespoon water

Melt butter in skillet. Add onion, bell pepper, and garlic, cooking until tender. Add beef and cook until browned. Add mushrooms and *cook until softened. Pour in broth and stir. Bring mixture to simmer; cover and cook 30 minutes. Add mustard and other seasonings. Mix cornstarch and water together, then add to pan. Allow sauce to thicken. Serve over mashed potatoes.*

◆　◆　◆　◆

Uncle Wes made himself scarce in midafternoon, saying he needed to fix an electric fence somewhere among the acres Nikki had not yet explored. She stood at the end of the sidewalk and watched him drive the ATV deep into the field beyond the barn.

She shook her head and said aloud to no one, "Wonder if he's coming back for supper."

The country music station kept her company. Promptly at five o'clock, Joyce arrived at the door with a bright smile and a three-pound bag of potatoes.

Nikki led her to the kitchen, where both aprons from the attic boxes waited next to the notebook.

Joyce stopped in the threshold of the kitchen and surveyed every inch of the room, as if letting a thousand cherished memories well up. "It's like a time capsule, this place," she said. "The counters are still the same. Goodness, the appliances! How are those still running?"

"I thought the same thing," Nikki said. "Those things are older than time itself."

"And that table." Joyce strode straight over to it as if pulled by a string. The sack of potatoes rustled as she walked. She ran her fingertips over the polished wood and sighed. "I must sound pretty sappy, but this really is a special place to me. It's like . . ."

"A sanctuary?" Nikki offered.

Joyce turned to her, eyes moist. "Exactly."

She had told Nikki how much Grandma Ann meant to her, but until that moment, with Joyce caressing the table and puckering her brow from emotion, it wasn't clear how much. What Joyce had found in that kitchen throughout the years was what Nikki tasted too, in far more infrequent bites. It was what had drawn Nikki to the farmhouse—as if pulled by a string.

Joyce's gaze drifted to the counter. She gasped. "Is that the notebook?"

"It is. Take a look."

Joyce approached reverently, lifting the potatoes onto the counter. She cradled the artifact and gently turned the pages. "This is incredible," she breathed. Her fascination confirmed she was the right choice to help with the recipes. "I love these little sayings," she said. "Someone put a lot of thought into this. It had to be written with someone specific in mind."

"Based on the note on the first page, I agree. We just aren't sure who."

Joyce flipped through a few more pages. "Regardless of who this was originally intended for, I'm glad it came to you. You're clearly the rightful owner now." She handed the notebook to Nikki.

The touch of the cover sent tingles up Nikki's arms, as if the past seeped into her veins, becoming part of her identity. Or, more likely, awakening the identity that had been there the whole time. Either way, the notebook would never be hidden away in an attic again.

Joyce smiled, then gestured toward the aprons. "Shall we suit up?"

"Let's do it."

Eighteen

Cooking has a magic to it. The taking of opposing raw things and step by step shaping them into something new and unified. Discordance is chopped, sautéed, and stirred away, until a melodious creation simmers in the pan.

As the potatoes Joyce had peeled and cubed bathed in their boiling water, the two cooks turned fully to the work of creating the beef sauce. Onion, garlic, and bell pepper sizzled in the rich puddle of melted butter—half a stick's worth because "it feels right," Joyce said. The beef soaked in the flavors of the vegetables as it browned, the aroma promising a soul-filling meal.

"Now the mushrooms." Joyce handed Nikki the carton of sliced baby bellas.

The pieces fell into a heap atop the beef mixture. Nikki methodically stirred in a figure eight, as Joyce had shown her.

"Cook until the mushrooms are softened," Joyce read.

"How long is that?"

"Basically until they have shrunk to almost half their size. We'll give it four minutes and see where we are."

Nikki made one more figure eight, then set the spoon on the rest. "Did you learn to cook from your mom?"

Joyce turned to lean her lower back against the counter and folded her arms. "Actually, I learned a lot by watching your

155

grandma prepare supper for the family. My mom would come to pick me up right about the time the boys started setting the table."

"What kinds of things did Grandma cook? I only knew her Christmas meals. I assume they didn't have baked ham and green bean casserole on a random Tuesday."

Joyce chuckled. "Hardly. They were simple meals. Pork chops, I remember. Mac and cheese. Hamburgers. Typical American farmer fare. She did make mashed potatoes quite a bit and taught me. And pie. She made a lot of pies. Did your mom cook when you were growing up?"

Nikki shook her head. "My mom relied a lot on boxed stuff. She worked full-time."

"My mom too, which was more unusual back then, but my dad was not around much." She took a fork from the drawer, not needing to ask which drawer, and tested one of the potatoes. The flesh pierced easily, so she clicked off the burner and let the boil begin to settle. "Would you guess, Nikki, that when I was young, I was a tomboy?"

"No kidding?"

"I loved to wear jeans and get dirty and did a decent job of holding my own during tag on the playground. So when my mom told me that Mrs. Werner was going to watch me after school, I was excited. Two of my playmates lived at Mrs. Werner's house."

Nikki smiled.

"But you know what happened? Your grandmother invited me to stay with her in the kitchen. That very first day, she asked, 'Joyce, would you like to have a glass of chocolate milk with me?' I said, 'Sure.' And she was the first person who sat with me and actually listened to what I had to say. She genuinely cared about how I was doing and how school was going and whether I was having trouble with anything. My own mom didn't have a lot of spare time for things like that, which I never faulted her for. She was busy trying to survive. But Mrs. Werner—she always had a glass of chocolate milk waiting for me and time to talk. That became my favorite part of the day. It got me through a lot of hard days too. She had a way of hearing the words but listening to the heart. You know what I mean?"

Nikki nodded. "Sounds like Grandma Ann lived out the proverb of haschee." She pointed to the notebook propped open on the cookbook rack. "She welcomed others into her home as a ministry and allowed it to be where others set down their burdens and rested."

Joyce's eyes twinkled. "Makes you wonder if she used this notebook, doesn't it? Even if not for recipes."

"It does."

Bubbles still broke the surface of the potato water every few seconds. Joyce waited a bit longer. "Her sons had a bit of that ministry spirit as well," she said. "Did you know your uncle once thought about seminary?"

Nikki's mouth dropped open. "No way!"

"In early high school, that's what he thought he wanted to do." Joyce stirred the potatoes with a wooden spoon, releasing a burst of steam. "Your dad, meanwhile, always had a soft spot for little kids."

Nikki closed her mouth and nodded. She turned to the skillet.

"The Eddner school was small," Joyce continued. "We had only one teacher for everyone. Us older kids would help the littler kids with their reading and math. Your dad loved doing that."

Nikki kept her attention on the meat mixture, trailing the spoon slowly through it.

"One year, I think when your dad was in fifth grade, he was paired with a first grader named Peter. Peter adored your dad, thought he could rope the moon. Your dad taught him how to field a ground ball and how to cross the monkey bars without stopping. He even showed Peter how to teach the pastor's old bird dog to give a high five through his kennel fence. The kennel was right next to the playground. I still remember the look of pride on Peter's face." Joyce laughed to herself.

Nikki kept stirring. A quiet descended.

Joyce peeked over at her. "I'm sorry. You probably don't want to talk about your dad."

She shrugged. "I just prefer to hear more about Grandma." Her gaze flitted to Joyce's.

"I understand."

Straightening her shoulders, Nikki pointed to the skillet. "Think these mushrooms are cooked 'until softened'?"

Like the gracious woman she was—and may have learned to be from Grandma Ann—Joyce smiled. "I think we can add the broth now."

For the next half hour, as the haschee cooked and the potatoes gave easily under the masher, they talked about Grandma Ann, her love for birds, her long walks up to the Eddner cemetery to say hello to her mother, and her adoration of hymns.

Her youngest son was never mentioned again.

◆　◆　◆　◆

It was strange enough having Joyce Kindstrom in his family's home again, smiling and chatting as easily as the wind blew, like nothing in the world hindered her from feeling at home. Stranger still how the mashed potatoes prepared by her hands tasted nearly identical to what his mother would pile on his Sunday plate, a pat of butter rivering down the peak.

Nikki and Joyce carried the dinner conversation, centering it on food. Whether the haschee was too soup-like to be a sauce, the differences between spicy brown and stone-ground mustard, if haschee was a viable option for the next church carry-in dinner.

"People may not know how to pronounce it, but I bet they'd eat it," Joyce said. Every time she smiled, tiny apostrophe-size wrinkles showed at the corners of her mouth. Lines invisible from the other end of the boardroom but ones that possessed a realness he had to fight not to stare at too long.

He kept himself from the conversation largely by stuffing his mouth. The fluffy potatoes slurped up the salty sauce even faster than he did.

"Do you think anyone in Eddner ever really ate this?" Nikki asked.

"I would assume so, at some point. The recipe had to come from somewhere." Joyce folded her potatoes into the haschee, creamy white slowly turning a light brown. "My aunt told me she doesn't remember much about what the immigrants used to eat, other than a lot of cabbage and potatoes."

As she enjoyed her meal, Nikki kept her gaze on Joyce. She clearly relished every moment, every mention, every clue.

"But my aunt was born toward the end of the Depression," Joyce said, "which is well after they had stopped speaking German. She wouldn't have a lot of context anyway. She did remember a story about your grandparents, though."

Nikki raised her eyebrows in anticipation.

"But maybe your uncle should tell it. The story of how and where they got married."

Both women turned to him.

He took a sip of milk before answering. "At the courthouse."

"Yes, but which courthouse?" Joyce prompted.

He pulled his brow low. What other courthouse was there? "In Redmont."

Her mouth pinched inward. The apostrophes disappeared. "Maybe I should have checked with you first."

He blinked. What was that supposed to mean?

"I think you have us both intrigued," Nikki said to Joyce. "You have to tell us."

Joyce looked between them. Her forehead wrinkled in question, quietly asking if he wanted her to proceed.

He nodded, as curious as his niece was.

Joyce laid down her spoon, extending the pause another moment. "Apparently they snuck off to Kentucky to get married."

Nikki's eyes widened.

Quickly Wes countered, "They moved to Kentucky after they got married."

Her reply was soft, almost hesitant. "According to my aunt, the move happened first, then the marriage. Then they wrote home to their families."

He shook his head. It didn't compute. His parents, rule followers and loyal, disregarding a tenet of family life? It couldn't be true. He would have known.

Wouldn't he?

"They lived in Kentucky the first two years of their marriage," Joyce continued. "They returned here because Lena died and Otto asked Henry to help him with the farm."

Nikki looked at him. "Is that part true?"

He nodded.

"But why did they sneak off?" she asked.

"My aunt said they both wanted more than Eddner could offer. Ann was twenty-three and itching to get out of her parents' house. Henry was the youngest of three boys and was told by his father in no uncertain terms that he would not be inheriting any land from him. So Henry decided to move to Kentucky, where his ancestors had first settled, and farm there. He convinced Ann to go with him."

Nikki furrowed her brow. "We're not saying Grandma Ann settled for Grandpa Henry, though, right? Because she wanted out of Eddner?"

Joyce looked at Wes. That part her aunt obviously had not covered.

"There, uh, there was love there," he said.

Nikki rolled her lips together. Based on what little she knew of her grandfather, no one could blame her for wondering.

His mother had always put extra butter on his father's potatoes. His father never said thank-you. His mother had moved back to the very place she'd wanted to leave. His father likely never thanked her for that either.

Maybe Nikki was right to be skeptical. Maybe there were many more layers to the Werner family history than he'd ever known existed.

And maybe he was more like his parents than he'd ever realized.

◆ ◆ ◆ ◆

After dinner, Nikki gathered the trash from the kitchen and hauled it out to the burn barrel on the far side of the yard. The screen door smacked closed the same moment Wes flipped on the kitchen faucet to start the dishwater.

Joyce brought plates, cups, and silverware over to him, arranging them with the other dirty dishes on the counter. Cups first. Then plates and silverware. Then cooking utensils. Last, the cookware. The same way his mother taught him. The only way that made sense.

It wasn't hard to imagine his mother influencing Joyce's dishwashing organization as well. Joyce clearly loved his mother and clearly had invested herself in the process of helping Nikki love her too. For that, Wes owed her, however weird it was to have her that close, however tight it made his muscles.

She started to turn to the stove to tend to the pan of leftover beef sauce.

"Um," he said, unable to get anything else out to stop her.

She paused, looked up at him.

"Thanks for helping Nikki. With everything. It means a lot."

That smile, soft and slow. "I'm happy to help."

He tore his gaze away and pulled the first of the cups into the water. They rolled briefly in the ripple of the pouring water before he turned off the tap.

Joyce leaned against the counter, fully facing him. "I am impressed how eager Nikki is to learn her ancestry. Many young people don't care even half as much."

"Some adults too." He dared to lift his face to meet hers.

Her shining hazel eyes brought heat to his cheeks. He began to wipe down the first glass.

"Wes," she said gently, "I'm sorry if I spoke out of turn at supper."

"No, no. It's, uh, it's fine. Nikki wants the truth."

"But you didn't know. That must have been awkward."

He shrugged, rinsed the cup. "Awkward for all of us, I suppose."

"I was surprised you didn't know your parents eloped. But now that I think about it, it makes sense you wouldn't. Your parents probably didn't talk about their past much, did they?"

He started on the next glass. "Our suppers were pretty quiet."

"Yeah." One small word, a depth of understanding. He didn't have to explain.

She spread the silverware into a single layer on the counter. "Your father had a lot of good qualities too, though. He didn't let them show often enough." She withdrew her hand and looked at him. "Or soon enough."

Their gazes met again. Hers filled with the grace that clouded around her like perfume.

In the years after he and Chris left, she had been there to sit with his mother. Which meant she'd sat with his father too. She'd seen and heard things Wes had not. Nor his brother. In so many ways, she was positioned to help them all.

The well of her stare invited him in, invited him to trust, as unflinchingly as a fellow soldier. The urge to lean in traced up his torso.

He swallowed and returned to the cups.

She waited by his side for several beats, long enough for him to rinse the next cup and set it in the drainboard. Then, wordlessly, she took a spare dishcloth from the drawer and wiped down the table.

Nineteen

Aunt Emma was back to answering his morning calls within two rings and with the usual cut to the chase. "My bones hurt today."

He set his bowl in the sink and rested against the counter. "You took a pretty nasty fall."

"Oh, that. No, I'm over that. It's all the jumping and whooping yesterday."

"Do I dare ask?"

"The bocce game!"

"Right. How could I forget. You did well?"

"The LLLs cleaned up. It was like no one else even showed up to the court. Boom diggity, as my grandson would say." She chuckled, bringing a smile to his lips too.

"The intimidation worked, I take it," he said.

"Like a charm. I wore my hair slightly ruffled for a little added effect. You should have seen the looks on the other teams' faces."

"I can only imagine."

"So, what's new up there?"

He gave her a quick update on the house, the new flooring arriving that week, the plans to install a new toilet and faucets. But it was the supper, specifically the story Joyce told, that he zeroed in on.

"Aunt Emma, I need to ask you something."

"I'm all ears and eagerness."

He gathered air into his lungs. "Joyce joined us for supper, and she claimed my parents eloped in Kentucky. Is she right?"

A short silence on the other end. Finally she answered, "You probably should have known before your fifties."

He straightened. "It's true?"

"I'm not surprised Ann never told you. It wasn't something she was particularly proud of. I think if she had to do it all over again, she would have taken a different path."

"What does that mean? Not marry Dad?"

"Oh, I think she would have married him, but in a different way, and maybe at a different time. They were both so rarin' to get out of Eddner. Your dad because he wanted to prove himself but felt he had no place there—only the oldest son got the farm and fortune. Sounds familiar, doesn't it?"

He tucked his chin to his chest. "Yes."

"That hard edge you knew in him was there from a young age, because it had to be. Meanwhile, Ann would have left home as soon as she turned eighteen if she could have. She had no suitor, though, and our father would not dream of letting her live alone. That's not something girls did back then. It nurtured a good amount of angst in her to break free. Though I was five years younger, even I could sense it."

Chris had always carried a similar angst as a kid, in spades. No small thanks to the favored-older-son mentality, the very thing their father had chafed against. History repeated itself, even one generation later.

Aunt Emma continued. "When Henry Werner and his determination caught Ann's attention, she took it as destiny knocking. They were together about six months before they left, and yes, they did leave suddenly without telling anyone."

"Why?" he asked. "Did your parents forbid them to marry?"

"Not outright, but they did express great concern about her rush into the relationship. Our mother in particular. In those early days, Ann loved the *idea* of Henry. I don't think her young, idealist

164

heart could comprehend the reality of Henry or the fact that he had an even stronger will than hers. Our parents did see that about him. They spotted it as soon as he walked in the door. I think Ann realized soon into marriage what our parents had tried to tell her. It especially hit home when Mother died."

Silence settled over them. Wes shifted his weight from one foot to the other.

"You okay, Fritz?"

"Just taking it all in. It's disorienting to learn things about your parents that change your narrative about who they are."

"Makes you more empathetic to our niece, doesn't it?"

Though Aunt Emma couldn't see him, he nodded. Somehow she always knew his response, spoken or unspoken.

"But despite her youthful choices," she said, "I want you to remember that the mom you knew was the true Ann. By the time she came back to Eddner, she had changed a lot, for the good. Faith had taken precedent in her life. She relished her Bible studies, I can tell you that, even if she didn't use the Bible I gave her. Then you arrived. Then your brother. The fierce loyalty she had to her church, her family, and her home was real. Whatever else happened, those three things brought her a peace for the rest of her waking days."

He rubbed his chin, the truth slowly sinking in. How much of their parents' history did Chris know? He deserved to know it. So did Nikki.

"Aunt Emma, have you ever wondered why we all eventually tune in to our ancestry?"

"Can't say I have. Have you?"

"Am now, watching Nikki."

"What are your thoughts?"

He stroked his chin once more, then tucked his hand into his front pocket. "Maybe we're wired to. God values families, so much so that he put Jesus into one."

"True," she replied. "And lineages are as common in the Old Testament as hellos."

"Exactly. It's like we have a hardwired desire—a need—to identify with a line, and the stories that carry forward on those lines are the ones that tend to resonate with us the most."

"Makes me think of the Psalms," she said. "They're full of reminders to the Israelites that 'your fathers' did this and experienced that. Then good ol' Paul reminded the church family that the saints before them did this and experienced that."

His gaze drifted to the portraits of the Baumanns in the dining room. "Seems family history is one of the most intimate object lessons we can receive."

"That's beautiful, my boy. Wholeheartedly agree. And I have no doubt your mother would too. In fact, if memory serves, her favorite Bible story is about family."

"Which one is that?"

"The prodigal son," she replied. "Seems fitting, no?"

He grinned. "Very."

On many levels.

◆　◆　◆　◆

Morning stretched its long, warm tendrils through the bedroom windows and nuzzled Nikki awake. *Welcome to Monday*, its embrace soothed into her dreamy state.

Welcome to her second full week in Eddner.

Slowly she sat up. The afghan slid down her front and pooled at her waist. She reached above her head, pulling her spine straight, and held for the count of five. If only she could reach beyond the shadow that hovered overhead. If only Isaac would reply.

Her phone lay on a large box doubling as a nightstand. As she had done every morning since her message to him, she held her breath and reached for it.

A text notification did wait for her, from her mom.

She blew out her breath, fought to keep her heart from sagging too far, and opened the message.

My new room.

Along with the words was a picture of a simple, mildly decorated room. A daybed, a dresser, a small work desk, and the collection of framed photographs her mom had gently wrapped in dish towels on the living room floor. Three decades of marriage reduced to about three hundred square feet. As small as the last four months must have made her mom feel.

Grief upon grief.

Nikki texted back.

> Looks homey. I love you. Will visit you when I can.

Her mom kept moving forward, no matter how painful it was, proving it was doable. Whereas her mom stepped into a reimagined future, Nikki needed to step into the past, toward the mothers who had slept in that bedroom before her, who had fed their children at the oak table. Women who had found their way through heartache and come out refined.

They had uncovered secrets to which she sought answers as well. Maybe one of those revelations could show her the way.

A walk to the cemetery, like Grandma Ann used to take, seemed like the very best way to start the day. Nikki dressed, tucked her phone into her back pocket, and followed the county road's curves through the canopy of shade trees.

Twitters from robins, the steady crunch of gravel under her feet, and an occasional whish of leaves. Every few strides, she filled her lungs with a new draw of clean air.

Peace.

At the top of the hill, she turned into the horseshoe drive.

Grandma Ann's wreath had blown cockeyed. She straightened it and brushed the dust off the cloth petals.

"I know how much you like to keep things clean," she said aloud. The dirt particles fluttered away.

She righted and stepped off to the side of the grave. Her shadow angled across the granite headstone, lapping the span of her grandma's time on earth, 1937 to 2005.

"Amazing. One little hyphen attempting to hold so much life."

The breeze kicked a strand of hair across her face. She secured it behind her ear.

"You left quite a few clues and treasures, though. Even your oldest son is stumped by a few of them, which is kind of fun to watch." She shoved her hands into the pockets of her shorts. "Your youngest son doesn't seem to care. Was he always this—" She bit back the lament. Though honest, it seemed inappropriate to say at his mother's grave. Pointless too. Grandma Ann knew the sting of his rejection.

"Mom said it wouldn't have mattered if you were still alive to confront him, but I believe it would have. Maybe you could have gotten him to wake up. None of us can. Least of all me."

A bird chirped in the nearby tree. The only other sound in the cemetery.

"It's probably silly for me to be talking to a headstone. I don't think you can hear me. But admittedly I'm murky on the theology of such things. What I do know is that it helps to talk to you—at you. Maybe that's why you would come visit your mother."

The wreath's petals bobbled in the breeze.

"You both fascinate me, Grandma Ann. I want to know more about you. I want to know what each of your hyphens contained. Is that why you left so much behind?"

Another chirp.

She sighed. "Whatever it is that you all left, I promise I will receive it."

A rustle of leaves. Then a bird winging its way through the air. It chose the direction of the farm.

◆　◆　◆　◆

Midmorning Wednesday, Wes handed Nikki his truck keys and the list of items he had on hold at Harman's. "Should all be at the front of the store, paid for," he said. "Ask someone to help you load the truck."

She grabbed her purse from the side table by the farmhouse door as she read the list. "You ordered a new toilet?"

168

"Figured if I have to take out the old one to replace the flooring, might as well put a new one back in."

She tucked the paper into her purse. "You're sure you don't want me to stay and help you rip up the flooring?"

"Things'll move faster if we divide and conquer. Don't want you to be without a bathroom too long."

"Fair enough." She promised to return around noon, with lunch for both of them.

The door closed behind her, and he headed to the bathroom. The freshly arrived vinyl floor tiles waited in their box in the hallway. Though relatively minimal, the bathroom flooring would require most of the day, and that was if the subfloor was in decent condition.

He grabbed a mallet and scraper from his toolbox and got to work.

The quarter-round edging the bottom of the baseboards came off first. Then the baseboards themselves. Last, the transition piece in the threshold. Within thirty minutes, all the trim was out and stacked in the hallway. He knelt near the threshold, where a slight gap had appeared between the linoleum and the subfloor, a perfect spot to begin prying up the old flooring. He wedged the scraper into the opening and hammered the tip of the handle.

Bang, bang, bang.

The opening widened as the glue gave way to the force. He moved the scraper a little to the left and hammered some more.

Bang, bang, bang. Specks and dust scattered as he chiseled.

Steadily, the linoleum peeled back, revealing a subfloor that appeared to be in good condition.

His knees soon ached. His neck muscles began to stiffen. But it was worth it, the labor of bringing new to the old. Someone who needed a blessing would find a home within the farmhouse the way he had, and his parents before him, and his grandparents before them. And then Nikki. And even Joyce.

Bang, bang, bang.

That smile. For years he had kept it at a distance, able to dodge away as needed. Able to deny that it drew him almost as equally as it put the urge to run in his feet. He had been able to deny that it had been going on far longer than anyone knew. Most of all Joyce.

Bang, bang, bang.

The ring of his phone cut through the noise. He laid his tools aside and pulled his phone from his pocket.

Chris.

He rose to his feet, knees protesting, and accepted the call.

"I'm at work," his brother said. "Only have a few minutes. Did you talk to Nikki? Father's Day weekend is next week."

"I did."

"And?"

He dug the toe of his boot under the loosened linoleum. "She needs more time, Chris."

His brother went quiet. Trust took time, but that wasn't what Chris wanted to hear.

"You could try calling her," Wes suggested.

"I told you, she wouldn't take my calls."

"What if she does?"

"She won't, Wes."

He tucked his free hand under his opposite elbow. There had to be a way to reach into his brother's heart. Maybe it would be with words from someone wiser than Wes.

"There's a notebook Nikki found among Mom's things," he said. "It has some German recipes along with wise sayings. One of them said something about considering what good you can bring to a place. That's the kind of thing Nikki's been thinking about while she's been here. I believe it's influencing her view of things. Makes her more open."

Silence on the other end.

Wes dug his toe harder under the linoleum, waited.

Finally, his brother sighed. "Listen, I have a meeting. I need to go, so . . ." His resignation was palpable.

It didn't have to be that way.

"Chris?"

"What?"

"I hope you'll try to reach out to her."

A long pause. "I need to go."

The call ended.

He shook his head and lowered his phone to his side. In the mirror above the sink, his reflection showed back to him. An ache clouded his face more than the dust.

"Never grow weary," he whispered.

◆　◆　◆　◆

"I have heard of scalloped cabbage, actually," Aunt Emma confirmed in their Friday morning phone call. "Mother made scalloped cabbage a lot when we were young. Ann never cared for it, but I loved it. I'm glad Nikki's going to try it out. Didn't realize it was German, though."

Wes washed down a bite of oatmeal with cold milk. "It may not be. But it's cabbage and has a lot of butter."

"Two of God's greatest gifts. Is Joyce coming back to help with the meal?"

"Yes. Arlene Rothfuss will eat with us too. Apparently Joyce told the Ladies' Aid at church about the recipes, which led to mention of Nikki researching our family. Mrs. Rothfuss offered to bring over 'some things'—her words—that she said might help."

"Sounds like an exciting weekend ahead. I have one of my own. A couple of the LLLs and I are leaving shortly for the Oklahoma City area. They are 'absolutely dying' to go to the store of that one cooking show hostess who lives out here. Something about specially designed spatulas or some such nonsense. I'm going for the food, which is how I usually travel."

"Same here."

"That's why we get along." She giggled. "And how's the farmhouse coming?"

"Flooring and toilet are in. Shower and sink fixtures going in next, then baseboards. Nikki's still deciding on the color for the walls."

"Sounds like a lot of progress . . . that I've yet to see in pictures that have been texted to me."

"I promise, I will. When it's done."

"Mm-hmm," she said teasingly. "Well, in the meantime, I'm wondering if you could send me Nikki's email address. I figure I'd spring myself upon her in a message. Maybe that would help break the ice. Plus, I'm champing at the bit to let my stories out. I'm old. I have to share while I'm lucid enough to remember them."

"I'll text it to you right after this."

"Thank you."

"Should I give her a heads-up you're emailing her?"

"It'd be more fun if you didn't. Speaking of fun, there's my friend calling to say she's coming to steal me away. Gotta go. Love you."

"Love you too. Don't complain too much on your trip."

"Fat chance."

❧ *Twenty* ❧

Scalloped Cabbage (Kohl aus Eddner)

You can either look at what you don't have and yearn, or you can look at what you do have and give thanks. A thankful heart is a friend of ingenuity. In the lean years of World War II, when rationing limited nearly everything and farmers prayed for a bounty from their gardens more than ever, this recipe was birthed in an Eddner kitchen, a blend of a popular recipe at the time and German sensibilities for cabbage and butter. This dish, lovingly dubbed "Kohl aus Eddner," was a small grace in the midst of a dark time and a staple at family celebrations. When it was served, it signaled a pause to reflect on how far God carries us, and to give thanks. Our God is always at our side; never shall he forsake us.

No matter how far away from the motherland, a German's heart is betrothed to cabbage (and butter). No matter how far from ease, a wise woman's heart is betrothed to gratitude. "Better is little with the fear of the Lord than great treasure and trouble therewith" (Prov. 15:16).

¾ cup butter

½ head cabbage, torn into bite-size pieces

2 sleeves buttery crackers, finely crushed

1 sleeve buttery crackers, coarsely crushed

Salt and pepper

2½ cups fresh cream

1 egg, beaten

In a stockpot, melt ¼ cup butter. Add cabbage and cook until translucent. Butter a 2-quart baking dish. Add 2 sleeves of finely crushed crackers, forming crust along sides and bottom. Layer cooked cabbage on crackers. Season with salt and pepper. Cube remaining butter and dot over cabbage. Top with sleeve of coarsely ground crackers. Pour cream evenly over casserole. Pour egg evenly over top of crackers. Bake uncovered at 350 degrees for about 45 minutes until liquid is absorbed and crust is golden.

◆ ◆ ◆ ◆

Nikki held up the spare floor tile between the two splotches of paint on the bathroom wall. Joyce stepped back as far as she could, the backs of her knees bumping into the freshly installed toilet. She tilted her head to the side, as if that would help her better study how the two colors coordinated with the tile.

"I think I like the Tundra Frost." Joyce pointed at the lighter tone on the right.

Nikki leaned back as far as she could and tilted her head too. At last she nodded. "I think you're right. Decision made. Thank you, Joyce."

"My pleasure."

Nikki returned the tile to the stack of extras on the floor, and they retraced their path through the farmhouse.

"I'm surprised how much work you all have been able to do in a week," Joyce said as they went. "You must be working night and day."

"The bathroom wasn't too bad. The kitchen is next, though, and it will definitely take longer. A lot more cabinets to sand, paint, and seal, and then of course a lot more flooring to replace."

A buttery aroma greeted them as they arrived in the kitchen, the savory scent of cabbage slowly softening in butter.

"This smells so good." Nikki picked up the wooden spoon and stirred the wilting cabbage. When they first put it in, it had nearly filled the pan. The leaves had now shrunk to almost half their size.

Joyce looked over Nikki's shoulder. "Almost there. See how the greener leaves are starting to turn translucent? That's what we want. When those whiter ones are easily pierced with a fork, we're set."

Nikki traced the spoon through the cabbage once more, then laid it back on its rest.

Joyce examined the room. "You're right about how many cabinets there are. I never really noticed before."

"Six upper cabinets, eight lower, eight drawers, plus the tall pantry on one end," Nikki said. "The dark wood is going to take at least two coats because I opted for white."

"You like white."

"I like brightness. Makes the house feel lighter."

"Fair point." Joyce took up the partially used stick of butter and began greasing the glass baking dish waiting on the counter. "Did your uncle not want to get new cabinets?"

"He said it was a waste of good money."

Joyce chuckled. "Sounds about right. Your grandma would have said the same thing. Wes used to say she kept the same foil pan for decades."

"She didn't, did she?"

"No, but she wasn't one to waste a thing. If it could serve a new purpose, then it did. If she could salvage something that was broken, torn, or expired, then she did."

"That would explain these appliances." Nikki scooted the box of crackers closer to her and popped open the top flaps. She took a sleeve out and started to open it as well.

Joyce stopped her. "You can crush them in the packaging. Watch." She used her fingertips to break apart the first two crackers. Enough gap formed for her to crush the next few. She handed the sleeve to Nikki. "No mess this way."

Much like with Uncle Wes, everything about Joyce was efficient and fueled by years of practice.

Nikki copied her technique. The waxy brown paper crinkled as she squeezed. The crackers inside gave easily, breaking into small pieces.

"Joyce, can I ask you something?"

"Of course."

"Did you ever want a family of your own?" The question teetered on too personal.

Joyce turned the dish to butter the remaining sliver of clean glass. "I did. In fact, I almost got married when I was twenty-one."

"Why didn't you?"

Joyce shrugged. "God often closes doors because he can see what's on the other side. I'm glad he closed that particular door before I walked through it."

"The man wasn't right for you?"

"I wasn't meant for him." Joyce smeared the last of the dish and put the butter aside. "Marriage is a big thing."

The stir started in her gut. She nodded. "Big enough to hurt if you get it wrong."

"Yes, I suppose that's true." Joyce reached into the box and pulled out a second sleeve. "But marriage is also big enough to be the most noble role you'll ever have."

Their gazes met.

Joyce smiled. Then she touched the bottom of Nikki's chin with the love of a mother. "You know what I think?"

"What?"

"I think we're ready."

Until Joyce nodded toward the pan of cabbage, the words seemed to mean something completely different.

◆ ◆ ◆ ◆

Wes eased his truck through the intersection at Eddner, taking the turn slower than usual to avoid rattling his passenger.

Arlene Rothfuss sat as prim as you please in the passenger seat, "pocketbook" (not purse) perched on her lap, both hands over top. A bag of treasures for Nikki rode on the seat next to her.

"You do a good job keeping up those grounds, Wes," she said as they slid past the line of Eddner buildings.

"Thank you. The grass grows faster than I want it to sometimes."

"If grass is growing, crops are growing." She looked out the passenger window at the corn drinking in the late-afternoon rays. "How're the Voepel boy's crops doing so far?"

"Coming in green and healthy. You'll get a look at them when we get to the farm. Got a bright future ahead of him."

"A good head on his shoulders, that one. Reminds me of you at that age."

"You're generous, Mrs. Rothfuss."

They chatted more about the small things of a small town—the need for rain, the health of his herd, Trennen's plans for a second hay cutting of the summer. Eddner slipped farther and farther behind them.

They were halfway to the farm when she turned to him and asked, "So what're your intentions with Joyce?"

Cold sliced through him. "I'm—I'm sorry?"

"Women read things differently, you know."

He kept his eyes on the road. "I, uh, there's not . . ." Whatever it was that needed to be said eluded him.

Mrs. Rothfuss tsked and looked out her window again. Response enough to tell him he'd better think on the question some more. His secret angst had been showing the whole time he thought it was hidden.

177

His breath came in shallow draws. Neither of them spoke.

They rounded the final bend. The farm lay in front of them. The grazing cows, the old farmhouse, the rambling yard—and the car of the woman whose smile made him recoil and lean in simultaneously.

Mrs. Rothfuss spoke one more time. "Hearts tarry far longer than they should, Wesley."

◆ ◆ ◆ ◆

Mrs. Rothfuss forked a dainty bite of brat. "Wes, you sure are a lucky fella to have these two wonderful cooks feeding you."

Uncle Wes flashed what could be considered a smile at their guest. "Very lucky." He stuffed his mouth immediately with a heap of scalloped cabbage. All meal long, his answers had been more perfunctory than usual.

Nikki exchanged a look across the table with Joyce. They both clearly noticed the difference.

For her part, Mrs. Rothfuss continued unabated, chewing her small bit of meat while slicing another. She had proven to be a much more considerate dinner guest than a church-landing conversationalist. Funny, insightful—and most of all, silent on the subject of a certain man. Perhaps Joyce, via her aunt, had something to do with that.

"Do you recognize the scalloped cabbage?" Nikki asked her. "I don't think it's authentic. More like a spin-off."

"I do remember something like this." Mrs. Rothfuss tapped her fork on the small helping of casserole. The butter and cream had soaked into the crushed crackers, making a gooey bed for the soft cabbage, a tantalizing combination of flavors. "Maybe Mrs. Baumann—your great-grandma—brought it to a church carry-in or two. I don't remember Ann ever making it, though."

"You were good friends with Ann?" Joyce asked.

"I was. We were in the same confirmation class. Which reminds me, Nikki, dig in this bag here." She pointed at the tote between their chairs.

Nikki reached in and pulled out a thin spiral-bound book with a manila envelope tucked inside. She laid it on the table between them. The book had the church building on the cover with a title announcing *Hosana Lutheran Church, 1869–1994.*

"That envelope has some pictures I wanted to show you," Mrs. Rothfuss said.

The paper crinkled as Nikki pulled out a collection of photos, most of which were the same square shape as those from the freezer bag she had organized into albums. The picture on top had suffered creases down its front, and chunks were missing from the edges. But in the middle, clear as day, was a baby girl in a flowy white dress and matching bonnet, enthroned upon a decorated wagon. An older girl held the handle.

"That's my mother pulling the wagon. And that"—she pointed at the baby—"is your great-grandmother Lena."

Nikki leaned closer to the photo. The baby girl had the dark eyes of the woman in the rose-adorned apron.

"This was the harvest parade they used to have in Eddner," Mrs. Rothfuss said. "Lena won the Beautiful Baby Contest that year."

"There used to be parades in Eddner?" Joyce asked.

"There used to be a lot in Eddner. A post office, hardware store. They would have events throughout the year. The harvest festival was a big one." She pulled the next photo from the pile and handed it to Nikki. "This is our confirmation class. Ann is the third from the right, front row. That's me next to her in the plaid dress."

Grandma Ann stood several inches taller than her friend. Both young teenagers held a Bible and stared into the camera with an earnest determination, as if they glimpsed the future and were bent on facing it head-on. The photo was dated 1951.

"Is my grandpa in this picture too?" Nikki asked.

"He would have been confirmed earlier, in the late 1940s. We can find his exact date in this registry." She tapped the book. "All the old church records are in here. The baptisms, confirmations, and weddings. I marked the ones for your family."

Nikki laid the pictures aside and opened the registry. The pages squeaked against the metal rings as she searched, at last landing on a page with a small sticky note affixed under a familiar name. Henry James Werner, confirmed in 1949. On the facing page was another sticky note next to another familiar name. Ann Ruth Baumann, confirmed in 1951.

"Would you like to see your great-grandparents?" Mrs. Rothfuss gestured for Nikki to turn back several pages. Two more sticky notes marked the confirmation dates for Lena Ann Schoenborn (1929) and Otto Joseph Baumann (1928).

Nikki turned to Uncle Wes. "I didn't realize Grandma Ann got her name from her mother."

He nodded.

"Family names were big in Eddner," Mrs. Rothfuss added to his nonverbal answer. "Some babies had three names but went by a middle one to avoid confusion with other family members who had the same given name. And of course, some names changed after World War I."

"Changed how?" Nikki asked.

"Americanized. Otto is an example. Go back to the baptisms and find him."

Nikki turned the pages until the sticky note marking his baptismal record came into view, from 1914, about three years before America entered the war. His given name was recorded as Otto Josef.

"See all these names around his?" Mrs. Rothfuss pointed to several examples: Katharina, Elisabetha, Ludwig. "By the time these babies were confirmation age, many of their names had changed to the English spelling."

"That's about the time they dropped German at the church and school too, wasn't it?" Joyce asked.

"And in their homes," the older woman replied.

"They wanted to disassociate from Germany that much?" Nikki asked.

Mrs. Rothfuss shook her head. "I think they wanted to be seen as American that much."

Changing names. Changing languages. Changing what they ate. German hymnbooks replaced by English ones. German books packed away, never read again. The notebook's opening letter talked about the "pressures of assimilation." War half a world away had amplified that pressure.

"No wonder the recipes faded to the background," Nikki said.

Mrs. Rothfuss folded her hands in her lap. "I have to say, it is refreshing a young person like yourself wants to learn about these things from so many years ago. None of us got where we are by accident. There's a reason we have the names we do, the language we do, the appearance and place in the world we do."

"Sometimes we have to look back to discern the way forward," Joyce added.

Nikki picked up the picture of Great-Grandma Lena, one child in the generation that came of age in the bull's-eye of the pressure. Surely Lena had written the notebook—an attempt to capture the culture she knew before it disappeared completely. But also to point to the hope and faith and the love of butter that must have sustained her, like her mother before her.

She nodded to Joyce. "I believe you're right."

Twenty-One

Mrs. Rothfuss stayed for an hour after supper, regaling Nikki with stories from her own childhood. The wood-burning stove that had warmed the schoolhouse, and the older boys taking turns each day to bring in the logs. The outhouses. The church coming together to repaint the parsonage and install new windows to save on labor costs.

Those were all scenes and experiences that her grandmother had carried too. The images were so real, Nikki could almost step into them wearing the same stiff leather shoes worn back then.

By seven o'clock, the dishes were done, food put away, and goodbyes given. The farmhouse basked in the afterglow.

Nikki settled onto the couch and called Hannah through video chat to tell her all about it. Her sister listened to every word, smiling in all the right places.

"So this cabbage dish was actually pretty good?" Hannah asked.

"Mrs. Rothfuss said it reminded her of something Great-Grandma used to make."

"That has to make you happy."

"It does." She nestled deeper into the cushions of the old couch. "What's going on there? Is Mom doing okay?"

"As good as can be expected. She went to church with us this morning."

"Hopefully she liked it."

"She seemed to. Everything's still so new for her, though. How's Uncle Wes?"

"Good-hearted as ever." She grinned. "And I think maybe in love."

Hannah's eyebrows shot up. "You're kidding."

"Unless I'm reading it wrong, but I don't think I am."

"Adorable. It's like a Hallmark movie."

They laughed together, the first time in so long. It filled Nikki in ways butter-drenched food couldn't.

Until her sister's smile drew in. "Speaking of romance . . ." she started.

The rest of the sentence didn't need to be spoken. Nikki grabbed a throw pillow and held it to her chest. "He hasn't returned my text."

Hannah looked down for a moment. "He posted pictures the other day. Some camping trip he took with friends outside Portland."

A thread poked out from the pillow seam. Nikki batted it with her forefinger. "Glad he's enjoying himself."

"Are you going to text him again?"

She shrugged.

"I still think you should."

"Maybe."

Hannah looked at someone or something off to the side, then nodded. "That's Tyler. He wants to take us for ice cream and cheer Mom up a bit."

"You have a good man, Han."

Her sister's smile returned, smaller than before. "So do you, Nik."

For a long time after the call, Nikki sat on the couch, gaze fixed on the window. The shadows grew longer. The crispness of the trees fuzzed with the evening colors.

The daylight in Oregon would be going strong still.

It would do no good to search for the post. It wouldn't result in anything productive.

She did it anyway.

There he was, in a collection of five pictures. In a canoe wearing only swim trunks. Making a goofy face with two of his buddies next to a campfire. Tossing a football with a friend. Holding up a freshly caught fish. Walking solo on the shoreline, his back to the camera, his face to the setting sun. All the things a guy would do when free from commitments.

He had captioned the pictures, "Out finding the sun. The only way to live."

Pain sliced through her chest. He was happy. He was happy without her.

"We'll both have space to figure out where we go from here."

Every pulse through her veins was more razor-like than the last.

She closed out of the app. Then she deleted it off her phone.

◆　◆　◆　◆

Instead of a phone call on Monday morning, Wes received a text message from Aunt Emma, along with a picture.

As he set his oatmeal to cook in the microwave, he opened the message.

> I'm back. I'm safe. I'm slightly tanned, and I'm not in any legal trouble. Overall, good trip. Here's a picture of my new spatula. Yours will be arriving for Christmas. No need to send a thank-you letter. Taking a nap this morning then emailing Nikki (shhh). Still waiting on those bathroom pictures.

She punctuated it with ten kissy-face emojis.

Always a hoot. And always with something good to say. If nothing else, Aunt Emma was a bridge among generations—the exact thing Nikki needed.

He made a mental note to ask Nikki later if she had heard from her great-aunt.

◆　◆　◆　◆

Monday, June 10, 7:05 a.m.
To: Nikki
From: Aunt Emma
Subject: About your grandma

Nikki—

You don't know me well, but I am your grandma's sister. Wes gave me your email address, a subterfuge I hope you do not hold against him. It was my idea, and I may have twisted his arm. He told me that you desire to learn more about Ann, and I wanted to offer up my services in that department.

I am five years younger than Ann, born smack-dab in the middle of World War II, 1942. Five years is enough of an age difference that we could be friends, though sometimes she did mother me a bit too much. I had ways of letting her know she crossed the line. Like when I coaxed our hen, Bertha, to roost on her chair at the table. I got more heat from our father than from her, though.

Mothering came second nature to Ann. She was the oldest girl, and that came with a lot of responsibility she didn't ask for. She took it in stride most of the time, but as she got older, she started to want other things. I couldn't blame her one bit. She was expected to help run the house. She helped Mother clean and cook and look after me, which could be quite the challenge, I admit. Because of that, she didn't have a true childhood. At least, not the same way I did.

She was an obedient girl, wanting to please, so on those rare occasions when she did let her horses run, it was so ridiculously delightful. I loved seeing that side of her.

One of my favorite memories of Ann was the night I convinced her to sneak out of the house to lay under the stars. I nudged her awake about midnight, and we slipped as quiet as church mice out the door and down to the pond across the road. We laid on the shoreline next to the foxtails, our nightgowns glowing in the moonlight and our hands behind our heads for pillows. The sky was so clear that night, the stars like perfect pinpricks in the floor of heaven. We took turns finding the constellations as we nibbled on the cookies I had swiped from the kitchen right before bed when our mother wasn't looking. We stayed like that for a long time, what felt like hours, talking and laughing. I loved making her laugh, and she had the most contagious laugh.

The only thing I distinctly remember discussing was what we could do if there was no one to tell us what to do. I remember clear as that night sky Ann said, "I would see what else is under these stars."

I felt sad because I knew that meant she hankered to leave our little corner of earth. She must have been sixteen or so, and I could tell she was already keeping one eye on the door. If it had been anyone else, I wouldn't have been as perceptive at eleven years old, but that was my sister, and I knew my sister. As I'm sure you know yours. You can tell her things without ever saying words.

I am happy to tell you as many stories about her as you can stand, and then a few more.

May I also tell you one your grandma once shared with me when we were grown? It's not about her, though. It's about your dad.

When he and your uncle were in school at Eddner, an older boy started picking on Wes, always making fun of him for one thing or another. Never gave him a moment's rest. Your dad reached his boiling point one day and hauled off and socked the kid right in the face. Gave him a shiner to remember. Your grandpa wanted to whup your dad, but Ann intervened. She said Chris did what brothers were supposed to do, and his father couldn't punish him for that. She always believed siblings were born to look out for one another.

That other boy never bothered Wes again. In many ways, I think Wes has been returning the favor ever since.

Well look at that, I've written a novel at this point. Hopefully you got something good out of it. Please drop me a line sometime. I'd love to hear from you.

How are the recipes going? How many have you fixed so far? Anything stand out to you?

Now you have to write me back. I've asked too many questions.

Love and hugs,

Aunt Emma

◆ ◆ ◆ ◆

Later that morning, Wes stepped off the curb in front of Harman's and followed the angled parking line alongside his truck. He kept his cap pulled low over his face, low against the reach of the morning sun and low against any looks or whispers that might have him at their center. Otis Harman knew his hidden business. So did Arlene Rothfuss. He'd been fooling himself that his business had been or could stay hidden at all in a small town where everyone could name everyone else and their family members.

He swung the two paint cans into the truck bed, tucking them against the back of the cab. Redmont may have been his stomping grounds, but he'd never wanted to escape back to the farm more.

A voice cut through the air. "Morning, Wes!"

So much for shielding himself. He turned toward the call

Trennen partially blocked the other side of Main with his truck and leaned out his open window. "Never seen you in town so often in my life!"

"It's what happens when you're fixing up a house," Wes called back.

"You going to be working on the house next week?"

"Probably. Why?"

"Need a driver for my hay crew out at your place. If the weather holds."

"Just tell me what day."

"I'll get back to you." Trennen ducked back into his cab as a city truck rumbled around him. He waved to the passenger then reemerged. "What did Nikki make yesterday?"

"Brats and scalloped cabbage."

"Any left?"

Wes huffed. One-track mind on that boy. "I'll have her save you back some."

"'Preciate it! I better split. I'll be out your way tomorrow, more than likely."

Wes nodded and sent Trennen on his way. Then he climbed into his truck and gratefully went on his own way, cap still low.

◆ ◆ ◆ ◆

The aftereffects of Isaac's post clouded around Nikki in a dreary, sagging gray, the kind encapsulated by the tear-in-the-beer country songs serving as her companions as she prepared the bathroom walls for their first full coat of Tundra Frost.

Isaac was out finding the sun, finding the joys of his space halfway across the country from her. Where he apparently wanted to be.

She affixed the end of the blue tape to the top edge of the sink backsplash and slowly smoothed it into position.

The front door unlatched. Uncle Wes called, "Nikki?"

"In the bathroom."

The familiar thump of boots fell on the wood floors. She pulled on a smile, trying to mask the dullness if only for a few minutes.

Soon he appeared in the doorway. "Paint delivery." He set the cans on the toilet lid. The thin metal handles clinked against the sides.

"Thank you," she said.

He glanced around the bathroom. Tape protected nearly every edge except the tub and its surround. "Saw Trennen in town. He wants to stop by tomorrow for some leftovers."

"Figures." She chuckled and sat next to the tub to start a new strip of tape at the spot where the porcelain enamel met the wall.

188

"Aunt Emma email you, by chance?" he asked.

"She did this morning. She said you sent her my way."

"Hope you don't mind."

"Not at all. She had good stories to tell." Nikki eased the tape up the side of the tub. "She told me one about your school bully, which I have to say surprised me."

"How so?"

She turned to him. "You don't strike me as someone who needs a defender."

He shrugged one shoulder and hooked his thumbs into his front belt loops. "We all need one eventually."

"Did you know Aunt Emma knew that story?"

"No. But your grandma told her everything."

Nikki grinned. "Sisters do that kind of thing." She returned to taping, moving inch by inch to create smooth, straight lines.

"Nik, uh . . . I was thinking. This Sunday's Father's Day."

Her fingers paused briefly. "I'm still not going, if that's what you're asking."

"Would you want to call him?"

She lifted onto her knees, better positioning herself to continue the progress. "I don't really have anything to say to him."

The tape peeled easily from the roll, smoothed easily onto the lip of the surround.

"This is a chance," Uncle Wes said gently.

She tore the tape and turned to him. "He won't hear anything I have to say. So what's the point in trying?"

He rocked on his feet. "Maybe he is ready, though. He asked to see you."

Her jaw set. On that, Uncle Wes was wrong. He hadn't seen the haggard look in her mom's eyes or the empty walls of their home. "He wants it for him, not me." She pulled a new strip off the roll and resumed edging the surround, the work that needed to be done to keep a clear line between things that should remain separated.

Eventually the boot thumps trailed away.

◆ ◆ ◆ ◆

Wes closed his bedroom door and sank onto the edge of his bed. Nikki had no idea how like her father she was. The German language may have faded between their family's generations, but the stubbornness held strong, as woven into the DNA as the brown eyes.

Neither of them saw the other the way they needed to be seen. Too blinded by hurt. Too lost in reacting to the hurt. Playing right into the hands of the enemy of their souls.

He bowed his head, covered his eyes with his palms. His fingers pushed his cap back on his head. The ache in his chest poured out in a long, deep exhale.

He could not weary of doing good. He could not stop asking the glorious Father to give his brother and his niece the spirit of wisdom and revelation, as Paul did for the hardheaded Ephesians. The enemy was tireless in his prowl.

But waiting for divine whacks tested the faith of even the strongest saint.

Twenty-Two

Wednesday, June 12, 9:19 a.m.
To: Aunt Emma
From: Nikki
Subject: RE: About your grandma

Aunt Emma—

Thank you so much for reaching out to me! I don't hold it against Uncle Wes that he gave you my email address. I don't hold anything at all against him, except maybe his taste in décor and breakfast food.

I love the details you gave about Grandma Ann. As you know, I don't have a lot of memories of her since I only saw her at Christmas, but what I do remember of her, I treasure. She was a great cook, I remember that, and a gracious hostess.

The lady here in Eddner who is helping me with the recipes, Joyce Kindstrom, said Grandma Ann used to walk up to the cemetery nearly every day to visit her (your) mother. I've been trying to do that myself. It makes me feel closer to them both. Like Atticus Finch says in *To Kill a Mockingbird*, I try to see things from another's perspective by walking around in their skin.

This morning when I went on my walk, I couldn't help but look at the pond across the road as I passed by and picture two naughty girls

191

laying on their backs and counting the stars. The thought of it covered me with such a warm feeling, like I was snuggled there between you. I would have loved to have been there!

What was Grandma Ann's sense of humor like? She seems like she would have been a fairly practical and straightforward kind of lady. What were her favorite games as a child? Did she have a favorite outfit or toy? Favorite book? Hymn? What was her favorite thing to cook? Why do you think she had this notebook? Who do you think wrote it?

I'm so full of questions. I'm thankful you're full of answers.

So much is going on in my life these days. I'm sure you know at least some of it, maybe all of it. Some days I don't know if things will ever go back to normal. Some days are so swirled with gray I forget the sun is out.

But being here in the farmhouse where Grandma's life was shaped gives me hope mine can be too. This broken, unrecognizable gray can be formed into something bright and—dare I say—redeemed.

Is that too idealistic of me?

With love,

Nikki

◆   ◆   ◆   ◆

Nudges, not whacks.

The phrase seeped into Wes's dreams in the small hours of Thursday morning. It surfaced again with the dawn light splashing across his porch. Blossomed more as he swung the pasture gate closed behind a full trough.

Nudges. Strategic, consistent, from various angles, on various fronts, using various mechanisms. With various allies tactfully maneuvered into position.

Pieces of a plan began to snap into place so cleanly there was no mistaking what to do or who the allies should be.

And that was what made him avoid his phone for most of the day.

Finally, after chores were done, lunch eaten, bills paid, he set his phone in front of him on his desk. He reached to pick it up once and retracted. Twice, retracted. On the third time, he sucked in his breath and dialed.

A woman picked up his call. "County Mart. How may I help you?"

Wes fought his mouth's resistance to move. "Bakery, please."

"One moment."

Hold music filled his ear. He took shallow breaths. Too deep of ones might have deflated what thin courage he clung to. After what seemed like a full year, the music abruptly stopped. A rattle of the phone, then the familiar voice.

"Bakery. This is Joyce."

Wes licked his lips, suddenly so dry. "Hi, Joyce."

"Wes?" Her frown was evident in her tone. "Everything okay?"

"Yeah, fine."

The clangs of pans in the background. An announcement through the PA system. She was in the middle of her workday. He had to get a move on.

He swallowed. "I was wondering if you would be willing to do something. For Nikki."

"Of course. How can I help?"

In one question, Joyce demonstrated effortlessly why her name had risen to the top of the ally list.

His grip loosened on the phone. "I'd like you to post some pictures."

◆ ◆ ◆ ◆

Wes's request for Aunt Emma was nearly as simple as his ask of Joyce. He called her as soon as he finished with Joyce and jumped right to it. "Nikki told me you emailed her," he said. "Thank you for doing that."

"Delighted to. I was right, she seems to prefer written conversations with me. She opened right up, and she's so eloquent, as

I'd expect a book lover to be. Of course, my endlessly charming personality probably helped."

He chortled. "Without question. And I thought of another way you can help in the battle, if you'll consider it."

"I'm already considering it. Tell me."

"Would you call Chris and tell him that you and Nikki are now talking too? Tell him how eager she is to learn about family history, particularly of Mom and Eddner, and that she comes alive when she hears these stories? Maybe if he knew all this, and he knew that Nikki now understands about Dad, then maybe it would stir him in the right way."

"Fostering empathy. I like it."

"I hope it works. He's not in a place where he can hear reason or rebuke, but these things I believe he will hear. And from you."

"Some dots only stories can connect," she said.

"Exactly."

"Brilliant boy, Wes. I'll call Chris today."

◆ ◆ ◆ ◆

Friday morning, Nikki flipped on the bathroom light and waited in the hall for Uncle Wes to pass through the doorway. Priming and painting the walls had taken her a few days. Save for the baseboards and quarter-round, the room was complete.

He stepped inside and inspected the walls and corners, each one coated twice in Tundra Frost. "You even got behind the toilet."

She leaned against the jamb. "As far as I could reach."

He ran his fingertips along the lip of the tub surround. "Great edging."

"I like painting. It's satisfying." Particularly in the longest hours of the night, when unwanted thoughts were at their loudest.

Uncle Wes turned on his bootheel and faced her. "Glad you think that. Lots more to go."

"I already have the kitchen cabinets measured for primer and paint. And I found some pulls and knobs online I hope Harman's can match."

He grinned, clearly tickled with how much she had picked up in a short amount of time. He trusted her, invested in her, gave her a reason to keep stepping forward. Everything family was supposed to do.

"Want me to pick anything up at Harman's?" he asked.

"I'll do it. I'm headed to Redmont for groceries."

"Have Harman's charge it to me."

"I really don't mind helping—"

"My cost," he insisted.

She couldn't argue. "Noted."

He picked off a piece of tape still stuck to the side of the surround. "What's the recipe this week?"

"Potato pancakes and applesauce. Apparently they're served together, and I'm not sure how I feel about that."

"Me either. Heard of it, never tried it."

She crossed her arms and pushed off the jamb. "Each one takes a while to make, so I'm thinking of asking Joyce to come tomorrow to help with the applesauce, then on Sunday to do the pancakes. Seems more manageable that way. Don't you think?"

"Sure. Yeah. Good."

The slight pucker of his brow hinted that he was selling himself on the "good" part.

He slid his hands into his pockets and surveyed the room again. "Guess I better get to these baseboards if we're having company."

She hid her grin. Hopefully she'd helped give him a reason to keep stepping forward too.

On her way to her car for the trip to Redmont, she texted her mom a selfie from earlier that week, when she had a paintbrush in hand, her hair in a ponytail, and streaks of white on her cheek. She followed that with a note.

Miss you, Mom. Praying Salina is treating you well. Funny how doing the next thing takes you closer to who you are, even when you may be further away from what you know.

◆ ◆ ◆ ◆

Potato Pancakes (Kartoffelpuffer) with Applesauce (Apfelmus)

We cannot know what is around the bend. It could be sorrow or joy, riches or poverty, health or infirmity. But we can trust that contentment can be ours regardless of circumstance. The Father's heavenly storehouses are full of his comfort, and he promises to rain it down upon the earthbound souls who ask for it. You have felt such sweet drops of relief before, a honeyed embrace of the divine to soothe your weary body of dust. When trouble comes, ask for this meeting of heaven upon the earth. The One who commands both realms, who carves the paths of the rivers and gives light to the stars, will lead us in the way we should go and shine a lamp unto our feet. It is a promise to us who trustingly call *Abba!* "In the fear of the Lord is strong confidence: and his children shall have a place of refuge" (Prov. 14:26).

For Applesauce (Heaven)

5 medium sweet apples

¾ cup water

1 teaspoon vanilla extract

Juice from half of a lemon

1 tablespoon sugar

2 cinnamon sticks

½ teaspoon ground cinnamon

¼ teaspoon nutmeg

Peel and cube apples. Place in a large saucepan. Add remaining ingredients. Mix well. Bring to boil. Reduce heat to simmer; cover and cook until apples are tender, about 20–25 minutes, stirring occasionally. Remove from heat and discard cinnamon sticks. Mash with potato masher; applesauce will be slightly chunky. Serve warm on top of potato pancakes.

For Potato Pancakes (Earth)

6 potatoes, peeled and grated
⅓ cup flour
Salt
1 onion, grated
3 large eggs, lightly beaten
Butter
Oil

Squeeze water from potatoes (need to be dry). In a bowl, mix potatoes with flour, eggs, and onion. Sprinkle with salt. Mix well. Melt butter mixed with oil in skillet. Scoop potato mixture into pan with ladle. One ladleful equals one pancake. Press cake flat into pan with bottom of ladle. Fry for several minutes on each side until brown. Drain on towel. Keep warm until ready to serve. Serve topped with warm applesauce.

◆ ◆ ◆ ◆

Joyce's blazing efficiency was a wonder to behold. She deftly nudged the blade of her paring knife under the skin of an apple slice and pulled it toward her, using her thumb as a guide. *Shhhifff.*

197

All the way down. The peel dropped to her cutting board with very little white on the underneath side. Without ever putting down the slice, she chunked it over the saucepan between them.

Nikki's slices ended up cratered, and no way was she going to attempt to chunk anything without the help of her board.

"You're doing great," Joyce assured her. "The point is not perfection. It's learning."

Abundant truth in such a short response.

More freshly washed apples shed their drops upon the paper towels spread on the counter. Alan Jackson crooned from the radio about the muddy waters of the Chattahoochee River.

Each stroke of the blade through the fruit connected Nikki back to the way her grandmother and great-grandmother would have done things. Painstakingly. To the modern world, needlessly. Applesauce was plentiful, cheap, mass-produced, sold at gas stations and in convenient squeeze pouches. A copiousness so great it was taken for granted.

Putting her hand to the knife meant putting herself among women who knew what it was to bring much out of little. It invited contentment amid humble circumstances. A "honeyed embrace of the divine to soothe your weary body of dust."

Joyce showed Nikki the apple slice in her hand. "See this bruise? Reminds me of what your grandma would say when we were prepping apples for pies. She said the bad parts make the good parts all the sweeter." She carefully cut around the bruise. The mealy refuse dropped to the board.

"Did Grandma Ann ever make applesauce?"

"She may have. I don't remember it. My mother did a few times, though."

"What was your mother like?"

Joyce grinned as she peeled. "Beautiful. Never complained about anything. Always coming up with clever ways to have fun, which made our lives easier to bear. It was hard having a single mom, as you can imagine."

"What ever happened to your father? If you don't mind me asking."

"Not at all." She paused to shake the peel off her blade and chunk the flesh over the pan. "My dad was not well. Mentally, I mean. He wasn't in my life much. Most of what I know about him I learned from my other family members."

"Was what they told you good or bad?"

"It was realistic more than anything else. He couldn't be the dad I wanted. That's a hard thing for a little girl to come to terms with."

A big girl too.

Nikki transferred chunks from her board to the pan. "Did you ever have a relationship with him?"

"Relationships can look all sorts of ways. I had to learn where his capacity to love met with mine." She held up another bruised slice. "A lot of bad parts, but the good parts are still good." The complexity of her past reflected in her steady, humble gaze.

"You are far more of a woman than me," Nikki said.

Joyce shook her head. "I don't believe that's true. You're more than you think and capable of more than you think." Her stare lingered. She clearly meant more than with cooking.

Nikki put her knife to the skin of a slice and cut as cleanly as she could, as cleanly as she had edged the tub surround. Keeping separate what should be separated.

They worked in silence.

At last Joyce spoke again, tone more playful. "I think we need to chronicle our cooking, by the way. Mind if I take some pictures?"

Always the gracious friend. She too was beautiful, never complaining, and always coming up with clever ideas. It was impossible to resist such friendship.

"Chronicle away," Nikki replied.

◆ ◆ ◆ ◆

Nikki and Joyce knocked on Wes's door shortly before noon. "Lunchtime!" Nikki held up a dish of applesauce as she breezed by him into the living room. Joyce hung back on the porch, grinning.

"I thought that was for tomorrow," he said.

"Had extra for today," Nikki answered as she rounded into the kitchen.

Joyce giggled. "We may have made too much." Still she stayed on the porch. After a moment, her eyes moved to the living room, then back to him.

It took a second for the unspoken question to register. He stepped to the side. "Please, come in."

"Thank you."

Joyce Kindstrom crossing his threshold. Coming into the house only a handful of people had seen. He blew out his breath and shut the door.

She looked to every corner and piece of furniture. "This is nice, Wes. Did you design it yourself?"

"It was a prepackaged plan."

She clasped her hands at her waist. "You did well. I like the layout."

Her lips were accentuated in a rose color. Feminine and tender.

"Uncle Wes?" Nikki's call jerked him back to awareness. "Can I use this roast beef for sandwiches?"

"Yes. Go ahead."

The refrigerator door smacked closed. Silverware rattled.

The noise was a good cover for him to confer with Joyce. He spoke quietly. "How'd it go? Did you get . . . ?"

She nodded. "I posted the pictures a few minutes ago. I did ask Nikki before I posted, though. It seemed better to have her permission."

"Right, yeah. I'm, uh, I'm glad you thought of that."

"Want to see the post?"

He nodded, only to realize a second too late it meant she would come closer.

She stepped over to him, pulling her phone from her back

pocket. She stood within inches, so close he could hear the swish of her shirt and detect the notes of her perfume.

On the screen were four pictures, three of Nikki in various stages of applesauce making, wearing his grandmother's apron. The last picture was a selfie of the two cooks each holding up a wooden spoon. The caption for the photos talked about Joyce helping Nikki "discover her culinary roots."

"I tagged Chris," she said. "I'll let you know if he responds."

Hopefully he would. Aunt Emma's lack of response indicated she'd had trouble reaching him. Every good battle plan needed multiple points of advance.

Joyce lifted her gaze to his, the touch of it so soft it stole his words. "I think you're onto something with this," she said.

A thank-you would be appropriate. A thank-you for a lot of things. The only response Wes could muster, however, was a simple nod.

She smiled, without expectation for more.

Twenty-Three

No sooner had Wes sat down to watch the Saturday afternoon Cardinals game than his phone rang from its spot
on the end table next to his recliner. No sooner had he
answered than Aunt Emma began talking.

"Finally connected with Chris. Only took me two days."

He muted the television and cradled the remote against his leg.
"Wondered what had happened there."

"I couldn't get ahold of him. But then out of the clear blue sky,
he called me up a little bit ago talking about some pictures that
Joyce had posted. I had to go look them up for myself because
I wasn't sure what he was talking about. He wanted to know
why Joyce Kindstrom was back in the farmhouse—and with his
daughter."

"What did you say?"

"Everything you told me to. How Nikki is eager to know about
where she came from and about your family. I told him Joyce was
there in Eddner and had the memories to share, so it was only
natural that she would be among the storytellers. 'She is filling a
need Nikki has,' I told him. I don't know how it hit him. He was
quiet throughout it all."

Wes tapped the end of the remote on top of his thigh. "That
could be a good thing."

"Could be," she agreed. "At the end of our visit, I wished him a happy Father's Day tomorrow. He said he intended for it to be. I couldn't tell if it was a hopeful response or a cynical one."

They could only pray it wasn't the latter.

"Thanks for calling him," Wes said.

"Thanks for putting Joyce up to the posts. That was you, wasn't it?"

"It was."

"Clever. Quite a friend, this Joyce. And she sure has a lovely smile, don't you think?"

He cringed. Not Aunt Emma too. Why couldn't anyone understand he was perfectly happy with the life he had chosen?

"She does," he conceded.

A beat went by.

"Okay, that's all I needed," she said. "That, and the fact I'm having a great time emailing with our niece. I need to send her a few more thoughts today before they disappear forever from this slippery memory of mine. At this age, I can't take remembering my own middle name for granted. Off to my keyboard."

He thanked her again for her help and wished her well with her email. For the remainder of the afternoon, he kept his focus on the Redbirds, not daring to turn to the spot mere feet away where Joyce had given him the closest view yet of her smile.

He was perfectly happy with the life he had.

Perfectly and wholly.

❖ ❖ ❖ ❖

Saturday, June 15, 5:15 p.m.
To: Nikki
From: Aunt Emma
Subject: More stories

Nikki—

What pure bliss you found meaning in the ramblings of my last email. We all hope someone will listen to what we have to say. That proves truer the older you get. I have more ramblings for you today. Buckle in.

You are correct that your grandmother had a more practical nature and a more straightforward sense of humor to match. She did not like pranks, I can tell you that, which caused a wee bit of ado in our childhood. She liked humor that tickled the brain, like riddles or puns. She collected the corniest jokes too. When we were young, she wrote any she found or heard in a little spiral notepad. One of her favorites went like this: Of what use are the Great Lakes? To fill up the holes between the US and Canada.

Another one was: What time is it when a man scratches his head with one hand? Five after one.

She couldn't get enough of these silly, innocent laughs. As far as games, she loved to play pitch. Are you familiar with that card game? She and Henry both loved pitch and would play almost every week with friends. They had a tournament going among the couples at Hosana at one point. Pitch requires a lot of strategy and thinking. That's who she was, a thinker.

We didn't have many toys growing up, and what we did have was mostly handmade. Her most beloved toy was a baby doll named Sallie-Jane. She kept her in her cedar chest well into her teen years. I'm not sure what happened to Sallie-Jane once Ann left home. Or the cedar chest, now that I'm thinking about it.

Though we lacked toys, we had a wealth of baby animals to love on. Ann was always the first to bottle-feed a calf or warm a baby chick separated from its mother. One time, there was a chick that was particularly attached to Ann right from the beginning. She named it Walter. The thing is, you can't really tell the gender of a chick until it's a few weeks old. Come to find out, Walter was a hen. It didn't matter to Ann, though. "Walter can be a girl's name," she insisted. So it was. Walter was a good egg layer, and we had her a couple of years before the eggs stopped coming. Normally that's the point hens wear out their welcome, but our father allowed Walter to live out her natural life despite not producing, because she was Ann's little friend.

From a young age, Ann loved the hymn "What a Friend We Have in Jesus." We sang it at her funeral. You may not remember that since you were so young, but I remember sitting in that church on the hard wood pews and imagining Ann's voice in place of my own. She couldn't carry a tune in a bucket, mind you, but when it came to that hymn, all her singing was beautiful to me.

Ann took after our father in many ways. He was a practical mind too, a detailed notetaker, a keen observer of facts and situations, and quite careful with his money. He made it a priority to save back enough of everything each day so that we would have at least a little tomorrow. That is a proverb, I believe. A wise man leaves an inheritance for his children's children. His conservation was a big reason why the farm stood as long as it did, even today.

Our mother was more like me—or rather, I am more like her. She would match our father's practicality when she needed to, but she also needed a good laugh every day. She found it too, either through someone else or because she created it. She said dancing at the stove made the flavors meld better. She also threw open the door to anyone who needed a friend or a plate or a hug. Often they needed all three. That was the kind of home she worked hard to provide, one fully stocked and clean and ready to welcome.

"You never know who the good Lord will ask you to entertain," she'd say. "It could be angels." (This is Scripture too, by the way.)

Ultimately, that was what my sister wanted the house to be under her rule as well. She wanted it to be open and welcoming. Especially to her boys when they had gone off to their adult lives. She wanted it to be the refuge her mother had made it. I have no doubt Ann would be tickled that you find it to be just that. Especially in this gray and swirling season of your life.

You are not idealistic to believe your life can be shaped in the farmhouse. Many lives have been and will continue to be, thanks to your uncle. I suspect whoever wrote the notebook wanted it to be part of that shaping work.

You are on the right track, my girl. Keep going.

Praying for you,

Aunt Emma

PS—Would you mind sending me a picture or two of the notebook you found?

◆　◆　◆　◆

Wes should have been paying attention to the sermon. Should have been listening to the words spoken over him. His father would have been writing notes in his Sunday journal. His mother would have been listening with her eyes fixed on the picture of Jesus.

"Every sermon has an ordained Sunday," his mother would contend. That was her way of telling him to pay attention.

Once again, though, Aunt Emma's distant observation of Joyce and her friendship rang louder than anything else around him.

His ears strained toward the pastor, but his eyes drifted to Joyce, a devoted ally. She wore a blue top. Blue like the hymnal cover, a deep-sea hue. Her hair skirted the collar, bending like thin feathers when she moved her head.

Nikki repositioned herself next to him, drawing him back to their own pew, to his own body. He folded his hands in his lap, the calluses of his palms scraping against each other. Nothing about him was feather-like or ever would be. Joyce didn't seem to care about that. Just like she didn't seem to care about the simple nod he had given her the day before in place of words.

His mother would have cared, though. She would have been disappointed.

Wes tightened his hands together.

In a matter of hours, Joyce would be back on his farm, continuing her service to his family. Regardless of everything, he needed to recognize what she was doing for them. She could not leave that evening until she knew—through his *spoken* words—what her help meant.

◆ ◆ ◆ ◆

The mid-June warmth wrapped around Wes as soon as he emerged from the church after helping put away the communion elements. Nikki was already on the landing, enfolded by Arlene Rothfuss and the pocketbook pack. The lightness in Nikki's expression spoke to her newfound ease among them. She laughed. She touched Mrs. Rothfuss's arm as they conversed. She was, by nearly all measures, finding her way.

Trennen strode through the door behind him with his mother on his arm. "Morning, Wes."

He nodded to them both.

"Quite a sermon today," Beth said.

"Sure was." He proceeded with them down the steps.

"I've always loved the story of Jesus feeding the five thousand," she said. "It makes me hopeful God keeps working miracles."

"It makes me hungry," Trennen quipped.

"I'm not surprised in the least." Beth looked at Wes and shook her head.

He chuckled and stepped with them onto the landing.

"That reminds me," she said, "please tell your niece thank-you for feeding my hollow-legged son. He does nothing but rave about the food she gives him."

"None of it makes it home," Trennen added.

"It's true. I can only guess that he is actually eating something on those days by the fact my pantry's not as bare." She glanced up at her boy with the tenderness relegated to mothers, impossible to replicate in any other relationship.

The look Wes still ached for so many years later.

"Nikki sounds like a wonderful young woman," Beth said. "I'm glad she's here with you."

Across the landing, his niece peeked at him, nodded.

If Chris could see the way she not only fit but shone in Eddner, surely he would be proud. As proud as Wes.

"Me too," he said.

Trennen angled his mother toward the parking lot. "Weather's looking good this week for baling. Still up for it?"

"You bet," Wes said.

"Tell Nikki I'll be by tomorrow for the leftovers."

"I believe that's a given by now." Wes slapped the young man's shoulder and bid them both a pleasant afternoon.

When he turned to find Nikki, she was already on her way to meet him. The joy lingered on her face the whole way to the truck.

"Having a good day?" he asked as they climbed in.

"A good weekend," she replied. "It could have been really hard. You know?"

The bulletin had recognized Father's Day. They had not.

He turned the key. "I know."

He pulled onto the county road and headed back to the farm. A long, bright Sunday afternoon stretched ahead of them. In his childhood, Sundays had given him hours to himself to fill as he pleased, the world open and clear, the prerogative wholly his. Every child, regardless of age, should know that feeling.

Gravel pinged against the truck's belly. They glided past the cemetery—the wreaths in alignment over his parents' graves—then into the tunnel of shade. Nikki watched out the window, the remnants of her smile still on her lips. By then, she must have known every curve and sun spot along the road, the way he did.

"What time are you starting the food?" he asked.

"Joyce will come about four. Shredding the potatoes will take a while. Especially when we need to make extra for Trennen."

Briefly their gazes met, hers twinkling with jest.

In every measure, she had found her way.

At the start of the final bend before the driveway, they crossed into the sunlight. The glorious rays amplified the green of the grass and the blue of the sky. The farm came into view.

Wes slowed for the turn into the driveway. "What else do you plan to make?" he asked.

But Nikki had leaned forward, rigid. Attention fixed in the direction of the farmhouse.

A strange black sedan sat in the driveway, its back facing them. "Unbelievable," she seethed.

Her reaction combined with the out-of-state license plate answered every question he had about the identity of the guest.

Lord help them.

Wes crawled to a stop behind the sedan and cut the truck's engine. He and Nikki sat in tense silence for a moment.

"Want me to talk to him first?" he asked.

"Tell him to leave." Her jaw joint bulged. All trace of sunniness had evaporated from her expression.

"Let's at least see what he wants," he said gently.

She glared through the windshield.

Slowly he pushed open his door.

Chris's movements flashed in the rear window of the car. He was preparing to exit.

Wes took up position at the front of his truck.

After a moment, Chris stepped out and stayed close to his door. He barely looked like the man of Wes's memory. Hair cut close on the sides with a crisp sweep across the top, a big change from the mop he used to wear. Face stylishly stubbled under gold aviator sunglasses. The T-shirt and jeans of the past had given way to a designer polo tucked into khaki shorts.

They stood face-to-face for the first time in years, surrounded by the grounds and ghosts of their boyhood.

The sun glinted off Chris's lenses. He nodded toward Wes's passenger. "She getting out too?"

No hello. No handshake. Wes girded himself. "I wanted to talk to you first."

"About?"

"Come on, Chris."

His brother planted his hands on his hips, widened his stance. He jutted his chin toward the new house. "Nice place."

Wes straightened his shoulders, refusing the redirect, and waited.

Chris looked off to the side. Eventually he sighed. "I thought if I saw her—if she saw me—then it might . . ."

"Help?" Wes finished.

His brother shrugged.

"You showing up like this only tells her you don't respect her, which she already believes."

Chris pursed his lips, nodded twice. "You always know best, don't you?"

Wes kept his voice calm. "I know what I've seen from Nikki."

"Aunt Emma said I should talk to my daughter and tell her my side of things."

"Your side of things as in what?"

"As in my perspective. About what's happened."

A sinking sensation gripped his gut. Whatever Aunt Emma had said, that was not the intended interpretation. Nikki was in no place to hear Chris's excuses. Anyone with ears to listen could tell that.

"I think she meant your perspective about our family history, about growing up in Eddner."

"That's not what she said," Chris insisted.

Instinctively, Wes took a step closer to his brother, reinforcing the guard around Nikki. "Chris—"

The truck door slapped closed. Both men turned.

Nikki reached Wes in four strides. A vein trailed down the middle of her forehead. "I'll take it from here, Uncle Wes."

Twenty-Four

Uncle Wes looked between them, clearly reticent to stand down. Only when she gave him a nod did he take a step back.

"I'll, uh, I'll go up . . ." He pointed toward his house. Shooting Nikki one last look, an assurance he wasn't far, he returned to his truck and rolled slowly up the driveway.

She was alone with her dad and all that had happened to bring them to that point. The billow and roll thundered.

Her dad let his hands fall to his sides, then he quickly tucked them into the pockets of his shorts. He had changed his entire look. Only one reason seemed obvious.

She crossed her arms, fists balled, and bore her gaze into him.

"Kinda strange being back here," he said.

Her fingernails dug into the heels of her hands. His sunglasses made it hard to tell exactly where his eyes pointed.

"I brought you something." He opened his door and reached inside. He pulled out a plastic sack with a gas station logo. "Sweet tea and Mounds." A crooked grin pushed into his cheek.

"I hate coconut," she replied flatly.

The grin faded. "I thought you always got a Mounds on the way home on Christmas."

"That was Hannah."

He looked down at the treats as if trying to remember. He offered her the sack anyway. "They're yours if you want them. Share them if you want."

She didn't move. "What do you want, Dad?"

He lowered his arm to his side and shut his door. "I was wondering if I could take you out for lunch."

"I have people coming over soon." Not for four hours, but he didn't need to know that.

"A quick bite? So we can talk?"

"We can talk here."

He started to speak, stopped.

A truck door closed. He glanced up at Uncle Wes's house, at his brother watching from a distance. "Can we at least go inside?" He nodded toward the farmhouse.

Once again, she stayed perfectly still.

"Fine." He shifted on his feet. The bag rustled against his leg. "I know we have some bad blood, and I'm sorry about that."

Her fingernails dug deeper.

"We weren't happy, Nik. Your mom and I. Not for a long time."

"That's justification?"

He jiggled his leg. "I never pretended I was perfect."

"No. Just faithful."

His mouth closed to a tight line. Even with the sunglasses, it was clear he looked directly at her. A father asking for respect he hadn't earned. A daughter asking for real answers she deserved.

The clench of her muscles wrapped up and around her vocal cords. "Why, Dad? Tell me why. All of it."

He dipped his head.

"Say something."

"What can I say?"

He could say that he was wrong. That he had cut wounds into their flesh that would take years to heal.

Tears burned the backs of her eyes. Her hand begged to rip off the sunglasses, to pull away the veil and leave him as vulnerable as he had left them.

He tilted his head up to her. "Does it make a difference to you that I'm happy?"

Sheer fury surged through her. "Happy? *Happy?* You're happy that your daughters are heartbroken? You're happy that Mom is bankrupt and living in Hannah's basement? That makes you happy?"

He turned away.

Her pulse throbbed. She took a step toward him. "The kind of people who find happiness in the misery of others are the kind of people I don't want to be around." One more step closer. "Ever."

She left him there with his head down and her words screaming around him.

The farmhouse door slammed behind her.

◆　◆　◆　◆

As soon as Nikki stormed up to the farmhouse, Wes pushed off the side of his truck. Voices carried, especially on a windless June Sunday.

Chris lingered next to his car long enough for Wes to nearly reach him. The gravel crunching under his dress shoes cued his brother to his approach. Immediately Chris turned for his door handle.

"Chris, wait." Wes double-timed the rest of the way.

"I don't want to hear it, Wes. It's no use trying to talk to either of you." He threw open the driver's door and thrust the plastic sack inside.

Wes reached the car in time to grab hold of the door, keeping it open. Chris sighed heavily and faced him, the door between them.

They were so close, an arm's length away. Wes's eyes reflected in his brother's glasses. "She's been through a lot," he said. "She's hurt."

"How do you think I feel! Do you have any idea what it's like to—" He bit back the words and looked off to the side. "Doesn't matter."

"To what?" Wes pressed.

213

His brother's strong jaw seemed starker. The jawline of their father. His lips barely parted as he spoke. "To never be what's desired."

Pain had a distinct feel. Like a razor's edge.

Chris yanked his door free from Wes's grip. "I gotta go." He folded himself inside and shut the door.

Of all times for words to fail Wes, his brother driving away— isolated with the festering wounds of a lifetime—was the worst possible one.

◆ ◆ ◆ ◆

Nikki threw her purse onto the couch and let loose the guttural scream that had balled inside her. It reverberated off the bare living room walls.

How dare he! How dare he show up against her wishes and expect things of her that he refused to do himself. Like show respect to someone else. What would her mom say if she knew? Hannah? Isaac?

Her chest tightened. Isaac. With secure arms to shield her. A smile that melted every fear. Soft words to soothe a racing heart. What would it take to get those back?

Her chin trembled. She picked up her purse and pulled out her phone. The screen stared back at her, waiting.

She could ask him into this raw moment, share with him the way he had wanted her to share. Ask him to wrap her in compassion.

But what if he refused? What if he wanted to protect the time and space between them more than he wanted to protect her?

She scrunched against the burn flooding the backs of her eyes and dropped her phone on the couch.

The giant looming wave threatened to take her under. One swift sweep of the legs and away she would go, lost in the swell. Her hands needed to move. She needed to cling to something solid, reliable.

She rushed to the kitchen. On the counter sat the three-pound sack of potatoes.

"His children shall have a place of refuge," the proverb had promised.

She tore open the sack, a haphazard rip splitting the side. Potatoes spilled onto the counter. One dropped onto the floor.

One by one, she washed them, vigorously rubbing the water into their thin skins, every muscle in her forearms taut. She peeled with precision, then wrenched the naked potatoes across the grater with a force that pulsed through her arms, across her shoulders, up her neck. Her upper body jerked with each stroke against the grater. Her fingers nearly caught on the blades more than once. But the sweat forming on her brow was a release. More and more, she chased that promised place of refuge, where heaven met earth. More and more, she craved it.

After a while, Uncle Wes came to check on her. When he saw the sternness of her posture and the growing mound of shreds, he nodded, turned around, and let her be.

Like few others in her life, he understood without her needing to explain.

◆　◆　◆　◆

Wes paced the width of his living room. The clock on the mantel inched closer to two o'clock, closer to the hour of Joyce's arrival. Maybe Nikki had called her already, but maybe not. Joyce should know what happened. She needed to know.

He sat in his recliner, jiggled his leg. He didn't make a habit of calling women on their private lines who were not his relatives or widows under his deacon care. Especially Joyce. But the circumstances were not normal.

He stood. Paced.

The clock ticked. Two minutes until two.

Finally he sighed. "It's what needs to be done."

He marched to his office. The top middle drawer of his desk held his copy of the most recent church directory. He lowered into his chair and dialed her number, the second time in a week he'd called her unexpectedly.

She didn't seem surprised in the least when he greeted her. "I hope it's okay I'm calling you," he said.

"Of course, but should I be worried?"

"Well . . . maybe." He told her about the events of the afternoon, about Chris, and Nikki's furious potato grating.

"How painful," Joyce said. "Do you think she needs a friend or time alone?"

"Alone, I think."

"I understand. I might text her a bit later to check in. How are you doing?"

He blinked. "Me? Fine."

"This has to be hard. You love them both so much."

She caught him wordless. It was as if she had stood with him in the swirl of gravel dust behind the sedan, and also shouldered the haunting image of a grown-up little girl hugging herself in the light of his porch that fateful Friday night. She had an uncanny way of seeing what he saw, but seeing it better.

"Joyce, I—" The words he had hoped to sort out before she came to the farm that afternoon rushed to his lips. All the things he should have said long before. "I want to thank you. For everything. I can't begin to tell you how much . . . Thank you."

A flaming mess of a speech. Unlike anything it should have been.

Regardless, the grace was evident in her voice. "Your family means a lot to me, Wes. Always will."

His face burned. He stumbled just as magnificently through a parting, then hung up.

Her phone number lingered on his screen. Joyce had been in his home, been at his table. Now she was in his phone. The pieces of his wholly perfect life increasingly expanded to include her.

◆　◆　◆　◆

There had to be a trick to frying potatoes evenly. Joyce probably knew what it was. Without her tutor's guidance, though, Nikki couldn't keep the golden brown of the first batches from turning earth brown by the end, no matter what she tried. The most burned ones she dumped into a repurposed cottage cheese container, treats to be doled out to Bonhoeffer during their morning hellos at the start of her walks. Grandma Ann would have done the same for her baby animal friends, if she'd ever needed to be rid of evidence of failed cooking.

By the time Nikki loaded all the presentable pancakes into a foil lasagna pan, strands of her hair had peeled from her sleek ponytail and her lower back smarted from standing mostly in one spot for more than an hour. The tension in her muscles had worked through her pores, but the echoes of her dad's words remained.

He was happy. That was what he wanted to matter most to her. His happiness.

She ripped a sheet of aluminum foil from its box and sealed it over the edges of the pan.

Wherever her dad's happiness led him, it would not be toward her.

She cradled the pan in one arm and grabbed the container of applesauce from the fridge. The walk up to Uncle Wes's house carved through the site of the unwelcome reunion. All the perfect comebacks had arrived far too late, when no one was around to hear them.

Uncle Wes opened the door before she knocked. "Saw you coming," he said and took the pan like the gentleman he was.

"Do what you want with those." She handed him the container as well. "Here's the applesauce. I texted Joyce that supper was off."

He frowned. "You're not eating?"

"Not hungry." She turned to leave.

"Nik."

She faced him.

The wrinkle of worry folded the tender spot above his nose. "You need anything?"

She smoothed the flyaways against her head, which already refilled with reverberations of the day, and the many days before it. The only way to keep them from drowning her was to drown them first.

Behind her, the old farmhouse waited, plenty of distractions within it.

"I only need the next thing," she answered.

◆ ◆ ◆ ◆

"How's our niece doing?" Aunt Emma asked over Wednesday breakfast.

"About the same," Wes said as he poured himself a glass of milk. "Been working nonstop since Sunday, on the house and cooking. Even Trennen can't eat all the potato pancakes she made. Now she's taken off every kitchen cabinet door and drawer and is sanding them like crazy in the front yard, even in the heat."

"Anger is a great energizer," Aunt Emma said. "On the bright side, if the pictures you sent of the bathroom are any indication, the kitchen is going to be a dream!"

Wes set his glass next to his bowl on the breakfast bar. "Suppose you're right. She's got a great eye and takes direction well."

"I wish your brother had half a mind to. He called me last night."

Wes righted. "Really?"

"Mm-hmm. Told me his account of the visit to Eddner, which included more than a few opinions about you and your influence over Nikki."

If only Chris could see what he wouldn't see. Much like Nikki couldn't hear what she wouldn't hear. Wes rubbed his temple with his free hand.

"I listened quietly as he said his piece," Aunt Emma continued. "You can't talk to someone whose only intent is to be heard. When he ran out of things to say, I reiterated—directly and clearly so there was no more mistaking my intent—that he might try sharing stories with his daughter about Eddner and growing up. After all, I told him, she is a story lover by trade and by passion. 'If you want to catch her ear, try a story,' I said. I truly hope he does."

"Me too. She enjoys the stories you've shared. She told a few of them to Joyce last night."

Aunt Emma's voice tipped up. "Joyce was out to your place again, huh?"

The fact had slipped so easily, casually, from his lips. He quickly explained, "Helping Nikki with these German rolls she's making. They did a test run last night. Nikki's making several dozen for Saturday when Trennen has a couple of boys over to put up hay. Going to make slider sandwiches for them."

"I see." The reply was simple yet somehow seemed layered with meaning.

"Anyway," he said, steering them back to the point he was trying to make, "Nikki clearly appreciates your memories."

"No doubt she does. Stories are the universal heart language. They bring together what is scattered."

"Happen to tell Chris that?" he asked.

"Should've. I always think of the most astute thing to say long after the moment has passed. But I did have mind enough to ask Chris if he needed Nikki's email address. He 'had it somewhere,' he said, but I made him jot it down anyway."

"Here's hoping," he replied.

"And praying," she added. "We'll pray for God to work where we can't."

Twenty-Five

Basic Bread Roll (Brötchen)

Let us embrace the hard work of living and loving in this world. We need not shy away from it; it is evidence of how much greater than we is our God. He does in a single word what we must spend ourselves in labor to accomplish. In our toil and our striving, we worship a God whose might we cannot fathom, whose thoughts we cannot grasp, whose ways we cannot direct. When we till and when we mend, when we knead and when we harvest, let our minds dwell on God, who never tires or slumbers and whose best work happens in the depths of our splintered souls. "Commit thy works unto the Lord, and thy thoughts shall be established" (Prov. 16:3).

2⁄3 cup milk, lukewarm
2⁄3 cup water, lukewarm
¼ teaspoon instant yeast
3 cups flour, up to 1 cup more for kneading
1¼ teaspoons salt

1 teaspoon sugar
A bit of warm milk for brushing rolls
Plentiful butter for serving

Combine milk, water, yeast, salt, sugar, and flour into a bowl. Mix with a wooden spoon until well blended; dough will be lumpy. Flour countertop and knead dough for 10 minutes until smooth, firm, and no longer sticky. Put dough in bowl, cover with damp towel, and proof in warm place for 1 hour. Dough should double in size. Punch dough to deflate. Divide into 10 equal pieces. Roll pieces into ovals about 3 inches long. Line baking sheet with parchment paper and place rolls on sheet. Cover with damp towel and proof for 1 hour or until double in size. Brush tops of rolls with warm milk. Score each roll lengthwise. Bake at 450 degrees for 20 minutes or until golden. Serve with ample butter.

◆　◆　◆　◆

Nikki dumped the dough into the center of the flour swirled on the morning-kissed countertop, the way Joyce had taught her. She set the glass bowl to the side and stepped closer to the mound. The toe of her shoe bumped the stripped and doorless cabinet frame. The plastic sheet taped in the door openings to protect the contents from sanding dust fluttered with her movements. The work before her that Saturday would tax her muscles, expand her endurance, and in so many ways remind her of the God who never slept and who did his best work in the depths of splintered souls.

She sank her hands into the pale brown dough. It yielded at her command. A tremble of pleasure coursed through her core. She invited the peace it promised, then stretched out the ends of the dough like wings and folded them over the center.

Pull, stretch, fold, roll, repeat. Her fingertips to stretch, the heel of her hand to roll. The sinews of her forearms came alive. In the kitchen, she had control, the power to bring something good from little, to change the unformed into something beautiful. It was as close to God as she might get.

Whoever had written the notebook must have known that sensation. The work—the next thing—and butter conspired to heal all wounds.

Pull, stretch, fold, roll. Until sticky became smooth. Until her muscles were stiff and the dough supple. "That's how you know you've done it right," Joyce had told her.

Nikki smiled. Her final batch of rolls was progressing better than the previous three.

She formed the dough into a ball and set it back in the glass bowl under a damp dish towel. Like unborn human life, bread needed a warm, draftless place and time to flourish. She tucked the bowl in the tall pantry cabinet and noted the time. An hour to proof. Time to fill with other healing work.

After scrubbing down the countertop and her hands, she took the cottage cheese tub with the last two potato pancakes and her phone and headed for her morning walk.

It had been more than a week since she had heard her mom's voice. Even longer since she had seen her face. As she crossed the living room, she called her mom. The other line connected the same moment the front door closed behind her.

"Hey, baby. How's it going?"

"Not bad." She paused on the porch to run her fingertips over the cabinet doors lying on the drop cloths. Dry as a bone. "How are things in Salina?"

"The big news here is I found a job."

"You did? Where?"

"At Hannah's church, in the daycare. I'm helping with the three-year-olds in the afternoons. I start next week."

"That's exciting. Congratulations."

"Thank you." Though her mom clearly tried to keep her tone upbeat, the notes of gray were strong.

A rumble of a truck. Trennen turned into the driveway. A country-rock song blasted through the open windows, as did Trennen's off-key singing. He drove past the farmhouse, completely absorbed in concert dreams.

"What are you up to?" her mom asked.

"This morning I'm baking bread."

"You are? Wow."

She chuckled and stepped onto the sidewalk. "I know. I'm legit. I also made some potato pancakes that went over well. At least the ones that didn't burn. Fried potatoes and I haven't fully come to terms yet."

"They can be tricky," her mom said. "Sounds like you're making great progress. Hopefully you're still enjoying being there."

"I am." Nikki's stomach reflexively clenched as she approached the end of the sidewalk. Echoes still resounded there. "Dad came to the farm last Sunday."

"He what?"

"Came despite Uncle Wes explicitly telling him I didn't want to see him. He said he needed to tell me his side of the story."

"Which was what?"

"He said you all hadn't been happy for a long time."

Her mom was quiet.

Nikki started to speak, to walk back any unintended hurt, but waited. She turned toward the pasture.

"He was right about that," her mom said after a moment. "We weren't happy."

Her feet slowed, soles dragging on the gravel. "I never saw it."

"You weren't there enough to see it, Nik. You were in school, then you had your job and Isaac and a whole life."

A life that now lay fractured. Nikki lowered her gaze to the dusty drive.

"The empty nest amplifies the gaps in a relationship," her mom said. "The gaps had become so much bigger than we realized. We had neglected too many things for too long. I tried to work on them, but it takes two. The more exhausted I became, the more I started shutting him out—and him, me. Your dad liked to think we were fine. He kept telling me I made too much of nothing. I don't think he knew how to handle it."

Nikki huffed. "He picked a fantastic alternative."

Quiet descended once more.

How many silent dinners had her mom endured? How many instances of her presence being ignored?

Nikki adjusted her grip on the cottage cheese tub. "Mom, what would you do if Dad showed up at your door tomorrow?"

"I really doubt he would do that."

"But what if he did?"

Her mom sighed. "I don't know. I'm not sure I could say anything."

Nikki crossed the county road. From his spot near the pond, Bonhoeffer tracked her progress. The innocent little guy knew nothing of the hard work of living and loving in the world.

"Would you be angry?" she asked.

"I would be confused. I'm confused now, but seeing him would make me more so."

"Why confused?"

"Because—" She stopped as if needing to pull the words together. "Because I don't know what he wants from me. What's worse, I don't know what I want from him. Does that make any sense?"

Bonhoeffer's hooves patted the ground as he trotted up to the gate, big eyes already on the tub, eager. A sweet spirit in a world bent on destruction.

"That makes perfect sense, Mom."

◆ ◆ ◆ ◆

Wes kept his eyes on the hitch of the baler and wiggled his uplifted fingers to Trennen in a "keep coming" motion.

Trennen eased the tractor backward until the tongue of the Massey slipped into the grip of the hitch. As soon as the connecting holes began to align, Wes flashed the stop signal, though

Trennen didn't need the help necessarily. Boys who learned to captain tractors at age ten had the honed instincts of a veteran farmer by twenty.

Trennen cut the engine and came around to the back of the tractor. "Going to be a hot one today. You can already feel it."

Wes slid the hitch pin through the connecting holes and secured it into place. "Your boys bringing water jugs? Got extra in the house if they need them."

"I told them to, so they should. But I also told them to be here by eight thirty."

"What time is it now?"

"Eight twenty-nine." Trennen grinned. "Kids these days."

"Kids in every day, son." He knelt beside the hitch, his back to Trennen, and turned the crank on the jack. With each revolution, the hitch lowered onto the tongue. Before long, the full weight of the baler rested solely on the connection between the two.

"I'm sure they'll be here soon," Trennen said. "Until then, looks like we have other company."

Wes twisted to Trennen, who nodded toward the house. Nikki approached, carrying a plate.

"Wonder what she's got," Trennen said.

Wes rotated the jack up to storage position against the hitch frame. He had it pinned in place before Nikki reached them.

"Morning," she said.

"Morning," they answered in unison.

Wes rose and brushed off his hands. Four halves of rolls slathered in butter rested on the plate.

"Thought you might like a preview of lunch," she said. "I made these rolls for your sandwiches."

"Don't mind if I do." Trennen grabbed a half in each hand and wasted no time diving in.

She grinned, one of the few smiles she'd shown for several days.

Wes took the remaining two halves and pressed the butter sides together. "Thank you, Nik."

The crusty exterior gave way to a pillowy inside made sweet-creamy by the generous globs of butter. Huck Finn Dinette's rolls weren't nearly as sublime.

"These are so good!" Trennen said around his mouthful.

"Glad you like them," Nikki said. "There'll be plenty more for lunch. Are you still thinking you'll break around noon?"

"Hoping to," Trennen said. "If loading goes as planned."

"Joyce and I will shoot for noon too, then. Thanks for letting us use your kitchen, Uncle Wes. The farmhouse is basically one big drop cloth at this point."

"Yeah, sure." Quickly he bit into his roll to hide anything else that might come out.

Joyce had been in his house briefly, but not for an extended period, not long enough to learn her way around his cabinets, learn where he kept the pot holders and the extra trash bags. Inch by inch, she moved into his life.

Nikki tucked the empty plate against her side. "I better get going. Joyce will be here about eleven, and I want to keep sanding the cabinets until then. Good luck this morning, guys." She started to walk away, then paused and asked over her shoulder, "Uncle Wes, can Bonhoeffer eat a roll?"

Trennen looked between them, brow pinched.

"Maybe chunk it up," Wes replied.

That brought another grin to her face, and she continued on to the house.

"Who's Bonhoeffer?" Trennen asked when she was out of earshot.

"The calf."

The furrow deepened to a full frown. "She feeds people food to a bull?"

He shrugged and took another bite of his roll. "Doesn't hurt him, and it makes her happy. She needs that."

"Why?"

He tapped the side of his roll. "Because family can be rough."

Curiosity cut across Trennen's expression.

226

Wes directed them to another topic. "Having the vet come out next week to cut Bon—I mean, the calf."

Trennen chuckled at the slip. "So you're keeping him? Doing the steer thing?"

"Thought I'd give it another go."

"Is this Nikki's influence?"

"That a bad thing?"

"Not at all." Trennen wadded up the rest of his first roll half and chewed it. "Does she know what you have in store next week for her little friend?"

"Does it worry you?"

"She feeds him from the table, Wes."

He tore off more roll. "I think she can handle it."

Trennen lifted his eyebrows. "If you say so. But one thing I've learned about women is they can be fiercely protective of what they love."

Protective. Like Joyce of his family. She loved them almost as much as he did. And the very sparkle of it in her eyes flinted a strange sensation within him.

He blew the air from his lungs, chasing the sensation away. "Hook up the moisture gauge. We got more work to do."

Trennen pursed his lips, clearly onto Wes's maneuvering. He folded his remaining roll half lengthwise, shoved it into his mouth whole, then got busy.

◆　◆　◆　◆

Nikki paused in the yard with the tray of sandwiches in her hands as the hay crew trundled up the driveway. Trennen drove the tractor in low gear, careful not to sway the seemingly precarious train behind him too much. The baler was first in line, then three flatbed wagons loaded with precise stacks of pale greenish bales.

Uncle Wes followed in his truck with the two teen boys in the bed.

"How do they get the bales stacked so high?" Nikki asked.

227

Joyce looked up from the food table they had set up in the massive pool of oak tree shade. "It's an art form." She pushed the bowl of chilled apple slices closer to the sweating water bottles to make room for the sandwich tray. Nikki slid it into place.

The crew proceeded to the large white barn at the end of the drive.

"How much do those bales weigh?" Nikki asked.

"Each one? Fifty, sixty pounds or so."

Her jaw fell. The math was staggering. Fifty times all those bales. "That sounds exhausting." Suddenly the spread of sliders, chips, and apples seemed too minuscule to offset the crew's expended energy. "Do we have enough food?" she asked.

Joyce set a stack of paper plates at the edge of the table. "They won't want to eat much. Heavy meals and heavy labor in the heat don't mix. What we have is right."

Cool food. Cool drinks. Salty ham and chips to replace sodium. All the things Joyce advised they prepare. The science and precision demanded of farmers extended to the food they ate.

In that one small way, Nikki was helping keep the food supply churning, an experience the mothers before her knew by heart.

By the time she and Joyce had the blankets spread on the soft grass for the guys to lie down on if they wanted, the crew had arrived at the hydrant next to the garage. Even from a distance, the specks of chaff sticking to their clothes and skin were visible. Each crew member took a turn at the hydrant, rinsing off his arms and splashing his face. Trennen soaked his cap under the water and slung it over his head. The teen boys followed his example.

They approached the lunch spot as a group. The teens eventually broke for the food while Trennen and Uncle Wes came over to the women, each carrying two water jugs.

"Need refills?" Joyce stepped forward to meet them.

"Please," Wes said.

She took all four jugs, then handed two to Nikki. She had warned Nikki that the guys would not want to go into the air-conditioning and then back into the heat, the adjustment too hard on their bodies. Whatever they needed from the house, the two of them would take care of.

"How'd it go?" Joyce asked.

"Some twine issues with the first few bales, but eventually we got cranking," Trennen said. The front of his shirt was soaked with a mixture of hydrant water and sweat. Streams from his cap traced through his hair and down his neck. "Not getting as many bales per acre as I'd hoped, but I still think I'll end up with at least five hundred. Got just under half of that on the wagons now."

"Think you'll finish the field today, then?" Joyce asked.

"If the boys can keep working as hard as they have been." Trennen nodded at the two teens already settling onto the blankets with plates. "Maybe they'll be less talkative this afternoon too."

"Teen boys are talkative?" Nikki laughed. "Not at my school."

"These two are," he replied. "Gabbed nonstop about sports and some Netflix show, but especially about the Young Farmers dance and which girl they think they can fool into going with them."

Joyce laughed. "I'm surprised any guy would be so eager for a dance." Her eyes drifted to Uncle Wes, who quickly looked at his boots.

"Oh boy," Trennen muttered in the direction of the teens. One of them shoved virtually an entire slider into his mouth. "I better go tell them to slow down before they make themselves sick. Thanks again for the food, ladies."

Uncle Wes nodded in agreement, then he fell in behind Trennen.

Joyce smiled after them, the joy of provision written all over her face. For the first time, Nikki understood it too.

Joyce waved her toward the house. "Let's fill up these jugs."

"What's this dance he was talking about?" Nikki asked as they headed for the front door.

"The Young Farmers group in Redmont hosts a dance every Fourth of July. It's a big community thing. They provide meat, then everyone brings a dish. The electric co-op your uncle and I are on the board of helps sponsor it. He hasn't mentioned it?"

Nikki shook her head. "He's one of the non-excited guys, apparently."

Joyce laughed. "He's never been big on dances. Ada had to twist his arm to go to our senior prom."

"You knew Ada?"

"Of course. She was a friend of mine. In fact, she helped me out quite a bit the night of prom."

"How so?"

They climbed the porch steps, and Joyce opened the door. "My date stood me up. Ada insisted that I still go, and she rounded up girls who were willing to lend their dates for a dance with me."

"That's sweet. Was Uncle Wes one of them?"

Joyce closed the door behind them. "He was. Begrudgingly, but he was. For a slow dance, believe it or not."

"No way! Uncle Wes slow-dancing?"

Joyce giggled. "He can be a surprising guy."

They crossed the living room into the kitchen. Joyce screwed the lids off the jugs she carried and restocked them with ice.

"So are you going to the dance?" Nikki asked.

"I plan to. I'm bringing pie." As she finished with each jug, she handed it to Nikki, who took it to the sink to fill with water. The ice cubes cracked as they bathed in the cascade.

"Maybe I could make one of the recipes for the dance," Nikki said. "And convince Uncle Wes to come with me."

"I bet he would if you wanted him to."

Her assertion said something about his view of Nikki. As the next jug filled with water, she peeked over at her friend. If it was true she had such persuasion over her uncle, then perhaps she could use it to repay the woman who had invested so much in her—and him.

"Maybe I could convince Uncle Wes to break out his dancing skills too." She cut off the water and turned to Joyce. "For anyone who may be interested."

Joyce flashed a small smile. "Now that *would* be surprising."

Twenty-Six

Tuesday, June 25, 1:17 p.m.
To: Aunt Emma
From: Nikki
Subject: Books and baby animals

Aunt Emma

Sorry it's been so long. I've reread your email a couple of different times, absorbing it all. I have so much to say in response, but I had to narrow it down.

The more I know about Grandma Ann, the more I relate to her in ways I didn't anticipate. Like the love for baby animals. We had, at most, a dog growing up, so I haven't been around a lot of animals until now. Uncle Wes has the sweetest little bull calf that Grandma Ann would have loved too. We've named him Bonhoeffer (I assume you get the reference). Uncle Wes plans to keep the calf and raise him as a steer. You'll forgive me, but I didn't realize what "steer" entailed until Uncle Wes said the vet was coming to the farm in a couple of days. Funny how you hear words all the time and yet not understand the implications of them. Eddner has taught me a lot of good things, but it's also revealed to me my ignorance in so much.

Your stories of Grandma Ann are a treasure. Thank you for opening up her life to me like this. I wish I would have gotten the chance to cook with her. I keep a picture on the counter of Great-Grandma holding Grandma as a baby, and I like to pretend they are watching over me as I cook. But it's not the same. Some things don't translate over the gap. Kind of like trying to understand these German books I found. Though I can get a somewhat muddled English translation, it's not the same as possessing the language. Things get lost in the in-between.

But I'll gladly take what version I can get! The most important pieces do transcend time and culture.

You asked for pictures of the notebook. I'm including those. You'll see the inside and outside of it. I also included pictures of the German books. Does any of it look familiar?

Thank you for your prayers. I appreciate them greatly. Things at home are a big mess. Not only with my parents but also with my boyfriend, Isaac. I don't know what's ahead in either case. One of the proverbs in the notebook says that no matter what's ahead, we can trust God for contentment. That's what I aim to do. Trust God, and welcome peace into this little farmhouse. How's that for shaping my life?

I am thankful for this summer in Eddner. Every day I find a new reason to relish it.

All my love,

Nikki

Nikki smiled and laid her phone on the coffee table. Every word she had written to Aunt Emma was true. In particular, the last line.

It had been more than a week since her dad's unwelcome visit, and the aftershocks of it had finally subsided. Finally, she had found her peace again. She cranked up the radio, sang along to the songs that had already seeped into her muscle memory, and continued to prime the kitchen cabinets.

She had work, she had peace, she had a dance to look forward to. She had faith that she could lay down every worry about anyone and everything outside the warm cocoon of Eddner.

That is, until hours later, when she checked her email again.

Tuesday, June 25, 9:13 p.m.
To: Nikki
From: Chris
Subject: In case it helps

Nikki—

I don't know if this will help, but I thought I'd share a few memories of Eddner. Maybe they would be of interest to you.

We used to have summer baseball tournaments. They were one Saturday each month in June, July, and August, out on the ball diamond that used to be behind the schoolhouse. You might still be able to see the field where it was. Have Uncle Wes show you.

Churches from all over the area would come play against each other, morning to dusk. We didn't have lights on the field, so we started as soon as the sun came up and played until we couldn't see the ball anymore.

The people would bring fruit from their gardens and trees to sell as snacks, and the Ladies' Aid would make sandwiches to sell. Your Uncle Wes played center field, and I was third baseman—"the hot corner," it's called. We were both decent hitters. Uncle Wes once hit a liner into the stomach of an opposing player, who also happened to be that church's vicar. Wes was convinced the vicar would call down the wrath of heaven for that, but the vicar assured him that heaven was too busy laughing at his poor reflexes.

Grandpa was an umpire. He was crazy about baseball. You'd never met a crazier baseball nut. His father really encouraged him to play. Perhaps it helped prove his American loyalty. Either way, Grandpa bled dirt. Baseball was one of the few topics he and I could talk about easily. It might have been the only topic.

I'm not sure when those tournaments started, but I think it was during the Depression. They ended sometime in the 1990s, around the time the school closed for good, which I believe was 1992.

For what it's worth, that's my favorite memory.

Dad

◆　◆　◆　◆

Wes wriggled the pry bar, coaxing loose the finishing nails securing the baseboard to the kitchen wall. The gap widened enough for him to thread his fingers in and pop the board clean from its spot. It was the only sound in the kitchen, save for the whispered swish of Nikki's paintbrush against the upper cabinet frames.

The radio was cloaked in silence, and so was she.

He penciled a sequence number on the back of the board and added it to the pile next to the table. Over by the stove, Nikki splayed a snowy tone over the primed wood frame, her mouth turned down at the ends. Something had clearly happened, though she had insisted she was "fine."

The morning progressed with the dulled concordance of pops and swishes.

At noon, they broke for lunch and went up to the new house. Nikki sat at the breakfast bar with a plate of leftover sliders and chips. Wes set his plate on the other side and remained standing, his back and knees grateful for the extra time in the straightened posture.

Chewing and crunching replaced the noises of their kitchen work. The shadow still slung itself across her face. It couldn't go on like this.

He gathered his breath, then pushed out the words he had entombed all morning. "I can tell something's wrong."

The directness drew her eyes to him. At first, irritation showed back. Then, slowly, a surrender. Like she was caught in a searchlight and too tired to run.

"I suppose I should stop hiding. It's the grown-up thing to do, right?"

He tore off a bite of sandwich and nodded. He wasn't much better at the art of vulnerability, though.

She picked up a chip, tapped the edge against her plate. "My dad emailed me last night."

Wes paused mid-chew.

She took her phone from her pocket, opened to the message, then slid her phone across the bar, a silent invitation to take and read.

He did. Every word. His chest tightened.

"Of all the things he could say to me right now, why does he think I care about some dumb baseball tournament?"

Wes wrapped his free hand around the glass of water next to his plate. He was halfway between drinking and eating, halfway between keeping quiet and pointing out the parts she'd missed about the email. Chris should have apologized, no question. Should have made more of an effort to approach her humbly. But one thing stood out more.

Baseball was Chris's safe topic, his go-to when he was too uncertain to talk about anything else. It was a bid for connection with her, as it had been for Chris with their father. Those tournaments were the only days Chris reliably received a nod of approval from him.

Nikki did not seem to pick up on the reference her dad had made. Or the between-the-lines olive branch he had extended with an undoubtedly trembling hand.

"He thinks he can jump in and out of my life at any point." Her eyes narrowed at her plate, as if her dad's face showed back to her there. "I didn't even know he knew my email address."

She had a right to be upset. But she had a need to understand.

His Bible still rested at the end of the bar, where he had left it that morning between his quiet time on the porch and his oatmeal. The ribbon bookmark held the place where his mind had been centered as the new day emerged. The place where Paul reminded the drifting Ephesians that they were "created to be like God" and to start acting like it. A dressing down wrapped in love, in heartbreak over their blindness.

Wes tapped the side of his glass. For weeks he had prayed for the wise words to speak. There they were. Direct from the Father's own mind.

"Nik, uh . . ." Tap, tap. "May I say something?"

She fiddled with her sandwich. "Sure."

His pulse quickened. "It's not right, what your dad did. He was wrong. But he's also very lost."

She huffed. "Glaringly so."

The bitterness burned his ears. He laid her phone on the countertop and stuffed both hands into his pockets. "By lost, I mean faith. He has wandered off the path to the Father. That's what shows." His pulse thundered. "But you haven't."

She righted, met his gaze straight. "Is this a lecture?"

"An encouragement."

Her jaw flexed. "You're telling me I should forgive him."

"No."

"Then what?"

He cleared his throat. His voice was sure as he spoke. "I'm asking you to be the image of God."

Stark silence. The sound of a loving rebuke hitting square.

Nikki looked away, closed her mouth into a tight line.

Pain could be a security, hard to surrender, practically an identity. But if she were ever to know the height and depth and width and breadth of the mercy in which she was awash, she needed to give mercy too.

If only she knew how much he spoke from experience.

Suddenly she rose. "Excuse me." She left her nearly full plate next to the sink and returned to the farmhouse.

She finished painting the cabinet frames in less than two days.

◆　◆　◆　◆

Saturday, June 29, 7:45 a.m.
To: Nikki
From: Aunt Emma
Subject: RE: Books and baby animals

Nikki, my love—

You never have to apologize for needing time to think before you write. The most prudent people think before they speak. It shows compassion and discipline. So, go you. I wish I was better at it.

I certainly do get the reference in the calf's name. Dietrich Bonhoeffer was—is—a modern hero of the faith. He wrote great books too, so get you some of those. *The Cost of Discipleship* is considered a classic.

Speaking of books, I recognize all the German books in the pictures you sent. Wes told me about them a while back, and I wondered if they were the ones I grew up seeing on my grandmother's shelf. Sure enough, they are! I figured her books were long gone, much like most of her things. Interesting what people hang on to and what they choose to leave behind.

As for the notebook, there is zero question in my mind that it is in my mother's handwriting. Absolutely zero. She had a certain way of writing her capital *E*'s. I would know her *E* anywhere, having come to love the way she scrawled my first initial. Oh, what a treasure you have found! Gives me goose bumps.

I have not seen my mother's handwriting in so long. Seeing it now makes this old woman's heart throb with homesickness. A child never truly leaves childhood.

What strikes me is the date in the picture of the opening message—1951. I did a little math, which is the only amount of math I can stomach, and I realized that year, 1951, Ann would have been about thirteen, the age she was confirmed or about to be confirmed. I forget exactly when she was.

Why is that a detail you should know? Well, you may be aware of this about synod churches, but confirmation is, among other things, the rite through which a child is seen as an adult in the eyes of the church. I don't know my mother's true motivation for penning such a treasure, but if I had to guess, I would say it was for Ann as a confirmation gift.

It was a way for Mother to welcome her to womanhood and lead her into living as a woman of faith. It would not surprise me one speck on a fly's wing that Mother wanted to teach her the practicals of life as well as about our German heritage, which had taken a beating after two world wars.

Sadly, I don't think Ann paid the lessons or the notebook much heed. At least not when she was younger. She believed Mother wanted her to be things she wasn't meant to be. Age and experience showed her differently, though. Mother only wanted to share the pieces of herself that she felt could help Ann the most. That's what every parent wants.

It's what people like Dietrich Bonhoeffer want too. Let's circle back to him for a quick second.

You may know this too if you've looked him up, but he was executed in a Nazi concentration camp days before the camp was liberated. He continued to write while imprisoned. One of the things he wrote sticks with me to this day. He said, "Nothing that we despise in other men is inherently absent from ourselves. We must learn to regard people less in the light of what they do or don't do and more in the light of what they suffer." I had to google that to ensure I got it right. Quite a statement from quite a circumstance. Do with it what you will.

Off to bocce. Tournament play this week. Then the ladies and I are heading to the rodeo for the Fourth. I plan to sit front row for the bull riding. That's my favorite. What are your plans?

Giddyup,

Aunt Emma

◆   ◆   ◆   ◆

The days had lengthened noticeably, the sun rising earlier than it had when Nikki first arrived at the farmhouse. By the time she eased into her car, the heat of the new day gave clear warning to its intentions of setting the earth ablaze. The week bridging June to July would be another hot one.

She drove down the county road with her hand out her open window. Airstreams slipped through her fingers like invisible sand.

When she came over the hill at Eddner, she turned to the cemetery and the wreath-adorned graves. The notebook surely was a gift of significant cost, particularly in the writing of it because no writer penned anything perfectly the first time, or necessarily in sequential order. How many drafts had been written? How many scribbles on spare pieces of paper and hours claimed to get the words just so, to accumulate the research needed and find the most befitting verses? It was a deeply personal gift, and one originally received with typical teenage indifference. It had garnered no more excitement for its irreplaceable value than *The Adventures of Huckleberry Finn* usually garnered from a classroom of sophomores assigned to read it.

Something had clearly triggered a mind shift for Grandma Ann. "Age and experience," Aunt Emma had said. Perhaps that meant motherhood.

The cemetery gave way to the small cornfield before the schoolyard. Maybe that was where the ball field once was, the site of recess games and tournaments.

What a sight tournament days must have been. Crowds gathered along the edges. Smaller children scrambling around the playground as the adults and older boys competed. Her dad, ready at third, pumping his fist into his glove. T-shirt and jeans clean and crisp, because that was the way Grandma Ann would have sent him onto the diamond. Maybe he smiled. Maybe he cheered for his teammates or chanted or taunted, all in good fun. Maybe he had the time of his life. Maybe he was unrecognizable to the daughter who knew him decades later.

What was it about baseball that brought out the exuberance in him? Why didn't his family elicit that kind of reaction anymore?

She turned away from the field, rolled up her windows, and focused on the drive ahead.

She was nearly to the highway exit for Redmont when a call

from Tracy rang on her phone. She accepted it on speakerphone. "Tracy! What a nice surprise."

"Thought I'd check in."

"I'm glad you did. How's your summer going?"

"The Royals are disappointing me, but what else is new?" Her laugh was a small, sweet taste of what was good about Nikki's Kansas City life. "I haven't gotten any calls or texts. I'm hoping that's a good sign and your summer on the farm is beyond expectation."

Nikki's grin shrank. "It's definitely not what I expected. Good and not so good."

"That sounds like a whole conversation. Let's have it."

Just like that, a Gab and Grace session began, Nikki gabbing about all the events of the last month and Tracy gracefully listening. They covered her mom's sped-up move to Salina, Isaac's ignoring of her text message for thirty-one days and counting, her dad's brazen appearance first on the farm and then in her inbox.

"That's a hefty bad news category," Tracy said. "Please tell me there's even more in the good news."

"It's a long list," Nikki said. She turned onto the cozy stretch of Main Street, which took her past the high school and then between the historic homes and storefronts decked in patriotic bunting. As her wheels turned, so did her report, through the German books, the aprons, and the notebook. Through the cooking sessions with Joyce and the evasive art of frying potatoes evenly. Through the stories that brought Grandma Ann and her world to vivid life. And finally, through the email exchanges with a great-aunt she'd only previously known by name.

"Sounds like you have gained quite a bit," Tracy said.

"More than I could have seen, which is exactly what you said would happen, you future teller."

"More like a life liver or an experience haver. We usually do find the right information when we need it most."

Nikki slowed to turn into the County Mart parking lot and waited for a truck pulling a cattle trailer to pass. Aunt Emma's claim about Dietrich Bonhoeffer's view of people resurfaced. "Tracy, can I ask you something?"

"Shoot."

She turned into the lot. "Do you think we should look at people in light of their actions or in light of what they have suffered?"

"Can't it be both?"

"If you had to choose one." She pulled into a spot and shifted into park.

"I suppose suffering can beget action, so I'd say suffering. At least that's what they tell us in those PD seminars on trauma-informed teaching, right? We all have subconscious or conscious ways we interact with what's around us, informed by what's happened to us."

Nikki turned off the engine and pulled the keys into her palm. "But at what point does someone become responsible for their own actions and it's no longer the suffering talking?"

Tracy was quiet a moment, a sure sign her teacher mind worked over the concept. At last she replied, "I'd have to say when they understand enough about themselves to see the connection." She added with noticeable jest, "Or when the Holy Spirit knocks the revelation into them."

Nikki grinned and pulled her purse from the passenger seat. "We can only hope for either."

"That's right. For them and for us."

The addition hooked into her.

"So how are you spending the Fourth?" Tracy's question cut Nikki away from her pondering.

She followed her friend into lighter topics. As she shopped, she told Tracy about the dance and the dish she planned to make and the freedom she intended to find from all the drama, if only for a day.

But carried in the undertow was the echo: *For them and for us.*

Twenty-Seven

Monday, July 1, 7:53 a.m.
To: Chris
From: Wes
Subject: I should have said it sooner

Chris—

I would normally call you, but I have so much to say, and I wanted to ensure I said it correctly and completely.

First, thank you for emailing Nikki a story. Though I doubt she has replied, I assure you she read it. Would you consider sending her more? Even if she doesn't reply to any of them? The more she reads, the more she will know you. The more you share, I believe the more you'll also see how much you have to give her, how much you have to no longer hide. She needs you. You need her.

Second, when you were here, you asked me if I knew what it was like to never be what's desired. The question has plagued me ever since. Chris, you didn't get all you needed growing up. We had a good but flawed father. That, we can both agree on. Those flaws can be awfully loud when they want to be, even today. They bore deep holes into you. But what you need to fill those holes cannot be found in the places you're looking, with the people you're choosing.

You won't find what's missing by trying a new city or a new home or a new relationship.

The good news is father hurt can be covered by the Father's love, if you accept it. I'm being more direct with you than I have been. I love you too much to not speak the truth. Please hear it for what it is.

"I keep asking that the God of our Lord Jesus Christ, the glorious Father, may give you the Spirit of wisdom and revelation, so that you may know him better. I pray that the eyes of your heart may be enlightened in order that you may know the hope to which he has called you" (Eph. 1:17–18).

Your brother,

Wes

◆ ◆ ◆ ◆

Scalloped Potatoes (Kartoffelgratin)

Light is the head that retains no ill thought toward others, that lets an offense pass by. Soft is the bed of the one who is free from the heft of bitterness. Like the grainy starch of a potato softened in a bath of butter, let vexations melt from your grasp. They are not yours to hold. They are not yours to wield. "Say not thou, I will recompense evil; but wait on the Lord, and he shall save thee" (Prov. 20:22). Though evil closes in on every side, still his mercy will not fail you. Through slings and arrows, he is your shield, your hiding place, your freedom incomparable. Lay down the bitterness and trust the Lord's protecting arm to save you.

Butter
1½ cups fresh cream
Pinch salt

Pinch garlic powder

Pinch ground nutmeg

Pepper

5 potatoes, peeled

1 cup Swiss cheese

Slice potatoes thin, about ⅛ inch. Generously butter a rectangular baking dish. Spread potato slices evenly in dish. In small saucepan, combine cream and seasonings. Bring to brief boil, then simmer for 1 minute. Pour cream over potatoes. Sprinkle with cheese and dot top with cubes of butter. Bake at 375 degrees until fork-tender, about 45 minutes. Let cool, then slice and serve.

◆ ◆ ◆ ◆

The sesquicentennial memorial hall sat at the top of the county fairgrounds' midway like a long, brown beacon to local revelers. Wes had been to many of the community events hosted in the "sesqui" building, from wedding receptions to 4-H shows to parties. It seemed large enough to hold half of Redmont, and on Fourth of July night, it nearly did.

Hundreds of people milled among the two columns of folding tables adorned with plastic tablecloths. The main aisle in between spilled into the open area on the other end of the hall with a portable wood-tile dance floor and a DJ booth.

A Luke Bryan song thrummed from the elevated speakers strategically located at each corner of the dance floor. A disco ball hung dead center, suspended from a chain affixed to the wood rafters above.

"This is fantastic!" Nikki's smile was wider than the pan of scalloped potatoes in her hands.

To their left, the line of food tables snaked along one side of the hall. The side doors stood open to the barrel grills outside. The aroma of salty meat slowly caramelizing over hickory chips wafted in. Men with longneck bottles and shiny tongs worked the grills as tendrils of smoke curled above their heads. Inside the commercial kitchen, volunteers in red aprons buzzed about, dishing finished meat into large metal serving pans.

"I'm going to find a spot for my dish," Nikki said and stepped through the crowd.

People continued to flow through the main doors behind Wes. The excitement grew. One night to blow off steam and everyone seemed determined to do just that. Children darted between groups of chatting parents. A few people said hello to him as they passed or stopped to shake his hand. Then suddenly Joyce was beside him, two foil-wrapped pie tins in her hands. Even in a crowd, she found her way to him.

She smiled. "Quite a turnout, isn't it?"

He nodded. "It's full."

"Where's Nikki?"

"Somewhere over there." He pointed toward the food tables. "Setting down her potatoes."

"Hopefully they turned out okay. I was sad to miss out on helping. Did you get a taste already?"

"Wouldn't let me."

"Did you try?"

"Chased me away with a fork."

She laughed. The way her eyes gleamed stirred up a feeling in his gut that he wished away. He shoved his hands into his pockets.

Around them swirled the crowd of their neighbors and friends, people they had known all their lives and who had known them. Likely too much about them as of late.

"So," Joyce said, "any update on Nikki and Chris?"

"He emailed her a story about Eddner."

"That's great. A step forward."

He nodded.

"Want me to take pictures tonight and post them?" She clearly had not forgotten the mission. It was still hers as much as his. Women were fiercely protective of what they loved.

The sensation bloomed again in his gut. "If you want."

Nikki returned, relieving him of the need to say anything more. The two women greeted each other with happy chatter about "how exciting" the night was going to be.

"That reminds me," Joyce said, "there is someone I wanted to introduce you to. She knew your grandma." She turned to Wes and held out the pies. "Do you mind taking these to the dessert table?"

"Uh, sure."

Their hands grazed in the exchange of the tins. The touch drew his eyes to hers. The heat of her soft hazel gaze traced down his chest. The lock lasted only a moment before Joyce turned to walk away, but it was long enough to kindle the sensation a third time.

"I'll be back," Nikki said over her shoulder as she walked beside Joyce toward the main aisle.

Joyce had pinned her hair into an updo with several perfect curls spiraling down to the nape of her bare neck. Her long, flowy skirt swayed with the swing of her hips. Every movement radiated grace. Wholly mesmerizing. Completely—

Trennen's stare caught his attention.

The young man stood a few paces away. He looked at Joyce, then at Wes. A goofy grin quickly spread across his face. He wiggled his eyebrows.

Wes opened his mouth to say something, but there was no defense. Trennen had seen what he had seen.

Quickly Wes turned and headed for the buffet line.

◆ ◆ ◆ ◆

Conversations flowed around Nikki as easily as the soda and beer. The hall hummed from the effects, carried on the seemingly inherent friendship that bonded small-town life together. Everyone in the building shared food from their own kitchens and laughter from their own joy. Easy and relaxed. An intoxicating air of not caring that yesterday had been filled with worry and tomorrow would meet them with more. For as long as it was night, they feasted, letting "vexations melt."

God help her, Nikki would join them and find a "freedom incomparable," whatever that entailed, starting with food.

After loading their plates, she and Joyce claimed seats several rows from the dance floor. Joyce sat with her back to the floor. Nikki sat opposite her, reserving the chair next to her for Uncle Wes. Eventually he made his way to them, plate in hand.

It took nearly the entire meal for Nikki to relay to him all she and Joyce had learned about Grandma Ann from Otis Harman's wife, Barb. Specifically about her young womanhood years tucked between graduation and marriage.

"Did you know she worked in an egg factory?" she asked him at the end.

He ate the last of his pulled pork and shook his head. "Knew she worked some, but not at a factory."

"Mrs. Harman said the factory paid women the highest wages of all local employers. And Grandma was trying to save up as much as she could. She and Mrs. Harman and a couple of other girls had hopes of getting a place together."

"Can you imagine what that would have meant to them if they had?" Joyce asked. "Girls today take such things for granted."

"Take what for granted?" Trennen slid sideways through the row of seated diners near Joyce.

"Freedom," Nikki told him.

"Don't we all." He plopped into the empty chair across from her.

"Speaking of free." Joyce looked at him. "No date tonight?"

"Nah, flying solo. Even my parents skipped out on me. They went to Minnesota to see my aunt for a week."

"Why didn't you go with them?" Nikki asked.

"Can't. It's wheat harvest time. I'm baling up a few fields for some guys this weekend after they're done combining."

"From hay to straw," Uncle Wes said.

Trennen shrugged. "Fun never ends."

"Just be careful." Joyce aimed her plastic fork at him. "The heat is supposed to be worse the next few days."

He waved away the concern. "Won't be any worse than any other July." He turned to Nikki. "How you liking your first Young Farmers dance?"

"It's definitely not like anything in KC," she said. "I like it."

"She made these potatoes." Joyce pointed the tines at what remained of her serving.

Trennen shook his head. "Should've known those were yours, Nikki. They were like silk. Well, if silk was creamy."

She chuckled. "Thank you." Though clumsy, his description was accurate. The cream-butter bath had softened the potato slices to a smooth, melt-on-the-tongue state. If any were left after the dance, she would devour them on the way back to the farm.

"I have a question for you, Nikki." Trennen folded his hands and leaned on the table. "We know you can cook, but can you dance?"

"You mean line dance?"

"Yeah. The party's about to start in full." He jutted his thumb over his shoulder toward the dance floor. "What kind of steps you got?"

They all watched her reaction, smiles beginning to form. She was clearly headed for something.

"I do like dancing," she admitted, "but I can't say I've ever line danced."

Waggishness welled in his expression. "That so?" He rose.

"Where are you going?" Joyce asked.

"You'll see." He winked at Nikki and made his way to the main aisle, then the DJ booth.

"Should I be worried?" Nikki asked.

Uncle Wes and Joyce exchanged a look. Then, in unison, they replied, "Probably."

◆　◆　◆

If Nikki had a single fret left, it didn't show on the dance floor. Her heartache was flung away with every spin, and her pain was heel-toed into submission. From the moment the DJ kicked off the dancing portion of the evening, Trennen ensured that Nikki was surrounded with people her own age, ladies to lock her arms with and guys to mirror. They scooted and slid as the strobe lights reflected off the disco ball and shot across the dimmed hall.

Under the table, Wes tapped his toe in time to the beat as he worked through his second slice of cake. The covert move was the most dancing he planned to do.

Joyce returned to her spot with her phone in hand and a victorious look on her face. "You have to see these photos," she said over the music. She sat and slid her phone toward his plate.

The screen displayed a collection of candids that spoke of the reprieve playing out mere yards away. Nikki with one leg swung upward and arm raised. One with her hair flying free as she twisted. One with her elbow linked into another young woman's as they circled. In each photo, her delight was broad and unmistakable.

Joyce leaned closer. "Doesn't she look amazing? Pure bliss!"

He grinned. Nikki had never been more lovely. He handed the phone back to its owner. "Those're great."

"She's inspiring, Wes. She's absorbed herself in this place. It's made me see Eddner differently in the process. Strange how you can be around something all your life and suddenly get new eyes for it." Her gaze centered on him.

The knotted sensation roused. Quickly he nodded and returned to his cake. She put away her phone and turned in her chair to watch the dancers beneath the bright lights.

Many years before, he and Joyce had been among such a crowd, in a high school gym decorated to look like the sea floor. Life had taken them such different directions since school, and yet, in the end, to the same destination.

Two songs later, Nikki reclaimed her seat next to Wes and grabbed her half-empty water bottle. Her forehead glistened, and her hair stuck to her temples. "I'm parched!"

"You look like you're having a good time," Joyce said.

Nikki nodded and gulped down the contents of her bottle. After the last swallow, she sighed contentedly. "Trennen's hard to keep up with. I don't know where he gets the energy."

"Youthful exuberance," Joyce replied.

"Must be. Are you going to get out there?" She pointed her empty bottle at Joyce.

"Me, do that? Goodness, no. I'd throw my back out." Her chuckle carried over the din, as bold as the woman she had become. No longer the wallflower of childhood. No longer the girl who hung back while others spoke and adventured.

"Maybe they haven't played your song yet," Nikki countered.

"Yes, I'm sure that's it." Even in the low light, Joyce's eyes shone. Amazing how they did that.

Out on the dance floor, the song churned, the lights throbbed, the crescendo built. The dancers kicked and swirled, spun and swayed, all the way to the tune's final chords. Cheers and whoops erupted from the floor. Joyce and Nikki joined in the clapping.

Wes stacked his own empty water bottle onto his bare plate and checked his watch. One hour until fireworks.

"All right, folks," the DJ said into his microphone. "We're about to slow things down for a bit. Grab your favorite partner. It's time for a Bob Seger classic."

A slow, aching piano riff looped from the speakers. Familiar. Reminiscent.

A few bars in, the memory unlocked. His breath caught.

Joyce's gaze drifted to his. By the way she enveloped him with that stare, it was obvious she remembered too.

Of all the songs the DJ could have chosen.

Every note revived a new detail of a long-ago scene. Her hand lying upon his shoulder, her feet shyly following his as Seger promised "we've got tonight" and Ada looked on, triumphant.

Nikki glanced between them. "You all know this song?"

Joyce lowered her chin, looking up at him from under her brows. "We danced to it at prom."

Nikki turned to him, a pointedness to her expression.

"That was a long time ago, wasn't it, Wes?"

His hands found his water bottle. He dug his fingernail into a groove along the side.

Joyce looked away, toward the couples floating on the floor.

Nikki bumped her knee against his, drawing his attention. She lifted one eyebrow, saying everything she couldn't say aloud. *Ask her.*

Heat rose to his face. Inch by inch, Joyce had found her way closer, deeper into his life, even in ways he thought were forgotten.

Dig, dig into the groove of the bottle.

Nikki watched him, waited. Her expression pleaded, *Do this for me.* The way Ada's had.

His duty was to keep Nikki's laughter bubbling, to protect her night of freedom from worry. Regardless how much the ask cost him. He could do it. He needed to do it. He couldn't face Aunt Emma unless he did do it.

He removed his hands from the bottle. Licked his dry lips. "Joyce."

His call brought those shining eyes back to him.

"Would you, uh, would you like . . ."

Mercifully, she didn't require him to finish. She nodded, smile already spreading. "I'd love to." She rose from her chair with regality.

Slowly he stood, stomach knotting.

Seger's vocals marched into the refrain. Wes slipped down the narrow space between the chairs as Joyce moved in parallel, glancing at him every so often from across the full table. A few people looked up as they passed. God only knew what they thought.

She stepped into the main aisle first. His boot caught on the leg of the last chair, and he half stumbled to meet her.

She chuckled, aglow from delight—from sheer happiness.

His pulse raced. They would be as close as they had been at prom. The closest yet. In full view of everyone.

She reached out her hand.

He reached back.

251

The touch of her skin. His vision blurred. The tightness crept into his chest. Pound, pound, pound.

But it wasn't the weight of expectation, like it had been at prom. It was different.

It exploded. To every part of him.

"I . . ." He pulled his hand away. "I'm sorry."

He did not feel his feet moving under him, but he knew from the blast of evening air that he had run.

Twenty-Eight

If their blood relation was any clue, Uncle Wes had done what she did when overtaken with emotion too tangled to unravel—he had found the quietest, most private place possible.

Nikki pushed through the main doors of the sesqui building and paused, turning to the right, then the left. Quiet and private could be any number of places on the resting fairgrounds. She opted for the right and headed for the truck, a logical first place to try.

Dusk wrapped its cool arms around the grounds, squeezing the mugginess out of the remaining daylight. The dwindling sun painted a purplish haze over the asphalt road leading to the parking lot on the far end of the grounds.

She followed the road down the full length of the sesqui building, then by the row of open-air livestock barns, each with a different arrangement of fencing below its roof. The dormant spaces undoubtedly resounded with moos and bleats and clanks of gates in the height of fair season, farmers scurrying between stalls with hay and feed. What a sight it must be. And the show barn—the tallest and widest in the row, with its dirt-floor arena encircled by portable bleachers—must be the draw of all draws outside the midway.

She would have to ask Uncle Wes when the fair was. Maybe she could come back to—

She stopped.

A man sat on the show barn bleachers, his back to the road, staring into the arena. The soft light highlighted the plaid pattern of his shirt, the same pattern Uncle Wes had worn to the dance.

She swung her legs over the cable barrier along the road and trailed through the grass between the barns. Her footfalls were as muted as the evening. The thick layer of dirt on the arena floor bore shoe marks and bike tracks. Local children apparently brought their own imaginary show to the arena.

Uncle Wes rested his elbows on his knees, his boots propped on the bench below him, gaze locked straight ahead. Her movement caught his attention.

Their eyes met. Quickly he looked at his clasped hands.

The wood bleachers creaked as she climbed up to him. His posture did not change. She slid onto the bench next to him and waited. If he wanted to talk, he would.

A cricket sang from somewhere in the dirt. Its searching song reached to the rafters.

At last Uncle Wes sighed. "She mad?"

"Perplexed, mostly."

A grimace pulled at his brow. From disappointment at himself, maybe. From regret, perhaps.

"She's taken care of," Nikki assured him. "Mr. Harman asked her to dance." The older man had been sitting on the other side of the aisle, close enough to witness everything. Before Nikki could get to Joyce, he'd taken her by the hand and led her to the dance floor. Like the gentleman Uncle Wes clearly wanted to be.

He ran his hand through his hair.

"Do you want to talk about it?" she asked.

He shook his head.

"Do you want to go home?"

"You're having fun."

"Uncle Wes, do you want to go home?" No one understood better than her. Surely he realized that.

The cricket sang a melody so similar to the ones that lulled all manner of life to sleep on the Werner farm. The sweet song of home.

"Yeah," he said. "I do."

"I'll go get my things." She rose and stepped down the bleachers slowly to keep them from shaking too much. She was nearly to the edge of the barn when he spoke again.

"It's funny . . ."

She turned toward him, silently asking for more.

"When I was young, I was so eager to see what else was out there. So ready to find it all. Do it all. Here I am past my prime, and what I really want . . ." His Adam's apple bobbed. "What I really want is to find out what else is here."

She took a step toward him. "Does that include a who?"

Pause. Then a nod. "Don't know what to do about that."

Another step. "You have been so good to give me advice. May I give you some?"

His eyes lifted to hers.

"Lean in. She loves you too."

He blinked.

She smiled, confirmed it was true, then headed back to the sesqui building.

◆　◆　◆　◆

They did not talk about Joyce the rest of the evening or the next day. In fact, Nikki barely spent time in the same room as Uncle Wes on Friday. He came to the farmhouse in the morning to pry the last of the baseboards off the kitchen wall and rip up one section of linoleum to check the subfloor. He didn't return for lunch or for supper.

Nikki filled in the hours by plunging into work on the front bedroom. The equation she followed would be repeated on all the other rooms she needed to paint. Scrub the walls, tape off the edges, prime, first coat. She left the bedroom to dry overnight, keeping the bed in the middle guarded by the trays and brushes.

By Saturday midmorning, the second coat was on, so Nikki

headed to Redmont. She needed more tape, some milk, and an opportunity to talk to Joyce. The latter two were at County Mart.

Joyce spotted her almost immediately as Nikki wheeled her cart into the bakery section. A mother and her toddler stood at the counter picking out donuts. The little boy rubbed his hands and practically his entire face on the glass case. Regardless, Joyce filled their order with her signature smile that rivaled summer itself.

When it was Nikki's turn, however, the smile was reduced to an obviously forced grin.

"Morning, Nikki." She slid the case door open, grabbed a tissue sheet, and began rearranging the donuts to mask the fresh gaps.

Nikki hung back by a display table. The wide berth seemed more respectful. "I wanted to see how you're doing."

"I'm good."

"But how are you really?"

Joyce straightened and shut the door. "I'm glad Otis was there." She wadded the tissue and tossed it into the nearby trash can. Her uninterrupted movement hinted at her wish to be out of the conversation.

If Nikki was going to speak, she had to do it quickly. "I'm really sorry about what happened the other night."

"Nothing for you to feel sorry about." Joyce reached into the compartment under the counter and pulled out a spray bottle and microfiber cloth. She came around to the front of the case and started to clean away the toddler grime.

"This may sound like a silly question," Nikki said, "but are you still interested in coming over tomorrow to cook? I'm making either rouladen or cookies, depending on what you're in the mood for."

Joyce finished wiping and returned to the other side of the counter. "I'll sit this one out."

Nikki smoothed the cart handle with her thumb. No one could blame Joyce for wanting to avoid the farm. Still, if she only knew the truth.

"You may not believe this, Joyce, but I don't think you should write him off."

Joyce returned the bottle and cloth to their spots and looked at Nikki. Her expression was as firm as her tone. "Love is heard in actions, Nikki. He's made himself clear. Multiple times. The other night was just the exclamation point."

"But—"

"I have bread in the oven. I'll see you at church, okay?"

Nikki started to reply, but her friend had already turned away. It wasn't Nikki she walked away from. It stung nonetheless.

Joyce was correct. Love was heard in actions. And she had been doing all the talking for so long.

◆　◆　◆　◆

Anything and everything that kept his hands busy on Saturday, he did. No matter that it didn't need to be done right then or that the heat index soared over the century mark.

Wes washed the grime and grass off the baler, towed his brush hog up to Eddner for a fresh cut, then washed the mower too. After lunch, he found the girls in the shelter of the tree line along the river and inspected their hooves and hides. He checked Bonhoeffer's wounds for signs of proper healing and drove along the fencerows, fixing the weak spots and the spots that gave only a vague impression of weakness.

He did anything and everything to keep his mind away from the fact that the next day was church and Joyce would be two rows in front of him. More so, Otis would be ushering, giving him a look as he passed through the sanctuary doors. Undoubtedly other people had seen that moment in the sesqui building. Undoubtedly tongues wagged in earnest.

His skin burned, and it wasn't from the heat of the sun.

Late in the afternoon, he piled his tools and extra fence wire back into the bed of his truck and returned to the house. His clothes were a swampy mess. They clung to his skin as if trying to infuse themselves into it. He peeled them off in the bathroom and took a long, cool shower. A blessed reward for a hard day.

When he dressed, he poured himself a tall glass of ice water and picked up his phone. A notification showed on the screen for a missed call from Graham Voepel.

Trennen's dad rarely called him. Graham hadn't left a message, but he returned the call anyway. The other end rang several times before Graham answered.

"You call me?" Wes asked.

"I did. Not urgent, but is my boy out there, by chance?"

"Haven't seen him. Believe he's baling straw for some guys today."

"That's what he told us too. His mother's been trying to get ahold of him. He was supposed to call his aunt for her birthday today."

Wes chuckled. "You know how fieldwork goes. And young men."

"That's what I told my wife. In any event, if you do see him, would you mind telling him to call his mother back?"

"Will do. Say hello to Beth."

"Thanks, Wes."

He put his phone on the counter and shook his head. One thing he could teach Trennen about women was to follow their lead on how to show them care. His mother had pointed that out to him when he was Trennen's age. "Women show you how they receive love, if you're attentive enough," she had said. Men only needed a few words, maybe brief eye contact. Women needed a look, a touch, a smile, a voice, a tone. They received with multiple senses and emotion. They also gave with multiple senses.

His mother did. So did Nikki.

So did Joyce.

The name panged in his chest.

He filled his lungs as full as they could go, pushing away the discomfort, then let the air out slowly. "Lord," he prayed quietly, "show me the next thing."

◆ ◆ ◆ ◆

They arrived at church later than usual, a fact Nikki left unaddressed. Uncle Wes pulled into a parking spot with only six minutes to spare before service. He kept his attention on the ground as they walked to the front doors, not daring to meet the eyes of others who probably knew the events of the Fourth by then, and he definitely did not check to see if Joyce's car was in the lot.

It was.

In the narthex, Mr. Harman handed them bulletins with a simple nod and "Good morning." Uncle Wes barely looked at him.

In the sanctuary, Joyce sat in her usual spot, hair perfect and a sheer royal-purple scarf neatly tied around her neck.

"Want to sit in the back today?" Nikki offered.

"No." He led her to their usual place and waited for her to enter the pew first.

The wood creaked as they settled in. With what little gap of time remained, he seemed intent on studying the contents of his bulletin.

Shortly after they sat, one of the deacons came up beside him. He leaned close and whispered, "Morning, Wes."

"Dave."

"Have you by chance seen Trennen? He was on usher duty today with us and was supposed to be here early to set up for communion."

Uncle Wes frowned. "I haven't, no."

Dave shrugged. "Must be sick. Or forgot. Thanks anyway." He patted Uncle Wes's shoulder and walked back to the narthex. He seemed satisfied. But Uncle Wes's frown tightened.

"What is it?" Nikki asked.

"Trennen's dad called yesterday looking for him."

"Think he's sick?"

Absently, he closed his bulletin. He shook his head. "I should check on him."

"Now? Service is about to start."

Pastor Vark emerged from the sacristy, Bible in hand and white robe flowing around him.

Uncle Wes shook his head again, harder. "Something's not right. I better go."

She grabbed his arm. "But what about—"

"I'll be back." He pulled free and calmly strode out of the sanctuary.

Across the aisle, Mrs. Rothfuss took notice. She smiled politely at Nikki.

Nikki returned the sentiment, then turned to the front in time to heed Pastor Vark's call to worship.

No one else seemed worried or bothered by a sense of urgency. She could only hope they were right and that Uncle Wes's sudden exit was motivated more by a desire to escape an uncomfortable proximity to the woman who brought out complex emotions in him.

Thirty minutes into the service, however, Uncle Wes had yet to return. Mrs. Rothfuss cast a few glances Nikki's way, increasingly curious. Each time, Nikki smiled and nodded despite the tension growing in her stomach.

The congregation followed Pastor Vark through the prayers, the hymns, the reading of Scripture. All the standard course of action, usual and predictable. Until the moment he invited everyone to sit as he settled into the pulpit for the sermon. In the lull, a scuffle of feet rose from between the pews in the back. Several heads turned, including Nikki's.

Two men quickly exited through the swinging doors at the rear of the sanctuary, phones tucked to their ears. The onlookers quickly refocused their attention on the pastor.

As Nikki turned with them, she caught a snatch of the hushed conversation between the couple behind her.

"EMTs," the woman said.

Nikki clasped her hands in her lap and tried to give her full focus to Pastor Vark's message. Surely it was a coincidence. Or maybe she misheard the woman, allowed her subconscious to play tricks on her.

When communion time came and the ushers took their turn at the altar, Dave accepted a serving of wine from Pastor Vark and leaned forward to whisper something in his ear.

The tension spread to her muscles.

◆　◆　◆　◆

"The Lord make his face shine upon thee and be gracious unto thee." Pastor Vark made the sign of the cross over the standing congregation. "The Lord lift up his countenance upon thee and give thee peace."

The organist steered the congregation through the three consecutive amens. Though Nikki's mouth moved, her heart had slipped elsewhere. The service was coming to a close and still Uncle Wes had not returned. She resisted the urge to check the swinging doors and risk another glance from across the aisle.

Like many around her, she prepared for the dismissal, reracking her hymnal, tucking her bulletin into her purse as the organ played a soft, reflective melody.

Suddenly the music stopped.

Pastor Vark's voice rang out once more. "If I could ask you all to stay a moment longer." He stood on the floor in front of the altar, hands folded and elbows at right angles.

A foreboding descended.

"I know this is unusual, but we have an urgent need to pray. I've been informed that our own Trennen Voepel was found this morning unresponsive in his home."

Heat surged through Nikki. Sharp gasps cut through the room. Several people sat, including Joyce.

"I don't have much information at this time," Pastor continued. "That will come in due course. For now, while we are all still together, let us go before the Lord for the sake of our young brother. I invite you to pray with me now for Trennen and for his parents, this family that has ministered so faithfully to this church. Please bow your heads."

Every head lowered.

Even locked, Nikki's legs wobbled. Even folded, her hands trembled. In her heart, she echoed the pleas of the pastor for mercy upon Trennen, the young man who had started to be like the kid brother she'd never had. Who three nights before had swung her around the dance floor and helped her find laughter in a place far from home.

For all he was to her, though, he was more to Uncle Wes. He was like a son to him. A son he always fought to protect and had instinctively known was in trouble.

Even closed, her eyes flooded.

Even filled with faith in a sovereign God, her soul cried.

What must Uncle Wes have seen?

Twenty-Nine

There was nothing more he could do.

That fact alone shattered Wes more than everything else. He hadn't been able to get to Trennen through the locked door. Hadn't been allowed to enter the house with the highway patrol officer who was the first to respond to his call.

There was nothing he could do except tell the officer how to reach Graham, and live thereafter with the searing images. Trennen's legs visible through the living room window, sprawled face-down on the floor, his work boots still on.

An hour later, the sheet-covered stretcher.

There was nothing more he could do.

Somewhere in Minnesota, Beth Voepel was surely collapsed in an inconsolable pile. Her mother's intuition had proven correct.

He should have paid closer attention, taken his focus off his own problems and read between the lines. It was not like Trennen to ignore his mother, fieldwork or not.

He should have listened. Because maybe he could have done something, gotten there sooner. Gotten there in time.

He drove home by power not his own, under grace he didn't deserve.

Nikki was waiting on the porch when he pulled up to the garage. Someone must have given her a ride.

She rose from the rocker, his Bible in her hands, church clothes still on her frame. She watched his every move as he came up the sidewalk. Though his feet fell on the path, they seemed to touch nothing at all.

She met him on the porch, her eyes searching his face, expression clinging to hope.

The only response he had was a shake of his head.

Her chin trembled. Face scrunched. She threw herself against him.

He gathered her to his chest, held her close for as long as she needed. Her tears soaked into his shirt and reached into the pain underneath.

◆ ◆ ◆ ◆

Wes dreaded making the call to Aunt Emma Monday morning. Not because he didn't want to talk to her or be soothed by her comfort, but because he would have to say the words, out loud, for the first time.

As soon as he said hello to her, she clearly could tell something was off. "What's happened?" she asked.

He told her. Like ripping off a bandage.

She gasped. "Oh, Wesley. I'm so sorry."

"Twenty-three," he said. "He was only twenty-three."

"Unfairly young." Her voice was tender. "How did it happen?"

"Heat stroke. Sometime Saturday evening."

"Goodness my."

He stumbled through the full details. How Trennen had been baling alone on one of the hottest days of the summer so far. How at some point he had gone home. How the first responders found a baggie of water next to him, likely a crude ice pack he had tried to take with him to the couch.

How he had died alone.

The pain in Wes's throat forced him to pause.

"Bless his heart," Aunt Emma whispered.

Joyce had tried to warn Trennen two days before about the heat. He, like every bullheaded farmer, ignored the caution.

Wes swallowed against the pain. "His funeral is Thursday. His parents have asked me to be a pallbearer."

"An honor I'm sure you'll fulfill to your utmost, my boy. How is Nikki? Were they friends?"

"Yes. She's shaken but okay. She's thrown herself into painting the living room and hasn't yet made a recipe this week. Said she'll make something for the funeral luncheon instead. She volunteered to help Joyce and the other Ladies' Aid members with it."

"Sweet Fritz, I wish I could be there to squeeze you both. God embrace you with his loving arms. We cannot understand why the young and noble must be called home so early, but we can trust that is where Trennen is now—home."

His faith told him it was true. But the ache in his chest refused to quiet. "Aunt Emma, I've lost many men over the years, some even younger than Trennen, but none of them hit the way this one does."

A moment of silence. When she spoke, a resolve edged her tone. "Wesley James, I need you to listen to me. Zero in on my words good and full."

He held his breath.

"You did not lose this man. You did not fail him. You did not fail anyone. You were a good mentor and friend to Trennen, everything you were supposed to be. You did what you were responsible for doing. Trennen's time was Trennen's time. Are you hearing me?"

The clench formed again, furrowing his brow with it. He nodded, trusting she could discern his unseen, unheard response.

"The other thing that needs to be said," she added, "is how wildly proud I am of you. You invest so much care and love in those around you, and it shows in how real your grief is for this boy. Never, ever, ever stop doing good. Especially when it gets hard. Teach our niece to do the same. She's watching you more closely than ever. You understand?"

He nodded again, sucked in air through his stiff windpipe. He pushed out his voice as sturdily as he could. "Thank you, Aunt Emma."

"No, Wes. Thank you."

◆ ◆ ◆ ◆

Mother Schoenborn's Raisin Nut Cookies
(Kekse mit Rosinen und Walnüssen)

This world gives enough reasons to fret. Be not one of them. Be the help. Smile to coax a smile from others. Laugh to stoke hope. Extend a gift of butter baked in sugar to invite friendship to grab hold. As the sun melts away the storm, so shall your help bring life into the vale of grief, and warmth into the shivering souls of the weak. "Withhold not good . . . when it is in the power of thine hand to do it" (Prov. 3:27). Someday you will need the return of the blessing. In fact, your day may be tomorrow.

I cup butter

1½ cups sugar

3 eggs, beaten

I teaspoon baking soda

I teaspoon cinnamon

½ teaspoon (or ¼ teaspoon) anise extract

I cup raisins

I cup black walnuts

3 cups flour

¼ teaspoon salt

Grind nuts and raisins together. Cream butter and sugar. Add beaten eggs and extract. Sift together flour, soda, salt, and cinnamon. Add to creamed mixture. Then add nuts and raisins. Roll out and cut with a rather sharp cutter. Bake on greased cookie sheets at 350 degrees until brown, about 10–12 minutes. These keep well.

◆ ◆ ◆ ◆

Nikki slowly panned her phone's camera across the farmhouse kitchen. "Cabinets are done," she told her mom and sister on the other end of the video call. "Once Uncle Wes replaces the flooring and baseboards, I'll paint the walls. In the meantime, I'm working on the living room."

"The cabinets are impressive, baby," her mom said.

"They are," Hannah agreed. "You all have accomplished so much."

Nikki switched back to selfie mode and propped her phone against the backsplash, side by side with the photo of Great-Grandma Lena and Grandma Ann. All the women in her line in one place, snuggled near the ingredients for the cookies named after Lena's mother.

She strapped on the apron. "Uncle Wes said he'd do the floor after the funeral tomorrow. I haven't seen him much. He's been low-key since Sunday."

"I can imagine," Hannah said. "He was close with this kid, right?"

"Very."

That morning when she'd returned from her walk, Uncle Wes was standing by the big white barn, arms akimbo, gaze fixed on the field of Trennen's corn. Just staring.

"Maybe these cookies will help," she said. "I hope they're good. They're unlike anything I've heard of, let alone made."

"The recipes haven't failed you yet," her mom said.

She grinned. "True."

"It's nice of you to pitch in with the luncheon," her mom added. "One thing Grandma Ann used to say about Eddner was how people came together in a crisis."

The baby version of her grandmother stared back at her from the gray-and-white past, eyes yet innocent of hardship.

"I'm sure she lived through several of those times," Nikki replied.

"She did. In fact, your dad told me about one of them."

She tensed at the mention of him.

"A farmer died in a tractor rollover accident," her mom said. "The other farmers took turns helping with his animals and property while the women helped his wife with the children and housework. Your dad was ten or eleven, but he had a job too. He cut their grass every Saturday."

"Really?" Hannah lifted her eyebrows in seemingly genuine interest.

Nikki busied herself with tearing open the bag of walnuts and measuring out a cup. Grandma Ann had probably made him do that. It wasn't heroic.

"Didn't he do the same thing for the woman who used to live down the street?" Hannah asked.

Nikki's hands slowed. A fuzzy image resurrected, of her dad pushing their mower down the sidewalk.

"Miss Regina," her mom confirmed. "Raked her leaves too."

He had spent hours on the front yard alone, tall trees on either end.

She shook the memories away and muttered, "Too bad he's not that man anymore."

The line went quiet.

Her mom lowered her gaze, lips pulled tight. Hannah shot Nikki a pointed look.

The comment helped no one. The bitterness helped no one.

Nikki sighed and pushed the walnuts aside. If it was within her power to do better, then she needed to do it. For her family's sake. At least for those short, precious moments they were gathered over video.

Next to the walnuts sat the bottle that had cost her a small fortune. She picked it up and brought it into the frame.

"Anyone ever heard of anise extract? I hadn't until today."

The antidote worked. They engaged once more in easy conversation, drawing closer together despite the distance between them.

Her family stayed with her as she measured and mixed, rolled and cut.

However the cookies ended up tasting, she was determined to bring life into the vale of grief. For all of them.

♦ ♦ ♦ ♦

Wes walked up the church steps in his black suit with his freshly shined oxfords tied neatly and his gold tie smoothed against his white shirt. Gold for Mizzou, Trennen's alma mater, and for the Army. A private homage to the intersection of their lives.

He sang the hymns Beth Voepel had selected for her boy. He sat under the Scripture Pastor Vark evoked for the reassurance of the full sanctuary. He kept his jaw tight against the well in his chest as the casket rested on his shoulder.

At the side of the waiting grave, he stood sentinel as Pastor led the recitation of Psalm 23 and the boy's mother sobbed silently on the shoulder of her husband. Graham wrapped his arm around her shaking frame. What strength he had, he shared selflessly with his wife.

Joyce stood on the opposite side of the grave as Wes, occasionally dabbing a folded tissue against her lower lashes. He ached to reach for her, to offer her a shoulder to catch her tears.

She never looked his way.

In the cool shelter of the parish hall, the mourners were welcomed to a buffet of comfort food typically found at the family table. Linen tablecloths and small arrangements of artificial flowers offered a touch of softness to the stark hall. The Ladies' Aid had done what they could to point to life in the midst of sorrow. They moved about the kitchen and hall, steady in their service. Joyce welcomed his niece into the fold, giving her tableware to restock and dishes to wash.

Still, she never looked his way.

The work before her gave her strength and purpose. His hands, meanwhile, remained unneeded. He attempted to fill them at the dessert table, selecting the last slice of rhubarb pie and a cookie Nikki had made.

Otis met him there. "Afternoon, Wes."

"Otis. How are you?"

"Considering . . ." He looked at the Voepels. Though each parent engaged in conversation with those next to them, their posture had curved under the weight of their burden. "It's hard to lose anyone," Otis said. "Especially a child."

Wes nodded. Though Aunt Emma had assuaged his fear of responsibility, the niggling remained. The older were always responsible for the younger. That was how it worked.

"Wanted to let you know, Wes, that some of the boys have plans to take care of Trennen's crops. So long as you don't mind them coming and going at all hours. They will cover as they can."

"'Course. They're welcome to my equipment too."

The elder nodded, looked again at the grieving parents. "The Voepels intend to pay you from the profit, you know. Honor the remainder of their son's rental agreement."

Wes shook his head. "They don't need to do that."

"It's important to them that they do."

In other words, it would be an insult not to accept. Trennen would have wanted it as well.

Still, it seemed wrong to keep the money. Wes shifted his weight from one foot to the other. "Is there a way I could set up a fund at the co-op? For customers who need the help?"

Otis's lips lifted in a half smile. "We can figure something out."

"Good," he replied quietly.

Across the hall, Joyce breezed out of the kitchen, carrying a cup of coffee. She made her way to Beth and leaned close, gently placing one hand on the woman's shoulder. Beth nodded at whatever she said and offered a smile. In one graceful movement, Joyce set the coffee down and picked up Beth's mostly untouched plate. Joyce's back was tall and square as she flowed to the kitchen.

Otis looked at Wes.

Wes cleared his throat and picked up a fork from the table. A week earlier, it had been him walking away from her. How quickly things changed.

"You know, son," Otis began, "it's none of my business, but one thing the past week has taught me is this." He cupped Wes's shoulder, caught his eye. "Our days are too fleeting to waste them on fear."

His hand and gaze stayed on Wes for a second. Then he turned and walked back to his wife. He encircled her with his arm, assuring her with the strength his old bones still possessed. A strength given to men to be given selflessly.

Thirty

Friday, July 12, 10:17 a.m.
To: Nikki
From: Chris
Subject: Sledding

Nikki—

Thought of another story.

When I was nine or so, a snowstorm came through a few days after Christmas and dumped about a foot of snow on the ground. We were so busy taking care of the animals that by the time we were done, it was too late to go out and play in the snow. So, in the middle of the night, Wes and I decided to sneak out our bedroom window and go sledding. Considering how creaky that old house is, I'm not sure how we got out without our parents hearing. Somehow we did, and we grabbed our sleds from the shed and headed for the river bottoms. The snow glowed with moonlight so brightly we could see each other's faces without flashlights.

I don't know if you've seen the bottoms yet, but it's a good hike from the house. There is a long, wide hill that dumps into a valley. The very northern edge, farthest from the road, has a good incline to it, perfect for a long ride on the sled. It was our favorite spot.

Though I'm not sure how long we stayed out there, it must have been a decent amount of time because all of a sudden, we look up the hill and there is our father. He was hopping mad. He made us march back to the house while he drove his truck slowly behind us. The whole way home, we knew we were going to get it. Wes was so upset, he was shaking. He hated getting in trouble. He always has been a rule follower.

When we got back to the house, our dad lined us up on the porch and got his belt. I told him it was my idea and Wes only went along with it because I made him. I must have been convincing, because he sent Wes to bed and kept me on the porch.

We both had to do extra chores for a week, but I still say it was worth it. That night was one of the few times I remember my brother being just a kid. I still think of that hill.

I hope this is the kind of thing you're looking for, and I hope it helps.

By the way, Aunt Emma told me about the young man who died. Did you know him well? My condolences to you and Wes.

Dad

◆　◆　◆　◆

Nikki smoothed the last stroke of paint on the living room wall, in the crook between the baseboard and the trim of the kitchen doorway. The bristles fanned onto the top of the tape shielding the baseboards as they plied color onto every millimeter of wall.

At last she laid the brush on the tray and stood. Second coat complete. She smiled and called into the kitchen, "Living room's done!"

Uncle Wes looked up from where he knelt by the stove, mallet and pry bar in position under the linoleum. "One more down," he said, his voice still fairly monotone.

"Two rooms to go," she replied.

With two full weeks left before she returned to Kansas City and Uncle Wes wanting to work practically nonstop to stay busy, the odds increased that she would enjoy the finished house, if only for a bit.

The hammering resumed. The snaps and pops of slowly breaking glue accompanied the song from the radio. The mask of noise meant Uncle Wes didn't have to talk much, nor did she press him to.

She lifted her arms above her head and stretched, pulling loose the kinks in her neck and back. Leaving the brushes and tray to rinse later, she headed for the smaller bedroom. Besides the kitchen, it waited its turn for a refresh. It still housed the boxes she had moved there as well as the "Keep" boxes from the living room. It was cluttered, ignored. On purpose.

She flipped on the overhead light. The weak beams joined the Friday afternoon sunlight streaming through the lone window, the escape route used by more than one generation. Sneaking out must have been the preferred way to buck the demanding system of farm life. And demanding fathers.

She hugged her arms to her stomach. The mention of a belt on cold skin shaded her dad's childhood in a new, darker hue. The way her dad took the punishment for his brother shaded him differently too. A shade similarly conferred by the fact he mowed for those who couldn't.

She turned away from the window and began moving boxes to the hallway. The top flaps of the third box she carried out slid open as she set it on the stack in the hall. Showing through the opening was a framed picture of her dad as a teenager. She pulled it free and held it with both hands.

His hair was neatly combed, suit crisp, tie a bright red. One side of his mouth angled upward, drawing out a faint dimple. The year of his high school graduation was embossed in the lower right corner. He would have been a newly minted eighteen-year-old, ready to be on his own. Eager to do so in ways she'd never had to experience. She hadn't wandered far from home; he'd moved hundreds of miles away, for reasons that increasingly became clear.

She tucked the photo into its place and searched the boxes

from the living room for the albums she had organized using the loose photos. One in particular called to her. She dug it out and opened to its contents.

Page after page progressed her through her dad's younger years. In every photo where Grandpa was with either of his sons, his face was stoic, his stare off to the side of the camera or dead center on it. He never smiled. Never rested a hand on a son's shoulder. Every picture of Grandma Ann, meanwhile, captured her in some degree of mirth, from the slightest upturn of her lips to a full-on laugh. Grandma Ann smiled to coax a smile, laughed to stoke hope. She gave the good that was within her power to give.

Their youngest son had inherited a mix of them both. A messy, conflicted mix.

She came to a picture of her dad taken in the schoolyard. His youthful face held a smile similar to his mother's. He stood at the site of his favorite Eddner memory, holding a baseball glove.

Somewhere along the way, that little boy became lost.

Her summer on the Werner farm was meant to draw her closer to the mothers of her line. The sharper they came into focus, though, the more the fathers appeared in the frame too.

◆　◆　◆　◆

Friday, July 12, 9:18 p.m.
To: Aunt Emma
From: Nikki
Subject: A question

Aunt Emma—

Forgive me for not having written back before now. We've been a little distracted, as you have heard. Uncle Wes is quieter than usual and hiding it in work on the house (which is nearly done!). Trennen is the primary cause of that, unquestionably. But if I can tell you in strict confidence, I also think it's lovesickness. Trennen's passing made it worse. I won't say who it is because I have violated Uncle Wes's privacy enough in telling you this much, but if you think of it, would you pray he finds the courage to "do the next thing," as Grandma Ann would say?

I definitely need a similar prayer. Which brings me to the question that finally prompted me to sit down and write this email to you.

I've been thinking a lot about what you've shared so far. There's a lot I still want to know, but one question has forced its way to the top this week. One simple but hard question. Aunt Emma, what is the hardest thing you have ever had to forgive?

Thank you, and I hope the bull riding was all you hoped it would be.

Your niece,

Nikki

◆　◆　◆　◆

Saturday, July 13, 8:14 a.m.
To: Nikki
From: Aunt Emma
Subject: RE: A question

Nikki—

So glad to hear from you again! I was beginning to think you lost my email address. Just kidding; I'd never let that happen.

I was distraught to hear of young Trennen's passing. Your uncle is a good and kind soul. His reaction to such a shock is unsurprising. Thank you for understanding he needs to work to process his feelings. Men are commonly like that. When something big and emotional happens, they go quiet and focus on something productive. It helps them recenter. Be patient and he will find his way.

I certainly will keep confidential what you said about his love interest. Will you keep confidential that I know it's Joyce? My nephew doesn't hide as much as he thinks he does.

Speaking of lovely people, I'm sending along the selfie I took with the bull rider I met at the rodeo. Isn't he a doll? His name is Chase, and he autographed a bocce ball for me. We're Facebook friends now.

On to the consequential matter at hand. You asked me what was the hardest thing I have ever had to forgive. I have had many hard things to forgive. I have been maligned, abused, insulted, neglected, shunned. Sometimes by those closest to me. I learned a long time ago—from your grandma—to come at this question from a different angle, though. Gird yourself because this will require me to wax poetic. Here it is: It's not what I forgive, it's why I choose to do it that matters most. The why is Jesus.

I myself am a maligner, an abuser, an insulter, a neglecter, a shunner. Yet I am pure, covered in the love of a scourged and rejected Savior. I love because I am loved. I forgive because I am forgiven. I am a saint because he became my sin. I cannot charge a penny debt to someone else when I have had millions erased.

Okay, that's all the waxing I can do in a single email. I need a cold beverage now.

In all seriousness, darling niece, please consider what Ann taught me. It is my belief she came to this wisdom too late for certain relationships in her life. She wouldn't want that for you.

Happy painting,

Aunt Emma

PS—Seems a ribbon-cutting party is in order when the house is finished. Maybe with some German food. Wouldn't that be a hoot?

◆ ◆ ◆ ◆

It was strange stepping back into Hosana Lutheran so soon after the funeral. Strange to see the Voepels' empty pew, Trennen's place as usher filled by another man, Joyce with a good-morning smile for everyone except Wes. If he could, he would rewind everything back to the way it was. Beth and Graham would not know the grief of a boy taken, and Joyce would not know the humiliation of his cowardice.

Because that was what it was. Otis had been right about the fear. The courageous stare down what makes them afraid, they don't run from it.

After the service, Wes and Nikki descended the front steps together. Joyce and her aunt were hived with the other ladies under the shade tree. Her back was to the steps and remained that way even as a couple of ladies broke away and conversations in general began to end.

By the time it was Wes and Nikki's turn to leave, Joyce had not moved. He took his keys from his pocket and led the way across the parking lot. They were almost to the truck when a voice called from behind them.

"Nikki, hold on!" Joyce waved from the edge of the concrete landing. "Wait there! I've got something in my car for you."

His niece glanced at him as if asking if he wanted to stick around or take cover. He held his ground.

A few moments later, Joyce approached carrying a silver tray. She kept her attention on Nikki. "You forgot this the other day. It looks like your grandma's, so I figured you'd want it back."

Nikki took the tray and tucked it under her arm. "Thank you. Come to think of it, I didn't have a single one of the cookies I brought on this tray."

"Me neither," Joyce said. "They must have been good, though. There weren't any left."

"They were good," Wes offered. The comment drew a nod from Nikki. Joyce, meanwhile, pulled the strap of her purse higher on her shoulder, no acknowledgment he had said anything.

"The whole luncheon was delicious," Nikki said.

"The ladies always do a good job," Joyce said. "We're all taking a meal to the Voepels on different nights of the week as well. I have tonight."

"Really? I'd love to contribute if you'd like. I could make a side dish from one of the recipes."

"That's very kind of you. I'm sure the Voepels would appreciate that. I'm planning on doing ham steaks, so whatever you think goes. I can come pick it up later today."

Nikki paused. "Actually, I was hoping we could cook together."

"Oh?" Joyce moved her eyes halfway to Wes, her thoughts obvious.

He squeezed the keys into his palm.

"It sounds like you might have a full afternoon," Nikki said, "but it would mean a lot to me if we could have one more session at least before I go. It's my last two weeks in the farmhouse."

"Is it really that soon that you leave?"

Nikki nodded.

"Goodness, summer went fast. I guess you can't take for granted that people will be around." Once more, her eyes moved halfway to him.

He dipped his head. He had to find a way to tell her how much he never wanted to take her for granted again. Or all they had shared, all they had experienced, all they loved and cared about, together.

"So will you come over?" Nikki asked.

Joyce rolled her lips together. Then she nodded. "For you, I will."

A wide smile broke across Nikki's face. But there was no mistaking that Joyce had made her motivation clear.

"I'll be there at four." Her gaze briefly touched Wes's. Long enough for the hurt to show in her expression. She loved Nikki enough to face what wounded. Quickly she said her farewell and walked back to her car.

When she was out of earshot, Nikki elbowed his forearm. "If you're going to tell her, today's a great day."

Thirty-One

Crispy Egg Noodles (Spätzle)

Spätzle comes from the German word for "sparrow." It is a befitting name. When collected onto a plate, these noodles give the appearance of a bird's nest, a safe cocoon for the Lord's delicate creatures of flight. The sparrow has nothing of its own to sow or reap, yet its every need is met lavishly. The sparrow constructs its home with grasses of the field and borrowed ingenuity from its attentive Creator. Does he not love us more than a sparrow? Are we not more valuable than they? His Word is sure; he is our provision in all, big and small. Whatever we lack, we need not fear our Father won't see, be it clothing or shelter, love or rescue. He sees, and he gives. "Whoso putteth his trust in the Lord shall be safe" (Prov. 29:25).

I cup flour
I teaspoon salt
¼ teaspoon ground nutmeg
2 eggs

1 cup cold milk

Butter

Parsley

Combine flour, salt, and nutmeg in a bowl. Make a well. Add eggs and milk. Beat with whisk until batter drips slowly from wires. Add flour or milk as needed. Let rest 10—15 minutes. Boil a large saucepan of salted water. Meanwhile, melt butter in frying pan. Working in batches, spoon batter into colander or onto smooth side of a grater. Press the batter through the holes into boiling water. When noodles rise to the top, remove with slotted spoon and fry in melted butter until golden and crispy. Drain on towel. Sprinkle with parsley and serve. Pairs well with gravy.

◆ ◆ . ◆ ◆

Nikki poured the milk and eggs into the nest of flour mixture. Under the command of her whisk, the two folded together in a smooth, nutmeg-speckled batter the hue and consistency of pancake starter. She lifted the whisk from the bowl, and the goo eased off the wires.

"Think this 'drips slowly' enough?" she asked.

Next to her, Joyce looked up from the ham steaks on the cutting board and watched Nikki dip and lift the whisk a second time. "Probably needs to be a bit thicker." She glanced over her shoulder, in the direction of Uncle Wes's living room, the third time since she'd arrived.

Nikki almost told her—again—that he was occupied in the farmhouse installing the flooring. It was, after all, the reason they had to use his kitchen. She kept mum and whipped in another scoop of flour. When she lifted the whisk, the batter didn't drip so much as slog toward the bowl.

Joyce nodded. "Looks good."

281

"This is why I'm glad you're here. I really am going to miss cooking with you." She knocked the whisk handle against the rim of the bowl to coax off the excess batter.

"Me too. You've put my culinary knowledge to the test." Joyce grinned and rubbed a brown sugar mix into the grain of the meat.

"I won't miss frying potatoes, though," Nikki said.

"Give it time. I have faith in you."

"Misplaced faith." She laughed and took the whisk to the sink. "This batter needs to rest for a bit."

"Perfect. So do these ham steaks. We can prep everything while we wait." Joyce rinsed her hands then dried them on a paper towel. Once more, she cut her eyes toward the living room. Once more, it was empty.

Nikki grinned to herself and retrieved a pot from the cabinet. "Joyce, can I ask you something?"

"Of course."

She took the pot to the sink and started to fill it. "Do you still love him?"

"Who?"

Nikki swiveled to Joyce and pursed her lips.

The older woman pulled her gaze away and busied herself with setting up the electric skillet for the ham steaks. "To be honest, I don't know how I feel about him, other than it's hard to trust someone who leaves."

"Totally relate to that." Nikki transferred the filled pot to the stove and salted the water. "Do you think maybe it was not knowing how to handle it all that made Uncle Wes leave? Because I believe deep down he does love you, despite him being terrible at showing it."

"Interesting theory." Joyce turned to face her fully. "Do you believe that's true about your dad?"

The question plowed into her. She opened her mouth to object, to say the two situations were completely different. But the parallels rapidly solidified, like they had been there all along, waiting for someone to notice. Her dad's attempts to engage were ill-timed

282

and awkward, but they were attempts. Was it possible deep down he still loved her? Possible that insecurity was a factor? What if he longed to be the dad who snuggled his little girl on Christmas Day, despite being terrible at showing it?

She lowered her head, flipped the saltshaker lid open and closed with her thumb.

"Nikki," Joyce said gently, "I wasn't trying to shame you."

"No, I didn't take it that way. It's . . ." She pushed the shaker away and turned around to rest her back against the edge of the countertop. Uncle Wes told her to be the image of God. Aunt Emma told her she had a noble why.

So why did it hurt so bad? Why did it feel like a piece of her body would be ripped out?

"I don't know how I feel about my dad either," Nikki said.

Joyce joined her in resting against the counter. She folded her arms. "Anything I can help with?"

She shrugged. "Maybe tell me how you did it."

"Did what?"

"Learned to love your dad."

Understanding settled into her expression. "How to love the unlovable?"

"Exactly."

Joyce smoothed her hands down her apron and tucked them into the pockets. "For me, there was no magic flip of a switch or anything like that. It was a years-long process, with lots of frustrations along the way. But it's not about perfection, it's about learning, right?"

"Right," Nikki agreed softly.

"It came down to me accepting that he could only be what his maturity allowed him to be. That maturity grew over time, but I realized I still could not expect certain things from him."

"Like what?"

"Like an 'I love you' or a birthday card. Those were not in his capacity. It wasn't until I leaned closer to him that I began to understand where his capacity really was."

"Where was it?"

She crossed her feet at the ankles. "When I was younger, it was in the way he became calmer when I visited. That was something the institution staff pointed out to me. As I got older, it was in the way he didn't pull away when I took his hand. And when I was in high school, it was in the way he painted for me. Little canvases of swirls and basic shapes. When I visited, he would give me one." She paused, stared at a spot on the floor. "When he passed, my mom and I went to collect his things. We found seven paintings he was saving for me."

Nikki smiled. The aching beauty of a daughter's final memory of her father. Their relationship could have ended so differently—for them both. The way Aunt Emma said some relationships had for Grandma Ann. More than likely, one of them was with Great-Grandma Lena.

"To your question of how I did it," Joyce continued, "I suppose I started with deciding I did want to have a relationship with him. Then I found the connecting points and nurtured them as best I could, even if it meant sometimes I felt like I had to lose in order to gain. Believe me, in the end, I counted it all gain." She looked at Nikki. "Does any of this help?"

"It does. Yes."

"And lots of prayer," Joyce added. "I wouldn't have grown maturity of my own without it."

Nikki nodded.

"Good." Joyce turned back to the skillet. She searched the counter as if missing something. "It's just occurred to me, I neglected to bring a foil pan to transport these steaks to the Voepels."

"I've got an extra at the farmhouse. I'll go get it while we're waiting." Nikki started to turn. "You'll be okay here alone, right?"

Joyce chuckled. "Trusting the Lord."

❖ ❖ ❖ ❖

Nikki cut across the front yard, far enough away to not notice Wes in his truck gathering the shopping bags. He had run to town for more supplies without either her or Joyce knowing he had left.

Nikki appeared to be on a mission herself, distracted by whatever coursed through her mind. She was to the end of the yard by the time he stepped out of his truck.

He needed to get to the farmhouse too. Work waited for him. Time ticked away. But his own front door vied for his attention. Inside his house, Joyce was alone.

"If you're going to tell her . . ."

"Our days are too fleeting . . ."

Time ticked away.

He bit the inside of his lip, tensed against the urge to cut across the yard himself.

Enough of running.

Enough of fear.

The day had come.

He pushed toward the door. Up the sidewalk, onto the porch. With every inch gained, words abandoned him more and more. Still, he pushed forward.

He turned the knob, entered.

What would he say? How would he do it?

The door shut behind him.

"Did you forget something, Nikki?"

Joyce's voice carried from the kitchen and trembled through him.

He pushed across the floor. His mouth went dry.

"You know what we did forget?" she called through the house. "Music."

He righted. Music.

Joyce, as usual, completed every one of his gaps. His many awful gaps.

He laid the bags on his recliner and slipped his phone from his pocket. In a series of taps, he cued up the song that, by any grace of God, would bring her smile back to him.

"Nikki?" Footsteps approached.

He checked the volume, sucked in his breath, and pressed play.

The opening riff waltzed through the house. George Strait, "I Just Want to Dance with You."

The footsteps halted.

He came around the corner, phone in hand.

In the middle of his kitchen, wearing an apron and a perplexed frown, stood the woman who had his heart. Regal, even in the everyday. Graceful, even with the pucker of her brow.

"Wes?"

He stepped toward her.

She leaned back. "What are you doing?"

Closer, closer. Each step landing in time to the beat. He passed the breakfast bar, slid his phone onto the surface, and stopped an arm's length from her. At the moment George began the titular lyric "I just wanna dance with you," Wes extended his palm.

She blinked. The song, the actions. Too foreign to compute. He was not who she normally saw.

He held his gaze to hers. "Joyce," he said, "may I have every dance?"

The crease across her brow faded. Her perfect lips drifted apart.

"Please," he added.

Slowly, as if in a dream, she reached for his hand. Her skin as soft as the down of her hair.

He pulled himself to her, and she to him. The music soared into the chorus.

He swayed them to the right, then left. His feet moved sure and steady, more so than any other time in his life. She followed him through every step, syncing her rhythm with his. A harmony as strong as the turn of gears.

She giggled. The sweet sound soothed his racing pulse. He wanted more. He lifted her hand above her head and gently propelled her into a twirl.

"Oh!" she yelped as she spun. Her church skirt swirled against her legs.

He caught her against him, bringing her so close he could see the tips of her lashes. Her eyes gleamed.

"Oh, Wes." She laughed, her mouth pulling back high and wide. All the years of waiting for him, for the scales to fall from his eyes, melted into one breathless moment before he twirled her again.

Her laugh filled the room.

For the rest of his life, he would never again let her languish when she wanted to dance. He would lead her, uphold her—love her.

What a liar fear had been.

◆　◆　◆　◆

Nikki stepped across the threshold carrying the foil pan. The moment she grabbed the door to swing it shut, laughter bubbled from the kitchen. Joyce's laughter.

Then, Uncle Wes's voice, tender and bemused.

How had he gotten—

More giggles. More indiscernible words.

She frowned. Softly she shut the door and tiptoed across the living room.

"Should we tell her?" Joyce whispered.

"Tonight," he replied.

Quiet.

She eased up to the wall between the rooms and craned her neck to peek into the kitchen. Her eyebrows shot up. She clamped her hand over her mouth to block the gasp.

There, in front of the ham steaks and spätzle batter, the two of them embraced, heads touching, chins nestled against shoulders.

Quickly she doubled back to the porch, careful not to rattle the pan. Once outside, she dropped the pan on the swing and said to no one, "Oh . . . my . . . word!"

Uncle Wes had done it.

"Where did he even come from?"

It didn't matter. He had come. That was the point. She grinned so wide her cheeks hurt. The afternoon seemed suddenly clearer. The oak tree's limbs sashayed as if cheering along with her.

Truly the Werner farm, the small slice of earth, was a humble mechanism for knitting together what had unraveled. If only Grandma Ann could witness what unfolded in her son's kitchen. How thrilled she would have been. Whatever was needed—including love—God saw, and gave.

Then her smile began to fade.

What about her love? Did he see that too?

Isaac. All the words said and unsaid, offered and unreturned. Mistakes made. How would their story end?

She needed to reach him, to reach across the space and the miles. If Uncle Wes could cut through the fear, so could she.

Her phone was still next to the bowl of batter. She would go back inside—loudly in forewarning—get her phone, and text Isaac. No backing down. No giving up.

She turned on her heel, strode to the door.

A strange and mighty warmth brought her to a stop. With it, an unmistakable truth. She needed to connect, but not to Isaac. Not yet. Not first.

Restoration had to start at the point things first began to crumble.

Thirty-Two

Tuesday, July 16, 3:35 p.m.
To: Chris
From: Nikki
Subject: What you should know

Dad—

Let me start by saying I am angry. I am angry at the choices you made. I am angry at how much pain your choices inflicted upon me and those I love. I am angry that you have not apologized or taken responsibility in any way. I am angry that you cut me out of your life only to expect me to let you back into mine at your will.

But you know this already. So let me tell you things you don't know.

You don't know that we ate spätzle the other night and I couldn't stop thinking about how much you've missed about our rich and marvelous heritage.

You don't know that every time I pass the schoolyard, I picture you running to the field with your glove.

You don't know that Uncle Wes speaks of you only in ways that make me see you as human.

You don't know that I realize now why Eddner became a place you avoided.

You don't know that I can relate to the holes in your heart that are jaggedly scarred over, if filled in at all.

You don't know that I believe under all the wounds you have borne most of your life, you have an enormous capacity to love. You don't know how badly I want for you to prove my belief worthy.

Lastly, you don't know how hard it is for me to write these words. The anger wars against the hope. Every hurt I carry wants to scream back at you, but every assurance I have in Jesus tells me to be still. I am caught in the tug.

"These hearts of ours are curious and contrary things," Louisa May Alcott wrote. I've never understood that sentiment more than I do now.

I started by saying I am angry. I will finish by saying I am trusting God to show me the next thing, because honestly, I'm still conflicted on how to feel about you.

I will also say thank you for the stories, and if you want to share another, I will read it.

Your daughter,

Nikki

◆　◆　◆　◆

The last time Wes prepared to call Aunt Emma, dread had accompanied him. A week later, the opposite was true. He set his Wednesday breakfast dishes to dry with the George Strait song on his mind and a lightness in his step. He crossed the kitchen floor, passing through the warm reminders of Sunday, and picked up his phone from the breakfast bar.

Aunt Emma answered within three rings. "Well now, there you are! It's been *ages*."

"Hopefully you weren't too worried."

"Haven't seen you on the evening news, so figured you were all right. Been thinking of you. The LLLs have been asking after you as well. How is everything and everyone?"

He settled onto a barstool and gave her a quick recap—the conversations about Trennen's crops, Nikki starting on the kitchen painting. "When she's done, I'll reinstall the baseboards. Then we will 'dress up the place,' she said—whatever that means."

"It means you're about to spend a lot of money you won't think you need to."

He huffed. "Great."

"A woman's eye, my boy. Keep your opinions minimal and your credit card handy."

"You've got me spending lots of money these days, Aunt Emma. I hear the ribbon-cutting party was your idea."

"She talked you into it, huh?"

"I thought it'd help get the word out about the farmhouse being for rent. We'll invite some folks from church and town. The party'll be a good send-off for Nikki too. We'll have it the afternoon of the twenty-seventh, the day before she leaves."

"Sounds like a good time in the making."

"Want to come?" he asked.

"Wish I could. We've got a bocce tournament to reign that day. But I expect reams of pictures of both the house and party. Don't disappoint me."

"Nikki would never let me."

Aunt Emma hummed contentedly. "She's been good for you. And you for her. I'm sure it'll be strange not having her on the farm."

"It will." He pulled in a breath, girding himself for the biggest news of the past week. His eyes wandered to the middle of the kitchen floor. A grin sprang loose. "I won't be alone much after she leaves, though."

"What do you mean by—" She stopped. Her tone switched to playful. "I mean, do tell."

His smile widened. "Joyce and I will be spending more time together."

Her girlish squeal made him laugh.

"So you knew?" he asked.

291

"Of course I knew! I've been waiting for you to catch up! Lord have mercy, you took your time."

"You approve, then?"

"I'm happier than a dog with two tails! Joyce will be even better for you! Now I doubly wish I could come to the party."

"Maybe I could bring her to Oklahoma sometime. You could take her to your favorite cooking store for a spatula."

"Ha! I vowed never to set foot in that place again, but if it means I get to meet her, I will turn cartwheels the whole way there."

They both laughed. Joy tingled through his veins, a sensation he was learning to embrace.

"Goodness, goodness," Aunt Emma said. "This has been one wild summer for you. Loss and love, nieces and brothers. God hasn't wanted you to be bored for a second."

"He's kept us both on our toes."

"Probably why my ankles hurt so bad." She giggled. "Which reminds me, I got a curious question from Chris last night. He asked me which novel Louisa May Alcott wrote. He wouldn't say why he wanted to know."

"Interesting. Wonder why."

"If I have my wits about me, which is usually a big if, I'd guess this summer has one more twist yet."

◆　◆　◆　◆

The last of the feed cascaded from the bucket into the trough. Wes swung the bucket upright and moved away. "Happy Friday, girls."

Reddish bodies filled in around the meal, snouts rooting for the best spot to grub. Off to the side, not far from where Connie had stood moments before, Bonhoeffer watched Wes's every action.

"Hey, guy. How're you healing?"

The calf trained his eyes on him, clearly having no intention of engaging without a good and delicious reason why.

"You're going to make me do it, aren't you?"

A swish of the tail.

He sighed and set down the bucket. "Nikki spoiled you, you know that?" He pulled a baggie of apple slices from his pocket and held it out for Bonhoeffer to see.

The calf twitched his ears, stare locked on Wes.

Only at the sound of the baggie seal popping open did he move one front hoof a few inches forward.

Wes harrumphed. "Come on, then. Let's eat." He pulled out a slice and wiggled it in the air, enticing the young Angus.

Bonhoeffer padded closer, slowly at first, then at a steady gait.

Wes dropped the slice on a patch of short grass and dumped the others on top. He stepped a few paces off, giving his young charge plenty of berth. Steadily the calf came forward to sniff out the treat. When he began to munch, Wes inched to his side.

"Good boy," he soothed as he leaned down to check the wounds. "Easy." Everything seemed to be healing nicely. The way it should. Wes righted and stuffed the empty baggie into his pocket.

Apple slices sloshed around the calf's mouth, along with a few grass blades.

"I'm going to regret giving you that, aren't I?"

Bonhoeffer lifted his gaze to him and continued to chomp. Apples would be an indefinite addition to the grocery list.

The hum of an engine made Wes turn to the road. Coming around the curve was a late-model SUV marked with a US Postal Service logo.

Wes returned the bucket to the Polaris and was through the gate in time to meet the carrier at the mailbox. "Early today," he said to the man.

"Getting a head start on my weekend. Never too early, if you ask me." He handed Wes a stack of envelopes on top of a small box.

"Have a good one," Wes said.

"Same to you." The carrier waved and proceeded down the road.

The envelopes contained the expected bills and begrudged credit card offers. But the box brought him to a halt. It was addressed to Nikki with rush postage, from an unidentified sender in Oklahoma.

"Oh boy," he mumbled.

A few moments later, he climbed the farmhouse porch, box in hand. He poked his head through the door. "Nikki?"

"Come in!" Her voice came from the kitchen, loud enough to rise above the radio music.

He crossed the living room to the doorway. The kitchen wore a full coat of primer and an armor of blue tape. Nikki knelt on a drop cloth next to the table, stirring a can of Slate Gray paint, a tone she claimed matched the brushed-nickel pulls and faux-marble floor tile "with outright perfection."

"Delivery for you." He held up the box.

"From who?"

"It's not signed."

Her brow crinkled. She let the stirrer rest and rose to meet him halfway. When she took the box, she held it for a moment, staring at the return address. "That's not Aunt Emma's address, is it?" she asked.

"No."

Her mouth pulled into a straight line. There was only one other person in the Sooner State who knew the farm's address.

She tucked the box under her arm. "I might open it privately."

"'Course. I'll, uh, I'll finish my chores."

Nikki nodded a thanks, then watched as he backed out of the kitchen.

Once again, Aunt Emma had been right. The last days of Nikki's stay could bring anything.

◆ ◆ ◆ ◆

Three days had passed since she sent the email to her dad. Three days of no reply and wondering if he had read it. And if he had read it, did he understand what she meant? Understand what she asked of him?

The box in her hands surely held a clue.

294

She took it to the living room, grabbing a pair of scissors from a drawer on the way. The country station played a car dealership commercial, annoying at all times and especially incongruous to the moment. She switched off the radio, and the morning quiet embraced the room.

She sat on the couch, placed the box on her lap. The tidy print spelling out her name stared up at her. Nikki Werner. Two names given to her by the man who had written them.

She sliced the tape and pulled open the flaps. Inside, under a layer of balled-up grocery store circulars, lay a business-size envelope on top of a rectangular item wrapped in layers of white tissue paper. She lifted the envelope, broke the seal, and slid out a single sheet of folded notebook paper. Black-ink words lined the page.

Nikki—

You said you would be interested in another story. Your email inspired one. It's about you. One of my favorite memories. In high school, you set out to collect as many classic novels as you could. You insisted on using your own money, which meant you often went to thrift stores and garage sales. Some of the copies you bought contained the notes and markups of the previous owner. You said you enjoyed those because they allowed you to experience the story from a different perspective. You said that was the best part of reading—how you could follow the same sequence of action as someone else and come away with different meanings. That's what made you a lover of stories then and a great teacher of stories now.

I was proud of you then, and I am proud of you now.

I know I have a lot to make up for, and this one small gift is a drop in the ocean. But I hope it's a drop that counts.

Love,
Dad

Nikki pursed her lips. He had read her email. That part was clear. But his message was hardly an apology. It was barely an acknowledgment of wrong. The story he shared, though, was spot-on. He had remembered things she didn't know he had noticed. Such a paradox, that man. Alcott's assertion that hearts were "curious and contrary" proved all the truer.

The tissue-wrapped gift waited in its nest. She laid the letter aside and picked up the cloaked object, a shape and weight altogether familiar. She tore away the layers of paper—and froze.

In her hand was a copy of the classic novel by the woman she had quoted to her dad. *Little Women*.

A collector's edition.

Casebound, snow white. Delicate blue ivy trailed elegantly over the cover between debossed gold accents. As formal a keepsake as the German books. A treasure by any measure.

She traced her fingertips over the cover, followed the indentations of the gold. She turned the book to the right, past the spine—uncreased—all the way to the back, where the ivy flowed uninterrupted.

Not a smudge or nick sullied the pristine white.

Nikki rotated the book until the stack of gilded pages faced her. A piece of cardstock stuck a fraction of an inch higher than the smooth edges. The book opened easily to the marked spot. The makeshift bookmark turned out to be only the business card of the bookstore, but on the page it denoted, a light touch of a pencil underlined one passage: "I shall be infinitely prouder of a lovable daughter with a talent for making life beautiful to herself and others."

The words of Mr. March, about his youngest daughter.

A swell bloomed through her chest. It flooded her eyes.

She had wanted her dad to prove that her belief in his capacity to love wasn't foolish.

He did.

Thirty-Three

Hannah came to a halt in her office parking lot and stared open-mouthed at her screen. "He sent you that?"

"It's a collector's edition. Look at that design." Nikki held the book closer to her phone's camera. The ivy and gold picked up clearer in the video feed.

"It's stunning. *I* am stunned. How did— Where—" Her sister shook her head. "Wow."

Nikki laid the book on the coffee table and tucked her feet under her on the couch. "It arrived this morning. I didn't know what to expect when I saw the package from him."

Hannah resumed her after-work trek to her car. "That's one of your favorite books, isn't it?"

She nodded. "And it's not lost on me how apropos the novel is to us."

"To us? How so?"

"Daughters learning to thrive in the absence of their father, helped along by the guidance of their wise mother's timely proverbs."

"I just got goose bumps a little bit."

"Right?"

Hannah arrived at her car and piled in. The door thumped closed. "Did Dad know what the book was about?"

The penciled line on the marked page was a clear signal he knew enough about the plot. Enough to know the quote was there. But her dad reading any book, especially a tome aimed at females, didn't seem likely.

"I don't think he knew anything about the book until he bought this copy," she said.

The reality of that took a moment to sink in. Her dad must have sought help in understanding the book. He had done that for her.

"So what are you going to do?" Hannah asked. "How are you going to respond?"

The gift was the biggest effort yet in his attempts to connect. It had come on the heels of her reaching back.

She told her sister about the ribbon-cutting festivities they had planned, complete with the favorite German dishes from the summer. "I might invite Dad," she said at the end.

Hannah was quiet. Too quiet.

"Bad idea?" Nikki asked.

Another moment of silence, her older sister clearly studying all the angles. At last Hannah replied, "You should do it."

Nikki released a breath, not realizing she had been holding it. Having her sister's support would never stop mattering. Neither would their mom's.

"You don't think it will upset Mom, do you?" she asked.

"Considering she has been praying every day for you to find your peace with him, I highly doubt it."

"She's been praying for that?"

Her sister nodded. "For both of us."

Her chest hitched.

"I hope you do invite him," Hannah said. "I hope he comes . . . And I hope that I can get to where you are someday too."

"You will, Han. You know how I know?"

"How?"

"Because wanting the relationship is the first step."

◆ ◆ ◆ ◆

SATURDAY, JULY 20, AT 3:22 P.M.

Nikki

Thank you for the gift. We have a lot to talk about. Uncle Wes and I are hosting a party next Saturday to celebrate the finished farmhouse. It's my last full day in Eddner. Want to come?

SATURDAY, JULY 20, AT 4:58 P.M.

Dad

Yes.

◆　◆　◆　◆

Wes leaned over the top cap of the stepladder and secured the new curtain rod into the final bracket. The hem of the thick drapes Joyce had selected trailed over the floorboards under the picture window.

"How's that?" he asked his supervisors. Both women stood near the couch, heads tilted, eyes squinted.

"What do you think, Nikki?" Joyce asked.

Nikki put her hands on her hips as if this was one of the hardest judgment calls of her life. Finally, she nodded. "Looks straight to me."

"Me too. Well done, Wes." Joyce's voice wrapped around his name had become his favorite sound.

He smiled at her without hesitation, then descended from his perch. "That's the last of the curtains, right?"

"The last of the curtains, the accent rugs, the pictures to hang." Nikki looked around the room. "Too bad we can't do something about this couch before Saturday."

He pushed off the last rung and folded the ladder. "Still a perfectly good couch, Nik."

"For an eighty-year-old matron, maybe."

"We can always replace it later," Joyce cut in. "Two days isn't enough time to find the right one."

"We" and "later." Words that referred to him and her, and a

299

future. He carried the ladder to the wall by the front door, barely feeling its weight. Bliss lightened every burden.

"On to the next thing, then." Nikki sat on the supposedly heinous couch and picked up the notebook from the coffee table. "Are we thinking cookies or cake for the party?"

Joyce joined her on the cushions. "Maybe your uncle should decide."

Both of them looked his way.

He knelt next to his toolbox and began to put away his tools. "Aunt Emma said something about a cake my mom used to fix that still makes her salivate."

"What kind of cake?" Joyce asked.

"Not sure."

Nikki searched the pages, marking a few with her fingers. "There's a recipe for a plum cake. Did Grandma's have plums in it?"

"Don't think so."

The pages rustled. "There's something called a bee sting cake with almonds and honey."

"My dad couldn't stand almonds."

She turned to the last recipe she had marked. "That leaves streusel something-or-other, a crumb cake."

"Streusel, yes," he said. "Aunt Emma said it had a streusel topping."

"Goodness, look at how much butter it uses!" Joyce pointed at the recipe. "Nearly two sticks."

"Clearly that's our winner, then," Nikki said. "Let's look up what this salivation-inducing cake looks like."

As the two of them searched for an image on Nikki's phone, Wes snapped the toolbox's latches closed and set it next to the ladder.

"Found one," Nikki said. "This even has a pronunciation guide with it. Apparently the cake's name is pronounced *shtroy-zuhl-koo-kin*."

"That's one golden cake," Joyce commented.

"Here, Uncle Wes, does this look familiar?" Nikki rose from the couch, phone screen extended to him.

Before he could touch it, a chime filled the room. The screen cut to a notification for an incoming video call. Bold white letters announced the caller's identity.

Isaac.

She looked at the screen. Went still. Lips parted.

"You should answer," he said.

Her eyes lifted to his. Her expression comprised part fear, part hope.

"You should answer," he repeated.

Another ring.

He nodded, a simple, silent way of telling her everything would be okay. To trust. To lean in.

She closed her mouth into a tight line, then quickly strode toward the front bedroom.

Joyce watched her leave, a frown pulling at her brow. "Everything all right?" she asked Wes.

He sat next to her, took her hand in his. "Let's pray it will be."

There was nothing more they could do but wait and trust.

◆ ◆ ◆ ◆

The backs of her hands felt as if finishing nails were being hammered up her veins. For weeks she had prayed for the moment Isaac responded. There it was, waiting on the other side of the ring.

She shut the bedroom door. Her thumb shook as she lowered it to the screen. Accept.

A pause. Bated breath.

Then his face. His searingly handsome face.

How quickly the heart ached again for what it had pushed aside.

Her voice cracked. "H-hey."

His expression was unreadable. "Had a break. Thought I'd call."

She lowered onto the bed, a slow movement that concealed a million charging thoughts. One of them shot to her lips.

"Isaac, I'm so sorry. I was a fool." Tears welled in her eyes. But he looked away.

Her chin trembled. A plea rose in her throat for him to hear, but a constraint not her own kept her still, waiting, listening.

"Nikki." His gaze was still averted. "I've been doing a lot of thinking and praying this summer. I've sought wise counsel. It took me a long time to sort through the advice. Longer than I wish it had." He peered at her. "The truth is, my heart has changed. I can't keep going like this."

The air was sucked from her lungs. Her cries begged to spill out, but nothing could carry them.

"The path we're on—it's not a good one. I see that clearly now."

Her brow wrenched. What had she done? "Isaac," she murmured.

"That's why I have to tell you something."

She hid her face, unable to bear up against what encroached.

"Nik, look at me."

She shook her head.

"Please. Look at me."

Of all the torturous requests he could levy, that was the most brutal. But maybe if he did see her, he wouldn't do what he was about to do. Maybe he would look closer and understand how contrite she was. How gnawingly sorry.

With all she could muster, she moved her eyes to his. Though only pixels across wavelengths, his stare bored into her, bringing heat to her face.

"I need to tell you," he said, "that I'm sorry too."

The room went quiet. Even the air didn't know which way to go. "W-what?"

He ran his hand through his slicked hair and let it fall to his lap. "I did the same thing to you that you did to me. I shut you out."

She blinked.

"That's not who I want to be. That's not what I want us to be. And I need to know if you agree with that . . . and if you'll forgive me too."

Too. He said too. Which meant—

"You forgive me?" she asked.

His lips tilted up into that sideways grin he reserved only for her. "Of course I do. I love you, Nik."

Relief rushed out as a laugh. "Isaac Chao Sarn, I love you so much!"

"Does that mean you accept—"

"Yes!" She laughed again and raised her voice to the ceiling. "Yes!"

She would scream it into the sky if she had to. Go up on the tallest mountain. No joy could be brighter than that of forgiveness received—and given.

"I have missed you more than I thought possible," he said. "I cannot wait to see you again in real life."

"Me too. And I—" The words came suddenly and unplanned, but they were as right as the morning breaking over the farm. "I want to pick up where we left off."

His smile widened. "No more hiding."

"No more hiding." She wiped the drops from her lashes. "I'm so glad you listened to that wise counsel. Where did it come from anyway?"

"My grandpa. He talked some sense into me."

She dried her hand on the afghan that had kept her warm and safe in the house of her mothers. She nodded. "Grandparents are good at that."

Thirty-Four

Crumb Cake (Streuselkuchen)

A harvest is the reward of seeds wisely sown. It is impossible to reap what you have not nurtured. "Streusel" bears from the German "streuen"—to strew or scatter. Crumbles of flour and sugar kneaded into butter are scattered across the supple "kuchen" (cake) dough. A talented baker employs the pantry ingredients; a wise woman adds a divine one. With every crumble she shakes from her palm, she pours a prayer from her lips. Each buttery seed is a petition for the souls who will partake in the bounty of her labor. She intercedes for their health, their healing, their sanctification, and their lives. Friend or enemy, she loves them with butter and prayer, putting off all bitterness and discord, hoping after the glorious crown in heaven for herself and for them. She sows seeds of love onto hate, mercy onto hurt, hope onto gloom, giving freely of the faith she possesses. "To him that soweth righteousness shall be a sure reward" (Prov. 11:18).

For Cake

2½ cups flour, plus more for kneading

1 teaspoon instant yeast

¼ cup sugar

½ cup warm milk

1 egg, room temperature

5 tablespoons butter, room temperature, cut into pieces

1 teaspoon vanilla extract

Pinch of salt

Warm milk for brushing dough

For Topping

1⅔ cup flour

⅔ cup sugar

11 tablespoons butter, softened and chunked

1 teaspoon ground cinnamon

In a large mixing bowl, mix the flour, yeast, sugar, and milk until well blended, using a stiff spatula or scraper. Add egg, butter, vanilla, and salt. Use spatula to mix dough until it no longer sticks to side of bowl, gradually adding more flour as needed. Dough should be supple, not firm. Use hands to form into a ball. Cover bowl with towel and set in warm place to rise 1 hour.

Line 9x13 metal baking pan with parchment paper. Remove dough from bowl and quickly knead on floured surface. Then gently press into pan, working dough to edges. Let it rest for another 15 minutes.

In separate bowl, add all ingredients for topping and press into a crumbly dough. Break apart dough into pieces no bigger than a bean.

Brush top of dough with warm milk. Sprinkle topping evenly over dough. Bake at 350 degrees for 30 minutes or until lightly golden brown. Let cake cool on counter. Best served fresh.

◆ ◆ ◆ ◆

Nikki pulled the tray of steaming brötchen rolls from the oven and paused to let herself bask in their aroma. Peace had a scent. It was warm and golden, found in places like a farmhouse kitchen with an oak table awash in sunlight. An intangible gift she would take with her, a treasure far greater than the hollow gains of the world.

"How do they look?" Joyce asked over her shoulder. She wound a wooden spoon through the sautéing cabbage.

"Perfect." Nikki carried the rolls to the table and left them to cool in the afternoon beams.

Uncle Wes buzzed by the window with the mower, momentarily drowning out the twangy chords from the radio. All the ordinary elements of life on the Werner farm embraced her on the bright final day of her stay.

Though one dish was done, many more party preparations remained.

Scrubbed potatoes awaited the peeler. Sleeves of crackers lay next to the buttered casserole dish. Ground pork and beef rested in the refrigerator. And the oven, ripe and ready, hankered for the cake.

Nikki went to the pantry and retrieved the jelly roll pan of cake dough from its proofing hideaway. She slid it onto the counter beside the large bowl of prepped streusel. "Joyce, will you come look at this?"

Her tutor set aside the spoon and stepped closer.

The pale brown pastry Nikki had pressed to each corner of

the pan hadn't risen noticeably, the surface still wavy from the indentation of her fingertips.

"Is it supposed to be this thin?" she asked.

"I'm not sure. In the picture, it didn't look very tall. Not like American cakes, anyway."

Nikki poked at the center. "It's definitely not as puffed as the dough for the rolls gets."

"Maybe that's why you add so much streusel—to give it lift."

The glass bowl next to the pan was nearly half full. A stick and a half of butter tediously pinched together with flour, sugar, and cinnamon to form crumbles the size of peas and beans. Her hands still ached from the effort.

Joyce wrapped her arm around Nikki. "It's going to be wonderful. Keep going." Not once had her teaching steered Nikki wrong, nor her encouragement failed to galvanize.

Nikki nodded.

They each resumed the work before them, each committed to bringing good to the humble home.

Nikki brushed the dough with milk, creating a sticky sheen upon the surface. Then she took up the bowl, nested it between her arm and rose-print apron, and gathered the first handful.

The mothers looked on from their perch against the backsplash, delighted gazes fixed on the young woman who shared their eye color and now their vision.

In gentle, easy movements, Nikki scattered the topping upon the dough. Each crumble fell into place accompanied by prayer, as the divine proverb of streusel had enjoined.

Prayer for the people of Eddner, that they would all come to know the wealth they possessed.

For Mrs. Rothfuss and Mrs. Dutzow, whose experiences and recollections filled gaps.

For the Voepels, that they would see God do his best work in the depths of their splintered souls.

For Aunt Emma, that one day they could share a German meal together, bound by unbreakable ties.

For Hannah, a fellow daughter learning to let vexations melt from her grasp.

For her mom, that she would never stop doing the next thing in hope for better.

For Joyce, that her heart would be forever betrothed to gratitude—and love.

For Uncle Wes, that he would always desire to be the image of God to those around him.

For Isaac, that he would continue to pursue wise advice as they pursued each other.

For her dad, that he would have wisdom to seek what he was missing most.

For herself, that she would always crave the feeling of love, pardon, and light scattering from her palm.

The finished layer of streusel stood thick upon the dough. Like a tall, noble crown.

And when the first knock fell on the farmhouse door an hour later, she requested that she answer it alone.

She faced his searching expression without company, but a heart full.

She pulled the door open wider, as wide as the hinges allowed, and said, "Hi, Dad."

Addendum (Nachtrag) by Nikki Ann Werner

In honor of her grandmother—and for the daughters to come.

Fear not tomorrow, child of the King,
Trust them with Jesus, do the next thing.
Do it immediately, do it with prayer;
Do it reliantly, casting all care;
Do it with reverence, tracing His hand
Who placed it before thee with earnest command.
Stayed on Omnipotence, safe 'neath His wing,
Leave all results, do the next thing.

Minnie Paull, 1897

Author's Note

Readers often ask authors where they get ideas for their books. In many cases, authors start within the context of their own experience. They speak from what they know because that is the most authentic kind of story to tell. The kind that resonates.

Though not autobiographical, *The Divine Proverb of Streusel* was inspired by my own family's history and heritage. Those who know my family and the northeast Missouri hamlet in which they sank their roots will recognize the real-life influences on this fictionalized story.

Some pieces of this book do remain entirely true to life. For instance, the recipes for Scalloped Cabbage and Mother Schoenborn's Raisin Nut Cookies were taken directly from my grandmother's collection, which were passed to her. The German-language books, including the tattered hymnal, are real family artifacts. The loss of the German language, spellings, and culture in our hamlet largely due to the effects of World War I is also true.

That said, my goal in writing this book was not so much to explore heritage (though that was fun, not going to lie). My goal was to build an altar of remembrance.

Like Nikki, I struggled in the aftermath of my parents' divorce, particularly in how I viewed and treated my dad. Hurt led to hardness.

But God.

My heavenly Father steadily chipped away at that hardness until I saw my earthly father through eyes of mercy.

The last words I said to my dad on this earth were "I love you." I still choke up in deep, abiding gratitude for the rewrite God did in our relationship. Above all, this story is meant to be a testament to the fact that I, too, learned "no joy could be brighter than that of forgiveness received—and given."

Turn the Page for a
Sneak Peek at Sara Brunsvold's

INCREDIBLE FIRST NOVEL,

The Extraordinary Deaths of Mrs. Kip

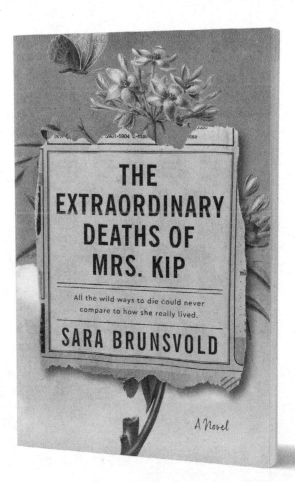

One

Clara Kip had prayed repeatedly to die in São Paulo. It truly seemed the smallest of requests. People died in Brazil every day. What was one more? Especially one who had dreamed of the country most of her life.

The Lord, however, gave her Kansas.

She watched the white line edging the Kansas City interstate pass by her window. It gently carried her toward a facility she'd hoped she would never need in a city she never thought she'd still be in, and she could only trust that the Lord was up to something. Because he usually was.

The facility's shuttle driver—a small, meaty man with a dark complexion and a nameplate above his head that read "Trey"—hummed softly as he drove. The notes floated into her imagination. She smiled, reshaping little blips of music into the dramatic, soul-tickling sounds of samba. Beats that made feet move on impulse and hearts soar with anticipation. Her weary bones enlivened, the way they had when John taught her the dance steps.

Just once she would have loved to samba well past sundown in São Paulo, or walk along the Avenida Paulista strip, or enjoy a golden-fried *coxinha* hot from a street vendor's cart.

She looked at the Kansas sky stretched above her, streaks of clouds still tinged faint orange from the fading sunrise.

315

But not my will, Lord, she prayed.

Around gentle curves and over hiccup slopes, they traversed farther away from the little house that had been hers for decades, until the doctor had shown her the scan and said "aggressively metastasized." The annoying pain in her abdomen that had landed her in the hospital a week prior wasn't the UTI she had insisted it was to him and all those ER people.

After delivering the prognosis, the doctor refused to let Clara travel outside the country. Clara had called him a square.

Somewhere at a facility in the far southern outreaches of the city, her hospice team awaited her arrival.

Eventually the driver merged into an exit lane and peeked at her in the rearview mirror as they came to the stoplight. "Beautiful morning," he called back.

"Sure is, young man. God definitely got creative with that sunrise."

"That he did."

Clara considered his response. "Tell me, honey. Do you know Jesus?"

The driver's eyes twinkled. "Yes, ma'am, I do."

"Good. I can conserve my energy then."

He chuckled. "I suppose so. Although I never mind talking about him."

"Good for you, Trey. Talk about him a lot, especially when others seem uninterested. He loves that."

"Yes, ma'am." He turned onto a side street, slipping closer to their destination.

Outside the window, she caught sight of a young mother herding her kids into the SUV parked in their driveway. The littlest one skipped behind her mother, a pink backpack jiggling on her tiny shoulders. Off for another day of running headlong into new life. So much to learn and explore and discover. Clara pictured her friend Mai surrounded by her sweet little ones, specifically that one day at the airport, when their months of separation had come to a glorious end.

Only one reunion could be sweeter, in Clara's estimation. She turned back to Trey. "May I ask you something?"

"Of course."

"What do you think heaven will be like?"

He thought. "I really don't know. Bright?"

"No doubt there."

They rode in silence, then Trey asked, "What do you think heaven will be like, Mrs. Kip?"

Clara grinned. "Oh, honey. I think heaven will be the wildest ride yet."

◆ ◆ ◆ ◆

Trey parked under the awning of the main entrance to Sacred Promise Senior Care Center. The one-story building sprawled away from the main entrance in both directions. One side comprised assisted living apartments with their own little porches, and the other, skilled nursing residence rooms with large picture windows. A thick screen of trees wrapped around the property, giving it an appearance of seclusion from the busy shopping center beyond. Of the various facilities the kind people of the University of Kansas Medical Center had shown her in brochures, Sacred Promise seemed to offer the closest proximity to unadulterated nature. One of many reasons Clara felt drawn to it. That, and they took Medicare.

Trey hopped out of his seat and pulled her leather suitcases from the rack at the front of the shuttle. "Let me take these to the sidewalk," he said as he headed for the steps. "I'll come back to help you."

Clara grunted at his subtle suggestion that she wait. She had been walking out to get her mail just fine until a week ago. She rose and ambled after him.

When he caught sight of his passenger hobbling down the steps, he rushed over with arms extended. "Please, Mrs. Kip, let me help you."

"Honey, I'm only dying. I'm not an invalid."

Regardless, he insisted she take his arm, which she did, but only because a lady never declines chivalry.

317

Safely on the sidewalk, she peered down at her suitcases. Poor, sad things. They had waited with her for more than half a century to see the ends of the earth. Sacred Promise wasn't even the ends of Kansas City.

Trey lifted them by the handles and nodded to the entrance. "After you, Mrs. Kip."

Clara gazed at the sliding glass doors of Sacred Promise. Such an odd feeling to know that once she walked in, she would not walk out. She clung to the belief the Lord had something for her here, so she shuffled forward.

The doors opened to reveal a small foyer that tried ever so hard to look homey. Burgundy wingback chairs, a grandfather clock, and floral print wallpaper made her wrinkle her nose. On either side, a hallway led to the respective wings. And in the middle of the foyer stood a young woman with fiery hair and an expression that fell somewhere between moderately welcoming and completely bored.

"Good morning, Mrs. Kip." Her voice registered minimal inflection. "Welcome to Sacred Promise."

"Thank you. How are you today?"

"Fine, thanks. I'm from administration. I believe you've been speaking with the social worker, Rosario."

"Yes." Clara started to ask the gal what her name was, but she seemed intent to get on with their business.

"Rosario is out today, so I'll be the one helping you settle in."

"Fantastic," Clara replied with a smile aimed at drawing out the friendlier side of the woman. Surely she had one.

But the gal turned on her heel and said over her shoulder, "Right this way."

Clara looked at Trey, who raised his eyebrows, clearly thinking the same thing she was.

"She seems fun," Clara whispered.

He laughed quietly.

Admin Gal led them through a door on the left side of the foyer. An etched gold plate on the wall identified it as the office.

When they arrived at the woman's desk, Trey set the bags down and stood close by as Clara lowered into the visitor's chair. "Can I be of any further assistance?" he asked her.

The gal cut in. "We can take it from here, thanks."

Trey started to respond, but Clara touched his hand. "You've been a blessing, honey. Thank you."

He smiled and dipped his head congenially. "God bless, Mrs. Kip."

"Same to you." She watched him walk away. "Such a sweet young man."

The gal gave what could be considered a smile. "Shall we begin?" Her pragmatism obviously was there to stay.

"Definitely," Clara replied. "Can't wait."

What Admin Gal lacked in pleasantries, she made up for in blazing efficiency. The paperwork blurred by.

At the end of it all, she stacked papers into a manila folder with Clara's name on it. "You'll be meeting Rosario and the rest of your care team within the next two days." She then rattled off the names of the doctor, nurses, and chaplain who rounded out the team, none of which stuck in Clara's memory.

Clara nodded nonetheless.

"Any questions?"

Even if Clara did have questions, the gal likely lacked the where-withal for them. "I think I'm okay for now."

"In that case, let's get you to your room. I'll page an aide to help with your bags."

Five minutes later, their small parade exited the office—Admin Gal as marshal and a baby-faced aide named Jimmy bringing up the rear. *He* actually smiled, making him instantly delightful.

They trooped down the hallway toward the skilled nursing side and soon came to the activity room, the wing's central hub. Save for the buzzing nurses' station on the opposite end and a small aviary of chirping birds nearby, the room was graveyard quiet. Three other hallways radiated out from the room, one each to the north, the east, and the south. The floral wallpaper carried forward, coordinating with the cherry-finish dining table in the middle and the gaggles of emerald green–striped armchairs. Bouquets of silk flowers dotted the room, attempting to bring a semblance of nature—and life—into the place.

Had it not been for the silver tray of chocolate chip cookies waiting on the dining table, Clara would have written the place off entirely. She salivated at the sight of her favorite treat. She was tempted to break for one, but Admin Gal barreled onward to the north hallway, seeming to gather steam the closer she got.

Clara did her best to keep up, but despite her efforts, she quickly fell behind. Subsequently, so did Jimmy.

As if sensing the widening gap, Admin Gal looked over her shoulder and came to a stop. "I can get you a wheelchair if you'd like, Mrs. Kip."

"I think a race car would serve me better, honey."

Jimmy chuckled but quieted the instant Admin Gal shot him a look.

"If you believe a wheelchair would help you, I can get you one," she repeated. "We want our residents to be comfortable and safe." The words rolled out like a party line.

"I appreciate it very much," Clara replied. "If you could just hold back the pace a bit, that would do the trick."

"I'd be happy to," she said, her expression not matching her promise.

They walked the rest of the way in silence, lumbering along at Clara's slow pace. Her legs already felt the pinch.

Thankfully, only a few doors into the north hallway, Admin Gal stopped. "Here we are." She pushed open the door to room 303 and motioned for Clara to enter.

Upon first glance, the four-hundred-square-foot space seemed comfortable enough. A private bathroom adjacent to the door. A spacious chest of drawers and a small square table with two dining chairs. A comfy-looking loveseat and reasonably comfy-looking armchair, both next to the picture window. Clara skipped right over the bed—the place to avoid as long as possible—and focused her attention on the view through the window. And her heart sank.

The window gave only an acrimonious view of the front parking lot.

"The loveseat folds out into a double bed, and the armchair
by the window can also recline into a . . ." Admin Gal said more
words, but Clara tuned out.

That view. A fat eyeful of nothing God-created.

Clara shook her head. "Excuse me, honey."

Admin Gal's monologue came to an abrupt end. "Yes?"

"I'd like a different room, please."

"Is something wrong?"

"There are no trees."

"I'm sorry . . . *trees?*"

"Or grass. The brochure promised a serene lawn, wooded acre-
age, and hummingbird sightings." Clara pointed at the window.
"That's not it."

The gal looked from the window to Clara. "I can assure you,
Mrs. Kip, all of our rooms are identical."

"And they are lovely indeed, but surely they don't all face the
parking lot, do they?"

"Well . . . no."

"Then I'd like a room that does not." To put an end to the
matter, she called upon the gal's own words. "It would make me
comfortable."

Admin Gal looked at Jimmy as if asking him if she'd heard
correctly.

He put on a confused expression for her benefit, but as soon as
she looked away, a smile inched onto his lips.

Clearly he and Clara were meant to be friends.

"Let me see what I can do," Admin Gal replied. With brisk
movements, she stepped into the hallway.

When she was gone, Clara gave Jimmy a wink and said quietly,
"I'm a troublemaker."

"Clearly," he whispered back.

Acknowledgments

I am indebted to many for the inspiration, creation, and production of the book in your hands. Books are a team effort, and I will do my best to thank all those who played a key role.

To my agent, Cynthia Ruchti, for always making my wild-hair ideas make sense and seeing what I cannot.

My editor, Rachel McRae, who prayed for, encouraged, and advised me. This story is stronger because of you, and I am a stronger author because of you.

The entire crew at Revell, especially Michelle, Brianne, Jessica, Laura, Karen, and Barbara. You pour your hearts into sending good stories into the world.

Ruthie, for invaluable feedback in early versions of this story that helped shape what it became, and for always being so quick to support.

Rebecca and Elisha, whose prayers storm heaven on behalf of this writing ministry. I walk onward in confidence.

Tanya Kelley, for keeping my German translation on the nose.

Grandma Kaden, whose oak table, scalloped cabbage, and lessons on how to pray will forever be among my happiest memories. I hope I have represented well all you have taught me.

Carol Ann, whose copious notes, records, and documents of

family and local history brought new depths and details to the story. I hope you recognize your influence in these pages.

Harlan, who came alongside the facts and drew out stories to further shape my understanding of family and heritage.

Aunt Kathy, whose family treasures inspired many pieces of this book, including those handwritten recipes.

Aaron, whose heart never truly left the farm and whose ag know-how I have long admired. Thank you for answering my specific and weird questions.

Mom, my first and faithful reader, who assured me this story was worth telling and who generously shared her memories, even hard ones.

Dad, who years ago nodded with approval when I said I wanted to write a story based on ours. If only I could put a copy in your hands. I miss you.

Robert, whose insight filled a critical gap, who gladly and repeatedly took on supper duty, and who stands guard around my writing time. Thank you for your love and for growing with me in this writing thing.

My daughters, who tried out all the German food I made and helped determine which recipes should go in the book. We chose well. May this story enrich your understanding of the heritage you have—in every sense of the word.

To every reader who sent an encouraging message throughout the writing process. You have no idea what those words mean. I cherish them for the gift they are.

To you, reader. You are the reason I wrote this. May God use this story to complement what he is doing in your heart and life. May he open your eyes and mind to all he has for you. Thank you, always, for reading.

Above all and because of all, to God. The one who carves the paths for rivers and turns on the stars also guides my steps. You are the lamp unto my stumbling feet.

Sara Brunsvold is the author of the Carol Award–winning novel *The Extraordinary Deaths of Mrs. Kip*. She creates stories that speak hope, truth, and life. Influenced by humble women of God who find his fingerprints in the everyday, she does the same in her life and her storytelling. Sara lives with her family in the Kansas City, Missouri, area. Learn more at www.SaraBrunsvold.com.

CONNECT WITH
SARA

SARABRUNSVOLD.COM

SHARE STORIES THAT SPEAK

 SaraBrunsvoldAuthor Sara_Brunsvold

Be the First to Hear about New Books from Revell!

Sign up for announcements about new and upcoming titles at

RevellBooks.com/SignUp

@RevellBooks

Don't miss out on our great reads!

LET'S TALK
ABOUT BOOKS

Beyond the Book

Visit our Facebook page, where you can join our online book club, Beyond the Book, to discuss your favorite stories with Revell authors and other readers like you!

facebook.com/groups/RevellBeyondTheBook

Revell Roundup

Subscribe to our specially curated weekly newsletter to keep up with your favorite authors, find out about our latest releases, and get other exclusive news!

bakerpublishinggroup.com/revell/newsletters-signup